OUR COUSIN VERONICA;

OR,

Scenes and Adventures over the Blue Ridge.

BY

MARY ELIZABETH WORMELEY,

AUTHOR OF "AMABEL; A FAMILY HISTORY."

"No, thou art not my first love—
I had loved before we met,
And the music of that summer dream
Is pleasant to me yet.
But thou—thou art my last love,
My dearest and my best,
My heart but shed its outer leaves,
To give thee all the rest."

NEW YORK:
BUNCE & BROTHER, PUBLISHERS,
No. 126 Nassau Street.
MDCCCLV.

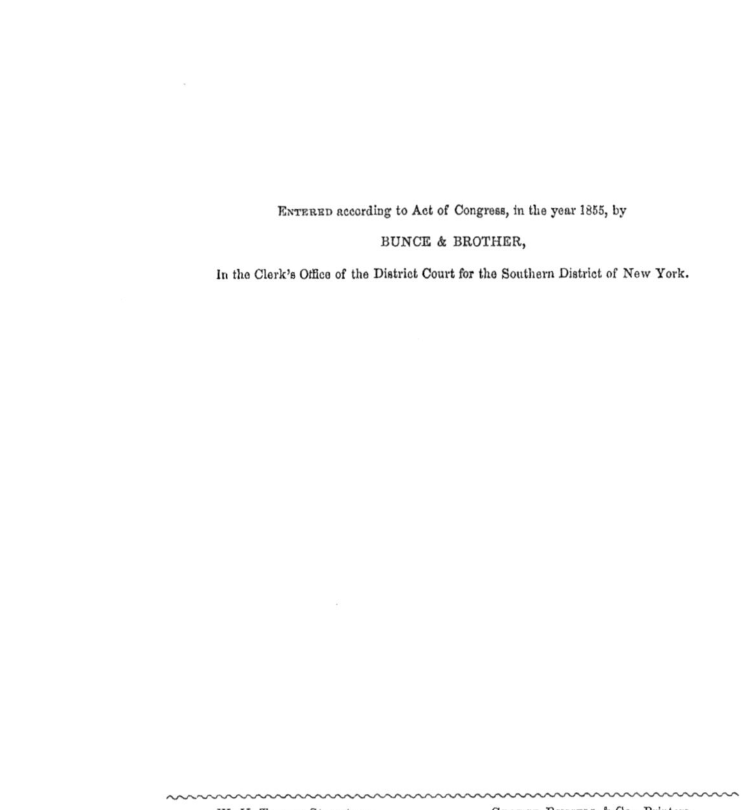

W. H. TINSON, Stereotyper. GEORGE RUSSELL & Co., Printers.

TO

MY COUSIN MARY

(MRS. S. G. WYMAN),

WHOSE LIFE IS DEVOTED NOT ONLY TO THE WELFARE,

BUT TO THE HAPPINESS OF ALL AROUND HER:

WHOSE BRIGHT EXAMPLE

TEACHES THOSE PRIVILEGED TO WALK IN THE

LIGHT OF IT,

THAT FRIENDS AND STRANGERS, KINSFOLK AND ACQUAINTANCE,

THE NEEDY AND DEPENDENT,

MAY DAILY BE ENRICHED BY THOUGHTFUL KINDNESS,

THESE PAGES, WHOSE PROGRESS SHE HAS

ENCOURAGED BY HER SYMPATHY,

Are Affectionately Inscribed.

PART FIRST.

The first inconstancy of unripe years
Is Nature's error on the way to truth.
H. Taylor, *Edwin the Fair.*

OUR COUSIN VERONICA.

CHAPTER I.

Oh! the little birds sang east, and the little birds sang west,
Toll slowly!
And I said in underbreath, "All our life is mixed with death,
And who knoweth which is best?"
MRS. E. B. BROWNING. *Rhyme of the Duchess May.*

"MAX, my boy," said Col. Mandeville, as the pony carriage, one English autumn evening, came round to the front door, "I am going to the coach office to meet our cousin Lomax. If you wrap yourself up warm, and are a good boy, I will take you."

"Oh! papa, may not I go with you?" I cried.

I was two years younger than my brother Max, and I think the favorite of our father. His courtesy to the sex extended itself even to a female child, and I often made use of his feelings upon this point to obtain little advantages over my brother.

But this time he answered, "No my dear; cousin Lomax takes no interest in little girls. He does not want you, Molly, he wants Max. To-morrow morning after breakfast will be time enough for you."

"Oh! but papa, I want to ride with you. I want to go with you. Do let me come too."

My father's kindliness was a fertilizing stream which watered his whole life. "I want to go *with you*," plead strongly in my favor. After all Max was less his own child than I was. Max by a family arrangement of long standing was old cousin Lomax' heir. Mr. Lomax had vested rights in him; was consulted upon all his educational arrangements; and I—poor little Mary Mandeville, my father loved me better because I would have no inheritance except such dower as he could economize from his pay as an English Officer.

"Mary, it is too cold for you," said our father's wife. Max and I had lost our own mother.

"Not too cold under papa's cloak. I am going to keep close to papa."

"Tell Nurse to get you ready then. Don't keep the pony waiting," said my indulgent father.

"Is she going with us?" said Max. "Make haste then Molly."

I made great haste, and in a few moments Max and I, wrapped snugly from the dews of night, were sitting in the back seat of the four-wheeled pony carriage. Bruin, the pony, had been bought during the last months of our poor mother's life-time. Our father had remarried eighteen months after her death, but he had been led into his second marriage chiefly by the desolation of his home. Bruin had been the "horsey" of our dear mamma, and I do not think we, any of us, well liked to see the second Mrs. Mandeville in the pony carriage. He belonged to a Welsh race. He was shaggy and black like a dog of St. Bernard's. His mane stood up like bristles. The harness sank into his winter coat and made deep furrows in his hair. Max said it was longer than his own, for he had measured some.

We sat together in the back seat of the pony carriage, close swaddled in the heavy folds of a military cloak of our father's.

My head was pressed against my brother, and his arm was round me. Peeping from our nest, with eyes whose light was bright like star-light, Max and I gazed on the wonders which opened at every turn upon our view. I had never been abroad after the dusk of the long English twilight had deepened into darkness; after the lamps were lighted in the shops and streets, and Uriel had set his watch of starry sentinels along the darkening sky. It was a voyage of discovery into a land of mystery. Familiar things loomed out along the streets in unfamiliar forms. Shadows became solid as mason-work—the size of every object was increased by indistinctness of outline. As we drove along a miserable alley in the marine suburb of the county town near where we lived,—foul and unwholesome with decaying garbage, bordered by sailors' eating-houses and slop-shops with strange scarecrow garments flying idly in the wind—these forms and the dark figures that passed by us, half illuminated by the lamps of our little carriage, seemed like unearthly shapes—like night-mare visions which disturb our rest when the "terror walketh in darkness," and the veiled figure of Calamity which the imagination shapes from real events, stalks in the dim illimitable future. Children who live nearer the Ideal world than we have frequent glimpses down many an abyss of mystery. Over the spirit of a thoughtful child, fall shadows projected from events beyond his knowledge. He trembles on the borders of the Valley of the Shadow of Death from which a life of three score years divides him.

We left our cottage full of interest in the voyage of discovery we were about to attempt into the darkness; but interest soon deepened into awe. At first Max clamorously pointed out the lights amongst the shipping in the harbor, but long before our drive had ended we sat hushed. My head lay quietly on the arm of Max: we gazed with silent terror at the vague uncertain lights and shadows of the earth, then lifted our eyes up to the open firmament. Earth limited our view of Heaven, it is true, but between the roofs of houses, squalid, dark, disreputable (as from their situation they must have been no doubt) the answering eyes of angels smiled down into our childish hearts out of the starry sky. We drove under an archway,—under a brilliant lamp with a red bull's eye. The rumbling noise and change of light burst the bubble of our reverie. We found ourselves in the coach-yard of an old, strange, rambling hostelry.

"Mail not in yet, hostler?" said our father.

"No sir; but the morning papers is come down by the Shannon. Shall I lift out the young lady, sir?"

"No," replied our father, "not yet, I am obliged to you. Hold the pony as they sit here, and see that they are safe till I return. Max, take good care of Molly—do you hear? I am going into the reading-room. I shall be back before the mail arrives."

We had the kindest father, and children are better, perhaps, for not being tended too assiduously. Still what would our mother in her grave have said to see us left alone by night sitting in the pony-chaise, in that strange court-yard? We had a kindly, hearty nurse, a woman of warm feelings and considerable powers of thought, who gave us homely, hearty, unintellectual sympathy. Health, happiness, and holiness should be the Trinity of childhood. We had them in our nursery. Nor have I ever considered it disadvantageous that we were permitted, more than is common amongst English children of the highest ranks, to associate with persons in stations of life below our own. The atmosphere of our nursery was so refined, that ill things died away and left us pure. We loved our nurse so dearly, we confided in her so unreservedly, that her influence counteracted anything that might have sullied our minds, or made our manners coarse in association with other servants or farm people. I am glad to remember that we played daily in the fields and stables with the groom and the gardener, exchanged greetings and claimed sympathies with the children at the lodge of the great Park, tumbled over in the hay amongst the haymakers, gleaned amongst the gleaners, and gave them what we gathered, and rode on the harvest wain, with wheat garlands round our hats, receiving homage from the harvest-men. Our father was not willing we should be taught to isolate ourselves from human sympathy, under pretence of station.

So Max and I, left alone in the coach-yard, were probably less afraid than many other children would have been. The court-yard was very large. The inn had been a princely mansion in Queen Anne's days, when neighboring gentry had town houses in the county-town, and their daughters looked forward to the Assize Ball or the Races. The inn-yard, paved roughly with small stones, but now disfigured with wooden wings added to the stone stables, and useful but irregular out-buildings erected for purposes connected with the service of the inn, had been the former pleasaunce and court-yard.

The inn-keeper had had a forge put up, the blacksmith doing all his farriery in consideration of his living free from rent, and picking up his profits from the patronage of the neighboring gentry. Nothing delights children like watching the proceedings of a blacksmith. The horses waiting to be shod inspire them with sympathy. There is mystery in the Pandemoniac glow proceeding only from the forge or from the red-hot metal. Their sense of beauty is awakened by admiration of the ruddy light, and of the sparks flying about in every direction, striking the smith upon his brawny arms and face as well as on his leathern apron. They are interested by the contrast of the limited circle of fierce light around the forge, with the blackness of the material, the person of the smith, and the dim dusk of the windowless smithy. There is a mysterious sense of creative power and strength, a sort of sympathy with human triumph over difficulty, as the black bar, glowing red in the fierce heat, is shaped into the form desired. Not that children analyze, or ought to analyze, these sensations. They are present very vaguely to their minds, they heighten the interest of the moment, and years after, if we are wise enough to remember the feelings and experiences of infancy, we apprehend what we then felt, with a certain reverence for our own childish thoughts. It seems as if the angels whispered solemn thoughts into the heart of childhood, or rather, as if, like the sea-shell, which, they say—

> "Remembers its august abodes,
> And murmurs as the ocean murmurs there,"

a faint remembrance of secrets brought out of the land of mystery lingered round our spirits in our infant days.

So Max and I watched the broad-shouldered, swarthy smith, bending into shape a shoe for one of Sir Harris Howard's carriage horses. We extricated ourselves from the folds of the warm cloak, and knelt upon the seat of our little carriage, watching the beautiful showers of great sparks struck out by every blow upon the anvil—admiring the smith as Max, a few years later in his boyish life, learned to admire every great conqueror. A "blessed is he that overcometh" was in our childish hearts. May the echo of that truth, in its sublimest sense, be in my heart when the gates of life are closing behind my steps, and I catch the first faint vision of the great White Throne!

We had watched the smith ten minutes, when the guard's horn sounded in the Market-place. The sound brought our father out of the reading-room. He was afraid the pony might prick his ears when the mail came through the archway.

"Stay quiet, children, till I come to you," he said. "Max, hold up your head, and speak to your cousin Lomax. Say, 'I am glad, sir, to see you back from Virginia.' You must be half a head taller since he left Castleton."

In came the mail—a sight which in those days gladdened the heart of every Briton. An express-train is as national, but we don't gaze on it with equal pride, thundering along with iron hoofs, its smoke, like the tail of the pale horse, floating, as it hurries on over hamlet, field, and river.

"Max, look after your sister," were our father's parting words, as he went towards the coach-door, already surrounded by a crowd of stable people.

My eyes were still attracted to the smithy, where there was more to interest me, than in cousin Lomax, a small, grey-haired, blue-eyed gentleman, who had never honored me with notice of any kind. I saw the smith take up the red-hot horse shoe with his pincers, and hold it over the hoof of Sir Harris Howard's horse. I trembled with sympathy for the poor animal if he should let it fall, and was turning round to impart the apprehension to my brother, when the smith gave an exclamation, and I followed the direction of his eyes. There was a bustle round the mail. I saw a figure—the embodiment of bogy—very black, with large gilt ear-rings pendent on its neck, with a strange turbaned head-dress, without bonnet or hat, wringing its hands by the coach-door. I was frightened at first, and pressed closer to my brother.

"Nonsense," said he. "It seems like the Arabian Nights; something is going to happen I dare say. Don't you remember the black slaves who waited upon Zobeide and all the other Sultanas?"

"Is it a black woman? How do you know that, Max? Oh! what a frightful face!" I cried. "But we are in England and not Damascus. Max, what sort of people do you think sultanas are now-a-days?"

"They must be very beautiful, and they have spells and enchantments, and can order people about and turn them into things; and at first they may be very kind to you, but afterwards, if you offend them, and rouse them, they may turn you into birds, or beasts, as the Princess Giahaure did King Beder. Don't you suppose that the Princess Giahaure was a flirt like that Miss Wells, who treated Captain Sparks so when he wanted to marry her?"

"Look, look, Max, what has papa got in his arms?"

He was coming out of the crowd, which opened before him, carrying a white bundle very tenderly. It was a little girl, perhaps six years old—one year younger than I, three years younger than my brother.

Our father set her down in the pony chaise, and said—

"Take hold of her little hand, Max, and cheer her up. Don't let her get away; take care of her till I come back. She is your cousin Veronica."

Our cousin Veronica! We looked curiously at the tiny figure dressed in white. I even lifted one of the golden curls. She was a slight child, very fair, and at this moment very frightened—too frightened even to cry. She was more delicate and fairy-like than English children. We were ruddy little creatures, with firm, round, stout limbs, protected by warm clothing. Her white dress struck us as unseasonable, and yet it gave her an aristocratic air.

"Did you come with cousin Lomax, cousin Veronica?" at length we said.

After a moment she began to cry, "Oh! my Mammy! oh, my Mammy! Where is my dear Mammy?"

But she gave us no answer.

"You shall have her presently," said Max. "Your mother will be here soon. Stay here, dear; you *must* stay here," with emphasis, as she tried to get out of the little carriage.

"Oh! there is my Mammy!" she said, stretching out her hands after the black woman. "She is going in there, into that house; let me go after her."

"No, no, dear; she'll come back."

"Oh, my papa, too; they are carrying my papa, too!" interrupted Veronica.

"Never mind, dear; he will come back. Stay with me and Molly; we'll take care of you. Sit down, you poor, cold, shivering little thing; sit right down at the bottom of the chaise, upon the cloak, and I'll make a little nest for you. Watch those beautiful big sparks flying all about; I wonder they don't put out the blacksmith's eyes! See him strike them out with his big hammer. Mammy will soon come to you."

"Mammy is her nurse, I suppose," he whispered to me. "Papa had a black nurse in Virginia—Old Aunt Sukey. Everybody has black nurses in Virginia, you know, Molly."

As he said this, he was gathering the thick folds of the military cloak about our charge, till she was really in a little nest.

"Now, Veronica," said he, "you can play at being changed into a little bird, you know."

A more frightened and ungenial a playfellow could not be imagined. She had sat down, with her eyes turned from the sparks, and fixed on the inn-door. They were pretty, soft blue eyes, but now, to use our nurse's phrase, they looked "as wide as saucers;" and though she did not sob aloud, nor cry, she made a little moan. Max sat down at the bottom of the chaise, and put his arms about her. All soothing questions, or attempts to win a look, were quite without avail. She kept her eyes fixed steadily; and, no doubt, the poor little heart sickened with hope deferred as nothing came. At last the curtains of the blue eyes slowly drooped. The little creature was worn out. Once or twice she opened her eyes with an effort, and fixed them earnestly again upon the door, through which she expected her father and her mammy would return. Then, wearied out by the day's journey, and the lateness of the night, she sank into an uneasy slumber. Max held the cloak around her.

"Molly," said he, "come down and sit here too. You can creep into the nest. I will put a corner of the cloak over you."

"And over you, Max?"

"No, I am warm enough," said he; "cover yourself up in it. We must have been here an hour I should think. Listen! The Tower clock is striking ten. What will Nurse think of us? How she catches her breath. She is very pretty. Prettier than any little girl at dancing-school, I think. How very white she is too."

Time slowly passed. Sir Harris Howard's horse had long been shod and led into his stable. The blacksmith had shut up his forge. The great clock of the Tower Church had chimed half-past ten. I too had gone half asleep, when a couple of officers whom we knew, drove noisily into the court-yard.

"Hallo! what's Mandeville's old trap doing here at this hour of the night?" said Captain Sparks to Lieutenant Jarvis, "Quite a family trap,—full of children I declare. Look here young Mandeville what are you after?"

We hated Captain Sparks. He was a man from whom children, brought up as we had been, would shrink with instinctive aversion. At being wakened rudely by his voice and touch, and smelling, as he peered into my face, his hot breath redolent of brandy, I began to feel myself quite powerless in his hands. I fancied that our father had forgotten us, and given us up; that he was never—never coming back again; that like the Babes in the Wood, we were alone and lost. The tide of utter desolation swept over my spirit. I seemed to stand at one end of a perspective glass, and view the life before me stretching lonely into eternity. Infinite vastness of misery opened before me in a moment—infinite loneliness. I began to shriek aloud; to call for "my papa—my own papa, my dear, dear papa." My cries woke up Veronica, who with responsive lamentation demanded her lost Mammy. The officers half tipsy, stood amazed and much annoyed by the clamor they had awakened. In vain they coaxed and threatened us to make us silent. The stable-yard resounded with our cries. I was unmanageable with terror. Max indignantly reproached Captain Sparks for waking us. I insisted on getting out of the chaise and finding my papa. And Captain Sparks, very willingly to annoy Max (who having just learned to repeat "Cassabianca" was bent on obeying orders, and detaining us in the carriage till our father's return) said; "Come to me, little Miss Mary, I will take care of you, you little witch, and we'll go and find papa." He lifted me out, screaming and red in the face. He carried me in his arms, holding the hands with which I attempted to push away the blood-shot eyes and horrid lips with which he tried to kiss me. Lieutenant Jarvis took up Veronica. Max, like a dog whose puppies are borne off, was sullenly compelled to follow us.

The officers were perfectly acquainted with the old Inn and its stone passages. Captain Sparks led the way and shouted "Waiter!" with his loud hoarse voice. Boots came at the summons, loud and coarse, reverberating along the passages.

"Waiter, hold the light!" and he went on with tipsy oaths to order him to conduct him to Colonel Mandeville, for that I—(to whom he applied a very uncomplimentary epithet) kicked, screamed and struggled "like the very devil." "And I say Boots," added he, "better ring a bell and wake 'em up, if you've got any more children in the house you know."

Boots, with his cat-like steps, went on before. At length, after some windings and turnings, for we had entered the old building by the kitchen, he stopped before a door, and said in a hushed voice, "It is here, gentlemen; had I not better call out the Colonel?"

"Call him out? No! hang you! I'm not the fellow, am I Jarvis? to call out my commanding officer."

As Captain Sparks said this, with a great ringing tipsy laugh, the door before which we stood suddenly opened, and a servant of the house came out, with some towels in his hand, and with a pail of water. He looked up in the reveller's face with grave reproof, and something awed both me and Captain Sparks in his hushed manner. But at that instant, Veronica caught sight of the turbaned head of her black nurse. She sprang from the Lieutenant's arms, and was in the apartment in a moment.

"Oh, my Mammy! Oh, my dear Mammy!"

She clung fast to her neck, and sobbed—and sobbed as if her little heart would burst. It was not struggling, frightened grief, like mine, but something much more piteous. It was such an indulgence of grief as in times of great repression one has yearned for, saying, "Ah! when all is over—when the clouds have broken, and the storm is past, I may lay down my weary head, and weep and weep, and, tell then, for the first time, how wretched I have been."

Max and I saw our father and cousin Lomax also in the chamber. The officers, sobered, had drawn back; but our father beckoned us, and Max and I went in. The window was opened on to the clear night, and full into the chamber shone the frosty stars. What was it made us shudder as we stepped in lightly, drawing closer to each other, holding our breath, and clasping each other's fingers? We stood for the first time face to face with death; and though no person told us what had taken place, we recognized by instinct traces of the Destroyer.

We knew that rigid solemn whiteness in the centre of the room (they had removed it from the bed on to a couch) was the dead body. Awful, awful outline of what had been life, lying under that white sheet waiting for its coffin!

Cousin Lomax and our father, with awestruck, solemn faces, stood apart from it. They spoke with hushed voices; they trod with hushed feet. They were still men, and this cold clay had also been a man, *but was a man no longer*. To us, children, it seemed as if we heard the very rushing of the wings of the Death Angel; the cold air in which we shivered had been parted by his flight; he had quenched the spark of life—borne off the soul—left *that* behind (ashes to ashes, dust to dust) to be gathered to its earth, and taken his strong flight to the immortal stars. Our father stepped forward, folded back the covering from the awful face, and turned to us. "Come," said he, "and look at him."

That icy look froze itself into my heart. I have seen death since, but this first view remains my type of it. It was a man apparently about fifty years old, tall, and grey haired, with a high forehead; even in life the features must have been sharply chiselled. He had probably been out of health for some time, for he was much attenuated.

Oh! awful to our childish hearts was the unbreathing, frozen stillness which had settled on his features. We realized that darkness lay under the lids of those closed eyes; we realized those rigid hands could never be drawn apart. The soul had put off this her tabernacle. Nurse had taught us heavenly truths. I instinctively realized the *necessity* of immortality, and ever since that moment this conviction has been prominent in my thoughts, whenever I have stood beside the dead.

Every line of his fixed face came out as the blood retreated further and further from his features. Every little scar, even the hurts of infancy, over which his mother, long since in her own grave, may have grieved, revealed themselves as flaws upon the livid whiteness. The features had been drawn into a smile, not natural, I should think. A smile they never were to lose, day nor night—long days and many nights—till they changed with dreadful change such as one dares not even think of—changing in the dark—in the closed coffin.

The old black Mammy, in her strange, quaint dress, sat at the dead man's feet, and about her clung Veronica.

"Oh! look at him, honey," she cried. "Thar'll be a change in his dear face. Look at him, honey; look at him!" she repeated, finding the orphan did not stir. "Honey, your pa is dead. Your poor, poor pa is dead; you's 'lone in all de worl', honey. We's far from old Varginny, in a strange, new land. You's nobody left you now, 'cepts your poor Mammy."

Veronica would not look up. We could see by the strained muscles of her rigid little hands how tightly she had clasped them round her nurse, who also held her close, laying the child's cheek on her ample breast, and rocking herself to and fro.

"Oh! honey, to think he should have brought us all this long way, honey—over the seas, and in the ships, and just to die so mighty soon. An' all 'lone, too, honey. None of his own servants, nor nobody 'bout him, 'seps poor Mammy. Oh! my dear Mas'r! The Lord he knows! The Lord *he* knows! Take dis stroke 'way, Lord! Oh! my dear Mas'r. Oh! honey, be a good girl, honey, and den when de Angel Gabriel's a comin'—comin', darlin', for to fetch away poor Mammy—ah! you's be 'lone den—all 'lone. All 'lone, in this wide worl', widout Mammy. And de worl' mighty big, and mighty bad worl' my sweet honey! Oh! honey, look at his poor face. Look at his face, dat allerst had a smile on it for us, honey. I'se gwine to sit by him. I'se gwine to watch by him till dey's come put him in de coffin. You hasn't got nothin' else left, honey; nothin' else left now but poor old Mammy, chile; and he was mighty rich, mighty rich once. I tell you he was, honey! When I was a little, black gal, jus growed up, tendin' on Miss Edmonia, your grandma, honey, thar warn't no kind a young man in all our section o' country was any kind o 'count compared with my young Mas'r. And he's lying dead here, an' I'se laid him out. Lying dead, honey, an' no soul but old Mammy dat knowed him, 'seps his brother. I'll sit by him till he's buried, honey. Ole Mammy ain't gwine to leave him, honey. She'll sit by him all this blessed night, an' don't care if de witches comes. Dey won't scare Mammy 'way from her ole Mas'r, honey."

Cousin Lomax approached, and was about to lay the sheet over the face, but Mammy rising, with her burden in her arms, stood by him, and prevented him.

"Not yet, Mas'r Thomas. She must look once more at his face. Vera! look up at your poor pa. Look at him, honey."

She forced the child, still clinging to her breast, to raise her face. It was a cruel kindness. She gave one quick glance, then shrieked, and went into convulsions in the nurse's arms.

CHAPTER II.

> The thought of our past years in me doth breed
> Perpetual benediction
> For those first affections,
> Those shadowy recollections,
> Which, be they what they may,
> Are yet the fountain light of all our day.
>
> WORDSWORTH.

I DON'T remember well what happened next. There was confusion in the inn as well as in the chamber. A doctor, who had been somewhere unperceived, came forth, and took up our little cousin. They put her in a warm bath, and, by-and-by, wrapped in a blanket, they laid her into our father's arms, who carried her down stairs to the carriage.

When I opened my eyes, very late in the morning, nurse was sitting by the fire, altering my pen-ultimate merino frock. I was not lying in my bed, but on a temporary couch, made up on chairs, while my own place was occupied by Veronica.

I lay quiet a few moments. My mind was slowly piecing together the *disjecta membra* of the recollections of the night. I recalled the hours in the frosty night air waiting in the coach-yard—my dread of Captain Sparks, which made me shudder—my agony at having lost all trace of my dear father—and tender, sympathizing pity stole into my heart, as I thought of the orphaned little Veronica. I recalled the loud moan of her colored nurse, "All 'lone, all 'lone, all 'lone, in dis wide worl' honey!" and my heart melted within me.

The nurse, though I had no time to think of her before, became one of the prominent objects in my retrospect. That figure in bronze beside the awful marble. At that period, West India Emancipation was the subject of the day. The newspapers, which, during my father's widowerhood, no one had restricted me from reading, had curdled my young blood by revelations of slave life in the colonies.

Many of the persons who came to our house took no sugar in their tea, because sugar had been raised by slave labor; and the question—could Veronica's old Mammy be a slave—and had Veronica the right to slap her, and ill treat her, and stick pins into her (for of such things I had read) agitated my mind exceedingly.

From this reverie, however, I was soon awakened. Nurse seeing that my eyes were open, suggested I had better get up. She was going to wake up Master Max, and when we were both dressed we were to breakfast in the parlor.

"And what are you doing with my frock?" I asked.

"Altering it until she gets her black one. She'd catch her death of cold in that white flimsy thing" said Nurse, pointing to the garments of poor little Veronica.

This made Veronica seem much more real than anything had done before. Very little would have persuaded me she had been but a creation of my brain, like daily visions, among which my life was passed, of the Princess Giahaure, Queen Gulnare, and the Sultana Zobeide, who, by the way, is a remarkable delineation of that to which the higher type of womanhood must degenerate under the blighting influence of the Zenana.

Max came stealing into the chamber holding his shoes.

"Oh! let me look at her," said he, and going up to the bed, he bent over Veronica. The child's cheek was flushed with sleep, a delicate faint bloom upon her tender skin made her exquisitely pure complexion even purer than its whiteness. Even in sleep you could have told that her eyes were blue, by the purple line under the fringes of her eyelids.

"Oh! Nursy, isn't she pretty?" exclaimed Max.

"Well Master Max," said Nurse, whose weak point it was to consider that the praise of other children disparaged her own brood, "if you ask me if I like those kind of looks, I don't. I like something much more healthy. I don't see any beauty in a sickly skin. Look at your little sister's rosy cheeks, and at your own; there's health, just what there ought to be. And *your* limbs is firm and round." Max and I discouraged by this disparagement, were rather ashamed of our taste. We felt quite grateful to nurse, when a few minutes after, as she brushed our hair, she spoke pitifully of the bereavement of Veronica.

"She is our cousin, Nurse," said I.

"Well," said Nurse, in a very chilly way, looking at Max, "not first cousin I hope. I don't see no likeness to the family." But by and by, when the poor little child woke up, Nurse showed her goodness of heart in all she did for her. Max and I thought she had never done so much for us; nor spoken with so soft a voice, nor cared for us so kindly, and could not help beginning to wish that we too, could be taken ill, for the sake of those caresses. She propped her up in bed, she made her a nice cup of tea in the gilt cup kept for good children. She called her "my poor lamb," and seemed as if she could not do enough for her. By and by, when she had made her comfortable, she called us to the bed, and told us that we might amuse our little cousin.

But the poor child was too listless. She did not ask after her Mammy, but her eyes turned wistfully to the nursery door. Max brought out his jack-straws, and emptying Nurse's needle-book when her back was turned, proceeded with his magnet to show how, as he said, "the needles would walk after it across the pillow," but even this wonder failed to excite any responsive interest in the little Veronica; till, by and by, tired of our ill-success, we left her to be amused and soothed by Nurse, and went into a corner by ourselves, where we repeated to each other, as appropriate, the Burial of Sir John Moore.

The third morning after her arrival, nurse dressed her in a new black frock, for which she had been measured the day she came. Our father came into the nursery during our breakfast, and took her up in his arms, and kissed her on the forehead.

"A very still and gentle little creature, Nurse, he said."

"Very still indeed, sir," she replied, "not one atom like Miss Molly."

"Well, keep the blinds well down till after one o'clock, for we shall pass this way. Mind what I tell you, children! don't you let your little cousin look out of the window," he added in a whisper.

Thus cautioned, we proposed to her to play at gipsies, an unexciting amusement, which consisted principally in sitting in the dark under a tent formed by four nursery chairs, and a green baize curtain. The blinds were down, as our father had desired, but as Nurse was very busy fitting up a chamber in the upper story, we had nobody to prevent our peeping out from time to time to see *why* our father had ordered us to keep them so.

About ten o'clock we heard several carriages going past the house at a slow pace, and desiring Veronica to stay close in the tent, and be a good gipsy, we lifted up one corner of the blind and looked out. It was a stately funeral. Four horses, coal-black, with black plumes upon their heads, and velvet trappings, drew the hearse. Three mourning coaches followed. All but the first was empty. That held our father, cousin Lomax and old Mammy. We watched the slow procession as it passed, admiring the prancing horses and the nodding plumes. As we looked, another breath beside our own was on the window pane, —another little face was pressed to the glass with ours.

"Oh! Molly!" cried Max, "*she* must not stay and look. Go back, Veronica, into the tent; indeed you must not look out of the window."

But the child did not obey him. She watched her father's funeral until it passed out of sight. I do not know whether she saw her nurse. I do not know whether she knew whose funeral it was, but she went back into our gipsy tent and remained perfectly still.

After an hour the sound of wheels was heard again, and Nurse came into the chamber. She hurriedly drew up the curtain.

"Here's her nurse arrived," said she, and we looked out. One of the mourning coaches drew up at the door. The mourners were getting out of it.

"Veronica, your Mammy is come," we said, and running to the tent we tried to pull her out by the hand. But she shrunk back, nor did she come out of the hiding-place even when Mammy, calling her, "Whar's you got to, my sweet honey?" stood at the nursery door. Either she associated her nurse with the painful scene of death, or her little heart had been sore wounded by her absence during days in which she had longed and watched for her. I think the latter was the case. It would have been in accordance with her character.

So Mammy and Veronica became inmates of our nursery. It never occurred to any one that Mammy should not take her meals with us, as our own nurse did. And though she frequently declared "she warn't 'customed take her food with white folks," hers was the only protest entered; but she ate with her knife, and I cannot say Nurse liked her.

Veronica, after the first moments of her estrangement, occasioned by the shock to her little heart, hung round the ample skirts of her black nurse, with a sort of watchful wistfulness and exclusiveness of affection. "Mammy ain't gwine leave her dear chile, honey," the old woman used to say. But Veronica would not separate from her a moment, and it was only holding Mammy's hand that she could be induced to go into the parlor.

Of an evening, sitting round the nursery hearth, in the long twilight, Mammy would tell us wondrous tales; how negroes, walking in the woods, or "stealin' white folks' corn," saw ghosts and witches—stories which irritated our own nurse, who dealt in legitimate fairies.

"Your papa wouldn't like you to listen to them things," she used to say. "There ain't no word of truth in anything she's telling you." Whereby we understood that a patent of veracity was taken out in favor of Tom Thumb and Cinderella, and the rest of her own stories.

Sometimes, at dusk, though Nurse said something about "spoiling precious eyesight," Max read aloud to us by the light of the glowing coals. The first series of the Tales of a Grandfather, then just published, with its glorious stories of Randolph and Black Douglass, and its wild, graphic pictures of border life, was his delight; as was also a book of stories of Lord Nelson. This latter was an American reprint, and the most moving chapter was the story of Prince Carraccuoli.

But, one evening, while Veronica was sitting with her head upon old Mammy's knees, and holding fast by her wide apron, Max and I a little apart, were bending over the Arabian Nights. Our story was King Beder and the Princess Giahaure. We read how the young king pretended to sleep, and heard the description of her beauty. How he became violently enamored of her, saying with the poet,

> "I loved her when her qualities were described, for sometimes the ear loveth before the eyes."

How he persuaded Saleh, the sea-green whiskered potentate, his uncle, to present him and his suit to Giahaure's father, "stupid, overbearing, of little sense, of great power, and niggardly of his daughter in marriage." How King Saleh and King Beder proceeded to the caverns of the sea; and how their civil suit accompanied with two leathern bags, "each a slave's load," "full of jewels, and jacinths, and oblong emeralds, and precious minerals of all kinds," in exchange for "the unique pearl—the Princess Giahaure—the jewel under the sea," was refused despitefully. How Saleh's men and captains, lying without the palace, rushed forward sword in hand. How Giahaure, waking in her harem, took to flight, and springing from the water, took refuge in an island above the surface of the sea. How Beder, "led by the destinies fixed before all time," sought refuge in the same lone spot, and beheld his *inamorata* sitting in the boughs of a great tree. How he made his suit upon his knees to the tree-nymph. How she, wondering at his perfections, was much disposed to fall in love with him. But soon discovering in him an honest suitor, who would have been a good match at any time, her pride perversely rose against accepting him. How to have him in her power, she "beguiled and spake him fair, with gentle words, and soft discourse, till his love for her inflamed, and he approached her to caress her," and then how Giahaure, flinging water in his face, said to him: "be changed from this human form into the form of a bird, the most beautiful of birds, with white feathers and red feet and bill?"

Again the question rose with us, "What was a flirt?" Had Giahaüre been a flirt? Had she treated King Beder as Captain Sparks had been treated by Miss Wells?

"Don't let me hear you talk such nonsense," said Nurse, when, after paying no attention to our discourse for some time, she began to perceive what we were talking of. "Don't talk of flirts, or anything of that kind. That is not proper talk for young ladies, and gentlemen such as you. As to that Miss Wells," she added, "she made herself the talk of all the officers. Never let me hear you speak of flirting again, either of you."

"Law's sakes?" said old Mammy, rousing up, "why flirtin' is what all our ladies does whar I'se come from. All de gals in old Varginny has beaux and plenty on 'em, an' dey winds 'em jist like dat," suiting the action to the word, and twisting the string of her apron round her fingers. "Vera, chile, you's have plenty beaux when you grows up, honey."

"Well," said Nurse, with a sharp toss of the ribbons of her cap, "I hope Miss Veronica will go back to where she came from before then. I should be very sorry to think I was ever going to have all the regiment talking of my Miss Molly. I don't like to have the children told about such things. I hope she will marry a good respectable man, when she's grown up. Flirting is a thing I can't abear. It is not accounted lady-like in my country. And while she stops in my nursery her papa don't wish any such talk as that should be put into her ears."

"Laws now! never hear'd tell dere was no harm flirtin'," said

Veronica's black Mammy. "Dere was a young gal over to our parts was engaged to two of her beaux to once. Her pa owned a farm down to Laurie's Mill—that way."

"But Nursey dear," said I, "just tell us what it is to be a flirt."

"To be a flirt," said Nursey, in a huff, "is playing off and on with a young man when a girl don't want to marry him. It is what no young lady, properly brought up, would ever be guilty of. It may answer," she said in a lower tone, "for people who live among blacks, and such as them."

Veronica sat looking at the grate, without appearing to notice what we were saying. Max said she was too young to understand the Arabian Nights, and he left me and went round to her and pulled her curls, which made her shake her head, and desire him to get away from her, which he did not do by any means, and before long, she was on his knees, and was letting him very shyly begin a game of romps with her.

There were frequent discussions in the parlor during the fortnight that they spent with us. I understood that cousin Lomax would have been glad to leave Veronica and Mammy to share our nursery. But our father objected. His wife was but a bride, and had taken the charge of his own little ones; he did not wish to see her troubled with another little girl and a strange attendant.

Cousin Lomax, after many hesitations, decided on taking Veronica and Mammy to his own bachelor home. It was a very splendid place in Yorkshire, in the East Riding. Max was its heir, and we had been there once during our mother's life-time. There were three hundred acres of fine land, a park, and a large house called Castleton.

Cousin Lomax invited us to spend a month with him when

summer came, and cheer our little cousin. Our father and he laughed. "Max," said cousin Lomax, "if I should tell you she should be your little wife, how would you like her?"

"I'd like her very much, if she'd like me sir," replied Max. Our father patted the boy's head, and said that was the proper answer.

"Aye, aye," said cousin Lomax. "She promises to grow up pretty, too. Her father was a good-looking man, and had a handsome wife. A remarkably good-looking man was my poor brother Alonzo."

CHAPTER III.

But let that man with better sense advise,
That of the world least part to us is read,
And daily how through hardy enterprise,
Many great regions are discovered
Which to late age were never mentioned.
Who ever heard of th' Indian Peru?
Or who, in venturous vessel measured
The Amazon huge river, now proved true?
Or FRUITFULLEST VIRGINIA who did ever view?

SPENSER. *Fairy Queen.*

THOSE who sneer at the passion for family in the Old Dominion, say that there are no "second" families in Virginia: that according to Virginians, every dweller in the State inscribes after his name an F. F. V. That is, a member of one of the First Families of Virginia.

Absurd as the truth embodied in this sneer may be, there is no better blood in Adam's family than may be found in the descendants of the old Cavaliers. Of late years, since the abolition of the laws of entail and primogeniture, so eloquently lamented by John Randolph, our late kinsman, Ichabod has been written over all their escutcheoned gate-posts and old hospitable doors.

The ancient lords of the soil—the ante-Revolutionary Aristocracy, left impoverished estates to be divided amongst their families. The children of their servants till the cotton lands of

Alabama, Louisiana and Mississippi, and the sons of overseers reign in their masters' stead.

Nothing is less interesting at the beginning of a book, than the genealogical vanities apt to commence biography. But it is absolutely necessary that I should give my reader some account of our own family history. It will not take him long to read how old we were, how rich we were, how proud we were in days of yore. Nor could he make the acquaintance of any Virginian, and escape being told parallel particulars at the beginning of the intimacy. Mine is a true record; very similar to that of all the other old families who flourished before the Revolution in the Colony. Under the present go-a-head conditions of society in America, rotation in family is a principle as fully established as that of rotation in office. No family is entitled to more than two generations of prosperity. He who can count grandfathers, must go back to the ranks, and work his own way up again to fortune. The man who has been distinguished either as a member of society, or in political life, knows that the working of this law of rotation will give his family no right to occupy his position. His grandchildren will sink back into the ranks, and be lost in the obscurity from whence he sprung.

The family of Mandevil in England, is a very old one. Its ancestor was one of the Flemish auxiliaries brought over by the Conqueror. Worthies who distinguished themselves by their rapacity, and settled in Lincolnshire, where land was assigned them amongst the fens.

Sir John de Mandevil, of Lincolnshire, was in 1312 invested by the noted and turbulent Earl Warren, with the Manor of Hatfield, in Yorkshire, being part of a grant of land which that Earl had recently received from Edward II. On this estate, held by the honorable service of a pair of golden spurs, the family con tinued to reside and flourish, country gentle folks without historical distinction, till the sixteenth century, when the head of the family having acquired by marriage a neighboring estate at Riccal, removed thither. In the little church of Riccal, handsome monuments of the family may still be seen. The last, dated in 1800, records the death of Christopher Mandevil, last of his race, and an old bachelor. In him the English and elder branch of the family became extinct.

A cadet of the family emigrated to Virginia during the Civil Wars, very probably with some of the Lomaxes, the two families being neighbors in Yorkshire, and connected by intermarriages. The Mandevils were distinguished as staunch royalists. In the early Colonial history, the name of one or more of them is always to be found in lists of the Governor's Council, and on several occasions they put themselves forward on the side of the crown and prerogative. Their residence was Rosencrantz, on the banks of the Rappahannock. It was a princely house, built of red brick, said to have been imported from England. It had its private chapel, its picture gallery, and its thirty guest chambers. It stands looking over the river, two miles broad before the house. The garden has a high sea-wall, and men-of-war have been known to anchor under the windows which overlook the river. Every year the owner of this property dispatched his own produce in his own ship, to England, importing in return all the luxuries of civilized life. The elder sons were always sent to Eton and to Cambridge. It was not a family that ever had very many younger sons. Marmaduke Mandevil, our great-grandfather, commonly called the King of Virginia, had two sons, Marmeduke and John. Marmaduke he sent to England, after the fashion of his house. He was captain of Eton school, the contemporary and intimate associate of Charles James Fox, and the Lord Carlisle of that period. The three friends went together to Cambridge; their portraits were painted by Sir Joshua Reynolds, on one canvas, and the picture is still shown in the hall of the College.

Marmaduke Mandeville the younger, having received a learned education, returned to Virginia after a prolonged residence abroad. He had been distinguished in England as a scholar. He had lived amongst the wits of Johnson's time, and his return to Virginia was extremely distasteful to him. Even the refinement on which he prided himself seemed ludicrous to the persons with whom he was to pass his days, and wonderful stories are still told of the grandiloquence with which he used to issue his commands. He continued to keep up an interest in literary affairs, and was considered an authority on such points throughout the colonies. A letter of his, published in the Boston *Sentinel* of 1782, is in my hands, written in Johnsonian periods, on the authorship of Junius, which, he contended, could not be the work of General Lee.

On one occasion, Marmaduke Mandeville, our great grandfather, travelling on horseback, at some distance from his home, found himself at a little roadside inn, where lands beyond the Blue Ridge were being bid off at auction. It was a magnificent estate on the left bank of the Shennandoah, running west for several miles from Harper's Ferry, comprising what is now some of the finest wheat land in Jefferson and Clarke counties. The man who was anxious to dispose of it, had acquired it, it is said, in exchange for a fine horse imported from England. Our great-grandfather Mandeville joined in the bids, when the property was knocked down to him for a thousand pounds. But several persons having laughed at his new purchase, and assured him it was buying lands in the moon, he became quite uneasy about it in the night, and in the morning consulted General (then Colonel) Washington, who happened to be also at the same lone inn, on the subject of his bargain. The General's advice was, "Keep the land; I have surveyed it, and I know it to be as fine a tract as any in Virginia. But if you really wish to give it up, I will take it off your hands." Thus reassured, old Mr. Mandeville retained the property, went over to see it, and built a house calculated for an overseer's residence, or for a shooting box, to which house his son Marmaduke was soon after banished, having been one of Lord Dunmore's counsellors, a leader in all offensive measures up to the time the Revolution broke out, and "a very malignant Tory."

At the close of the Revolution, he married his first cousin, and died early in life, leaving his property to several sons. They squandered the estate, which lavish hospitalities had encumbered. Their descendants dwindled out; their lands became exhausted and uninhabited. Rosencrantz itself has been used as a tobacco warehouse, and its former glory has long passed away.

John Mandeville, our grandfather, was the second son of Marmaduke Mandeville, senior, and was not sent by his father to an English university. He was educated at William and Mary College, where, when yet a schoolboy, he fell violently in love with the beautiful Edmonia, daughter of the Colonial Attorney-General, niece to the President of the First Congress, and sister to Washington's first Secretary of State. The young lady became soon after engaged to an English naval officer, and our grandfather, in despair, quitted College, and took ship for England, writing to his family that he wished to learn French, and had gone to the French capital.

"The French language! D——n everything French!" cried

his father. "Be d——d if he shan't forget every word of French. It's an ungentlemanly tongue."

Trouble was brewing between England and her colonies at the time he left his home; the Revolution broke out, and he remained in England, the more willingly that the Colonial Attorney-General, parting on the sea-shore from his son, who took the side of the Colonies, fled with his daughters in the ship that carried Lord Dunmore to England. By this step the young lady's engagement was broken off with her English lover.

The refugees lived in absolute poverty at Brompton. A pension of one hundred pounds a year was given to the loyalist Attorney-General, and he was left to struggle as he best might with the wolf at his door.

Our grandfather, John Mandeville, meanwhile, had been made a captain in the newly raised corps of Staffordshire militia, serving at Windsor as body-guard to the king. After a hard courtship of some length, he married his beautiful *inamorata*, and seems to have had powerful friends willing to have assisted his fortunes. Lord George Germaine offered to put him on the pension list, which he declined, saying, "his family never took a pension." He was afterwards offered an office something like that of wholesale purser for supplying men of war in the Thames, an office which he could have had served by a deputy, and which would have brought him in one thousand pounds per annum; but with true Mandeville pride, he rejected it. "I have never had anything to do with commerce or trade," he said, "and do not think such employments becoming a member of my family."

At the close of the Revolutionary war, he went back to Virginia, but did not reach his home in time to see his father.

The old gentleman dying, left Rosencrantz, his patrimonial

property, to Marmaduke, and had given Stonehenge, the estate over the Blue Ridge, to his second son. Upon this property our grandfather hastened to take up his residence, and there, in 1785, our dear father was born.

Stonehenge, of which we had always heard him speak with such affection, that, until we saw it, Max and I had formed very magnificent ideas of the place, is a straggling, rough, yellow stone house, built on the borders of the Shennandoah on bottom land, with a wooded mountain rising abruptly on the opposite side of the river. The best road, till recently, to the house, was through the bed of a torrent, and in the field before the windows, is a graveyard, where our grandmother and seven infant children all lie buried.

On the last evening of our father's life, walking with us through the woods of Castleton, he was telling anecdotes of that mother, whose memory his heart had kept so green, and of whom, I have known him often speak with tears. On that last evening of his life, he told her grandchildren again of all her virtues, of her beautiful voice which still rung in his ears, singing "Pray Goody" and "Love among the Roses," of the ardent attachment that her husband bore her, and of her matron dignity. "She never left a salutation unreturned," he said. "Her kindest smile, and lowest bow, were for the humblest negro." He told us how all the neighborhood mourned her death, and wept over her coffin, and even after the long lapse of more than forty years, the subject affected him so much, that we walked on in silence, and were withheld from questioning him by a certain timid respect for a loss that had never ceased to be a sorrow.

Our grandfather was alone at Stonehenge when she died. Our father was his only living son. He had educated him in England, and in order that he might see the world before settling down to the monotony of a Virginia farmer's life, he had bought him a commission in the English army. After his wife's death, everything in Virginia became distasteful to him. His overseer could hardly get him to attend to his affairs. He pined for England and its associations. He disliked owning negroes—indeed his principal reason for the step he took, was a desire that his son should never be a slaveholder.

At this juncture, Alonzo Lomax, his first cousin and near neighbor, made him an offer to exchange against Stonehenge the reversion of the Castleton estate in Yorkshire, coming to him (Alonzo) on the death of an old lady upwards of eighty, and infirm.

The Yorkshire property was of great value. Yorkshire was the country of our family, and our grandfather's English friends, to whom he wrote, eagerly advised him in favor of the scheme.

He exchanged the estates, setting free eight of his negro families, and settling them in Pennsylvania, where they all did well, and their descendants may be living. One of the men—a blacksmith on our grandfather's return to Virginia, ten years after, made a long journey to see him, and told him that though they were all prosperous and happy, not one but would be willing to come back to his old master, if he would settle on his estate, and wanted them to return.

In parting with the estate to Alonzo Lomax, our grandfather made it a condition, that the negroes should not be sold off the place, a condition he had no power to enforce, when Alonzo sold the property; and having arranged his affairs satisfactorily as he thought, he started for England, taking leave of his married daughter, Mrs. Ormsby, and carrying with him, a bottle of rattlesnake oil for the crippled old lady, on whose decease the Castleton estate was to become his property. The rattlesnake oil preserved her life twelve years, during which time, our grandfather found himself reduced to poverty. Alonzo Lomax ran through his estate, and when at the death of the old aunt, it was discovered that Castleton (being entailed upon the elder sons of the Lomax family), never had been hers at all, and became the property of Thomas Lomax, the elder brother—there was no possibility of recovering any part of Stonehenge.

The knowledge of his error—the thought that he had been the ruin of his son, born to a princely property, broke the heart of poor John Mandeville. He had been struggling with poverty, and with regret at seeing his own fine Virginia property, passing from the spendthrift hands of the younger Lomax, parcelled into small estates and gradually sold.

Such fragments of property as could be saved from Alonzo's wreck passed into our possession. Cousin Tom Lomax, who had also been a refugee in England in his youth, came over to Yorkshire and established himself at Castleton. He came to see our father, Colonel (then Major) Mandeville, at that time quartered in the west of England. He severely blamed Alonzo, with whom he was not on speaking terms at that period; blamed our grandfather, who had been no man of business, for his share in the transaction, but, moved to compassion by the narrow country quarters of his cousin, ended by advising him to marry, saying that he himself should stay a bachelor, and should be glad (as Alonzo had been forced to dock the entail in consequence of an arrangement made to pay his debts), to see him with a son before his death, and that that son, as some compensation for past disappointments, should be the heir of Castleton.

Max was named after him, Thomas Lomax Mandeville. The old gentleman in yellow top-boots, and a buff vest, held his godson at the font, and gave ten guineas to Nurse, who brought us up with great respect for him.

Cousin Lomax showed no relenting towards Alonzo, who after all, perhaps was only more unfortunate than many other gentlemen of Virginia, who lived on anticipating their crops, with a note always in the bank, swallowing up the profits of their wheat crop by its interest, and leaving them nothing but the corn of the estate, of which John Randolph said, "The hogs, sir, eat the corn, and the negroes eat the hogs, and the master's profit sir, is always—nothing."

What reconciled Alonzo to his brother Tom Lomax, and brought them out to England in the same ship, after the brief visit cousin Lomax paid to his estate over the Blue Ridge, I never knew. I imagine that Alonzo intended to travel for his health; and that his death upon the road, was the effect of the gradual decay of his system, brought about by disappointment and anxiety. He was not a man of dissipated habits. He was only one of those of whom it is said, "He was nobody's enemy but his own." Yet he contrived to ruin us, to spend his own estate, to be the cause of endless misery among the families of his dependents, to embitter his wife's life, and to leave his little daughter penniless to the compassion of his brother.

CHAPTER IV.

"Et moi, quelque soit le monde et l'homme et l'avenir,
Soit qu'il faille oublier ou se ressouvenir,
Que Dieu m'afflige ou me console,
Je ne veux habiter la cité des vivants
Que dans une maison qu'une rumeur d'enfans
Fasse toujours vivante et folle."

VICTOR HUGO.

VERONICA and Mammy went to live at Castleton, and when the summer holidays arrived, and Max was released from grammar-school, he and I and our dear nurse went into Yorkshire.

We found Castleton a large, Italian house, standing upon rising ground. The velvet lawn, the care of one grey-headed, good old gardener, sloped down to a clear stream of water, widened into an artificial pond. Ornamental shrubbery was planted round this basin. A boat-house and swan-house had been built of mossy logs, under some willows on its margin. Two mute and stately swans, so tame that they would eat out of our hands, floated on the unruffled surface of the clear, still waters. On the other side of the lake, woods stretched into the distance. They were kept thinned out with pleasant paths opening through them in all directions to pretty points of view. The park was dotted with superb and vigorous trees. There was deep fern at the margin of the woods, such as the deer delight in; but there were no deer in the park, the pride of cousin

Lomax was in his cows. They used to graze about the park in a large drove, perfuming the air with their sweet breath. The heads of the whole herd always turned in one direction. They never molested us when we passed by them on the path, but raised their ruminating heads, their broad brows and their large eyes, and gazed at us, recognizing Veronica, no doubt, and Luath, her great stag-hound, a terrier in greyhound shape, with shaggy hair over the mild eyes that lighted up his face with such expression.

We found Veronica an altered child at Castleton. English air had given her a great appearance of health. Her step was more elastic, and her form more round, though she had lost nothing of the pure delicacy of her unrivalled complexion. She had creatures all around her. Half her life was passed with animated nature. The game-keeper had given her an owl, who lived and blinked in a cage made by the game-keeper's son, over a hole in a hollow sycamore. The peacocks spread their tails for her. The mother pheasant, who was bringing up her young upon the lawn, under a wire grating, ceased to gather her brood under her wings while the child stood and looked at her. the swans would follow her. She scattered corn in the barn-yard, and the fowls gathered round her, and she knew them all by name, and had endless little anecdotes of their individuality of character. The horses in their stalls, turned their proud heads when she came tripping in to pat their shining sides; the hunter let her tiny hands stroke his soft cushioned nose, as he bent down to her. All creatures seemed to recognize in her a natural sovereignty. Luath, the stag-hound, was her prime minister. She never stirred without Luath, who attached himself to her from the first. He was quite as much about her path and bed as her old Mammy.

None made her afraid. As the creatures owned her for their mistress, and seemed to do her bidding at a look or at the lifting of her hand, so all the men and women of the estate followed the example of the animals. The old place had been so still and stern without young life—and now she seemed to carrry gladness about the house and grounds with her. Had flowers bloomed wherever her light feet were set, it would scarcely have surprised the gardener. Her very presence gave good thoughts of Him who said that little children were less of earth than heaven. She seemed to

> "Bring with her blessing and a feeling,
> As when one reads in God's own Holy Book."

I have seen her retreating slowly from the lake side, followed closely by the largest of the swans for bread, which she could hardly hold out of his reach, fearlessly and composedly defending herself from him, not sportively nor affrighted, but quietly maintaining her ascendency, with a calm "you must not do so, Swaney;" while stately Luath waited at her side, ready to give her his assistance in emergency. And I have seen her in the drawing-room at Castleton, amongst a crowd of sporting gentlemen, many of them in their "pink," who had come there after a hard day's run with the hounds. And while it frightened me to be amongst so many men, Veronica was just as calm as she was amongst her birds and flowers. She received notice, and dispensed attentions to great bearded men, all subjugated by her winsomeness, with the same air of trustfulness with which she had appealed to the big swan. And yet, she was not an authoritative, willful child. She yielded on the contrary to both Max and me, in all our sports. I was often surprised to see how readily she adopted any new suggestion, from Max especially. Incorporating it into her own will, as it were,

> " She welcomed what was given and crave no more.
> Whate'er the scene presented to her view
> That was the best. To that she was attuned."

Max and I could hardly understand, at first, how the little child, so timid, sensitive, and listless when she came, could have so changed at Castleton. We did not perceive that it was because she was one of those flowers which only open in the sunshine, growing, unfolding, and expanding in the warm, bright summer days. One harsh word, one conviction sent sharply home to her young heart that people did not love her, would have blighted all her sweetness, as a premature first frost nips all the tender shoots, and devastates a garden.

She was so sweet that everybody loved her. She was happy as spontaneously as a little bird or lamb. Our cousin Lomax, who had given her a home with no idea that she would become an object of any interest at Castleton, had been won by the frank gaiety which seemed to develop itself into her crowning grace, as she grew in favor with the people round her. Cousin Lomax was a sportsman, very fond of animals, and he liked her when he found that Luath followed her, and that his old horse, Brown Tony, whinnied when she came about him. She was a Una who would have led her milk-white lamb, or tamed a lion. A little queen over birds, and beasts, and servants, Mammy, master and guests, at Castleton. A queen who preserved her authority by never stretching it, who commanded only when she was certain of obedience, who founded her pretensions on a sense of being loved.

Mammy was the only soul who contradicted her. Mammy's

temper was not equable. Though she loved Veronica as her own soul, she would sometimes get unreasonably cross with her. But this crossness never ruffled the child's temper, because, as she said once to Max and me, "Old Mammy may speak cross, but, oh! how much she loves me."

Max and I were astonished to hear her chidden by old Mammy, in a tone in which our own Nurse would never have spoken to her charges. It upset my childish theories of slavery, to see the position assumed by Mammy, with reference to her little mistress, and I was not old enough to understand how social distinctions being protected by the mere fact of color, it was more possible for Mammy to assume the ascendency over one who would be righted when time had adjusted their position, than it could be for our hired Nurse to presume on her authority.

We used to spend long summer mornings by the little lake, when the soft noonday breeze, like nature's sigh in sleep, rippled the water; or we sought refuge in the coppice where the thick hazel-boughs protected us from the heat, and shutting out the fiery glances of the sun above us, made a cool green light and freshness in the arbor-like retreat which we had chosen.

Our own Nurse, with brass thimble and a well-filled cotton-bag, would sit in the shade sewing. Old Mammy, with her elbows on her knees, her gaudy negro Madras handkerchief tied on her head, her huge hoop ear-rings shaking in her ears, and massive silver rings upon her knotted hands, would loll upon a mossy log, holding her chin and doing nothing, while we strayed about the wood in happy wonder, delighted by each new discovery of ant-hills, weeds, or many-colored mosses, pebbles, or gnarled roots of trees covered with gaudy fungi or gay lichens, with curious insects crawling in and out, and busy everywhere.

One day, when we had played till we were tired, and hunted

novelties till nothing seemed new any more, and were resting under the shadow of a spreading hazel-bush, so quiet, that our nurses did not know that we were near, we heard Mammy say to nurse,

"Law, sakes! ain't yer never tired sewing!"

"It don't matter if I am," said Nurse, who had as stern a sense of duty as a martyr. "I have got Miss Molly's frock here to let out, and have stinted myself to get it done before dinner-time; and I should say, Mrs. Nurse, though to be sure, it is no business of mine, that you'd do a great deal better if you did some work; or, least ways, taught that child to work. Don't they never work any where you come from?"

"Don't does much sewin' work 'way dar, honey, I reckon'," Mammy said. "Ole missus use do mos' all de sewin' her own self. Laws! you can't git nothin' out o' niggers, 'scepts you's all de time lookin' after them."

"Don't you know how to sew?" said Nurse.

"Laws, yes, honey. I knows sure 'nuff. Allers use to sew for my ole husband. Sunday clothes, an' that; other ones he done got from his mas'r."

"Were you ever married?" asked Nurse, with an awakening curiosity.

"Law, sakes! never knowed ole maid o' colour, any how," said Mammy, with a laugh. "Done married my first husban' when I wor nos'ing 'scepts a chile, and had a mighty smart weddin'. Ole missus, she comed down; there was right good times at dat ar weddin', honey. Ole mas'r telled Jim he'd give him mighty sound whippin' if he warn't kind to me. Ole mas'r married us hisself—but, laws, 'twarnt no great use, I reckon."

"How did he die?" said Nurse.

"Laws! he died . . . . who? Jim? I dunno as he's dead His mas'r moved to Missouri, way down south, an' took his negroes thar. He offered mas'r to buy me to go 'long, too, with him, but Miss Edmonia, she didn't want to give me up. So I reckoned I'd best stay with her. Mighty hard thing gittin' real good servants like them you has brought up. Jim got 'nother ole woman 'ways down thar, I reckon."

"Married again! Did you marry while your husband was living?" cried Nurse, in a fit of horror.

"He done gone. Warn't never comin' back. Never heerd on him agin," said Mammy. "Yes, I done married Blacksmith after that. We was man an' wife twenty years, I reckon."

"I thought you called yourself a Christian!" exclaimed Nurse.

"Laws! so I am. Done got religion five years sence. Ole missus, she thought a deal o' being pious, an' taught my boys a mighty heap o' things. One on 'em reads elegant. Wish't I was back in ole Virginny! I ain't no 'count here like what I'd be at home. An' I'd see my chil'ens too, I reckon."

Our nurse's last exclamation had been forced from her by her repression of indignation.

"Well! I'm sure," said she, "I think you'd better be back there than bringing up a child with such notions. And as to my young gentleman and lady, I don't know what their papa would say about their associating with you, if *he* knew you were such a woman as you represent yourself. I fancy you won't get *us* back here when *this* visit is ended. Come, children, I am going back to the house! Come along with me directly. Never mind your cousin, Master Max—her own nurse will take care of her."

"I dunno what you'se flouncin' roun' that ways for," said

Mammy, waxing wroth. "Here, Vera, come here, and let me tie your hat." Which she proceeded to do very roughly. "Wish't I was back over de Blue Ridge in ole Virginny. I ain't gwine stay here no how. I ain't no 'count here to what I allers done been 'mongst real white folks. I'se gwine home, whar I'se better'n white niggers any how, I reckon."

"Come along, Master Max—come, Miss Molly, do!" said Nurse, in a tone of irritation. "And don't you," she added in a whisper, "take example by anything you see her teach your cousin. I don't want you to have no more to do with Miss Veronica than you are obliged to. As for that black woman, all you have got to do with her is to be civil to her. She isn't fit company for little ladies and gentlemen."

This was the beginning of a feud between the nurses—our nurse insisting that as she was responsible for our morals in the absence of our parents, she should keep us apart as much as possible, out of harm's way. The quarrel grew so hot that it came to the ears of cousin Lomax, who sent for our nurse to his library, and held an argument with her which had no effect. His adversary drove in everything she had to say with a text of Scripture more or less well applied. Nurse fancied she came off victorious in this engagement. She could not understand that circumstances alter cases, and that a court of appeal from God's broad rules of morality might be found in the necessities and customs made by the laws of man. She told Mr. Lomax a good many home truths, too, and gave him some good practical advice about his duty to the child he had adopted; and though he laughed at the idea of good old Mammy, a respected member of the Baptist Church, being an unfit guardian for the innocence of her nursling, and though he called Nurse to her face "a meddlesome jade"—an expression she resented by declaring that after such language she would sooner lose her place than come again under his roof, to which he replied he never wanted to see her again at Castleton—he took into consideration the duty of providing some instruction for the child of his adoption, and paid a visit to old Dr. Dwyer, the rector of the parish, who, he vaguely hoped, might consent to educate her. But the Doctor, a grave gentleman, sixty-five years old, mistrusted his own aptitude to teach the primer, and suggested that a governess had better be employed. Mr. Lomax, however, had no relish for that alternative. He was resolved not to engage a governess, having an old bachelor's dread of introducing a woman of education into his house, who might, either by a bold assertion of Woman's Rights, or by a course of woman's management, succeed in obtaining "rule, supremacy, and sway" in his establishment. One or the other of the two old gentlemen at last hit on the idea that Miss Alicia, a sister of the Doctor, twenty years younger than himself, who lived with him and kept his house, might perhaps be prevailed upon to impart her own knowledge of spelling and reading to Veronica. Miss Alicia was appealed to, and consented to accept the charge, after a good many difficulties on the subject of compensation; for while it was very agreeable to her feelings to have an additional twenty pounds a year to dispense in village charities, her pride as a lady revolted from the idea of payment for an occupation which, as she said, would be a pleasure to a lonely woman, who loved children, during the solitary morning hours, when her brother was busy in his parish or his study.

A better choice than Miss Alicia, could hardly have been made. Writing an ordinary note of civility, was indeed to her a laborious literary labor, not performed without a dictionary, and many careful erasures. Spelling was not her strong point, and her acquaintance with the concerns of the human family, did not rise to the level of the information comprised in the histories of Mrs. Barbauld; but she was humbly pious, simple-hearted and affectionate. She taught Veronica better things than the old-fashioned accomplishments, which in time she superadded to the ordinary rudiments of a village school education—music as taught by Clementini, and French verbs as they were spelled before the Revolution, and the art of painting flowers in water-colors upon fancy cards. Miss Alicia taught her pupil to be open and truthful, to fear God because He always saw her, and to love Him because she saw his goodness everywhere. She taught her gentle kindnesses towards the children of the cottagers. She taught her to know all the flowers by their names, from the daisy of the fields, the shepherd's weather-glass, the bright blue-bird's eye, and the yellow pimpernel, to the tulips of her parterre, and the roses that bloomed in beauty and variety, upon the walls of the parsonage. Miss Alicia taught her to be pure in heart and simple-minded. She taught her to be wise with the true wisdom of childhood, which is love and faith; and womanly in word and deed and modest grace, as she grew older. She taught her to be loving and considerate for others, and at the same time, to remember her own place in life, and never to transgress the sweet proprieties, set like a fragrant hedge round the life of a true lady. If she taught her to *know* little, and to *do* little,—whereas better educated girls, are brought up for display, to *do* and *know*—she taught her to *be* good and gracious. *To be!*—ah! *to be* is to a woman worth all the doing and the knowing. To *be*, is in the power of every one of us. All God's best gifts are attainable by all; air, light, and natural beauty; human affection, goodness, holiness, his loving glances answering back the aspirations of men's hearts, may be the portion of us all. "Nay, rather," said the Saviour to those followers, who thought the mother placed in a situation unattainable by other women, must be blessed above all others of her race, "Nay rather, blessed are they that hear the word of God and keep it." Nurse was never required to return to Castleton, for, in truth, after this period, our father's family by his second wife, required all her services. She ceased to belong to Max and me exclusively. We went to school, and as our holidays were spent in Yorkshire with Veronica, we were very rarely at home.

CHAPTER V.

"My head runs round and round about,
My heart flows like a sea,
As ane by ane the thochts rush back
O' childhood and o' thee.
O mornin' life! O mornin' luve!
O lichtsome days and lang,
When hinnied hopes around our hearts
Like simmer blossoms sprang."

MOTHERWELL.

LET those who have been as happy as we were during the holidays we thenceforth passed at Castleton, thank God for the experiences of their Childhood. We can fill a child's cup to the brim with happiness, but afterwards the wine of life is bitter at the lees, we can but dash it with a temporary sweetness. The bitter taste is never lost, but by-and-by the palate gets accustomed to its bitterness. We learn to know its tonic properties, and we look forward to drinking for the first time since the cup was snatched from our lips in childhood, the pure wine of gladness in the Kingdom of God.

Little Veronica's cup sparkled in her hand. Kindness, security, affection, daily instruction, and such wholesome excitements as served to keep her interests awake, encircled her at Castleton, and the graces of her childish life happily unfolded themselves in an atmosphere as genial and as sunshiny as that of an English May. Child and queen as she was, the germs of her womanhood began early to develop themselves in our Veronica. "Women," says Teufelsdröck, "are born worshippers," and of all the figures that flitted across her camera obscura views of life, Max was the noblest object she could select for her devotion.

Poets have all felt the beauty of boyhood, and have done it reverence.

"Oh! dearest, dearest boy—my heart
For better lore would seldom yearn,
Could I but teach the hundreth part
Of what from thee I learn."

Veronica did not exercise over him the same sort of fascination she did over the grown people. They were excellent friends, and inseparable companions; but he quarrelled with her sometimes, and liked her the better because he always carried off the victory.

"Nature gives healthy children much—how much! Wise "education is a wise unfolding of this. Often it unfolds itself "better of its own accord."

Max was eminently an exemplification of this truth. Handsome, healthy, truthful, daring, and manly, with rigid adherence to a boy's code of honor, very little of his future character had been developed. That which was most prominent in him, was healthy growth. The discipline of life was to supply him training. He was a boy of remarkable simplicity and single-mindedness, vehement, impetuous, continually wrong, but always without guile. He seemed to have few intricacies of character; to dwell always in the sunshine. There was nothing moody about him; no *arrière pensées*—one always knew where to find him. You had no occasion to humor his peculiarities and fancies. There was harmonious adjustment and play of all his faculties—a "glad light from within radiated outward"—and those about him walked in the light of it. How great that blessing is in familiar intercourse, let those say who walk warily, treading in darkness on the tender places of a character, which lies under the shadow of reserve.

He loved me heartily, and Veronica very tenderly. A healthy boy twelve years of age, does not indulge in day-dreams, but he colors his panorama of the future. And wonderfully bright are the tints that he mixes on his palette (the brilliancies of Turner are nothing to it), and his drawing is as totally wanting in perspective as Hogarth' satire on Sir Edward Walpole.

Max's panorama had life and movement and triumph in it. In one part he was mounted on a war-steed, waving a blithe farewell to his cousin Veronica. In another, he was returning with laurels on his brow; but the acclamations of the multitude would have left him much to wish, had not his eye turned to a balcony above the street, where, witness of his triumph, was seen Veronica. No section of his picture could have been complete without her. She represented the womanly element which always enters even into a boy's visions of happiness. The multitude may shout man's triumph in the streets, but " only from one soul can he be always sure of reverence enough." His eye seeks out the woman he loves best, and his heart asks her sympathy, and her acknowledgment. Is it true that woman burns incense to "the golden-calf of self-love," as Jean Paul hath it?

Things went on among us in this way for some years after the death of Veronica's father. By-and-by, as Max grew older, aspired to the *toga virilis*, and attained the debatable frontier line of boyhood, he grew less sunny, frank, and single-minded. New notions began to develop themselves, which we could not fully understand. He associated less with me, and a good deal more with Veronica.

One warm, bright, golden evening, shortly before the close of the midsummer holidays, Max, Veronica and I, agreed to take our little boat, and spend some hours until twilight on the lake, gathering water lilies and reading poetry, of which, Max, though a school-boy of fifteen, was very fond. We had provided ourselves with a broad, flat, thin, and widely margined quarto from the library—a copy on India paper, of the first edition of the Corsair, and on the glad waters of our little, sunny lake, with a mischievous "*petit zéphir*," to blow over the leaves for us, we read of "the glad waters of the dark blue sea," while Veronica and I wove water-lilies into garlands, and Max, as he read, dipped his oar, now and then, into the lake, to keep us as much as possible in the middle of the water.

The shades of evening had begun to close over the landscape; Medora was consigned to early death; Gulnare had mysteriously faded out of the picture, to revive as mysteriously in Lara. Cousin Lomax, however, had concluded her life and history by writing at the close of his volume, "An Impromptu addressed by a wit to a lady who asked the fate of Gulnare, at a London party."

"Say what became of desolate Gulnare?
Ha! is it so? she cries. What? how? when? where?
A rope depending from the deck she views,
Swift to the end makes fast a running noose,
Then plunged despondent in the depth profound,
And died a double death—both hanged and drowned."

And I have questioned whether the fate assigned her by the London wit were not much more satisfactory than the Byronic ambiguity.

As Max concluded thus, we heard a shout, and looking up, saw Mammy on the grass, sending her prolonged, aspirative, negro cry of "Oigh! children—oigh, Vera!" over the water.

"What can Mammy be doing in the open air so late, with her bad cough?" said Veronica. "Make haste, cousin Max, and row us in shore."

As we drew near we heard her coughing. The ungenial climate had been telling very much upon Mammy. She had always had a grumbling wish to return to her own country. But now, when we used to talk to her of "ole Virginny," and tell her that some day she would go back to it, she had grown accustomed to say, "No, indeed, honey, Mammy's gwine furder." This did not make us unhappy, because Mammy had cried "Wolf" so often. She had always been full of complaints about her health. You could not possibly offend her more than by remarking that she looked well; and under these peculiarities of her race we did not trace the real progress of a slow consumption.

"What is it, Mammy?" we said, hailing her, as we approached the boat-house.

Mammy hailed back, in the intervals of her coughing, something about "Virginny" and "another Cousin."

We sprang on shore, and, as we did so, caught sight of cousin Lomax coming over the lawn that sloped down to the lake, accompanied by a young gentleman.

Veronica never had looked prettier. It was her birthday. Her bonnet hung upon her arm, and since the sun had set I had crowned her, like a water nymph, with a wreath of full-blown lilies. Her golden curls hung to her waist, and danced with every merry step, or the touch of every breeze. She had tied another wreath of lilies, like a girdle, round her waist, and her bonnet, hanging on her arm, was heaped with lilies.

Her first impulse, upon landing, was to give her Mammy an enthusiastic kiss, but cousin Lomax recalled her to propriety.

"Come here, my little girl; come here, Max and Molly too," said he. "Veronica, your cousin wants that kiss. This gentleman is from Virginia. His father owns Stonehenge, and was your father's second cousin. Your Christian name is James, sir, is it not?" he continued, turning to the stranger. "Your cousin James Tyrell! Give him a kiss, Veronica."

Veronica put on her air of a queen, and came up to him, offered him her cheek, and looked steadily at him, as if taking the measure of him. I struggled a little, and laughed, and pulled away as cousin Tyrell took my kiss. Whereat cousin Lomax scolded me for being coy, and told me to remember that "kissing was a cousin's privilege in Virginia."

At this moment came up Mammy, who had toiled up the slope less rapidly than we. Her black face shone a welcome, and at once struck cousin Tyrell. His eyes lighted with satisfaction. "Why, aunty," said he, holding out his hand as she came up to him, "I reckon you come, too, from old Virginia. I have seen nothing better than white folks since I left it, and it does me good to see an honest old black face once more."

As cousin Tyrell spoke thus, with his face half turned to cousin Lomax, Mammy was preparing him an unpleasant surprise. He found himself seized suddenly around the throat, and a loud kiss, five inches by three, was imprinted on his face by the ample lips of Mammy.

"De Lord be praised, mas'r, dat I done see one of our own folks from old Virginny! I knowed you sense you was mighty little chile, young mas'r. Laws! I nussed you monstrous sight o' times when my ole mas'r and my missis was living at Stonehenge, an' your pa and ma dey used to bring you over to our place, mas'r. Oh! mas'r Jim, dat place your'n now, mas'r. Ole mas'r done sell all, and leave nosing to dis chile 'ceps her old Mammy."

Tyrell, who had been a good deal startled by the embrace, but after the first shock seemed good-naturedly inclined to take it as it was meant, was put much out of countenance by this conclusion.

"The old woman is getting troublesome," said cousin Lomax, drawing away Tyrell; but the thought that Tyrell's father owned Stonehenge, jarred discordantly upon every one of us. Our father still took an affectionate pride in the old place, and often spoke to Max and me about the loss of it. We knew how bitterly he felt the alienation of his inheritance. We knew how much our own prospects in life had been changed by the careless, spendthrift habits of Alonzo Lomax. We by no means agreed with Mammy, that, setting the Tyrell interest aside, Stonehenge would belong to our little cousin. My heart brooded over my own share in the loss; for I had heard my father often say, "Cousin Lomax has promised to make all good to Max, when I am gone—but when I die who will provide for you? Your face must be your fortune, little Molly."

Cousin Lomax became thoughtful, pondering the prospects of his niece, or the misconduct of her dead father. Max put on an air of dignity to mark his sense of the pretensions of his family. But Veronica was gay and unconcerned. She walked beside cousin Tyrell, drawing from him a description of Stonehenge, which she wanted to compare with that given her by Mammy, until after a time, the stiffness consequent on Mammy's *accolade* passed off, and pleasant feeling was restored.

Cousin Tyrell was a youth barely nineteen, though he looked older. His eyes were blue—not cold blue eyes, but eyes blue like the sky warmed by the summer sunshine. He had "hair of an excellent chestnut color." A mouth firm, but its strength was tempered by its sweetness. A figure, not very tall, but closely knit. A step elastic. A gleam of pleasant fun about his eyes. Happy and thoughtful when alone—happy and genial when in company—nobody ever could have mistrusted him, or put a slight upon him. Nor did it take us long to get acquainted with such a cousin. Before bed-time we were the best of friends, and found that though graver than we were when grave things were discussed—riper than Max, better informed than any one whom we had ever met, and several years our senior—he was able to adapt himself to our society. We promised to take him all over the woods next day, and on the lake, and before we went to bed, we had Mammy into the parlor, and Tyrell told her news of the darkeys, and white folks, over the Blue Ridge, in Jefferson and Clarke Counties.

He semed to know them all, and to have endless anecdotes to tell of all of them. And cousin Lomax laughed till his chair shook under him, and Veronica drew close to Tyrell, and fixed her blue eyes upon his face, and Mammy kept up the ball of conversation as it hopped, as she stood behind his chair shaking her hoop ear-rings, and stretching out her long, lean arms; coming up to him at times, and putting her hands upon his shoulders, as she listened to what was told ostensibly for her benefit, but which was equally amusing to us all.

Nobody ever was so graphic in description as cousin Tyrell, nor was he above the weakness of enjoying a fair field and a delighted audience. He told all sorts of racy stories; he gave us negro imitations, *con amore;* he seemed to have inspired Mammy and cousin Lomax with new life, and sent us to bed regretting with all our hearts, that he could not stay longer than the next day at Castleton.

That next day we spent rowing over the lake and walking in

the woods. Tyrell, the gayest of the gay, exciting Max to many an enterprise which was to show off manly prowess, and develop manly strength. We never before had laughed so much, or walked so far, or gained so many new ideas, or enjoyed ourselves so thoroughly. Even after dinner, by moonlight, Tyrell would not let us rest, but had us off to the lake for a row, and sang plantation melodies, not known beyond the cornfield at that period. He made us join him in the choruses, and the echoes on the other side of the lake caught and prolonged the notes as they floated over the water. Veronica and I refused to sing one of his choruses, which Tyrell called "the new version," adapted to his experience of woman-kind, and present circumstances.

We protested that the sentiment was untrue; he asserted that it would be true upon the morrow; and the words, prolonged by voice and echo, seemed to linger over the lake, of the strange plaintive ending of each comic verse, which sent us into roars of laughter.

"Jim crack corn I don't care,
Jim crack corn I don't care,
Jim crack corn I don't care,
Cousin Tyrell's gwine away."

And true enough, cousin Tyrell shouldered his knapsack, and met the mail before daylight the next morning. He was on his way to a German university. An unusual destination for a young Virginian gentleman, but his father was an old diplomatist, and took a fancy to send his son abroad. He and three other young Americans, graduates of Harvard University, and also bound to Germany, were taking a preliminary pedestrian tour to the lakes of the North of England, and Tyrell had pushed on three days in advance, out of his way to York, to see his relatives at Castleton.

Max and I wrote about him to our father, who took pains to send him an invitation to come to the town where he was quartered, and to bring his party with him; but the letter failed to reach him; and when we parted from him at Castleton, upon the wide oak stair-case, with a last good-night, and a brief resistance, and a ravished kiss from each of his young cousins, and promises that we always would remember him, we saw the last of him that we were destined to see, till death and time had driven us from our retreat, and wrought a good many sad changes in our circle.

Dear cousin Tyrell! I am glad I can associate his visit with all the other happy recollections of our life at Castleton.

CHAPTER VI.

Let it not longer be a forlorn hope
To wash an Ethiope;
He's washt; his gloomy skin a peaceful shade
For his white soul is made:
And now, I doubt not the Eternal Dove
A black-faced house will love.
R. Crashaw. 1646.

Another winter holidays had passed—two other school half years, and Max and I were once more on the road to spend another six weeks at dear Castleton. Max had the box seat of the coach, and took the ribbons. For many holidays, Veronica, on her white pony, caracolling by the side of Brown Tony and cousin Lomax, had met us on the bridge which spans the little stream that runs by Castleton. This time, although the day was fair and bright, though the blue waters gurgled merrily beneath the old stone arches, and the little stream seemed all on fire with the red light of the sun, as we came up to the bridge, there was no one on the lookout for our arrival.

"Hullo! Mrs. Wilkinson," I heard Max say, as the coach stopped to leave a parcel at the toll-house. "Have you seen Mr. and Miss Lomax about, anywhere?"

And I heard Mrs. Wilkinson answer that the old black woman was ill up at the Hall.

The carriage waited for us in the village, at the foot of the hill.

The coachman confirmed the report. The doctor had confessed that day, that poor old Mammy could not live much longer.

"What will she do without her, Max?" I said; "Vera is as much of a child as she ever was, in some respects. She will be so lonely without her Mammy. It will be dreadful to be so lonely, even at Castleton."

There was a hush over Castleton, as we drove up to the house.

"Is she dead?" we asked the butler, as he came forward to open the carriage door.

"No, Miss, they think she'll linger."

Veronica had heard the wheels, and came running down, the stairs with traces of tears upon her swollen face, to bid us welcome.

"Oh, Max! Oh, Molly!" she cried, as she threw herself into our arms. "I try to be good and patient, and to trust. Mammy says I ought to trust. But what shall I do without Mammy. My mother is dead, and my father is dead, and I shall be all alone in the wide world."

She had caught Mammy's phrase, "all 'lone, all 'lone, all 'lone in dis wide worl', honey."

"You will not be alone, dear, darling Vera," said we. "We love you dearly, cousin Lomax loves you, everybody loves you, Vera."

Instinct taught us there is no human consolation to be offered to bereavement, except to pour into its wounds the balm of love.

And Veronica laid down her head and wept. "Don't stop my crying, cousin Max," she said. "It does me good. I try not to cry much in her chamber."

We went sadly to our rooms, and took off our travelling things. We dined alone with cousin Lomax.

"The poor child will have to go to school," he said, "when the old woman dies. There will be no one to take care of her."

Veronica's dinner was sent up to her. Towards sunset, a message was brought down that Mammy was awake, and wanted us to come to her.

The dying sunlight streamed over the bed, gilding the walls with its red, golden light. It fell upon the Bible in big print, from which Veronica had been reading that description of the Celestial City, in the Book of Revelations, which has an especial attraction for those of Mammy's race. It appeals more than any other passage of Holy Writ, to that which we consider a defect of taste, the love that nature gave them for the gorgeous.

Mammy lay quietly when we came in—her hands were clasped—how strange it seemed, as she lay in her white night-dress, on the white pillows and white sheets, that she should be black all over! She lay gazing earnestly at the going down of the summer's sun. It was sinking out of sight—going—Mammy knew not whither. Was she thinking that the next morning he would re-appear above the horizon to the eastward, in brilliancy and splendor, and that the other sinking light, would, when the night was passed, shine forth renewed in glory? I think that this analogy ranged above Mammy's powers of abstract thought; but she drew Veronica down, so as to bring her eyes on a level with her own range of vision, and pointed feebly to the west.

"Thar, chile, 's whar Mammy's gwine—thank the Lord. I see de towers and de pearly gates, an' de Lord is de light thereof."

"Yes, Mammy," said I—inspired by the recollection of a text to express a truth since deeply precious to my soul, but which I then hardly appreciated—"The Lord is our light and our salvation, whom shall we fear? The Lord is the strength of our life, of whom, then, shall we be afraid?"

"I'se not 'fraid to die, an' be with de Lord, honey." There was another pause beside the bed of death. The sun was sinking low behind the woods, flickering through the shadows of the leaves upon the grass, and Mammy watched it.

At last she said, "I done left all my chil'en. My chil'en over thar, honeys. Patsey, and Pete and Christopher, and Joe." She repeated the names slowly. At length she turned to Max, and said, "Come here, young Mas'r."

Max and I had been standing together full of awe, a little apart from the bed. He went to her and she stretched out her wrinkled hand, adorned with silver rings, over the Bible which lay open, and took his and drew him close to her.

"You'se been mose like my own chile, Mas' Max—you'se been mighty fond of Mammy, ever sense you was a boy, honey."

"I am very fond of you, and I always was, dear Mammy. Is there anything I can do for you? I'll do anything you ask me, Mammy," he said, perceiving there was something on her mind, and that she paused either to summon resolution, or to gain breath to ask him.

"Patsey, an Pete, an Christopher, an Joe," she repeated to herself, "and I done love dis chile of mine too well—too well, honey."

I think that what was troubling her, was a conviction that she had loved her master's child—her little white nursling—better than her own flesh and blood.

"We'll write to them," said Max, "and tell them that you thought about them to the last. But you will get better, Mammy."

"Yes, honey—but you'll never *sell* one of 'em for poor ole Mammy's sake, promise me that!" she said, rising in her bed with an energy for which we were quite unprepared, and grasping Max's hand in both of her own, and looking into his face wildly and earnestly.

"*I* sell them? what do you mean, Mammy?"

"Mas' Tom he lent money to my ole Mas'r, an he had my chil'en, Joe, an Patsey, an Christopher, an Pete. Dey's living all now up on his farm at Oatlands, way dar in Clarke County."

"Cousin Lomax wouldn't sell them, Mammy—you may be certain of that."

"An you?" she gasped. "He done make you his heir—you'll never sell them way dar down South—way from whar dey's born an brung up, way down de ribber, whar de cotton's grown? Promise me dat. Promise ole Mammy dat you'll never do dat ar, honey."

"Mammy, I cannot promise. I do not know what cousin Lomax is going to do with his Virginia estate. I do not suppose he will give his American property to me. It is only Castleton that I am to have," said Max, dreadfully embarrassed.

The old woman's face worked painfully, "De Lord have mercy on my chil'ens sure enuf," she said, "if any o' them Williamses gets hold on 'em."

"Oh! Max—Max," Veronica cried, "promise her, conditionally—promise to consult her wishes if ever you should own them."

"Veronica, it may be you."

"Mammy, dear darling Mammy," she cried, "listen to Max and me. Hear us both promise you. We do not know how it may be, but if ever we can, we will both do all in our power to help and be kind to Patsey, Peter, Joe and Christopher. And we will never forget our promise, but we will try and do our best to fulfill it, Mammy—and try to make a way to help them, and to do them good. Won't we, dear Max? Do promise her."

"Indeed I promise, I will set them free if they ever belong to me, Mammy."

"An' Mas' Max," she said, still keeping hold of his hand, "I done so love dis chile," looking earnestly at Veronica. "I'se gwine leave dis worl,' Mas'r. I 'spects you larnt to love my sweet chile mose well as her ole Mammy. Mas' Max, ain't you bin gwine to marry my Veronica? Tell me—ain't she bin gwine to be your wife, honey? I 'spected to live to see dat wedding day—but de Lord, He knows—de Lord, He knows, honey. Tell me 'bout it, chil'en—tell me 'bout it while I live, an den I shall die happy."

She had taken their two hands and pressed them together in both hers, over the open Bible. "Oh! Mammy, please don't say such dreadful things. Don't, don't say you are going to die," said Veronica.

"Dear Mammy," said Max, grasping Veronica's hand more firmly in his own. "We are very young, perhaps"———

"Yes—too young—too young," said Veronica, drawing away her hand to hide her face, and burying her blushes in her old Mammy's breast, which was unnecessary in the darkness. "No, cousin Max—don't, please, Max. Oh! Max, she is fainting away. Her head is falling on my shoulder, Max. Call help! Sarah! Molly!"

They laid the old woman, very much exhausted, back in her bed. The moon, passing out of a light cloud, shone full into the chamber of death, lighting up my brother's face, as he passed his arm around Veronica, and whispered in the ear, deaf to the promise that he wished to give, "Veronica and I together promise, always to consider your children's interests. Neither of us ever can forget how tenderly you have loved her."

She did not die that night, though she was dying then. The strength of her constitution was such, that death could not take the stronghold by assault. She lived into the next day, and then died quietly. The last sign of life she gave, was to feel about her blindly for the hand of Max, and attempt to unite it with that of Veronica.

"What was that last thing Mammy said to Veronica and Max?" asked cousin Lomax, some days after.

"About being married, I think, sir," I answered, with a blush. "But Veronica is too young to think of such things."

I was more than a year older.

"Old Mammy was a very uncommon woman," said cousin Lomax. "Trust an old Virginia servant for finding out the wishes of his Master! Veronica is mighty sweet—the sweetest thing I ever saw; and your brother will be a credit to his family. I mean to put him into the army, Molly."

So cousin Lomax, unsolicited, gave a tacit consent to the understanding between Max and Veronica. I do not suppose the children talked of marriage, and I never asked them, for I had been brought up in a very strict school of propriety, and taught that love-making was an improper pastime. But here was a case where everybody seemed to regard it with complacency. "All heavenly aspects" seemed to smile on this attachment. The naughty little god laid like a foundling at our gates, had been brought in, welcomed, dandled in our midst, and adopted by the family. He seemed to like his entertainment. He took the darts out of his roguish eyes, and laid aside his mischief. There were no signs of his little wings as yet. Max went nowhere unaccompanied by Veronica. Propriety apart, I used to feel a little lonely as I watched them walking up and down the gravel paths, at early morning or by moonlight, her pretty head a little bent, while Max, in a low voice, was talking to her. Adam and Eve, when they talked love, must have done it in a whisper.

And, being loved had a charming influence upon Veronica.

She was more winning than ever to her uncle; who was always throwing out hints of his approbation of the state of things between her and my brother.

They read out of the same books—they talked endlessly together. She would sing like a little wild song-bird, all the music that he liked, in the sweet English hour of twilight, which all lovers love. They rode together every day on horseback. They had a hundred merry jokes, for, after all, they were but children. I found them with a basin of soap-suds, and two long pipes, blowing prismatic soap-bubbles.

The world of Veronica, was Max; the world of Max, was Veronica. Had all the universe been blotted out, excepting an area of twenty miles round Castleton, it would scarcely have given either of them an uneasy thought.

Love rarely gives the right-hand of fellowship to laughter. Little dwarf hopes, and great, dim Genii-like fears, according to my experience, wait upon his steps and travel in his company. But for once he had given the slip to his grim escort, and had started off on a frolic by himself, before his usual waking hour.

Her dear old Mammy's death had tamed Veronica's gay spirits, and Love, when he first found her, had nestled at her side, with a brief show of sympathy. But very soon his inborn restlessness prompted him to stir up his young playmate, and before the holidays were ended, we had many a game of romps, in which the truant rogue played a gay part at Castleton.

Neither Veronica nor I ever dreamed of disputing the fact, that Max was the handsomest, wittiest, cleverest, bravest and most generous of human creatures. Max thought so himself very likely. He exercised a very absolute sovereignty at Castle, ton. Veronica was not even his queen-consort. She had abdicated in his favor. It was her pleasure to bring him incense, to wait upon him in a russet gown, and be his hand-maiden. I could see this disposition to worship, stealing over her in sober moments; while Max complacently put on the royal purple, cocked his crown jauntily, and made himself at ease upon his comfortable throne.

We might have got tired of this sport at last, and Love would have borrowed some trick of cousin Puck, or have rambled away by stress of *ennui*, had not the summer holidays come to a conclusion.

Max had left his grammar-school, and was going to study fortification with a tutor in London.

I was to return to the establishment of Miss Lucas, where my education was being "finished," as it was called; and cousin Lomax had arranged I should be accompanied by Veronica. During the last week of the holidays, our cousin's spirits drooped. She would steal up into Mammy's room, where Max often went in search of her. If there were tears upon her cheeks, he kissed them away; if the loss of her old Mammy's watchful love made her lonely at heart, it surely needed but few words from Max to fill the void. Yet many sad tears fell into her trunks as she was packing them. Mammy had had a personal regard for the pretty clothes over which she presided; very pretty clothes they were, trimmed with an unusual quantity of lace, which was one of the dainty fancies of Veronica.

She insisted on going everywhere, and taking a last leave of every one at Castleton. We knew how they would miss her at the Rectory, where the dust of the Doctor's study had been illuminated by her presence, like a gleam of daily sunshine. He took her into that *sanctum* by herself, away from Max, and me, and Miss Alicia, and meant to give her good advice, but, somehow, he could only press into her hand Mrs. Chapone's letters, his voice faltered, and he folded her in his arms, and gave her a loving blessing. The old square piano in the little, cold drawing-room, where she had been used to practice, would miss her daily touch, and the bottle of snakes in spirits of wine, sent home from India by a gallant son, now dead, in shaking which, she had daily wasted idle moments during her practising hour. And kind Miss Alicia Dwyer would miss her pupil very sadly, and was preparing a great basket of light pastry and rich cake to console her at the moment of departure.

At church on the last Sunday, kind looks followed her as she went weeping down the aisle, for all the people loved her.

The housekeeper and butler had a hundred directions given them about the pony and dear Luath, the swans, the owl, and all the other dumb, tame creatures, who would surely watch, with "hope deferred," for the brightness of her coming. And though cousin Lomax did not choose to say how lonely he should be without her, we saw he had hard work to keep his spirits up, and that when he told her over and over again that the change was for her good, he was speaking to himself rather than to her.

The hardest parting was from Luath. He knew that something was going on, and kept close to her. The butler had orders from cousin Lomax to put a rope through his collar, and to tie him up when we were gone; and when Veronica saw this preparation, as she came down the stairs on the morning of departure, her fortitude forsook her; she threw her arms round Luath's neck, and passionately kissed his hairy face, and sobbed so uncontrollably, that cousin Lomax was forced to disengage her arms, and put her almost fainting into the carriage.

CHAPTER VII.

"Ah! these children, these children!" said Mr. Churchill, as he sat down at the tea-table; "we ought to love them very much, now, for we shall not have them long with us." "Good heavens!" exclaimed his wife, "what do you mean? Does anything ail them? Are they going to die?" "I hope not; but they are going to grow up, and be no longer children."

H. W. Longfellow. *Kavanagh.*

At the first large town upon our route, we changed our carriage for the London mail, for the experience of life had taught more wisdom to cousin Lomax than to our grandfather, who was of one mind with that O'Flaherty, who boasted to the O'Flannagan, "that the founder of his house was not saved in Noah's ark, for that his family had never patronized public conveyances."

Towards the middle of the afternoon, we reached a large, lone inn, at the spot where the road into the eastern counties branched from that to London.

Here, our father, Col. Mandeville, who was to take Veronica and me to the Cathedral town, upon the outskirts of which stood Miss Lucas's establishment, was looking out for us. Max was to continue his journey to town with cousin Lomax. The parting was necessarily brief between him and Veronica.

As our coach drove up to the large, lonely, haunted-looking inn, we saw a very handsome barouche packed, but without horses, standing before the door. An elegant looking young man in a shooting jacket, was giving orders to a servant dressed in livery, and rather conspicuous arms were emblazoned on the panels.

"It is Sir Harris Howard's carriage," said our father, answering my inquiring look, as he let down the iron steps and opened the coach door.

During the brief moments while the horses were being changed, Veronica and Max stood together on the porch. Her veil was down, and she was crying. I went away and stood at my father's side, that I might not interrupt their parting.

"The Begum is here," said my father, "and is going to put her little girl under the care of Miss Lucas, at Fairfield. That young man is the nephew of Sir Harris, and heir presumptive to the Baronetcy. How do you do, Mr. Howard?"

And now the note of preparation sounded from the guard's horn on the back seat of the mail. Cousin Lomax hastily wrung our father's hand, and kissed Veronica. Max followed his example. They were gone!

"Come into the house," my father said, opening the door of the best parlor of the inn. "I suppose we shall find the Begum."

But on entering it I was disappointed, only a dark complexioned, weird looking child was in the room.

My father shook his head. "*Chee-chee*," he whispered. "I am too much of a Virginian to like that. It is common enough, though. There are plenty of them."

"*Chee-chee*, papa? What's that?"

"Hush," said my father, and as he said this, the door opened, and a remarkable looking female entered the room. She was a tall woman, with a very dark skin, soft, lustrous, East-Indian eyes, and on her head she wore a large white muslin turban. I knew her at once. Her husband's place was on the outskirts of our town. I had seen her often as she rode in her barouche, with her postillions and four horses. I had run to the window many times and gaped at the dusty vision. The good lady stood to me as an impersonation of royalty. There was about her in my childish eyes, some of the "divinity that doth hedge a king," rendered far more palpable and personal than any royalty, elective or divine, that I have seen since by a semi-orientalism of costume. The Begum's white muslin turban was, in my eyes, a crown. The cashmere shawl, in which her long, lean form was always wrapped, was her imperial purple.

My father was too much imbued with the spirit of the times, and the public opinion of the place, not to feel a sort of reverence for the swart wearer of the turban, not at all upon the grounds of her "majesty" or "right divine," but because she was the lady of General Sir Harris Howard, Baronet, proprietor of one of the most noble parks in England, which had been in his family since the days of the Conqueror. Sir Harris was the greatest man of our town. He noticed, with regal condescension, the officers in garrison. He lent the weight of his presence upon public days, as patron of his borough-town and president of her charitable institutions. The name of Sir Harris Howard gave sanction to subscriptions. His voice was awful on the magistrates' bench. He gave his countenance to high Toryism. His patronage was a tower of strength to our venerable establishment. Nay, I am not sure he did not patronize the King.

Our father had dined frequently at Howard Park, and saluted the Begum as she came into the inn parlor.

"Come here and speak to Lady Howard, Moll; she is going to take her little daughter to your school," said he, accompanying his speech with an admonitory look which said, "Hold up your head, Molly."

The Begum was a person of but few ideas, and of few words. I have no reason to believe she ever had received an European education. She was a sort of wonderful gilt doll at Howard Park, rather in keeping with the mystery and magnificence of that august establishment.

Veronica sat apart upon a sofa, with her veil over her face, while I endeavored to make acquaintance with the weird child, who was the daughter of the Begum. She asked me a few questions about Fairfield, and what Veronica's name was, and why she was crying. After which, she turned her back upon me, kneeling in the window-seat, and fixed her attention on her cousin in the shooting-coat, who was holding parley with the landlord, and commending the four splendid Howard bays to his especial care.

I turned to Veronica and tried to comfort her. My father was conversing in a low voice with the Begum. But Veronica refused comfort. She was at all times ready to share her pleasures. If any happiness were granted to her, she renewed the miracle of the loaves and fishes, making her portion for one multiply to the satisfaction of all around her; but when she was in trouble, she was always reserved.

I walked to the window and examined the names cut in the glass. I was uncomfortably impressed by the Howard superiority. The landlord and the landlady, the hostlers, postillions, chambermaid, and boots all bowed down to the barouche with the four horses.

As I stood beside Miss Howard, thinking thus, Mr. Howard came into the room, and summoned his aunt and cousin to the carriage.

"That is a fine young man," my father said, as they drove off.

"Very," I replied, "but I did not like the rest of them; I thought they looked down upon me and Veronica."

"Nonsense!" said my father, in a tone a little cross—I suspect he had been suffering from such feelings during his conversation with the Begum.

"But, papa," I persisted, drawing forth under the pressure of wounded feelings, a thought which I had never presented to his notice till that moment; "was not Pocahontas an Indian princess? And are not we descended from Pocahontas? And was not Pocahontas as good as the Begum?"

"Stuff, child! hold your tongue. An English lady is a *lady*, the Queen can be no more. Tell them you are a Miss Mandeville, of Virginia. That your ancestors were ladies and gentlemen, and spent their money royally, and owned and lost magnificent estates, while the grandfathers and fathers of half our would-be-aristocracy, sold farthing candles in small shops, or carried the hod. As to these Howards!—Don't let me hear again of Pocahontas. *My* family is tainted with no savage blood."

In spite of the tone in which my father spoke of this alliance with East Indian royalty, our officers would put off any other engagement to accept an invitation from Sir Harris Howard. Sir Harris, to be sure, kept a good cook, and was a distinguished general officer. He had served in early life in India, where he had been made English Resident at the court of some Nabob or Rajah, and had married the Rajah's or Nabob's daughter. The Resident thus connected by marriage with the native court, lived in regal splendor at his Residency, and on his recall to England, brought with him a large establishment of native servants, lakhs of rupees, strings upon strings of diamonds, pearls, and rubies, and his princess, the Begum. The servants, one by one returned to India. The jewels and rupees (converted into India Stock), renewed the long decaying grandeur of Howard Park; and the bride grew old, but never Anglified, amongst the stately magnificence of her occidental home. There was a solemnity about the grand old gloomy place, which may have suited her Indian hareemic notions of seclusion and propriety. She drove about the country with four horses, and her carriage and her "natives" astonished the natives of our neighborhood.

By degrees, the Begum grew a fixed fact in the history of that part of the country. She took little share in social interests and none at all in political or borough life, as the lady of Howard Park, under other circumstances, might have been expected to have done; but a real, live princess, was a credit to the neighborhood, and the little known of her by the public, was not of a nature to render her unpopular. She went to Church in state, with all her family. Her daughter had been Christianly baptized. She had borne Sir Harris several sons who had died in India, but this was not regretted in the neighborhood, where his orphan nephew, Harry Howard, the heir presumptive of the Baronetcy, was decidedly popular. He rode with the hounds, accepted invitations to the mess-table, and his acquaintance was in request among the younger officers.

Miss Lucas's establishment at Fairfield, was situated in a Cathedral town, and patronized by the best families in the Eastern counties.

I had been the pupil of Miss Lucas several years, and there had been frequent propositions on my father's part, that I should be accompanied by Veronica. But cousin Lomax, till old Mammy's death, turned a deaf ear to advice upon this subject, and Veronica was suffered to grow up unpruned and trained and clipped, while all my natural dispositions were subjected to unnatural educational processes. But I was always a perverse and sturdy plant, and never had been much of a favorite in the school, either with the scholars or teachers. I had no county influence, which counted for a good deal in the establishment. My father was suspected of Radicalism, and had American associations. I caught little of the "esprit du corps," led by the favorites and adopted by the masses. I was not a pretty child. My disposition was thought odd, and I always wore the red mark for "bad carriage."

Under these disadvantages, I was not the person to introduce Veronica favorably at Fairfield. A great fuss was made over the accession of so important a pupil as the daughter of Sir Harris Howard and the Begum, while the *entrée* of Veronica Lomax into the school ranks was comparatively disregarded.

I suppose some of the girls drew from Miss Howard, the new favorite, an account of what she had observed about Veronica and Max during the few moments she had watched them from the window, for after a few days I began to perceive we were looked upon with disfavor by the authorities, and were kept as much as possible apart from the other pupils.

I noticed this more than Veronica, who was wrapped up in her own thoughts, but I was very sensitive about popular consideration, and was anxious to persuade everybody that Miss Lomax, of Castleton, with her pretensions to family in the Old Dominion was "quite as good," as I called it, as Miss Howard, of Howard Park, the daughter of the Begum.

"Is Miss Lomax heiress of Castleton?" asked one of a group of elder girls with whom I had been discussing the subject.

"No—not in her own right; but she is going to marry my brother, who is to inherit Castleton."

As I said this, I became conscious that Miss Lucas, entering the room, had overheard me. It was the post-hour, and she had letters in her hand. She ordered me back to my desk, and distributed the letters, retaining one, however, in her hand.

Veronica came into the room and took a French lesson. When the school was dismissed, a message from Miss Lucas summoned both of us into a small room she called her *boudoir*. I knew that something dreadful was on the point of taking place, but Veronica, less accustomed than I was to the habits of the house, attended the summons with indifference.

Miss Lucas (I can see her now, dressed in red cashmere worked with little yellow dots, and a cap trimmed with yellow ribbons) stood, stern and forbidding, in the centre of the floor.

"I sent for you, Miss Lomax, to receive this letter."

The warm blood mounted in Veronica's fair face. Miss Lucas saw it

> "Come and go with tidings from the heart,
> As it a running messenger had been."

She turned the direction of the letter to Veronica, and said, "I wish to ascertain, Miss Lomax, if you know who wrote this letter?"

"Yes ma'am—my cousin Max," said Veronica faintly.

"Are you aware, Miss Lomax, that young ladies at Fairfield are not allowed to correspond with school-boys or with gentlemen? It is not the rule at Fairfield (whatever it may be in other establishments for the education of young ladies) for your governess to read the correspondence of your parents. From your parents we presume you can hear nothing wrong. But all other letters—letters from brothers, sisters, and young lady friends, are read by me, or by my sister, before they are delivered to our pupils. Correspondence with young gentlemen is absolutely prohibited."

Veronica hung down her head. There was poor Max's letter within reach, and its perusal was denied to her. The tears gathered in her eyes, but she did not say a word.

"Where is your cousin now?" said Miss Lucas.

"He has gone to a tutor near London, to study fortification, and by and by he is to go into the army," said Veronica tremblingly.

"You will not be permitted to hold any correspondence with him," said Miss Lucas. "For this once," she added, "I will break the seal, and if there is anything proper for you to receive I will give it you."

"Oh! if you please, Madam," said Veronica, frightened at the impression a rhapsody from Max might produce upon Miss Lucas, "I had much rather you would burn my letter than open it."

Miss Lucas quelled her excitement with a look; broke the seal deliberately, and glanced down the heavy, round-hand pages of the letter. When she had done she folded it lengthways and spoke, striking it across the palm of her left hand, to give emphasis to her words, "Miss Lomax, this is a highly improper letter."

Veronica was speechless.

"Miss Mandeville," said Miss Lucas, turning to me, "I understand you have been spreading a report among your companions, that a very improper state of things exists between your brother, Mr. Mandeville, and his cousin."

Miss Lucas paused for a reply, and I began. "If you please, ma'am, I never said but once, and that was to Miss Smith as you came in, that Max and Veronica were going to marry each other."

"Silence!" said Miss Lucas, with a frown. "Can you be at all acquainted with the character of this establishment, and believe that I would suffer any young lady to remain at Fairfield under such circumstances? Indeed, young ladies, I owe it to your innocent companions, to see that they are not corrupted by such influences. During the years that I have been at Fairfield, I have never detected a young lady receiving a flagrant letter of this nature before."

After a pause: "I shall write by to-night's post, both to Col. Mandeville and to Mr. Lomax, requesting them unless this . . . . unless all ideas of this nature are given up, to remove you from my establishment. I have duties to perform towards the other young ladies who are under my care. How shall I answer to other parents, if I expose their daughters to bad influences? What shall I say, for example, to Sir Harris and Lady Howard?"

"Oh! Miss Lucas," I cried in terror, "you are not going to expel us from Fairfield? It will be a disgrace for life to us!"

"I am very sorry ma'am," began Veronica.

"Take your pen, Miss Mandeville, and write to your brother what I shall dictate," said Miss Lucas, interrupting her.

"MY DEAR BROTHER:

"Miss Lucas desires me to inform you that she has taken possession of your letter of the 27th ultimo, addressed to Miss Lomax, and will take an early opportunity of placing it in the hands of Mr. Lomax, her guardian and uncle. She desires me to add, that all correspondence between gentlemen and her young ladies is strictly forbidden, and so long as Miss Lomax or I remain pupils in this establishment, she requests you will abstain from addressing communications of any nature to either of us. I remain, with kind regards,

"Your affectionate sister,

"MARY MANDEVILLE."

"You may go to your chamber, young ladies," said Miss

Lucas, "and will stay there until I receive answers to the letters I shall write your friends. Your meals will be sent up to you. I am sorry to disgrace you in the eyes of the school, but it is absolutely necessary for the sake of the unblemished character of this establishment, that misconduct of this nature should be put a stop to."

We passed a miserable week, as Pariahs and outcasts from the little school society. We were shut up in a bed-room by ourselves, as if we should spread infection among our schoolfellows. Miss Lucas visited us every day to hear our lessons, and while the others were in the school-room, we were suffered to walk for an hour out of sight in the lower part of the garden.

At the end of a dreadful week, during which we had learned "to have a proper sense of our conduct," as Miss Lucas expressed it, she sent for us again into the *boudoir*, and told us she had received letters from Mr. Lomax and Col. Mandeville, which were perfectly satisfactory. That we might be assured that our parents would never countenance behavior or conversation such as we had been guilty of. And that she had consented not to disgrace us by dismission from her school, on consideration that all correspondence with my brother should be given up, and on the assurance that we should be thrown little in his company during the holidays. We were also required to promise that we would never speak on the subject (for the sake of our own reputation, said Miss Lucas) with any of the young ladies of the establishment, and were admonished to dismiss all thoughts of it for ever from our minds, as vain, light-minded, and improper.

We promised, and went back to the ordinary routine of school-life and school society. But a dreadful blight seemed to have come upon us. We felt that intimacy with us was suspected by the teachers. There was a general order given, that we were never to walk with the same girls two days in succession, for fear of corrupting them by our conversation, and they were liable to be cross-questioned as to the nature of what we said to them.

Veronica's spirits and health gave way under this discipline, and towards the close of the half year, they had to be more kind to her.

We passed our winter holidays at my father's home, as cousin Lomax was making some repairs at Castleton. Max was with us in Christmas week, but Veronica was very reserved towards him. She had learned to look upon what had passed in the light of the public opinion of Fairfield, and before the barriers of her shyness and remorse were broken down, it was time for Max to return to his tutor, who only gave ten days of holiday at Christmas, and a long vacation in September.

Miss Howard asked us during these holidays to Howard Park. She was an ill-educated, disagreeable girl, and neither Veronica nor I liked her; but Mr. Howard was there, and very kind. He showed me a great volume of the Hogarth Gallery, which entertained me delightfully, and I went home coveting my neighbor's house, especially a room that Mr. Howard said that nobody cared for but himself—the magnificent oak library.

The next summer we spent six weeks at Castleton, but Max was not there, for our holidays did not agree with his vacation.

Veronica drooped and missed him everywhere, but it was pretty to see her meeting with Luath and the pony, the servants and the village people, the Doctor and Miss Dwyer; to all of whom, as well as to her uncle, her return had been an event of pleasing anticipation. Her room had been freshly painted and papered. The old gardener had brought his choicest flower-pots to decorate her balcony, and Mr. Lomax, viewing her pleasure in these changes with complacency, and guessing, perhaps, her secret thoughts, said, smilingly, "Now all we want, my dear, is Max, in spite of old Miss Lucas, and next year, when you come home for good, he will be here."

But before next year, Max had gone into the army, and his regiment had been ordered to Ireland. He stopped to see us, at Fairfield, on his way from Castleton, and paid us a stiff visit in the best parlor, under the frowns of Miss Lucas, in whose presence Veronica, though seventeen, dared hardly speak to him.

We left school when the summer came, but in vain expected him at Castleton. He was looking after Ribbandmen and stills of illicit whisky, and wrote word that it was impossible to get leave of absence for more than a few days. It was not worth while to come to Castleton till he could make a visit of some length. He had several tempting invitations from the officers of his regiment, who were Scotchmen, to go with them to the moors that autumn, and to visit their families. He talked a good deal of Lord de Brousse, who was his fellow subaltern, and had made several agreeable acquaintances, he said, since he had been in Ireland.

CHAPTER VIII.

"Behind no prison grate she said,
Which slurs the sunshine half a mile,
Are captives so uncomforted
As souls behind a smile."

MRS. BROWNING.

It is a woman's business to look beneath the surface of life, to search out hidden causes, "to resist the beginnings" of pain. How many heart-aches are never guessed at by those who are about our path, and about our bed, day after day! Questions are answered with a cheerful voice, even while they break in on agonizing thoughts, and from the inmost heart rises a cry of pain.

"Each in its hidden sphere of joy or woe
Our hermit spirits dwell."

Talk of voyages of discovery! you and I know as much of public opinion in Timbuctoo as we know of the feelings agitating the classes of society below us or above us. We conjecture more truly about the frozen regions than we do about the secret thoughts of the young girl at our side. She sits with us beside the evening lamp, silent, and sewing, and the thoughts worked into the worsted or the lace, are not guessed at as we watch the progress of the crochet or embroidery. Ours to her would be a mystery. She watered her couch with her tears last night, while our hearts were light in the next chamber. Her grief was not brightened by the reflection of our joy—nor did the shadow of her cloud fleck the sunshine of our happiness. The news which elated us would have fallen on her ear as a mere piece of intelligence. The column of the newspaper she turns to when she opens it we glance at indifferently, with careless eyes. We have no secrets in our hearts which make us eager about shipping intelligence. She would be astonished if she knew we read with interest the money market and city news. The thought which strengthened us when we laid down the Book of God, and sank upon our knees last night, is not adapted to her spiritual condition. The terror which walked in darkness round her bed is an enemy that we have met and conquered. Yet she knows nothing of that experience, and is painfully working out at heavy cost an experience of her own.

Veronica ceased to talk to me of Max. That the childish attachment formed for him was growing with her growth, and maturing with her strength, I only guessed. Max had not written to her since his letter was intercepted in our old school-days. I knew she did not consider it an engagement. But she never told me what was passing in her thoughts. I saw that she was growing pale, and that her step was less elastic—a sure criterion of the spirit's change—but she said nothing to me of any care or secret grief, and I did not like to ask her. We took no sweet counsel together now, her secret sundered us. She was afraid, perhaps, that I should read her heart, afraid to read my thoughts, and learn that my fears about Max gave countenance to her anxiety. A true woman's conduct is made up of apparent inconsistencies. Though with me she was reserved and self-absorbed to hide her secret, with others she became from the same cause sociable and friendly. She found it easier to talk to strangers than to her nearest friend. She grew fond of going out, and visiting about the neighborhood, and often the horses would be put to the carriage, and we would be driven fifteen miles over bad roads at night, that Veronica might have the relief of talking commonplaces with the neighboring county ladies. She grew weary at home of the effort of concealment, and was thankful to take her part in their mild chat, which drew off her thoughts from her home griefs without any effort of her own. She became suddenly busy with parish clubs and village duties, under the patronage of good Miss Alicia Dwyer. The Rector no longer found her sitting on his library steps, reading out of his biggest tomes, but she went daily to the Rectory, and held little committees, and made school tippets for the children out of cotton and list, and listened gladly to the village stories and kind common-place moralities of Miss Alicia. We never now heard her gay laugh—as glad as marriage chimes, ring clear along the passages—but her face, except when she was unobserved, was always lighted by a quiet smile.

In happier times she had loved to be alone, and you might often hear her

"Singing to herself like bird or bee,"

among the flowers in the garden—but now in her unoccupied moments she was always beside cousin Lomax; and the old man who was getting infirm, grew very tender to her. He liked to see her pretty face, and hear her soft sweet Southern voice, and probably had never been more proud and happy in the best days of his youth, than when she sat by his arm-chair and read aloud his daily paper. She knew where to pick out such parts as he would like. She knew how to modulate her voice, so as to suit his drowsy moments, and emphasized the passages she knew he wished to hear. I never knew her lose her self-command but once, and that was when he laid his hand upon her arm one night, and said, "God bless you, my sweet child. You are a comfort to me." She wrote for him, she kept all his accounts —he referred to her when he was at a loss—he leaned upon her arm as he gave his orders to the gardener, and tears, poor child, were smothered in her heart, while smiles were upon her lips. She was trying to bear everybody's burden, and nobody ever guessed that she was already overladen with her own.

She seldom set foot into the woods, except when she accompanied her uncle. Day after day the boy who went to the next post-town, was told to exercise her pony. The rope was rotting of the swing in the big walnut tree (put up by Max), where Mammy had been used to seek her "chile" whenever she was missed, and where nine times out of ten she found her, with the tip of one small foot touching the moss, swaying slowly with the motion of the branch, dreaming her summer day-dreams and reading poetry.

Except the newspapers, pamphlets, or books of travels read to cousin Lomax, she never opened a book now. She had no appetite for reading. Over every pleasant volume in the house, her curls had touched the cheek of Max. It was when speaking of the book they read together, that Paulo and Francesca told the poet:

> "Nessun maggior dolor
> Che ricordarsi del tempo felice
> Nella miseria."

There was another change in her. Formerly, she had loved the early morning hours, as happy children always do, or happy summer birds; now she was always late. When she made her appearance in the household, she was dressed for the day, the mask was fastened firmly on till night. No wonder she put off as long as possible the hour of resuming it. I went into her room one morning after she left it, and found upon her bed the Sacred Pages blistered with her tears.

They got up a Race Ball at Doncaster, and sent us tickets. "Let us go, Uncle," said Veronica, eagerly. Alas! with the heart-ache, we may be ever so restless, but little or no relief will come from change. If Veronica had proposed a trip to Paris or the Sandwich Islands, I believe that cousin Lomax would have essayed to start, and have drawn on his boot over his gouty toe. He performed this act of martyrdom at her bidding on the ball night, dressing at the inn where the assembly took place, and escorting Veronica, Miss Alicia, and myself, into the dingy ball-room.

Veronica was tall, and all her movements were composed and stately. At school, or when she danced with Max to Miss Alicia's old Scotch tunes on the old piano, her curls had danced as gaily as her feet; now she swept through each quadrille with elegance, but little animation. She looked extraordinarily handsome, and gave every one her smile, so that ten minutes after she appeared, she was the reigning favorite. I heard comments, often couched in sporting terms, upon her beauty, and her "points," among the gentlemen.

As the evening went on, her spirits really rose—there was a gleam of her natural gaiety, for her heart had connected Max with her triumph by the thought that she was glad the woman whom *she hoped* he loved should be admired by other people. She was dancing with more animation, and the expression of her face was less fixed than it had been of late. Her smiles were genuine and more flitting. Suddenly, she caught sight of cousin Lomax, who looked bored to death; indeed, his gouty foot in the dress-boot was beginning to pain him. I saw her go up to him at the close of the quadrille, and offer him her arm, and a moment after every eye was turned on them as they came down the room. Youth and decrepitude—beauty sustaining age! Not any one who was present at that ball, but must remember them.

They came slowly, as I said, down the middle of the ball-room. She was the taller of the two. Her dress was India muslin, made high in the neck—that was her fancy. A handsome coral ornament fastened it at the throat. She wore a coral bracelet, and coral had been twined in the blonde tresses of her sunny hair. It was the simplest dress in the room, but she looked like a queen in it and wore it regally.

A certain Captain Collinson, who had just been introduced to me, was standing by me. His invitation to dance was broken short by the general attention attracted to this beautiful vision. Nobody could have seen her with the soft light in her eyes, the bright flush upon her cheeks, guarding the old man who leant upon her—the clinging ivy that supports the wall—the prop of his decaying strength, and not have felt there was a holy beauty, rarely seen in ball-rooms, in the vision.

I declined the proposal to dance, and joined her and cousin Lomax. I took the arm of Miss Alicia, and Captain Collinson accompanied us into the cloak-room. Veronica soon found her scarlet and white cloak and hood, which were conspicuous; but cousin Lomax had gone for the carriage before I lighted on my wrappings. As I was tying them on, Captain Collinson said, "I believe I am acquainted with a brother of yours, Miss Mandeville. I have been trying to get near you all the evening, to ask you to dance. Have you heard of him since I left him at Castle MacIntyre?"

"It is not my brother," said I. "My only brother, Max, is in Ireland, at the dépôt of the 189th regiment."

"I mean Lieut. Lomax Mandeville, of the 189th. I left him in Scotland last week on leave, staying with Lord de Brousse at Castle MacIntyre. I had no idea I should meet his family in this place, or I should have asked him to honor me with some message or letter."

"Max in Scotland!" cried I. "What could have taken him to Scotland? If he is on leave, he ought to be at Castleton."

"You must not be too hard on him, Miss Mandeville, there are great attractions at Castle MacIntyre. Young gentlemen too often show bad taste by forsaking the society of their sisters for that of ladies much less charming. Lady Ellen MacIntyre is certainly a splendid woman, and my friend Mandeville, an ardent adorer."

I felt myself growing pale. The blood seemed curdling at my heart. I had not presence of mind to stop his foolish talk. I dared not look at Veronica. She saw my agitation, and solicitious to cover it, yet hear the worst, she mastered her own feelings. Her voice was almost steady as she asked, "How long has Mr. Mandeville known Lady Ellen?"

"Only a few weeks, but he fell over head and ears in love with her at once," was the reply.

"Is she handsome," said Veronica, quickly. "Brunette or blonde?"

"She is very striking. A tall, dark beauty, with a high complexion. Older than he is, I should say. One of your dashing sort. She leads Mandeville a very pretty love chase."

I looked up at Veronica. There was a burning spot of color in each cheek. Her eyes were very bright. The muscles of her face were very fixed, and the dilation of her nostrils gave her an expression almost fierce and very eager. Her head was thrown a little back, and her whole air was proud. She stood drawing the tassels of her cloak nervously through her fingers.

"Lady Ellen MacIntyre favors his suit? did you say she favors him?"

The Captain, who saw nothing beyond his own share of what was going on, replied readily: "Lady Ellen is so experienced a flirt, that nobody can tell. But I told Mandeville I thought he had a fair chance to go in and win. He has large expectations, at least so we have understood. This will further his suit with Lord de Brousse, and I dare say will be no disadvantage in the eyes of the young lady."

At this moment, cousin Lomax, who had been calling up the carriage, came back to where we stood. He heard what the young man said, and looked him in the face. The impudent young fellow whose tongue had been loosened by the wine-cup, suddenly perceived his error, and guessed at once whence the expectations in question were derived.

"I —— I ——" he stammered, "have only been repeating gossip, sir."

"And gossip," said cousin Lomax, "which I have reason to know, sir, is quite false. Come, Veronica."

The luckless young tell-tale gave me his arm, and we followed.

"Tell me," said he, "have I blabbed like a fool anything to injure your brother with the old gentleman?"

"I don't know," said I; "I think we had better know it all. Are you sure of what you told me?"

"Molly, have the goodness to make haste," said cousin Lomax in a sharp, quick voice. "Shut up the door, James, and tell the fellows to drive on quickly."

God knows what thoughts were tossing, raging, surging in

poor Vera's breast. I had enough to do to control my own. I was first conscious of insane purposes to strangle Miss Alicia, who went on chirping about the ball. "Don't you think so, my dear?" to Veronica. "Mr. Lomax, won't you put up your lame foot upon this seat?" "Mary, my dear, it was a pity we came away before your dance with Captain Collinson. Is he staying at Vere Park? I knew his poor mother a great many years ago."

Cousin Lomax growled at her. I sat and thought that I should like to choke her; and I hope Veronica was too pre-occupied to hear her. At any rate, Miss Alicia was neither checked nor offended. She went on talking without any answer.

It came on to rain. James and the postillions had taken a little too much drink. We stuck fast in a rut in a cross-road. Cousin Lomax threw open the carriage door and jumped out, with his thin boots and his incipient gout, into the cold. His Virginian temper was excited. He levelled imprecations at the servants—demanded how they dared to drive in that way when they were driving ladies—put his own shoulder to the wheel, started the carriage by the force of his excitement—jumped back into his place and shut the door with a bang which broke the handle, and he had to hold it all the rest of the way home.

Day broke just as we were entering the grounds at Castleton. As its first rays fell upon my cousin's face, I saw she had been sitting smiling in the dark, with the fixed look she had worn when listening in the cloak-room. The coral colored lining of her hood which had been becoming to her at night, now made her face look ghastly. A more miserable set than we were never got out of a carriage by daylight, limp, draggled, and dissatisfied, on their return from a ball.

CHAPTER IX.

"There is a change—and I am poor;
Your love hath been, nor long ago,
A fountain at my fond heart's door,
Whose only business was to flow—
And flow it did, not taking heed
Of its own bounty or my need."

WORDSWORTH.

REFRESHMENTS had been spread out for us, and Miss Alicia fancied she was hungry. We went with her into the dining-room. She sat down at the table, begging us to eat, but I had a choking in my throat, as if it would be impossible ever to eat again. Veronica stood over the fire. It was the chilly hour after dawn, and her dress was very wet from rain, which had found its way into the carriage. I poured out a glass of wine, and gave it to her. She tried to drink it, but the rising tears choked her, and she sat it down. She commanded herself sufficiently, however, to say with a steady voice, "I am very tired. I think I shall go to bed. Good night. Forgive me for leaving you, Miss Alicia."

She took a candle from the table, and left the room. Cousin Lomax looked at Miss Alicia (eating sardines) with great disgust, and moved away, desiring me, before I went to bed, to come into his library.

We were all bent on deceiving Miss Alicia, and yet in the midst of our wretchedness, irritation at her placid unconsciousness was the most prominent feeling of us all. When she had finished her supper she wiped her mouth and got up from table, but still she seemed disposed to chat about the ball.

I had no patience left for further conversation, and telling her abruptly that cousin Lomax wanted me in the library, I broke up the half hour of gossip which was the poor old lady's delight, and hurried her unwillingly to her own chamber.

I found cousin Lomax suffering agonies from his attack of gout. He had called up the housekeeper, who was ministering to him, but he sent her away when I came in, and told me to stand before him, and repeat, word for word, "what that fool had been saying." He had a bundle of Max's letters in his hand, and had been looking over those of latest date, while his foot was swathed by Mrs. Mayhew. I told him, word for word, what Captain Collinson had said. "And you," said he, looking me in the face, "have you heard a word from your brother about Lady Ellen MacIntyre?"

"No sir, Max writes so seldom"——

"Yes—hang it," broke out cousin Lomax. "And I write so seldom: I can't do it. It isn't in me. I never knew a letter-writing Virginian. And it's God's providence they don't write, for I never got a letter from Virginia in my life that didn't tell me something disagreeable. And so your brother makes so sure of Castleton as to bid it for a wife? He had better remember that I must provide for my niece, and that I will leave no unmarried woman my Virginian property."

"Cousin Lomax," I said, "I don't think that what escaped Captain Collinson ought to prejudice you against Max. What he repeated was mere gossip. I know Max is quite incapable of speculating upon your promise about Castleton. Max was never mercenary, and has always showed you affectionate consideration."

A twinge of pain convulsed cousin Lomax's face; when it had passed, he answered bitterly, "I am not speaking of any hopes he may have built on his expectation of my property. Old fellows must expect to have young ones looking out after their own chances. I am not quarrelling with human nature. But he had better make quite sure that I shall leave him this estate before he buys a wife with it. You will write to-morrow, and tell him this, Moll Mandeville. I shall write the same thing to another quarter. You will tell him that his sucession to the property depends on my good will—that I have another child of my adoption to provide for—nearer to me in blood—a girl who has not her rival for goodness or for beauty—that she has twined herself about my rough old heart, and I won't have him make her unhappy. I wished to see them married, and to leave my property to both of them, but if he plays her false, be hanged if he shall have one shilling. I shall write your to father to that effect, and you may tell him so."

"We do not know this news is true, sir—and it was such a childish affair between Veronica and Max, that perhaps"—— I hesitated, for I knew my supposition could be hardly true, "perhaps Veronica may not care for him."

"Ha!" said cousin Lomax, "do you know it to be so?"

"No sir, I know nothing. Veronica never speaks to me of Max. But I know she does not consider herself engaged to him."

The old man mused a moment, and then said, striking his hand upon the arm of his chair, "I have set my heart upon that match. But I would not make her unhappy. She must judge him for herself. Accept him or reject him as she likes—but he will not have Castleton except he wins her for his wife. Tell him that from me."

I bid him good night. He called me back to get him the Peerage, and turn to the De Brousse family. She was two years older than Max, this Lady Ellen MacIntyre.

The feeble rays of a November sun were struggling in at the East windows, when I went up to my chamber. As I passed that of Veronica, her door softly opened. She came out still in her ball-dress—still in her cloak and hood. Her floating robes and satin feet contrasted strangely with her face. She had been weeping bitterly.

"Mary," said she, coming out upon the landing, and taking me by the arm, "you have been with cousin Lomax. Is he angry with Max? What did he say to you?"

"Compose yourself, dear Vera. He did not tell me he was angry with Max. He is going to write to him and ascertain if this report be true."

"And sacrifice me," said Veronica passionately.

"How sacrifice you, Vera?"

"Sacrifice my pride," she said, "by letting him suppose I think of his old childish fancy. Mary, don't you know if *he* remembered it he would have been here long ago? A small excuse has mighty weight unless it is balanced by the inclination. A woman needs no better test of the feelings entertained for her. I have known it—I have known, long ago, that Max could have got leave of absence if —— if he had wanted to see his family. He cared more for his hunting in Ireland—more for his friends in the mess-room—more even for the novelty of his new military life—more for the pleasure-trip he took to the Lakes of Killarney. Max is not to be blamed for this. Max, as I have lately felt, is very young. He needed, perhaps, to have his manhood wakened into life by some strong feeling—such a feeling as he never had for me, and has towards Lady Ellen. All that has ever passed between us was a foolish, childish dream, entered into to please dear old Mammy. I cannot be expected to consider it anything else. He will marry Lady Ellen, and bring her here to Castleton, and I—I had better go away. After what has passed she will not like to see me."

"Dear Vera, you deceive yourself. We shall have no Lady Ellen here, I think. You must hear what Max can say. Oh! Vera, Vera, do not cry. Pray do not cry so bitterly."

The tears were streaming down her face, but its expression did not vary. I think she was scarcely conscious of her tears till I said this, and yet they were falling fast, like heavy rain, over her cloak and drapery. But as I spoke she started and looked up,

"And her foot trod in with pride,
Her own tears in the floor beside."

She turned from me without a word, and was reëntering her chamber when the string of her coral bracelet (her coral had been a present from Max) snapped from the force with which she dragged it from its fastenings.

"Oh! my coral!" she exclaimed, with a voice of anguish; but she did not stoop to gather up the beads. She went into her chamber and turned the key in the door.

I knocked softly and called her "Vera! dearest Vera!" But there was no sound in the closed chamber.

"Oh! Vera let me in; I am almost as unhappy as you." She would not accept my sympathy. "Veronica! Veronica!" I pleaded for half an hour kneeling at the door, nor was there even a sob to break the silence.

"Goodness alive! Miss Mary—whatever are you doing on your knees in that dress by Miss Veronica's door?"

It was the voice of the housekeeper going to the kitchen *en camisole* to heat hot water and give her master an early cup of tea.

I got up from my knees. "I wanted my dress unfastened, Mrs. Mayhew and Miss Veronica has gone to bed, and I can't open the door."

"Well! come to your own room and I'll undress you. Mercy upon us, you seem all chills and fevers, and you are all damp, and cold, and wet. Miss Veronica has gone to bed, and to sleep. She's a great deal sensibler, Miss Mary, than you." So spake the old housekeeper, privileged to speak her mind.

She put me to bed, for I was really wet and damp, and all my limbs were stiff when I rose up in my pink crape dress from the floor.

"Mrs. Mayhew," said I, "please don't say anything about my being up all night to cousin Lomax."

"Well, I won't," said she, "but I never did see such a set to go to balls, and so I was telling my master."

I could not sleep. I had shut out the day-light and darkened my chamber, but I could not shut out a thousand wakeful thoughts. What was I to write to Max? If he were really in love with Lady Ellen, would he listen to anything that I would say either from myself or cousin Lomax?

And what a disappointment it would be at home. What a change in the prospects of Max if he lost the inheritance of Castleton.

We had a growing family of half brothers and sisters, and to have Max with his expensive tastes and breeding thrown back on our small means would be a family misfortune. As Max grew up our father had congratulated himself more and more that his future was provided for. I knew that I should always have a home with Max, and the future had not troubled me; but if Max was disinherited what was to become of me?

Would Veronica have Castleton? I knew better now than ever that she cared for Max. Did people ever become happy again when they had loved once? Novels said *not*. Would she die year by year of some disease, called by another name, but in fact a broken heart? What would become of Veronica?

Oh! why had cruel Love brought this trouble on all of us? Why had he shot that burning arrow into the heart of Max from the bright eyes of Lady Ellen MacIntyre?

I pictured her glowing with health, and beautiful, and bright, but she did not shine in my imagination with a soft home radiance; the light about her was the garish brilliancy of ball lamps; there was no halo round her head of "dim religious light," but the flash of a diamonded coronet, and eyes that glittered bright as arctic stars. Oh! how could Max be led away by her from his allegiance to Veronica?

I had written to Max very rarely of late. Letters are links in the soft chain which binds the wanderer to the dear home circle. My carelessness had snapped those precious links, and had estranged my brother. I had written so little about Veronica. I lay and thought by what means I should win his confidence. God forgive me for my fault! Had I been more advanced in the experience of life—had I ever loved myself, I could not have resolved to do the thing I did. I could not have betrayed for any purpose the secrets of Veronica.

I made up my mind to tell him that she loved him. I composed an eloquent appeal to his compassion and generosity. I implored him to come back, and to make good our hopes, to remember implied promises, to be careful how he offended cousin Lomax, who might revoke his promise about Castleton.

I softened cousin Lomax's message so as to give it as little of the nature of a threat as possible, for I had the sense to know that the pride of Max would revolt against coercion. At break of day without having been to sleep, I started from my feverish bed and wrote my letter.

When I came down stairs, Miss Alicia had already gone home to the Rectory, and Veronica was not in the breakfast parlor. I was not surprised, for I expected she would stay in her room all day. I had not dared to knock at her door and ask her how she felt, as I came down stairs. Great was my surprise when the door of the breakfast-room opened and she came in booted and gauntleted, holding in one hand the folds of her cloth skirt, and in the other her riding-whip. Her face was very pale, nor was its pallor lessened by her black veil and beaver. I did not like to ask whither she was bound, and turning from the food I could not eat, said only, "Why Veronica!"

"Can I do anything for you in Doncaster?" she said, "I shall pass through it in going to Vere Park; I promised Margaret Vere to ride over and teach Kate a new stitch. She is still lame, and lies upon her sofa, unable to put her foot to the ground."

"But Veronica it is a ride of four and twenty miles, and it is raining."

"Is it?" said she, looking up indifferently, "it will not hurt me I suppose." And then with a faint laugh, "I do not fear a little rain; I am neither salt nor sugar."

"Then let me order them to put the saddle on my horse. If the day is fit for you, Veronica, it is for me; I owe a call to Margaret and Kate as well as you."

"No—no," answered Veronica in a hurried voice, "there is not time, I want to be off." And going to the door, she was in the saddle in a moment. She gathered up her reins—the folds of her riding-skirt fell into their place, and before I had time to think how strange it was, she was gallopping with the groom hard after her down the oak avenue.

Of late, Veronica had rarely mounted the beautiful white pony she had once loved as tenderly as any Arab loves his horse or child. Every ride in the neighborhood was associated with happy days with Max, and when she gathered up her reins alone, or the groom drew the drapery around her feet, she missed the touch of Max's hand. What could have taken her on so slight an excuse a ride on horseback of so many miles? Probably the recollection that there were visitors from Scotland at Vere Park, and she might be able in the course of general conversation to draw forth some further description of Lady Ellen MacIntyre.

"Dear! dear!" said Mrs. Mayhew, "my master wants to know whatever you let Miss Veronica go out for such a day as this—and she hasn't said a word about the dinner—and there's a poor woman to speak to her in the kitchen, that Miss Alicia sent—and she was to have written the names on the preserves while Sally put them in the closet. They'll get spoilt standing on the dresser and my eyes won't let me write them. Oh! dear—dear, these balls, how they do put about every body!"

"I'll write the preserves for you, Mrs. Mayhew," said I.

"Well, Miss," rejoined she, "I'll be obliged to you, and you may as well too go and see Mr. Lomax, he's dressed and in his library. He would get up all I could say; he's writing at his desk, and has been left alone this weary while, which isn't one bit like Miss Veronica."

The old gentleman was sealing a letter with a large red seal, stamped with the arms of his family. I asked if I should put it in the post-bag, but he laid his hand over it and told me, "No,

I might leave him to himself, and send Mrs. Mayhew." I went back into the housekeeper's room, sent her to cousin Lomax, called a young girl from the kitchen, and made myself busy with the pots of preserves.

While I was thus occupied Mrs. Mayhew came in and sent the girl to get the post-bag. She held in her hand the letter with the red seal, which she laid face downwards on the dresser. Cousin Lomax only sealed on great occasions with that seal, and I was curious to know to whom he had addressed this letter.

"Master bid me ask you if you had a letter ready, Miss Mary; he wants the boy to go to town at once and bring the doctor."

I went for my letter, and by the time I came back her hands were very sticky from a leak in a pot of raspberry jam.

"If you'll please, Miss Mandevil, to put it into the bag yourself," said she.

I opened the bag and lying with its face turned up was the letter with the big red seal, addressed in cousin Lomax's strong, stiff hand to Lady Ellen MacIntyre.

CHAPTER X.

Although thou must never be mine,
Although even hope is denied,
'Tis sweeter for thee despairing,
Than aught in the world beside,
Jessy! BURNS.

THINGS went on in the old way. The calm of our days was a mockery to the tumult of our thoughts. We had no new information to be fashioned into fears or hopes, but our imaginations continued like kaleidoscopes, to revolve the same old thoughts into new patterns. If Veronica gained any information about Lady Ellen at Vere Park, she did not communicate it to any one at Castleton. Cousin Lomax was confined to his room alarmingly ill. The autumn leaves began to fall, and Castleton had never looked more dreary. A dry wind whistled round the solid mason-work, stole in through the chinks and crannies of the doors and window frames, and wandered up and down the corridors, moaning to get out and play among the leaves. The sap shrank down into the roots, leaving the dry twigs crackling on the upper branches of the trees, whence the wind snapped them off and threw them wantonly away. He ruffled the breast of the little lake, and discomposed the plumage of its stately swan; he broke the dry flower-stalks across the garden paths, and scattered the seeds out of their husks and carried them for miles away, tossing them before him like his foot-balls.

More than a week had passed away since the ball-night, when one bitter autumn evening about sunset, I was hastening home alone from the little hamlet that joins Castleton. It was a windy night, the clouds were hurrying over a cold blue firmament, and I forced my way with difficulty against the wind, which seemed to have left off its mischief, and to have worked itself into a rage. At a turn in the road near a small cottage covered with green, damp thatch, I paused to pick my way. As I stopped, I heard the footsteps of a man, but as it was beginning to grow dark, I did not wish to notice him or look behind me.

A hand was laid upon my shoulder. I started and turned round with a half-scream. Max was beside me. His military figure which, since I had seen him last, had filled out in proportion to his manly height—his fashionable dress worn with a different air from any other in our quiet village, took my attention at first sight.

"Oh! Max—dear Max! How glad I am! How changed you look," I cried.

But when I raised my eyes and caught the expression of his face, I felt the change was greater than I thought. "What is the matter, Max?" said I, finding that while I threw my arms about him and pressed my lips to his cold cheek, he did not return the loving pressure.

"I want to speak to you alone," he said. "I hardly understand myself what the matter is. Oh! Molly," and he kissed me then, "I do believe you are my only friend."

"Come home," said I, "and we will talk. But it is impossible to talk in this wind."

"I am not going to Castleton," said Max, "I shall only make matters worse by being seen there. I came here to talk to you and am fortunate in meeting you. I never want to see cousin

Lomax again, and for the present had better keep out of the way of Veronica."

"Veronica is out on horseback," said I, "and cousin Lomax is ill in his own room. Oh! Max, come up to the house. We have both much to say. We can let ourselves into the great drawing-room, and have a quiet talk. But I cannot talk or even think in this abominable wind."

"Are you sure the coast is clear? That Veronica is out?"

"Perfectly. What can have happened, Max?" But Max drew my hand through his arm and walked on at a quick pace, without consideration for my shorter steps, or for the wind which blew my skirts about my feet, and my hair about my face, entangling and half blinding me.

When we were in the grounds, Max stopped behind in a clump of *arbor vitæ*, while I went into the house and opened the drawing-room window. I beckoned to Max, who, looking round and seeing he was unobserved, crossed the lawn and joined me. The room was a peculiar one. It was long, low, and would have been narrow had it not been for a very large bow-window looking towards the west, and opposite the fire-place, which made it a fine, airy, handsome room, though too large for home life, and indeed, it was only used as a state apartment.

Cousin Lomax had the American fancy for green blinds, and was always for excluding sun-light, and finding it impossible to fix green blinds to his bow-window on the outside, he had hit upon the plan of shutting off the bow when the afternoon sun shone into it from the west, by having his green *jalousies* inside the room, and when they were closed across the bow, it formed by itself a pleasant little apartment.

The room, as I have said, was not used except for company. The green blinds were generally closed to save the carpet. It never occurred to me that Veronica having found the wind too strong, had returned early from her ride, and that she was standing in the bow still in her riding dress, watching the rapid changes in the western sky.

Max entered by the south window. He put his hat upon the marble table, and flung himself into a chair. I went up to him and hung about him, throwing one arm round his neck, admiring his manly grace, his curling hair, his bright keen eyes.

"What is it, dear?" said I.

"What is it? Oh! Molly, I'm the most unlucky dog alive! Isn't it enough to be madly, wildly, hopelessly in love with the sweetest woman upon earth—a creature whom you can't even imagine, living here as you do in this hum-drum place, out of the world of fashion and society—but I must have her insulted by cousin Lomax—But I must have my love laid bare to her by common report before I was ready to declare it? Look here, Molly—look at this. It is the letter she received last week. It was given to me by Lord de Brousse, with an intimation that I had better leave the Castle. I will never forgive cousin Lomax. He may leave Castleton to whom he will. He may put a barrel of gunpowder in the cellar, if he likes, and blow it up, but I wouldn't forgive him such an insult, to such a woman, not if he went down before me on his knees in this very room—and bribed me with two Castletons."

Max drew a crumpled paper from his breast. I recognized the big red seal of cousin Lomax's letter. It was written painfully. I could see in the cramped hand the evidence of many a gouty twinge as he was engaged in its composition.

It ran as follows:—

"MADAM:

"The expectations of my kinsman and namesake, Lieutenant Thomas Lomax Mandeville, are derived solely from my verbal revocable promise to leave him Castleton. That estate, even if it were entailed upon him as my heir, would hardly meet your Ladyship's pretensions in the partnership of matrimony. As it is, however, I beg to inform you that the inheritance is contingent on his marriage with a beautiful young girl—my niece—his second cousin, to whom he has been long engaged.

"I have the honor to remain,

"Your Ladyship's obedient, humble servant,

"*Castleton.* "THOS. LOMAX."

Max gnashed his keen white teeth as I, with a scared face, perused the letter, and snatched it roughly from my hand when I had done, and read it aloud with emphasis. "There," said he, "imagine yourself insulted by getting such a letter." "And you too, Molly," he resumed after a pause, "that you should write in such a way! You seem determined, all of you, to drive me mad. I am not engaged to cousin Veronica. Ask her to tell you the truth. If she thinks I am bound to her in any way, I am ready to meet the claim, and blow my brains out when I've married her. She is a good little thing—a dear, pretty little thing—but Molly, she is not a woman like that other one—a glorious woman, whose touch thrills through your nerves, whose glance shoots straight into your heart. When I am with her, I feel at once bold as a lion and bashful as a girl. I never felt so with Veronica. She was a dear, kind, sweet, good girl, and I loved her—I always shall love her—or always should if you had not been busying yourself in making her the rival of such a woman as Lady Ellen MacIntyre. There are moments *now* when I could almost hate her for being the cause of my trouble. Molly, I could have waltzed all night with Veronica without any more sensation than I should have had of waltzing with you; but it's intoxication to have my arm round Lady Ellen's waist—to breathe the perfume of her breath and hair. Oh! you don't understand these things. You don't know how true that line of Byron's is

"The ocean to the river of his thoughts."

"I think of nothing else—I dream only of her—If I could only be a knight of old, and calm these thrilling nerves by rushing into danger for her sake! But this living in a fashionable circle in a shooting box—this following her round—this picking up her gloves and standing over her piano—this being jealous of every fool on whom she throws away a smile, was half-killing me, Molly. Oh! it is the veriest humiliation in these days for a man to court a beautiful, proud woman. He wants to snatch her from the crowd and bear her off—to do and dare for her. And he has to cringe and wait and curb his jealousy and passion, and take her frowns and wait her smiles. He must come and go, and fetch and carry—not of his own free will—not with the service of love—for God knows in that service nothing would be humiliation, but just to give her triumph—just to fulfill the conditions that society imposes upon a lover. He must be something other than he is to convince her he is true, it seems. And the worst of it is, we are so powerless. No man can tell how he is going to be treated by a woman. We go to work in the dark. Self-reliance does not help a man. Half our little ventures are stranded before we get them out of port. We want to do something to please you, and it turns out the reverse. Your one sole object is personal triumph, and half of you never accept a man till you are afraid of losing him."

"Max! Max! this is not true!" said I, to whom this kind of

experience was quite new. "I know this is not true! It cannot be!"

"It *is*, though," said Max, who had been learning in another school. "I don't know that I believe in any woman's love, except you conquer her."

"Oh! Max, think of Veronica!"

"Aye—think of Veronica," said he. "Is foolish, childish nonsense of that kind to outweigh all my happiness in life? Am I to be as I am—a miserable, ruined man at the very threshold of my life, because a little school-girl, reading sentimental books, connects me with her *héros de romans*, and fancies that she loves me? Molly, I have too high an opinion of Veronica. She must know that the follies of the nursery have been cancelled by our growth. No woman of right feeling and good principle, allows herself to become interested in any man until he has unequivocally declared his affection to her. I am ashamed a sister of mine should think otherwise. It comes of reading silly books. I have a better opinion of Veronica."

"Oh! Max, I dare not say you are not right. But that is a man's theory, and does not square with every day's experience—at least so it seems to me. I know but little on the subject, but I do not think the wisest and best women always wait to be quite sure of that. Else why is there in the world so much suffering from disappointed affection?"

But my timid little opinion was swept aside by the increasing violence of Max.

"Lady Ellen," he said, "thinks so. Lord de Brousse brought me this letter, saying that though Lady Ellen was at a loss to conceive what had given rise to it, she had consulted him as to the best course to pursue, and he advised my retiring from the Castle. I begged for a few moments' interview with his sister, only to say good-bye. After some difficulty it was granted me. I saw her cold, haughty, changed, and barely courteous. Only the night before she ——— I ——— I thought ——— I was a fool—a weak conceited fool, to fancy she could ever love me! I told her that if the devotion of my life could blot out the insult of that letter she might feel that it was cancelled! She said, in her cold way, that the contents of the note were of more consequence to me than they could be to her. I poured out all my passion, and she heard me without one change in her beautiful face, and said when I had done, that she was 'very sorry!' 'Very sorry!'—to have a woman 'very sorry!' is that any reward for a man's devotion—for the adoration of his whole being—for all a man can give a woman—heart and mind and soul? And she looked up into my face with her clear, glorious eyes (it seemed to me that I could see into their depths), and said, "She had not sought anything from me—my regard for her had been spontaneous—I need not blame her for my disappointment." Then in my folly I said, I know not what. And she rose up and said, "I had better resume my allegiance to my cousin." And I protested like a mad-man that I never had loved—never could love—any other woman. I tried to detain her—but she left me, saying that she could not accept my statement that I had never loved my cousin. 'No woman,' and she drew herself up proudly, 'would have given her relations reason to believe she was attached to any man who had not sought her love in secret as well as openly admired her.' "

"Oh! Max!—Max!"

"I am not going to carry any woman a false faith. I should despise myself, could I be bribed by Castleton, or any other bribe, to give up the woman I care for, and marry another. It is perfectly hopeless! I did not even ask her to marry me. Of course such a woman could never follow my soldier's fortunes. Let Veronica have Castleton. She will forget this childish nonsense which has cost me everything in life—and will marry and be happy while I am wearing out my youth in India, or the West Indies. Oh! Molly, how I wish there was a war that I might run my head into the cannon's mouth, and either win such fame as I should like to lay at Lady Ellen's feet, or have my head blown off and be done with this cruel life, which young as I am, has disappointed me."

"Oh! Max—how can you talk so!" I said, bursting into tears.

"No!" said he, pushing me from him gently, "do not kiss me. I can't bear it at this moment. It seems to me too hard that when I am so young, all my life should be ruined by this weak fancy of Veronica's. If she were taken up to town, and put in the way of seeing men, she would find a hundred others better worthy of her attachment."

His face was covered with his hands and his voice was almost a groan. Suddenly he started up. "I did not come to Castleton to say all this. These are wild thoughts which day and night float madly through my brain and make me wild. What I came for was to see you and know the truth. Tell cousin Lomax that I thank him for the kindness he has shown me personally—that I cannot sell myself for Castleton—that he has broken off all chance of my marriage with Lady Ellen—not that there was a chance, but I could not help hoping that there might be, you know. Tell him that I am going to exchange into some regiment on foreign service, and that I bid him good-bye. I hope he may provide for you, and leave Castleton by way of consolation to Veronica."

He pressed me in his arms, and as he kissed me, my face was wet with the drops upon his eyelids. "Good-bye little Molly," he said. "And good-bye, too—a long good-bye," he added looking round him with an earnest gaze, which seemed to take in all the place, "to dear—dear—dear old Castleton." He turned towards the window through which he had come in, and I, still clinging to him to the last, followed him through the dusk into the shrubbery.

When I came back, what were my feelings to see that one side of the green *jalousies* across the bow stood open, and that Veronica's ivory handled riding-whip was lying in the middle of the drawing-room floor!

CHAPTER XI.

I stand by the river where both of us stood,
And there is but one shadow to darken the flood;
And the path leading to it where each used to pass,
Has the step but of one to take dew from the grass.
One forlorn since that day.

Go! be sure of my love—by that treason forgiven;
Of my prayers—by the blessings they win thee from heaven;
Of my grief—(guess the length of the sword by the sheath's)
By the silence of life more pathetic than death's!
Go—be clear of that day.

MRS. E. B. BROWNING.

I DID not see Veronica any more that night. She sent me word that she was tired with her ride, and had a headache. One half the headaches in the world would be returned as heart-aches, if Congress were too move for a census of shams.

I cannot tell how Vera passed the night; it must have been a night of storm; thunder and rain and wind, each striving for the mastery—pride, tenderness and desolation.

The next day she came down to breakfast very pale. Her head still ached, she said, but she was going to be very busy. Five hundred things had accumulated in the parish. She thought it would be a good plan if she visited the day-school twice a week during the sewing time, and read aloud some pleasant story to the children. She had been thinking about it during the night—and was going to consult Dr. Dwyer and Miss Alicia. What sort of book would answer, did I think? And by-the-way, when she was in the Doctor's library, she meant to borrow Gibbon. Had I ever read the "Decline and Fall?" Didn't I think we should do well to give an hour every day to useful historical reading? If she borrowed the book, we could begin that very afternoon. After we had done that, we might read Hume, but Gibbon would last us some time as a *pièce de résistance.*

Oh! restless heart! When brain and frame are weary with the heavy cares of life, wilt thou beat less wildly for the increase of thy load? Wilt thou be happier when in the march of life, anxieties and occupations are treading on the heels of each other? Try it! Every sick heart has done so before thee. And if this is not a remedy, at least we know not where amongst all the thorns and thistles that *this earth* brings forth, another may be found.

So Veronica came home with her Roman History, and we read for an hour about the condition of the empire in the days of the last Romans. I am certain that Veronica left off with very vague impressions on the subject, for when I asked her the next day which of the Emperors built the Scottish wall, she answered, "Trajan." A reply that would have shocked even Miss Alicia, who professed to have grounded her in English History.

For the remainder of the week she neglected cousin Lomax, confining her assiduities to the school children, and the Decline of the Roman Empire, but by Sunday she had a fit of remorse, and Monday morning found her in his chamber, soothing his pain and bearing his caprices. I had written to Max the day after our interview, to say that I had neither the tact nor the courage necessary to make the best of his message to cousin Lomax, and that I begged he would write to the old gentleman himself, and tell him his determination. In consequence of this communication Veronica, during the week, took a letter out of the post-bag in Max's handwriting.

She held it a few moments in her hand with her back to her uncle Lomax, and then said in a constrained voice, which she tried in vain to render natural, "Uncle, I think this is a letter from Max. I dare say it contains something that you will think romantic nonsense about Lady Ellen MacIntyre. You are too ill to care about it at present. Let me read it aloud."

"Read me that letter? . . . . No, indeed. What the devil! . . . . The letter is a letter of business. Bring it to me."

"But the business relates to me, I think," Veronica replied. "Uncle Lomax, I have been wishing to say to you, that I think you quite misunderstand how it is between me and Max. It is not usual," she continued, with the blood mantling in her face, "for a lady to refuse a gentleman before he has asked her, but uncle, forgive me if I go contrary to the kind wishes that I fear you have formed for me, when I say that Max is not a person I would marry. If he asked me a thousand times over to be his wife, my answer would be no! I am sorry, dear uncle, to say anything that you will fancy hard of Max. I am sorry to do my part towards disappointing you,"—she laid the letter on the table and knelt down by his chair—"but love is a thing that cannot be controlled. And since I would not marry Max if he were free, why should he not court and win Lady Ellen MacIntyre? Kate Vere says she is handsome, energetic and accomplished. I think Max, by such a marriage, would give Castleton an admirable mistress, and you and I could travel over Europe, or better still, go over the Blue Ridge and see our cousins in Virginia."

The old man put down his hand and turned up the brave young face that was trying to smile.

"What do you say to my plan? Will you take me to Virginia? Shall we pay a visit to the Old Dominion, uncle?"

"I do not believe you," said he. "I believe your face. I think you care for Max. And I begin to doubt if the rascal is worthy of you."

Veronica's face flushed up.

"I do not care for Max," she said. "Uncle, I speak the truth. Max is not the person I could marry. Take me to London. Let me see more people. We see few here. When we were children, no doubt Max and I played at being in love as children will play with each other. But neither he nor I wish to remember that old childishness. If there had been anything of a positive nature between us, I could write to Max—could tell him it was over now, that we are older and wiser. I could tell him that I hope he will marry Lady Ellen MacIntyre."

"I am not going to let Max throw himself away upon that Scotch woman," said cousin Lomax, "before he knows what is good for him."

"Max is twenty-one," pleaded Veronica. "What period do you fix upon for his coming of age in discretion?"

Cousin Lomax made a pause. "I think you will laugh in your sleeve at your old bachelor uncle, if I tell you that I doubt whether any young man (I know nothing about young women) comes of age in discretion till after his first experience in love. He wants that kind of thing to bring out his character. I am not much concerned about this fancy for my Lady Ellen Mac-

Intyre. I think his disappointment in that business may end by making him more of a man and a better husband for you."

Veronica rose up from her knees, and proudly drew herself to her full height. "I have said once for all what I shall say to the end of my life, that Max and I shall never marry."

"Pshaw! that is a girl's nonsense."

"Not at all, uncle; it is the resolution of a woman."

Cousin Lomax looked her full in the face, and her blue eyes met his, but did not fall under his gaze for several moments. Each seemed to be measuring the other's strength of purpose. Cousin Lomax very likely thought of his old will, and pondered several important clauses in his new one. Presently Veronica's eyes fell; a softer look crept over her features. She took a newspaper from the table, and said, "Uncle, I am going to read to you."

"No," said he, "I do not care to be read to at this moment. Veronica, you are not old enough to know the influence for good or evil that the character of the woman he knows best exercises on every man. Take care you do no harm to the man who loves you. If you prove proud, disdainful, selfish or worldly, if you destroy or lower a man's standard of what constitutes a good woman you inflict an injury which nothing but another woman's better influence can repair."

"Uncle, a woman cannot marry every man that asks her—she cannot return all the love that may be offered her."

"No," said her uncle, "but she need not injure him as well as disappoint him. A man is not the worse for a love disappointment (pshaw! most men have had dozens of them) provided he comes out of it unembittered against women. You wonder what I know about it. I *did* grow bitter under that influence . . . ."

"Dearest uncle!"—her arms were round his neck, and her tears were falling fast—"let me love you and be always with you. I wish for nothing better than to be dear to you."

But then remembering that his love for her might injure Max, she checked herself, and raising her wet face from his breast she somewhat coldly withdrew.

The next day he called her to his side, and putting a letter into her hand addressed to Max, asked her "if that would answer."

MY DEAR KINSMAN:

"It is not worth while to answer your last letter, which I excuse because you are a young man under the influence of your first fancy. I believe in your good heart, and think everything will turn out right when you have got rid of this folly. I think you do very well to go abroad and see the world. Stay two years on active service, and my word for it you will be glad enough to come home to the friends who will be waiting your return at Castleton. You very prematurely resign all claim to my estate or my allowances. The latter will not be withdrawn. I shall make no alteration in my will at present. It is but right to tell you that your late conduct seems to have resulted in the estrangement of your cousin, who "swears her pretty oath by yea and nay," that she will never have you. Any man who takes no for an answer from such a woman while she remains unmarried is a fool. You can draw for the usual remittance quarterly, and may write me a letter from your new quarters. Your cousin and your sister send their love, and I remain,

"Your friend and kinsman,

"*Castleton.* "THOS. LOMAX."

I did not stay long enough at Castleton to begin Hume; and only long enough to read two volumes of Gibbon. I was summoned home by sickness in our family. When I left Castleton, cousin Lomax's health seemed very much broken up, and Veronica had grown so pale and changed, that my father pronounced her "quite a wreck," when he came on to escort me. She did not seem to mind my loss so much as I should have expected. My knowledge of her secret, put a restraint upon our intercourse. I dare say I was continually reminding her of Max—who, by the way, by that time had written us a short letter from Gibraltar.

My memory paints her as she stood upon the steps of the Italian porch the morning that we drove from Castleton. I thought she looked like a broken lily.

"I do not think she will live long," my father said; "she is so slight, and if cousin Lomax continues in his present mood, her death will be Max's best chance of inheriting Castleton."

Castleton without Veronica—what would Castleton be? I pictured a robust, proud, dark-haired woman sweeping through its halls. The presence of such a person seemed unnatural. Veronica seemed identified with the place. She had grown with the growth of everything, dumb creature and green herb, that lived and grew there.

I could not fancy what it would become without her presence. I looked back upon her as she stood leaning against the florid stone pillar of the porch, and as long as she could be seen, I watched her. Old Luath, faithful to the last, waited beside her. Spring flowers bloomed in quaint, stiff parterres at her feet. Could my father's prophesy be true? Would these flowers, the next spring put forth new life, and she not be at Castleton to rejoice over them? Would the same sun fall across the porch, and lose no beam before it reached the pavement in illuminating her hair? Would the stag-hound lie lonely with his paws crossed like a statue on the threshold, caressed only by the servants for the sake of her who was gone? Would the village bells she loved, ring out their evening chime, though she could never hear them? Would the poor pass by the gate by which they had been wont to enter? Would the village children whom she taught, grow up with only a dim remembrance of some one fair and slight, with golden hair and a light step, and draw from faint impressions of this vision of their youth their notions of an angel? Would the rose over old Mammy's grave grow raggedly luxuriant for want of training? Would her place know her no more? Should I pay lonely visits to old Castleton? Would the sound of her piano make our hearts ache? Would her white pony whinny for her step and never hear it more?

It was a true prophecy—a morning dream which as we wake catches something from real objects. I came back to Castleton alone the following spring, and as I drove up the avenue and saw everything unchanged excepting the one great change, that Veronica "was not," the vision of the spring before became a painful reality.

She continued to write to me, but her letters were short and unsatisfactory. Any body who has ever tried writing familiar letters from which the whole of that which gives tone and coloring to one's daily life must be left out, will understand why the correspondence wearied her.

Late in the autumn she wrote me an account of Dr. Dwyer's death. He died very suddenly of apoplexy and cousin Lomax she said had been very kind to Miss Alicia, and begged her to make Castleton her home.

In a succeeding letter she told me of the arrival of another clergyman. A different person it appeared from Dr. Dwyer, who was a divine of the dry old school, and preached sermons culled from Warburton and Tillotson, and other sapless trees of controversial divinity. I do not intend to paint the influence which this gentleman's discourses had upon her—for, indeed, Veronica has never declared it to me. I saw it in after years in the fulfillment of that verse, "If any man be in Christ he is a new creature—old things have passed away—all things have become new."

There was at this time a new principle imparted, a new motive acquired, new hopes, new aims which were to tune the discords of her life, and bring it into harmony with the works and nature of our Father in Heaven. The new leaven was hidden in the measure of meal, and the whole lump was being quickened by the influence of that leaven.

Whoever thinks that the improvement of character even under Heavenly influences is not progressive, has either had no experience of the work, or will find himself fatally mistaken.

But while these new hopes dawned upon her life, while "let there be light," was spoken to her soul, her physical frame, as my father had foreseen, gave way under the influence of her conflicting feelings. Miss Alicia, soon after she came to Castleton, found herself called upon to nurse Veronica with all her skill and tenderness. Happily the sickness was sharp, positive, and short; in cases like hers it is more often weary, indefinite and long.

They despaired of her life for nearly a week, during which time, as Miss Alicia told me afterwards, "she kept repeating over and over some scene between you and your brother, poor dear, in her delirium." Another delusion was that everything about her room was dark, and from the darkness glowed letters of fire a thousand times repeated, waving, floating, above her, around her, behind her, scorching her by contact, dazzling and blinding her, the words "Lady Ellen MacIntyre."

When she was better, the physician recommended change.

"Oh, Dr. Denny," she said, when this was first made known to her, "order me back to Old Virginia. I feel sure I should get better if I could breathe my native air. The blue hills of our Valley which I faintly remember, are the back-ground of my fancies. Everything would be right (since I must live), if I could go back to Virginia. I have a letter from my aunt Edmonia, begging me to pay her a visit. Dr. Denny, please ask uncle Lomax to let me go."

By-and-by I had a letter from her in a weak hand.

"Dear Molly:

"You have heard, I dare say, of my illness. Miss Alicia and Mrs. Mayhew nursed me with the kindest care; but for them our beautiful village chimes would have tolled for me as they are now doing for old Goody Rowe. Molly, I wonder they don't ring their happiest chimes for a believer's funeral. I do not mean to repine at what appears to be God's will. I take back His gift of life, and will try to give a good account of my stewardship, and to use it thankfully. Our new Rector has been here talking to me this morning. He says that when people have had losses in life and trust in God, He makes up in Himself what they find wanting. He says that is the meaning of the verse which says, "if we bear the loss of houses and lands, and wife and children for His sake, we shall receive an hundred fold now in this present time and in the world to come life everlasting." He says too, we may find compensation for many griefs in Christian fellowship. He has lent me a sweet book particularly adapted to soothe such restless feelings as I have had of late. It is called "The Christian Year," by Mr. Keble. Our Rector has suffered very much himself, we hear, and so he knows how to understand a great deal that does not seem to be alluded to in sermons. Luath, all through my illness lay at my door; they could not get him away. They have cut off all my hair. They brought all the ice left in the ice-house at Vere Park and put it on my head during the week I passed in a state of delirium. What I want to tell you is, that I am going to

Virginia. A lady and gentleman whom uncle Lomax knows, are going back this spring in one of the new ocean steamers. Dr. Denny says I must go back to my native air. We have written to aunt Edmonia, and some of my cousins will meet me in Baltimore. Dear old Mammy! I wish she could have gone back to 'Ole Virginny.' Tell Max when he comes to Castleton, to see that her grave is kept in good repair. My chief regret is in leaving my dear uncle. Miss Alicia will take care of him, but he wants better companionship than Miss Alicia. What I want you to do is to write to Max, and tell him how very feeble uncle Lomax is, and that you think he had better get leave and come at once to Castleton. Uncle will find in his society great comfort—so shall I, to think that he is there. Uncle Lomax is not pleased with my going to Virginia, and I dare say I am not so ill but that I could live here still, but I have been wishing for some time past to go there. I suppose I shall not see you, dear Molly, as we go up to London as soon as I can travel. Oh! Molly, how can I ever bear to leave dear Castleton? Do write to Max by the next post to come and comfort uncle Lomax. I have written in great weakness, and have said several things I did not mean to say. If I had strength to write another letter for this post, I would tear this up. Good-bye, dear Molly—I am very tired.

"Your affectionate cousin,

"VERONICA LOMAX.

"P. S.—Pray write at once to Max. It is important, I think, that he should be at home. Please not to allude, if you write, to anything I have said about feeling depressed. It is only weakness. If I could, I would re-write my letter."

END OF PART FIRST.

PART SECOND.

He who for Love has undergone
The worst that can befall,
Is happier, thousand-fold, than one
Who never loved at all;
A grace within his soul hath reigned
Which nothing else can bring—
Thank God for all that I have gained
By that high suffering!

R. M. Milnes.

PART II.

CHAPTER I.

I might reprove thy broken faith,
  I might recall the time
When thou wert chartered mine till death
  Through every fate and clime;
When every letter was a vow,
  And fancy was not free
To dream of ended love;—and thou
  Wouldst say the same of me.

R. M. Milnes.

Three years have passed since the close of the first part of this *narrative* shall I call it?—or *biography?*

"Happy are the people whose annals are a blank," says Carlyle, quoting from somebody. I do not think Veronica's were very happy, but I know very little about them. She was in Virginia, and I at home, living in a quiet country town only enlivened by its garrison; reading everything readable that could be found; doing a good deal of fancy work; attending any stray concerts, bonnet shows, or lectures, or even a travelling menagerie; grateful for a card party where the lawfulness of life insurance was discussed over the whist table; or a share in entertainments given by the "other set," where the prophesies of the Apocalypse were adapted to the latest information about the state of Europe in their three days old Times newspaper, and delivered in short expository lectures over tea and toast, by "Dear Dr. Bogg."

Max returned to England a few months after the departure of Veronica, but he was gloomy and dispirited, and out of favor at Castleton. He hunted with the hounds of the East Riding, and fished a good deal in the river, tossed over the old books in the library without an appetite, yawned, and was poor company for cousin Lomax, who watched him shrewdly enough for a week or two, then told him he was "no good," and had better go back to his regiment, or travel abroad. The latter proposition was very agreeable to Max. He recovered something of his former animation when he told us of the project. This travelling about the world without an object, is rarely of great service to young men; and it was better for him, I think, when he found himself once more with his regiment, which went into garrison in the Eastern counties. I rarely heard from Veronica. The Virginia disinclination to write letters seemed to have seized upon her. She wrote regularly to cousin Lomax, but her correspondence with him confined itself principally to the prospects of the crops, and general news about people over the Ridge whom I had never heard of. She told us nothing about herself, except that she was living with her aunt Edmonia. She never spoke of coming back, and cousin Lomax would not ask her to return to Castleton. He had penetrated her motive, and had been much dissatisfied with her for going away. I had an instinctive impression that she was very wretched, but she never hinted at a secret grief, and I did not feel at liberty to ask her. The estrangement between her and Max blighted our intercourse. My spirit too was not in tune with any kind of misery. I stood in the first warm glow of my life's sunshine. The cloudless dawn of nursery days had given me a happy promise, but the promise was nothing to the brightness of its coming. All the earth seemed full of its glory. "Every leaf in every nook," glowed with fresh beauty in its golden light, and glittered in its gladness. Every clod of common earth gave back the reflection of my happiness. Hymns went up from my heart to the Father of Lights.

Some years after our regiment moved away from the town in which it was quartered at the opening of this history, it was joined in a quiet garrison town at the North, by the handsome nephew of Sir Harris Howard.

I am not writing my own biography, but the story of my brother and Veronica. It will be quite enough to say that Mr. Howard thought himself attached to me. He told me so, and I was very happy. I never had the power of winning. I never knew the secret of that pleasure which some women take in effecting what is called a conquest. God gave me only the power of loving. He rarely gives them both. My happiness had sought me out. I never thought of securing his regard till I was conscious I had won it, and then with trembling thoughts of my unworthiness, and fears lest I should never rightly guard the treasure of his preference, I gave myself up to the enjoyment of a happiness which seemed in the fullest sense the gift of God.

It was a match, too—looking at it *as a match*—very far above my fortunes. My father had hinted no disapproval of the courtship (my step-mother had openly encouraged it), and I was pleased to think my future place in life would gratify the ambition of my family.

There was nothing to break in upon my happy dream except

the thought that I was so unworthy of my happiness. I could hardly bear the presence of those less happy than myself. It seemed to me that they must feel it hardly right that I should have been taken while so many had been left to loneliness and sorrow.

Such were my feelings at twenty-one. Other women are more formed at that age, I dare say, and have profited more than I had done by experience and education, especially American women, who are born, I think, with a knowledge of the world.

Mr. Howard was little like other officers in the regiment. He liked quiet home ways, and was pleased to be admitted into our family interior. He had been sent to Oxford, which he quitted from a deficiency of application—but his acquaintance with *belles lettres* was much greater than that of any person with whom I had ever been thrown, and a girl is as easily dazzled by acquirement as reputation.

We first became familiar over a book of sonnets. I said I could take no pleasure in the formalities and perfections of a sonnet. That whenever my fancy painted Poetry it was with "robes loosely flowing, hair as free," not starched and hooped, and dressed by rule, with patches and powder. He replied by repeating Wordsworth's sonnet in defence of sonnets. Then he introduced me to those of Milton which I had read carelessly; explained to me the principles which regulate the composition of the sonnet, and showed me that the greater part of those which bear the name are excluded from competition by defects in their construction. He brought me English sonnets in a dozen books. He encouraged me to attempt the severe composition of sonnets. He brought me beautiful Italian ones; and when he found I only half understood them in the original, he insisted on helping me to study Italian. We read Dante, and Petrarch together.

How driest books and common themes blossomed into interest and beauty when he talked about them! I had been beginning to fancy that life was a dull round of petty daily cares. He opened for me the book of Art, and quickened my perceptions of the Beautiful. It seemed to me that he knew everything, and that I knew nothing. But he was eager to teach, and I delighted to learn. He fancied I was *piquante*. I had natural uncultivated taste and power of appreciation, and had ability enough to follow where he led.

He lent me piles of beautifully bound books; among his other cultivated fancies was a love for handsome print, and handsome bindings. My little writing-table was polyglot. Poetry in all languages; Essays on Plato and Michael Angelo; boxes of models from Italian gems; selections from the Elizabethan Dramatists; La Mothe Fouqué; Prosper Merimée; Souvestre, and Villmarqué; Books of ballad poetry; chronicles in old black letter; reprints of the Roxburgh Club; an essay on the Basque dialect (his own composition); another on the Pythagorian Theory of numbers; and other productions, MSS. and printed, of his own.

There was another thing that acted strongly on my feelings in our intercourse. I was too young to distinguish between religious sentiment and religious principle. He had a good deal of the former, which generally accompanies a true sense of art.

After several months of happy intercourse, sanctioned and approved of by my family, he was called away one morning when we were reading together the Vita Nuova. He laid down the book, supposing it was regimental business, promising to come back in a few moments.

He never returned. He was wanted by his uncle, who had learnt that he was paying attentions to a girl with little personal beauty and no fortune. His family had other views for him. It was in every way desirable that he should marry our old schoolfellow, the little Indian, the daughter of Sir Harris and the Begum. Howard Park without her stars in the East India Company's book to keep it up would be a barren inheritance. He did not like the "nut brown bride" they had in store for him. He had often joked with me about the plan of his own family, and had quoted the coarse proverb of the 18th century, that such a marriage was "*de mettre du fumier sur nos terres.*" But I never supposed they would really oppose his marriage with the daughter of my father. We Mandevilles had been accustomed to consider ourselves equal to any one in point of family—and except to pass reflections on the worthlessness of wealth, I did not think about money. My father was not rich, but I had always had enough to spend and spare. General Sir Harris Howard carried his nephew away from me. I believe he found a pretext in the illness of the Begum. Mr. Howard wrote me a letter the next day, enclosing it under cover to my father. It was an offer of marriage. He confessed the disapproval of his uncle; but time he said would soften opposition from that quarter, I must have faith in him, and wait the end.

When my father saw this letter he forbade all future intercourse. He said that no one should suppose he had made use of his position as commanding officer of the Regiment to marry his daughter to a man above her station.

He wrote thus to Mr. Howard himself. I could not write. The answer was one of entreaty, tenderness, and despair. Mr. Howard reminded me that I was his by every tie of affection. He implored me not to be conventional, to consider myself engaged to him in spite of the opposition of our families. He should consider himself bound to me till by my own hand or from my own lips he learned that my decision to part was voluntary.

I told my father that we could not give each other up; but I submitted to his wishes so far as to promise that until Mr. Howard obtained the approbation of his uncle, or occupied a position independent of his family I would not see him nor write to him.

My father was a wise man. He had full confidence in my word, and was satisfied not to put too great a strain on my obedience. If we took any satisfaction in considering ourselves bound to each other when such an engagement was not acknowledged by our families, we were at liberty to fancy ourselves engaged, provided we refrained from intercourse with each other.

Every body was very kind to me; but it was one of those cases in which change of place and occupation is the only possible alleviation to the ever-present pain.

While things were thus with us we got an express one morning from Max, summoning our father to the death-bed of cousin Lomax at Castleton. The old gentleman had had a paralytic stroke, and could speak very indistinctly when our father arrived. Almost the only sentence those around the dying bed could understand was addressed to him on entering the chamber.

"I hope you will be satisfied, Colonel, with my provision for your son."

"Of course, sir—quite satisfied," said our father, who was the least selfish man in the world.

So the old man on the 14th of October, 1841, went to his rest, and they buried him under the Chancel in the little church at Castleton—far away from his father and his mother, and his baby sisters who had loved him, sleeping under the green sod of old Virginia, in the little road-side church yard, beneath the willows and the yews.

He had been a good landlord, but never was personally popular. The people never looked on him as a legitimate lord of the soil. He had not been brought up among them. He was cold and aristocratic. He neither shared their interests nor their prejudices. There was nothing John Bullish, but his top boots, about him. They always felt he was a foreigner. Max had been a very popular heir presumptive, and the sun-flowers of the neighborhood turned their faces readily to the rising sun.

Two days after the funeral our father returned home from Castleton, leaving Max behind.

It was cold weather, and the coach came in about nightfall. When I saw him coming through the gate with ruddy cheeks and an icy glow about him, I ran out to meet him.

"Dear papa," I cried, "tell me about Max! Has cousin Lomax left him Castleton?"

"Yes—yes," said my father, "it is all right. The old gentleman has made a very judicious will. Max will have Castleton."

"And Veronica?"

"Will marry Max, and live there too. He is going out to court her as soon as he can make arrangements to leave Castleton."

"I am so glad of it, papa."

"And so am I. We could not wish a better little wife for him. She is a sweet girl, and it was a match cousin Lomax had set his heart upon. I am glad to find that Max had been thinking about her for some time before he was made aware that any proviso was attached to the possession of Castleton."

"What proviso is attached to Castleton?" I cried.

"That he should marry Veronica. Do you want to see the will? Here it is—I took a copy of it."

"Poor old gentleman!" said I, "I wish Veronica had been at Castleton when he died. He never quite forgave her for going away."

"He was a good kind-hearted man," said my father, "without the power of attracting human affection. There is a 'magnetic influence,' as you call it, about that sort of thing. Every body served him from a sense of duty, and there was an end of the relations between them. Did you ever know, Molly, that he was attached to Veronica's mother?"

"Is it possible?"

"Yes—and he felt her loss very much when she married his brother. Women always choose the man who has some dash about him. You all go in for the showy, every one of you, like your mother who wants me to buy a French polished dining table—instead of that set at Dawson's—good solid old-fashioned mahogany."

"Was that the reason he adopted Veronica?"

"I cannot tell. I believe he was very much displeased with his sister-in-law as well as with Alonzo. He thought she ought to have had better judgment and to have given him the preference. Perhaps she flirted. However, I believe the marriage was rather an underhand thing. Every thing was underhand that was managed by Alonzo. The old gentleman had no communication with either of them until after her death. Had Alonzo lived, there never could have been any cordiality between the brothers."

My father said all this as he was taking off his outer wrappings—hanging up on its accustomed peg a military cloak, in which he used to travel on cold days, with a brass chain to fasten it about the neck, and a red camlet lining. He patronized scarlet, which he used to say no civilian had any right to wear, any more than he had to sport mustachios,—both being the perquisites of English cavalry officers.

I opened the paper containing cousin Lomax's will. It ran as follows:—

"I, Thomas Lomax, bachelor, of the Parish of Castleton, in the East Riding of Yorkshire, being of failing bodily health, but of sound mind, declare this to be my last Will and Testament.

"1st. I desire that all my just debts shall be paid.

"2dly. I leave to all of my servants who at the time of my death may be resident at Castleton, three years' wages, to be paid out of my personal estate, within one year and a day after my funeral.

"3dly. I give and bequeath my estate of Castleton, in the East Riding of Yorkshire, together with all my personal estate that I may have in England at the time of my death, to my kinsman and namesake, Thomas Lomax Mandeville, Captain in Her Majesty's 118th Regiment of foot, to have and to hold to him and his heirs in fee, *Provided*, that the said Thomas Lomax Mandeville, shall, within one year after my decease, marry my beloved niece, Veronica Lomax, daughter of my late brother, Alonzo Lomax, Esq., of Virginia, in the United States of America.

"4thly. I give and bequeath to my beloved niece, Veronica Lomax, my Oatlands Estate, situate in Jefferson County, Virginia, together with all property, landed or personal, of which I may die possessed in the United States of America, to her and to her heirs in fee, *Provided*, that the said Veronica Lomax shall marry, within one year after my decease, my kinsman and namesake, Thomas Lomax Mandeville, Esq.

"5thly. Should the said Veronica Lomax, having received proposals of marriage from the said Thomas Lomax Mandeville, remain unmarried to him more than one year after my death, I will and desire that my Estate of Castleton shall be sold, together with all my personal estate, of which I may die possessed (always excepting such slaves as I may own in Virginia), and the proceeds of such sales be divided between the said Thomas Lomax Mandeville, and my said niece Veronica. Also, I declare all other provisions of my present will, saving only the 1st, 2nd and 7th clauses to be null and of no effect. And I give to my sister

Barbara, widow of William Williams, Esq., of Clarke County, Virginia, my Estate of Oatlands in Jefferson County, Virginia, to her and to her heirs in fee, together with all the negroes of which I may die possessed, desiring always that in any disposition of my property the negroes shall belong to whomsoever shall inherit my landed estate in Jefferson County, Virginia.

"6thly. Should the said Thomas Lomax Mandeville, disregarding my wishes on this subject, make no proposition of marriage to the said Veronica Lomax, within one year after my death, then revoking all former dispositions in his favor, I will and bequeath to the said Thomas Lomax Mandeville, my Oatlands Estate, situated in Virginia, together with all property, landed or personal, that I may die possessed of in the United States of America ; in which event I give and bequeath to my before-named niece, Veronica Lomax, my estate of Castleton, to have and to hold, to her and to her heirs in fee, together with all personal estate in England of which I may die possessed, revoking all former provisions of this will, excepting only the 1st and 2d clauses; provided always that whosoever of these, my heirs, shall be possessed of my Virginia property, shall pay out of my Oatlands Estate, the sum of five hundred dollars, yearly, to my sister Barbara, widow of William Williams, Esq., of Clarke County, Virginia.

"7thly. I appoint the Hon. James Edmund Tyrell, late Governor of the State of Virginia, of Stonehenge, Jefferson County, Virginia, and Lieutenant Colonel Mandeville, of Her Majesty's Dragoons, Executors of this my last Will and Testament.

"Signed,

"THOMAS LOMAX.

"Witnesses,

"ALICIA DWYER, Spinster,

"JOHN DENNY,

"JOHN HUGHES."

CHAPTER II.

See how yon flaming herald treads
  The ridged and rolling waves,
As, crashing o'er their crested heads
  She bows her surly slaves;
With foam before and fire behind
  She rends the clinging sea,
That flies before the roaring wind
  Beneath her hissing lee.

With clashing wheel and lifting keel
  And smoking torch on high,
When winds are loud and billows reel,
  She thunders foaming by;
When seas are silent and serene
  With even beam she glides,
The sunshine glimmering through the green
  That skirts her gleaming sides.

O. W. Holmes.

Max's salutation when he returned from Castleton was, "Well, little Molly, are you getting ready to go with me to Ole Virginny?" And then, as if to relieve himself of an embarrassment, he seized upon one of our little brothers who was running through the drawing-room, and sang him

"The sea was so broad and the land was so narrow,
He was forced to bring his wife home in a wheel-barrow."

"When do you talk of going, Max?" said I.

"Not until the spring," he answered. "There will be business arrangements to attend to here; besides which, winter is hardly the time to be in that part of America. They never shut a door my father says, in 'ole Virginny.' I shall apply for six months leave of absence from next March, and I hope," he added seriously, "that you intend to accompany me."

"I don't know," said I in the objective case. "It is a long journey, and I feel very little interest in Virginia. I hardly know enough of our relations over the Ridge to invest them with any personality."

"Yes—but my dear child travelling will do you good. I have been talking with the governor about it." And then passing his arm about my waist, "my dear, little sister," said he, "I think about your trouble a great deal, for as you know, Molly," and his voice became pretty serious, "I had a touch of the same fever several years ago myself, about Lady Ellen MacIntyre."

"Yes, Max—and since you profess to have been cured of that, you never seem to me quite the dear fellow that you used to be. You make fun of women. You never seem to trust us, or to think we are sincere, or ———"

"It is the experience of life, Molly. I was glad when I met Lady Ellen at court last spring, that Colin Nasmyth and not I had married that showy, heartless woman. You think me a harum-scarum, flirting sort of fellow—as I am—but there are better things in me which a good wife might bring out. I should be a worse man, too, if I had not had a good sister. There are plenty of quiet moments when I sigh for better things, and feel," (he turned his face away and his voice fell to a whisper) "that I should like to have a dear, little, good homekeeping wife—somebody who would love me, somebody it was my duty to love."

"I love you dearly—darling Max," said I.

Max smiled. "I want to be loved *best*," he said. "People marry and alter, and go away, and throw you over, and there is no stability for a man except in the affections of his own home."

Thus saying, he took up a ball of sewing cotton, stuck the points of my scissors through it, and cut several yards of it with deliberate care and measurement into useless shreds. "I will tell you who I think was quite sincere"—he said at length—"that is Veronica. Somehow nobody can go to Castleton without missing her. Her pleasant laugh, and pretty ways were like the sunshine of the place. The people about there are for ever telling me of all her little kindnesses—and Miss Alicia (she is a good soul, Miss Alicia) used to talk to me of her. There was a bundle of her letters written to cousin Lomax, as dear, pretty, womanly little letters as you could see—with plenty of good sense in them. They seemed to bring her back to me as in old times, with her pleasant, quick way of doubling upon you with some sauciness, when she fancied she had been showing too much feeling. I took the little bundle down to the old boat, and pushed out into the pond and looked them over. The old swannies came sailing round the boat as if they thought she ought to be there too, and I could not help promising the old couple that I would do my best to bring her back again. Somehow the old place got a more inhabited look after I imagined her return there. I cannot tell you," he went on to say, "how glad I am that I feel thus about it. I would not have sold myself to any woman I did not like, even to own Castleton; and now I will confess to you that if cousin Lomax had left me the estate without restriction, I should have gone to Virginia and offered myself to Veronica."

After a pause, and the destruction of more thread, "you are pretty sure she used to like me, Molly?" said he.

"I am quite sure of it, dear Max—I could give you twenty proofs of her regard for you."

"She acted a very generous part," said he. "It was a noble thing of her to go away, especially if she cared so much for such a good-for-nothing scamp as me—poor little soul! Do you think that I can win her now?" And he threw a glance into the mirror at his own handsome face and soldierly figure. "Does she often write to you, Molly?"

"Not very often—and her letters are quite short. She is living at Clairmont with aunt Edmonia."

"You ——— you don't think there are 'other Richmonds in the field?'" said Max. "You do not think she favors any other lover?"

"I cannot think she does. There is no indication in her letters that she cares for any one in Virginia."

"Well," said Max, smiling, "cousin Lomax's earnest wishes for our marriage almost defeated their own object. And I wish he had not tied us down. The will has made quite a sensation in the parish. They all know that I am going to Virginia. Won't the old chimes ring out a merry peal the day I bring her back there?"

Max spent a good deal of the winter at Castleton. Not as its proprietor, but as agent of the executors of the will, Governor Tyrell and our father. Still he felt himself the master of the place, and everybody considered him so. I was with him part of the winter. He gave up hunting and his boisterous tastes, and liked nothing so well as talking to me, or to kind, prosy Miss Alicia, about Veronica. He went over all the old rides and walks they used to take together. The trees were leafless, and the ploughed fields bare. "I'll tell you what, Molly," said he,

"I have a great mind to ask her to be married in the summer, and then she will come back here when the place is in its beauty. Can I persuade her to be married in July, do you suppose, or will the wedding finery take too much preparation?"

The old hound was alive, and Max used to go and pat it for her sake, for it never left the stable after she went away. He set me to work in the village to find out her old pensioners. The women dropped courtesies as we went through the hamlet, and made bold to ask "when Mrs. Mandeville might be expected at the Hall."

Max laughed out heartily the first time that this was said to him, and gave the old woman who said it half a crown. Of course, after that he was constantly subject to the inquiry.

The old gardener had an order to get his grounds trimmed up, and have every thing as Miss Veronica liked it by the beginning of the summer. He was constantly touching his hat to Max, and saying this or that was his "lady's fancy." And Max had confidential consultations with him about the tastes of Veronica.

"Take a lesson from me Moll," he said, when he found me crying by myself one day. "A man does not know what is good for him. I can never be thankful enough that I am going to marry a quiet good wife, whom every body loves, rather than my old flame Lady Ellen. She never would have liked a country life, and is leading her husband a pretty dance of fashion."

At last the spring opened. My heart ached at the thought of setting the Atlantic between myself and him who occupied my thoughts, but Max was in the highest spirits—made light of the perils of the deep, and rallied me.

I had several letters from Mr. Howard. I did not know but that I ought to send them back to him, and carried them honestly to my father—who did not exact the sacrifice. He only said that he was glad I was going out of the reach of that folly. I received one in Liverpool, and happy in the possession of its loving words, I was rocked to sleep on the first night of our voyage—the great ship panting remorselessly upon her way, putting thirteen knots between us every hour.

It blew that first night—and as I lay upon my narrow shelf, listening to the creaking, and the straining of her tiller ropes and bulkheads, and all her other thousand noises, and heard

> The beating of her restless heart
> Still sounding through the storm,

I prayed to God to make me happy. A girl's prayer! And He "whose way is in the sea, and whose paths in the great waters, and whose footsteps are not known," was drawing near, although I could not trace His steps, to answer in the end that vague petition. Like the Apostles James and John, I "knew not what I asked," but He who heard me gave my words a meaning.

Max was very kind to me during our voyage. He insisted on having me a great deal on deck. We used to sit behind the wheel-house, watching the beautiful wake of the great swift ship, acqua-marine and blue, and malachite and white, like a glacier from the Alps, in life and motion. Or we stood upon the paddle-box, at night, and watched the glowing funnel with its glittering sparks, and the beautiful phosphoric gleams among the silver foam, thrown off by the great paddles. I was disappointed in the beauty of the boundless ocean. The sea should be looked at with dry land to stand on. And the unbroken world of waters is only beautiful by moonlight, when a golden path seems paved across it to God's sapphire throne,—or rather when each glittering wave becomes a link of the celestial chain let down to earth out of the starry sky.

The discomforts of our life below were wonderfully great. As I lay in my berth, almost without life, during the first few days of our voyage, I had just wits enough left to wonder vaguely whether a personal reminiscence of sea-sickness had animated the Psalmist, when in the course of his description of the perils and deliverances of those "who go down to the sea in ships and occupy their business in great waters," he said, "Their soul abhorred all manner of meat, and they were even hard at death's door."

After a few days I was again on deck, enjoying the daily doings of the little world around me; accepting kind attentions from the gentlemen—learning helplessness as became a semi-American female (for short frocks and pantalettes were in that day the legitimate dress of the present race of Bloomer); but what I liked best was to have long talks with Max. I was admitted more fully into his character and confidence than I had ever been before. I saw that under a rattling exterior he had good sense, deep feeling, and a generous temper; and our chats upon the poop, however they might begin, always ended in confidential whispers about Veronica.

"What will strike me most on landing?" said I off Sandy-Hook, to an agreeable New Yorker.

"You will be first struck with our national costume," was his answer. "It is calculated that there are in the United States about two millions of white males of years and means sufficient to entitle them to wear 'waistcoats,'—as you call them. Of these two millions, 1,999,000 wear them of black satin."

We had left England before the spring had put on her mantle, and I never can forget the glory of the greenness of Staten Island and the heights of Hoboken, as we went into the harbor of New York through the Narrows.

We had no motive to linger in New York, and so soon as our luggage could be rescued from the Custom House, we set out for Baltimore. We passed the night in Philadelphia. The United States' Bank had failed recently, and the city (never a very lively one) was the abomination of desolation. We walked about the streets feeling ourselves aliens in the land of our fathers—with none to bid us welcome, where half a century earlier our relatives had been the great men of the day.

We stood before the superb marble structure left desolate by the failure of the United States' Bank. I was delighted with its pure Greek architecture, and asked Max what it was copied from? He answered in a whisper, "from the Temple of *Mercury*, with modern improvements."

My spirits rose as we went out of Philadelphia. Each railroad car was in that day drawn to the outer Depôt through the streets by six magnificent grey horses. All the railroad arrangements seemed so very queer!—especially the carriages themselves, long omnibus-shaped cars, holding sixty persons seated two and two on horse-hair benches, the conductor walking up and down the aisle; the noise precluding any genial social feeling, or cheery travelling intercourse among us. Every man sat grimly in his place, with his ticket in his hat-band. Nobody was travelling for pleasure, but going straight ahead towards a predetermined destination. And every man "aboard the cars" was doubtless thinking the same things he would have thought sitting at home in his store, or in his counting-room.

After leaving Philadelphia I missed the candy boys, who the day before had astonished me as they plied their trade among us. Great bearded men were grimly buying their variegated wares and craunching candy, not flattering the palate by sucking it deliberately. The consumption of peppermint, chickoberry, sassafras, crude apples, and lozenges, by adult travellers in the New England railway cars (or States that border on New England), is quite a feature in Trans-Atlantic travelling. Around every Legislative Hall that I have visited in the Eastern States —little boys hawk rolls of lozenges for the refreshment of the legislators. I, as a Briton, of course, had a provision of ham sandwiches in my travelling bag.

It was so strange to me to find the railroads unenclosed; to hear the whistle blown to frighten cattle off the track, and to know that ahead of the engine we had a "cow-catcher!" It made me nervous to be running at half-speed through the centre of small towns where rails were laid down in the main streets, without any sort of fencing or protection.

When we came to the Great Gunpowder, Max called me out to look at it. We were crossing a shallow, muddy stream, about a mile and a half in width, but not on anything that could be called a bridge. Piles had been driven about three feet apart into the river's bed, and rails were laid on top of them! And so it continues till this day (no accident having ever happened at that spot), upon the principal trunk line of railway between the Atlantic cities.

I was astonished when we crossed the Susquehannah, to notice with what business-like celerity the American officials effected every change. Instead of a distracted hunt for baggage at every stopping-place or break of gauge, which I had been accustomed to in England, the admirable check system of America left the traveller unconcerned about his trunks until their safe delivery at the end of his journey.

Soon after crossing the Susquehannah, the appearance of the country changed. The dazzling white houses looking as if cut out of card-board, sharp and uniform (Grecian temples with green blinds), gave place to low log-cabins with mud chimneys—neat fencing to the hideous worm fence; or in many instances to fences made of the roots of trees. I would as soon see an emerald of price set with the roots of teeth, as such an enclosure round a meadow. Max, who had been standing on the platform with the conductor, came and touched me. "We have fairly crossed Mason and Dixon's line," said he. "Delaware was hardly a slave state, but we are now in Maryland."

How I shrank from the black figures in short, ragged petticoats, which offered apples for sale at the next stopping-place! How I looked with a compassion they would not have understood, into their black, shiny, *nonchalante* broad faces—and shuddered at the thought that they were *slaves*.

Our journey was beautiful through the Maryland woods; where, however, the crowding prevented any development on the part of individual trees. The effect of the early verdure of the forest foliage, contrasted with the bright tints of the flowering shrubs which spread like underwood beneath the trees of larger growth was new to me and very pleasing. I was sorry in spite of the publicity of such travelling, and its manifold discomforts, when our car was again harnessed to six handsome horses, and we were dragged through a long mile of suburban streets into the dark "Old Depôt," in the heart of Baltimore.

My *impressions de voyage* are nearly over. Bear with me while I say one word about the Monumental City. I walked with Max, that evening into Franklin Street, Cathedral Street, and Park Street. The night was clear, the moon was bright as daylight, and the marble fronts of the superb aristocratic-looking detached houses, glittered in her beams with singular advantage. I thought Baltimore—and think her now—the very Queen of the Atlantic Cities. In 1842, there were but one or two half-finished streets of this singular beauty. In 1855 miles of new streets, as wide, as marbled, and as handsome, stretched beyond them, over lands which, at the time of which I write, were country farms, or nursery grounds, or virgin woods. Imagination keeps no pace with the growth of an American city. Fancy toils breathless after statistics and finds herself behind the truth, even when she thought she had been dealing in *hyperbole*.

But the glory of Baltimore is not in her streets of marble palaces, but in those streets which contain the dwellings of her poor. Broad, airy, wholesome and well paved; each tiny house with its white doorsteps and green blinds, and alley leading to the yard behind, is a mechanic's home. The squalid back streets of New York or Boston, or the hideous Black Quarter of Philadelphia, are as horrible as Saffron Hill or Monmouth Street, or old St. Giles; but Baltimore would be the joy of Dr. Southwood Smith, or any other Good Samaritan devoted to that branch of philanthropy which I believe is more than any other to work permanent good—the construction of decent dwellings as the houses of the working classes, or Model Lodging Houses for the more destitute poor.

We had another stage to make to complete our journey, and the next day took the Baltimore and Ohio Railroad, winding along the banks of the Patapsco, through corn-land and woodland, high rocks, covered with flowers of all hues, on either side of us, or the silvery foaming waters of the river that we crossed and re-crossed, hastening over shoals and rapids to the sea.

When we neared Harper's Ferry, Max, by especial permission of the conductor, took me outside upon the platform, and astonished me by showing me how the road was scooped under an overhanging mass of rock. There was not a foot of spare space, it seemed to me, from the right hand car window to the blasted wall of rock, nor more upon the left hand to the Chesapeake and Ohio Canal, which ran along the bank of the Potomac at the very margin of the river. Such railway work was awful—was wonderful! Ten miles beyond the Point of Rocks, Harper's Ferry opened on our view. Yonder on the other shore of the Potomac was Virginia, where the great smooth, rounded mountain swells out of the river into a mighty cone, washed at its base by both the Potomac and the Shenandoah. The old Ferry is now crossed by iron railway tracks. As we thundered into the Depôt, under a wooden covered way, the conductor told us that that spot was the Gretna Green of the Valley of Virginia.

We left the cars at Harper's Ferry, and as I was standing bewildered on a fork of the bridge belonging to the Winchester and Potomac Railway, dreading the sudden coming of some wandering locomotive, while Max with his great coat over his arm was hurrying up a negro porter with our baggage, a gentleman passed along the platform who excited my attention.

He looked at me earnestly for a moment, then at Max. His look was a little uncertain and troubled, but the cloud on his face cleared off, the sunshine broke out warmly, and with a pleasant smile he came forward to greet us. I had known him at once; it was our cousin Tyrell.

He said that our letters from New York had not been received at Clairmont, and that our relations were uncertain what day we should arrive, so that he feared there would be no carriage nor cousins at the Depôt looking out for us.

"Oh! Max," said I, "we had better wait here a few days, and send them word. Perhaps they have not room for us. I should not like to take them by surprise if they are not expecting us."

Cousin Tyrell laughed out heartily. "My fair cousin Molly,"

said he, "is not so good a Virginian as she ought to be, or she would know that our houses and hearts are inexhaustible in their capacity. A Virginian has a welcome for any friend at any moment. Your Clairmont cousins would never forgive the slight you put upon their hospitality, were you to carry out your plan of spending the night at Harper's Ferry. I'll send a boy on horseback from the Charlestown Depôt, and give them half an hour's notice of our coming."

Tyrell was the first person we had seen since we left England who was not a stranger, and I clung to him in all confidence as though he had been a dear old friend.

He took us into the hotel, and wanted us to get some dinner at the Ordinary, but my appetite was taken away by the crash and rush and scramble and din. I shrank back from the door to the diversion of Tyrell. "I have some dinner in my bag," said I, "and had much rather eat it quietly."

"Can you climb?" said Tyrell. "We might go up to Jefferson's Rock and improvise a pic-nic. You have two hours to wait for the Winchester train."

"What! the rock from whence Mr. Jefferson saw the view that he said it was worth crossing the Atlantic to get a glimpse of?"

"The same. —— Will you try it?"

"By all means," said I. So we went forth, piloted by Tyrell. The way was pretty steep, though we went up at a smart pace; but Tyrell carried my bag, and he and Max helped me and encouraged me.

"Have you forgotten our ramble through the woods?—Do you remember Castleton, and its pretty lake?" I said, as we paused breathless on the height above the Arsenal.

"Of course—of course," said he.

"And Veronica?" said I. "You have not told me anything about Veronica. Is she very much changed?"

"Veronica is staying at Clairmont," said cousin Tyrell. "If you stand this way, Miss Molly, you may see Washington's Head, on that hill on the Maryland side of the Potomac. There! don't you see his cocked hat?"

In the excitement of trying to do the impossible thing—to make out a fanciful outline, clear to the eyes of another person, I forgot the string of questions I had been about to put to him about Veronica.

We mounted the steep grassy summit of the hill, and the whole glory of the view broke suddenly upon us. The Shenandoah and the Potomac lay glittering at our feet—the "abounding and rejoicing" rivers. The Shenandoah pouring its waters into the Potomac, seemed to have cloven its outlet through the hill on which we stood, and rushed impetuously over shoals and rapids, sparkling and glistering with silver foam into the embrace of her sister river. The Potomac, too, had cleft its way through a spur of the Blue Ridge. All around the Ferry were high, steep hills (mountains almost), overhanging the water, which opened broadly out into a sort of bay, now lying glad and glittering in noon-day sunshine, blue, touched with silver where the water's course was ruffled by the rapids. These rapids extended nearly half a mile, commencing about a mile below Harper's Ferry. The whole surface of the river was covered with masses of rock, which I have since seen showing above water, when the stream was low, but this was the season of spring freshets, and they were nearly all submerged, their only sign the dash of the white spray made by the water foaming over them.

"Are these rivers navigable, cousin Tyrell?" said I.

"Formerly," he answered, "they were navigable for flat bottomed boats, built expressly for navigating these waters, and all the produce of the Valley passed this way. Before our Revolutionary War, there was a company of gentlemen, at the head of whom were your great grandfather and General Washington, who obtained a charter for the Colonies of Maryland and Virginia, for improving the navigation of the Potomac—their highway to the sea. At that time many boatmen were employed upon the river, a hardy adventurous class, resembling the Canadian Voyageurs, though Tom Moore wrote no song for them. The boats they used were built somewhat after the fashion of the gondolas of Venice, from which they took their name, corrupted by the boatmen into gunlows. It is an expression still familiar in this neighborhood."

Here Tyrell paused and added, pointing down the river:—"Many a fine boat has been stove among these treacherous rocks and boiling currents, and many a fine fellow has been drowned there."

I shuddered. "I do not like to connect ideas of death and danger with a scene like this. Those noble streams and mountains draped with woods, and the blue sky, with its faint golden haze, and the living sparkling beauty of everything around us, seem to me so full of joy and of the promise of gladness."

"Yes, but there are often things concealed under the smiles of nature. There are few things in the world without associations of sadness. I am glad to believe, however, that your life has never known the chill that comes over us when the sun withdraws himself."

Then changing his tone, he repeated in his full, rich voice, the feeling of the moment adding to its sweetness, a verse from Longfellow's "Wreck of the Hesperus," then just published:—

"She struck where the white and fleecy waves
  Looked soft as carded wool,
But the cruel rocks they gored her sides
  Like the horns of an angry bull."

Max joined in the conversation with some talk about American poetry. I opened my bag and spread our feast upon the rock. Tyrell gathered me a sprig of a small, modest, yellow wild flower, to grace our dinner table.

"Oh!" said I, "it is the pleasantest thing I have seen since I landed. It reminds me of home. It is an English pimpernel."

And I kissed the little blossom. The tears came into my eyes. It was dear to me, and I rejoiced over it. Tyrell stood watching me with his penetrating look, and his grave, kindly smile.

"Join to the English remembrance, that has made it dear," he said, "the thought that it is the first flower gathered for you on the soil of Old Virginia."

I gave it another kiss when he said that, and hid the modest, yellow first-fruits in my bosom.

CHAPTER III.

Honor to him who first "through the impassable paves a road."
CARLYLE. *Death of Goethe.*

WE came gaily down the mountain when our dinner was done, and were soon travelling along the banks of the Shenandoah, in the slow Winchester train. The beautiful green maize was about a foot high in the fields on either side the railroad. I remarked at once a change of countenance among our fellow passengers. The dress of most of them was extremely seedy, though Tyrell pointed out several as large landed proprietors; but there was something in the air and manner of these men which irresistibly attracted me. There was something native to the soil (something Indian) about them; in their tread, and in their height; in their prominent nose, with the thin nostrils; and above all in their foreheads, strongly perceptive, but without the reflective fullness which indicates severe habits of abstract thought. All wore their hair, which was mostly black and long, brushed back from their temples. Many were men yet in the prime of life who were prematurely grey. All were spare, sallow, and sinewy. There were some men "mountain men," as Tyrell told me, dressed in coarse green frieze, looking as wild as untamed colts—the roughest people both in manners and appearance amongst whom I had been ever thrown; disgusting in their habits—but indeed to say the truth, chewing tobacco seemed to be the error of even the most aristocratic-looking men among our passengers. There was one, a little "tight," as Tyrell called it, who persisted in quarrelling with the conductor. "Well, sir," said this functionary, "I refer you to Mr. Tyrell, son of Governor Tyrell, of Stonehenge. There is not a man who stands higher in general estimation in our section of the country. You may ask Mr. Tyrell if I am charging you more than the ordinary rate for your passage."

The other muttered something about "d—d dear, and d—d bad travelling on that line of railway."

"By no means, sir," said the conductor, confidently, "Mr. Tyrell will inform you. I appeal to Mr. Tyrell."

"He is right, sir, he has asked you only the legal fare, " said Tyrell, gravely, but with a gleam of mischief in his eye, "I consider this the cheapest railroad in the United States, without any exceptions.

"There, sir!—I told you so," said the conductor, as the defaulter sullenly pulled out his pocket-book and paid the money.

Several gentlemen had gathered round Tyrell, who turned to them with a funny look. "I really do," said he. "It is the only railroad that I know of, on which you can travel all day for the small sum of two dollars."

A great loud hearty laugh exploded through the cars. Tyrell was evidently a great and privileged favorite. Even this facetious observation, which they relished very much, did not impair his dignity. The "roughest customer" treatedhim with respect. though more or less he seemed to have a passing acquaintance with every one about him. Several of the landed proprietors gathered round our seat and asked Tyrell to introduce them to us. Each of them hoped I should decide on making Virginia my residence, and promised me a choice of lovers! Such speeches were so contrary to the taste of the society in which I had been bred, that I was a little uncertain how to receive them. "As for you, sir," said one or two of them to Max, "we hear you are coming out here to court one of our most distinguished Virginia belles. We think she must have left her heart in England, for she never has been known to favor any of her *beaux*. Eh, Tyrell?

"Miss Veronica is a prize worth striving for," said Tyrell.

"Aye, indeed," said an old gentleman. "It was thought at one time you were the horse that was bound to win. But I don't know how it was, I believe you did not make up to her. Why didn't you court her? It would have been a first rate match. If I were a young gentleman I wouldn't suffer such a girl to be carried out of the Valley of Virginia."

"Courting Miss Veronica is mighty skittish sort of work," said one of the youngest of the party. "I tell you it's like catching mules. She don't give a fellow time to get up to her before she's off, and he's knocked over on his back, with nothing to do but to get up and be laughed at," and he rubbed his shoulders, as if he well remembered such an overthrow, and had not relished the experience.

"Let me look out here, gentlemen, if you please," said Tyrell, "we are just approaching Charlestown. I want to see if any of my boys are about."

The train was slowly coming up to a rude platform, beside which several strange country carriages were waiting. Tyrell looked out of the window and addressing a darkey with a shining black face, wearing a singularly bright plaid waistcoat, much too large for him, cried, "Oigh, Diggory!—all right—That's you!"

"Yes, Mas'r Jim," said Diggory, with a gleaming ivory grin, taking off his hat with a true negro sideways bow—one of the cast-off graces of the last half century.

"Look you here," said Tyrell. "What horses have you got in my buggy? Tom and Jerry?"

"Yes, sar."

"Well, take out Jerry—do you hear? and tell somebody about here to drive Tom and the buggy to the inn, and send over for them before breakfast to-morrow morning. You mount Jerry—Are you listening?"—Diggory's eyes were rolling all about, and had settled on my face.

"Yes sar."

"Mount Jerry, and ride as hard as you can go to Clairmont, and tell your Miss Edmonia that Captain and Miss Man deville, from England . . . . What am I saying?"

"Cap'en 'd Miss Mandeville from England." Diggory's eyes opened wider on me than before.

"Captain and Miss Mandeville, from England, will arrive at Simpson's Depôt this afternoon, and I shall bring them over to Clairmont. Now be off.—Don't stop to watch the corn grow."

"I'se gwine, Mas' Jim."

But he stopped to point us out to another darkey, and to take a wider stare at Max and me, so as to make his arrival acceptable at Clairmont, by carrying with him a full description.

Several bystanders came up to look at us, and I heard one of them, an old negro, in the coarse drab clothes worn by slaves in Virginia, say, "Laws! ef that ar ain't Miss Vera's beau—done comed all de way out of de North—way dar somewhars, just to see Miss Vera Lomax. Mighty hansum lookin' fellar, any how."

The speaker was pushed aside somewhat rudely, by a tall,

white man in a long great-coat, who sprang upon the car platform just as the train was getting into motion. He looked about him, stared at Max and me, then came and took a seat in our vicinity, and touched his hat to Tyrell, who returned the salutation somewhat stiffly.

He looked as if he had been drinking. His eyes were wild and his hair was in disorder. After a few minutes he called out to Tyrell.

"Jim—what's your prospect of a corn crop?"

Cousin Tyrell answered shortly, but a conversation was opened, and the stranger, looking me disagreeably in the face, said: "That young lady is a relative of mine. She favors her father's family at Clairmont. Be so good as to introduce me to my cousins."

He got up and came beside me. Tyrell was obliged to say, "Mr. William Williams, of Clarke County."

Mr. Williams shook hands with us. Slapping Max upon the back, he said, "I am cousin Veronica's nearest male friend in this section. You will have to apply for my consent before you marry into the family."

"Really, sir," said Max, who had been chafing two hours under this kind of thing. "I don't see what business it is of every man I meet whether or not I am a suitor to my cousin."

Will Williams laughed right out. "It's mighty particular business of mine, I reckon. By the terms of the will, if you don't marry her within a year, I shall come in for a slice of that cake of my old uncle's."

Neither Tyrell nor Max answered. I understood at once that this was the son of "Barbara, wife of William Williams, Esq., of Clarke County," and sister to cousin Lomax, who had never liked her husband and had had no intercourse with her.

"My uncle Lomax was a mighty queer old fellow in his latter days," said Mr. Williams addressing me. I thought that anything was better than that he should have any words with Max, and answered with some alacrity that he was considered quite eccentric, certainly . . . . when Tyrell abruptly interrupted me, calling my attention to the country on either side of us. Presently the train slowly came to a full stop beside an unfinished looking frame house on the edge of a wood; with a rough boarded platform, covered with bales and flour barrels. Tyrell looked out. "This is the depôt," said he. "And yonder is your cousin Philip Ormsby. And there's old uncle Israel with the carriage. They have got your letters and are looking out for you."

As he said this, our cousin Philip disappeared from the platform, and a moment after we saw him come into the car, and look round dubiously till he caught sight of Tyrell.

"All right. Here we are!" said he; "come along, cousin," tucking my hand under his arm, after shaking it violently. "How d'ee, cousin Max. Everybody at home is on the lookout for you. Where did you have the luck to fall in with them, cousin Tyrell?"

So saying, without waiting for an answer, he hurried me out upon the platform. He was very handsome, very kindly, and his manners very cordial and winning. His hair was a little rusty, perhaps, about the ends, and his whiskers wanted trimming; there was none of the precise neatness of an English gentleman about his dress, which was more of an evening than a morning suit, with the eternal black waistcoat forming part of it, but there was something altogether fascinating about him; and he was quite the gentleman. He was six feet or thereabouts in height, with a figure tall, agile, and well-proportioned. His face was one a sculptor might have been glad to copy for some statue of the young Acteon eager for the chase. Such beautiful brown eyes, so sweet a mouth, a nose so delicately shaped I had never seen before. His complexion was very dark. Darker than that of many a mulatto slave on plantations in that neighborhood.

There was no waiting-room, of course. He carried me into the house, which was a shop or store, and left me leaning against one of the casks, while he went and brought the carriage. Such a carriage! I did not then know its appearance was the pride of dear, good-natured cousin Phil, who had spent some hours furbishing it up for so important an occasion as the arrival of English strangers. Its wheels were heavy with orange-colored clay, and it was spattered with blotches of red mud, from its foot-board to its whiffle-trees.

When he opened the door a strange noise issued from inside. The body of the carriage was blocked up by a large deal box which gave forth an uncertain sound.

"What have you got there, Phil?" said Tyrell.

"It's a sucking pig. Old Mammy Venus wants a lot of citron, mustard, and a vanilla bean. They are out of all such truck down at the store in Fighterstown. Uncle Israel get this pig out! Cousin Molly don't be shocked. This isn't what you have been used to, I reckon, in the 'marble halls' of Castleton, but you must put up with 'corn bread and common doings,' and 'hog and hominy' in all shapes, as cousin Veronica has done."

Here Uncle Israel, a white headed old negro, sauntered slowly up to us. "Uncle Israel," said Philip, "this is Miss Molly Mandeville, the lady I am bound to marry, before she goes away. The daughter of your Master Charles."

"Laws, yes, Mas' Phil," said Israel, holding out his hand. "Wish't she would marry you an' git fixed down among us. I like her face. Its real Mandeville. I'd a knowed her any whars for one of the family. How she do favor her pa."

I shook hands with Uncle Israel, as he seemed to expect it. I put my fingers into that great wrinkled black hand, yellow in the palm. I was ready to wish the African race all good, I was ready to desire immediate emancipation, but I was not prepared to shake hands with a negro. I had never shaken hands with any of the servants at home.

However, I got over it after I was seated in the carriage, and was jolting over what, in Virginia, is called a "dirt road." Philip was driving with a great expenditure of exhortation to his animals. Max sat with him in front. Tyrell and I with the exchange for poor piggy, in mustard, citron, vanilla and other spice occupied the interior of the carriage.

We wound down a hill. The road was cut through a stiff orange clay, and wound irregularly round fields protected by worm fences, or found its way as it best might through the heart of noble woods in all their summer verdure.

"Don't be afraid, Miss Molly," said Tyrell, as the carriage gave an awful shake. "Phil is the best driver in our country, and can turn his carriage round the edge of a dollar."

"I reckon I could," said Philip, flourishing his whip and turning round with a laugh, "provided anybody had a dollar to lend me for the purpose. I hav'n't seen one so long that I should be glad to renew the acquaintance. Specie is mighty scarce just now in these parts, or I shouldn't have let Simpson had that little hog, I reckon."

Away we rattled down a hill, rough as a staircase, with great limestone ridges running across the road. Over these we went gritting and slipping. Phil talking to his horses, and reining them up to let us down easily, two wheels at a time, over great rocks of limestone. Every now and then, we plunged into a mud-hole. Down went the horses over their knees in mud. Then came a scramble—horses dragging up the other side, as if they would drag themselves out of their ragged harness; but it held firm: as Phil said, "no city gear was ever half so strong." Then our fore wheels went in with a sudden jerk and splash—the hind wheels followed with a creaking strain on every bit of wood or iron. "Oigh, there, Liz! Ge' up there Barney?" The horses' hoofs are striking and slipping on another limestone ridge; they can hardly keep their feet. Philip continues to gesticulate, never using the whip, and with a long pull and a strong pull from our unflinching little quadrupeds, the carriage is jerked at length all safe upon another ridge of limestone.

I trembled all over every time we came to such a place, and held on to the side of the carriage with both hands.

"This isn't bad," said Philip, with a laugh. "Cousin Molly, I will introduce you to some of our back roads. We've got a fine bit of turn-pike macadamized with black marble from Clairmont to the river."

On we went over six miles of travelling such as this, past fields of waving wheat, and clover scenting all the air with its sweet perfume, and corn just beginning to swell into ear.

We passed through woods of noble but neglected trees, their beauty not impaired by any undergrowth, and everywhere the landscape was shut in by its frame-work of blue mountains.

We skirted a straggling town with muddy streets; we found ourselves on the "black marble" highway. Philip and Tyrell pointed out Clairmont, a white house on an elevation overlooking the valley, and visible itself for miles away, standing out in bold relief, with its extremely handsome Grecian porch, and its green back-ground of woods, stretching like wings on either side of it.

We turned into the avenue, with rougher jerks over the tall limestone ridge, which made a sort of staircase at the gate, than any former shocks that had befallen us.

"Why in the name of sense, don't you set to work and blast these rocks?" said Max.

"Mr. Morrisson has been thinking of it," said Phil, "and he's been fixing up lately. Last week we got the gate-posts up, and after harvest he expects to get the gate hung. We are obliged to keep a boy about, to keep out the neighbors' hogs which eat up everything. There they are again! Oigh, Tom! Tommy Tadd! run boy, and drive those hogs out! Drive them well down the road."

"How came the fences broken down?" said I.

"Aye Phil," said Tyrell, with his funny look, "tell us how it came so?"

"Well," said Phil, "when I was a boy it was getting into a pretty bad state, and the negroes have torn down some of the rails to save themselves the trouble of chopping wood after nightfall. And there's a mighty bad mud-hole just beyond, where carriages and carts get mired in the spring, and they used up the fence rails prying them out; and so pa got tired of putting up new fencing. But Morrisson has got a great idea of fixing up.—Next year, cousin Molly, you will see!"

Tyrell responded to this by singing a stave of

Old Virginny nebber tire,
Stick a hoe-cake on him foot
And hole him to a fire.

Meantime we were driving under splendid oaks, black walnut trees, locusts and hickories, which kept in order would have made an avenue a king might envy, and as we turned on to the grassy opening beside the house, the glorious view, with mountains, valley, and the rising moon, broke full upon us. I gave an exclamation of delight, interrupted by several figures running down from the porch towards us. "Welcome, cousins! Glad to see you Tyrell. Your Diggory got over here half an hour ago, having ridden Jerry most to death to be the first to tell us to expect our cousins. Cousin Max, did you ever hear before of sending a man and horse in advance of the railroad? We are so glad to see you. We got your letter last night, cousin Moll. You don't look the least like what we thought. What do you think of our roads in Old Virginia?"

With pleasant hearty greetings like this from our cousin Virginia Morrisson (*née* Ormsby), and introductions to her husband, Mr. Morrisson, and to a distant cousin, Weston Carter, a superb looking fellow, just from the Florida swamps, with the air and dignity of an Indian, we were carried up the steps of the portico. Sitting upon the upper step, surrounded by several gentlemen of the neighborhood, was our cousin Veronica. She rose at our approach, and came down the steps to meet us. She kissed me, but without much warmth. Her greeting was very different from that of cousin Virginia. She gave Max the tips of her fingers. As she stood in the soft moonlight, in a lilac muslin dress, with a red Indian shawl, which had been her mother's, folded around her to protect her from the evening dew, I thought I had never before seen any vision of earth so gloriously and proudly beautiful. Her queenliness had developed itself, and half her childish winsomness had disappeared. She took us up the steps on to the porch, and presented us to aunt Edmonia. Dear aunt Edmonia, too infirm to totter down the steps and bid us welcome, who rose up tall and stately from her rocking-chair at our approach, laid her hand upon my head and gave me her kind blessing.

CHAPTER IV.

Mine own dear land
With its mountains wild and blue.
MOULTRIE.

WE sat round the long hospitable tea-table at Clairmont, piled with delicious biscuit, hoe-cake, and hot corn cake, "fruit cake" (Virginian for plum-cake), and other votive offerings, by which sacrifice is made to the lean goddess Dyspepsia, who is thus invoked on altars of hospitable mahogany through the length and breadth of the land.

Veronica was seated between two gentlemen of the neighborhood, and appeared engrossed by their conversation. Max tried every now and then to win her notice, but, without being in the least rude to him, she treated him with great *nonchalance*, and put his attentions aside. I sat between Weston Carter and cousin Tyrell; both bent on supplying me with amusement and indigestion. The mistress of the house, on "hospitable thoughts intent," sat at the head of the table, directing by word and gesture the movements of three little negroes, two girls and a boy, whom she was bringing up as house servants, and who had so much personal interest in the fresh supply of guests, as to require continual ordering to prevent their standing gazing at us with great eyes, instead of attending to the service of the table.

"I declare, cousin Tyrell, you haven't eaten one thing yet. Do try some of old Marm Venus's corn cake—it's elegant to night—though your old Mammy Pomona makes it so good at home. I declare, you have grown quite a stranger at Clairmont since last Fall. Mr. Morrisson and I were talking about it. Perhaps cousin Molly's being here may attract you, as you seem to have taken a fancy to your English cousins. I reckon you expect we have none but common doings in our ash-heap. Cousin Molly you will have to put up with a great deal. We can't fix up things in the style you've been accustomed to at Castleton."

The conversation was very animated, and, with the exception of the by-play between Veronica and her two gentlemen, it was very general. We were ten persons at table; Phil and the children of the family, including an intelligent and gentlemanly little boy from Baltimore, taking their tea at a side-table. Good eating, good humor, and a good understanding seemed to prevail everywhere. Perhaps Tyrell was less talkative than when we had him by ourselves, but he sustained his part in the conversation sufficiently. He was a man of much more observation, cultivation, powers of thought, and knowledge of the world, than any of the rest of the party. His superior education blended delightfully with their talent for anecdote, and genial gaiety. Weston, or the Great Western, as Tyrell called him, on account of his extraordinary height and proportionate development, was paying me Western compliments, telling me I was "some pumpkins, certain," and "a whole team with a big dog under the wagon," when cousin Virginia made the signal, and we rose from the table.

The two gentlemen of the neighborhood, who had come over on business with Mr. Morrisson (it was an affair of five minutes, as I learnt afterwards, and they had been at Clairmont seven hours!) took leave of us upon the porch, and attended by Phil and Tyrell went to the edge of the wood where their horses had stood under the trees, hitched to a ring in an old rack, since their arrival in the morning. They mounted, and rode over the grass up to the porch, caracolling as they waved a farewell to Veronica, while Phil with shouts and gestures tried to excite their horses, and a crowd of little darkies all agape, enjoying "Mas' Phil's fooling," filled up the back-ground.

When they rode off, Veronica called the children round her, and entrenched herself in the midst of them, apparently engrossed in attention to the explanations of the little boy from Baltimore, who, convinced by her cordial, earnest way, that she was deeply interested in his information, was explaining to her with some animation, the programme of out-door amusements throughout the year, adopted by Young America all over the Union. How ball, and hockey, marbles, and kites came into fashion, each on its own day in the calendar, as regularly as our own moors in August, or partridge shooting on the 1st of September. Max, whom she had shut out from the conversation, but who was standing near the group, broke in on Walter's naming marbles, with "Don't you remember what a famous hand you were at marbles, Veronica? And don't you recollect the little shop, just as you go into the hamlet, kept by the one-legged sailor who had his marbles in glass jars, like sugar-plums?"

"Did he?" said she. "I hardly recollect; it is so long ago. Tell me some more about your sports. I am quite interested, Walter."

There was a brief moment just as we were about to separate at night, when Max found an opportunity of saying to me "Did you ever see any one grown so handsome? But what makes her so cold?"

I answered in a whisper, "It is an awkward situation for her."

"Very true," returned Max. "In a day or two that feeling will be over."

The elastic sleeping accommodations of Clairmont were a great wonder to me in after days, but at present I knew too little of the family arrangements to give a thought as to the shifts and changes that would be necessary to accommodate a bushel of company into a peck measure of room. I went up stairs to share the apartment of Veronica, with rather a regretful feeling that I was not to be alone.

The room was a very large one, with four ill-fitting and uncurtained windows, opposite each other, and two double beds. A little negro girl was piling brands on an enormous glowing fire of hickory logs in the wide chimney. I had never seen such an incomparable fire, and though it was nearly June, it was not unacceptable, for the house stood upon high ground, and chinks in the windows let in plenty of night air.

Veronica did not seem disposed to talk, and I was so tired with the varied impressions of the day, that I hardly allowed myself to sit a moment over the glowing hearth, but was in bed and fast asleep, while Veronica was still brushing the golden tresses of her beautiful hair. I awoke somewhere about midnight, startled by the downfall of some broken brands, and turning towards the firelight saw Veronica in her white dressing-gown seated on a low stool beside the hearth, with her head bowed on her hands. It was an attitude of such utter misery and self-abandonment, that I yielded to my impulse of compassion, and springing out of bed I crossed the room and threw my arms around her. Her first impulse was to repulse my sympathy, and then I suppose the barriers of her pride were swept away by the surprise and suddenness of the movement. She laid her head upon my breast and burst into tears.

"What is it, dear Veronica?"

"Nothing—nothing Moll," she said, "only I feel so very desolate. Uncle Lomax, who loved me so, is gone; and I was not with him when he died. I might have made him happier in his last days if I could have made up my mind to go back to Castleton. I acted for the best, but it is very hard to know what the right course is when one has no adviser to depend upon. Oh, Molly! Mammy's words came back to me continually, "all 'lone, all 'lone in dis wide world."

"Dear, dear Veronica look up and tell me if you can, how many people love you?"

"Yes, but that is no comfort. That is another cause for suffering." Then suddenly the anguish in her face, from worldly trouble, ceased, and a smile lighted it as she laid her hand upon a book upon her knee. "'In quietness and confidence shall be your strength.' There is help and comfort here."

"What book is that Veronica?"

She put into my hands the 'Christian Year,' repeating:

Nay rather steel thine aching heart
To act the martyr's sterner part,
And watch with calm unshrinking eye
Thy darling visions as they die,
Till all bright hopes and hues of day
Have faded into twilight grey.

"Molly, I wish there were such things as Protestant nunneries. I am one of the persons who ought to enter one. I have no natural ties. I do harm to every one who cares for me. It is hard not to wish I was in that quiet grave under the old apple-trees."

She had risen and gone towards the window. I threw a shawl over my night-dress, and followed her. A glorious moon was lighting up the landscape till night was luminous as day. The valley before us was set into a frame-work of mountains; the nearest about six miles from our window. Close under the foot of the Blue Ridge ran the Shenandoah, but its course was masked by woods along its banks, and it formed no feature in the landscape. From the river to the spot on which we stood the valley sloped up gradually, till Clairmont was nearly at the same elevation as the summit of the Ridge. Between the river and the house lay Fighterstown, glittering white in the calm moonshine. Every ragged outline was softened by the moonlight; the woods, and rolling country, and the fields of waving wheat, the winding road, the distant roofs of other country-houses with their barns and "quarter," all were distinctly visible for miles around at midnight as we stood together at the window, the griefs of earth subdued by the surpassing beauty of the scene.

"Yonder is Stonehenge," said Veronica, pointing towards the river.

"Yes, cousin Tyrell lives there. I am very glad that cousin Tyrell has the place. Veronica, I like cousin Tyrell exceedingly."

Veronica turned and looked at me. "He is a gentleman and a Christian," said she. "But you do not know him yet. Not half his good points will come out till you have tried him."

"Veronica you speak very warmly."

"I feel very warmly," she said. "By the way that is more than you can do. Why Molly! you will catch your death of cold. Go back to bed immediately."

With such kind scolding, and with gentle force, she obliged me to lie down, tucked me up cozily, and bent down and kissed me as my dear nursey far away at home, tormented by the after-crop of children in our house, was wont to do whenever, after I retired to rest, she came into my chamber. I had risen to comfort Veronica, and yet, though she had not repelled my sympathy—nay had rather invited it for a moment—she had in her own quiet way turned the tables on my purpose and was as usual bearing another's burthen without relinquishing her own.

I lay awake some time watching the dying fire-light, and wondering about Veronica. What she had said in praise of Tyrell gave me an uneasy feeling. I tried to remember whether she had talked with Tyrell that evening, but I could not recollect that I had seen them exchange a word. Tyrell had been talking to Mr. Morrisson upon the porch, and when we went into the drawing-room had been devoted to cousin Virginia. Another thing I asked myself: had Veronica any suspicion that I knew she had overheard the conversation in which Max had revealed to me his semi-boyish love for Lady Ellen MacIntyre?

I had never told Max that she had overheard it. I had just discretion enough to know by instinct, though I had not then read Carlyle, "that speech is silvern—silence golden." When it occurred I felt that it would wound his feelings to know his confidence had had a listener. I comprehended perfectly why it was Veronica had been unwilling to appear when we first came into the drawing-room at Castleton, and why she had been still less willing to show herself after our conversation had begun; and I could easily imagine that her delicacy would be wounded by the thought that Max knew that she had overheard his confidence, and in all our conversations I had guarded this little secret; more, perhaps, because I was afraid to tell it, afraid of the annoyance it would be to Max, than from the same motives of delicacy which had influenced me in the first instance to guard the secret as if it had been mine own.

CHAPTER V.

In Memoriam.

My impressions of the beauty of Clairmont were not less vivid by day than they had been under the light of the summer moon at midnight. The fir-clad mountains bounded the landscape, looking like a trim and mighty hedge around a garden of the Titans.

We breakfasted at six, to accommodate the gentlemen who professed themselves busy about agricultural affairs. Tyrell was at the breakfast-table when I entered, but nothing more than ordinary civilities appeared to pass between him and Veronica. There was another guest who ate his breakfast silently at the foot of the table, between Cousin Phil and Mr. Morrisson. He was an old man, very tall, and fashioned in proportion to his height. His silver hair was parted in the middle of his head, and hung long and slightly curled over his coat collar. He was dressed in a complete suit of gray cloth. His mild, sweet mouth, his gently-lighting eyes, and the simple dignity of his manners, drew my attention immediately. He was not introduced to me, however, when I sat down to breakfast; but when Veronica came in, shortly after, her face lighted up when she saw him, and going cordially across the room, with her pretty hand held out, she greeted him with her brightest smile. Cousin Virginia made a very funny face, and motioned me to observe the greeting. The old man rose and took Veronica's right hand gently and tenderly in his left, saying in a soft voice, but in a nasal key—

"It is always an honor and a happiness to be permitted to find myself in this young lady's presence, whenever my good fortune conducts me into the bosom of this amiable family."

As he spoke, he waved the fingers of his right hand slowly in the air.

"Who is it?" whispered I. "What a striking-looking old gentleman!"

"It's a beau of Veronica's," said cousin Virginia. "He holds her in such reverence, that he won't even speak her name. Mr. Felix, won't you let me hear you say my cousin's name? Make the effort, to oblige me, won't you?"

"That young lady is acquainted with her own name," he replied, with a quiet smile. "I trust she may be fortunate in her choice, whenever she concludes to exchange it for another."

I looked at Tyrell. He had called up a pointer dog of Mr. Morrisson's, which had been lying on the hearth, and was giving him a bone.

"Tell me who he is," I said to cousin Virginia.

She was interrupted in her answer by the arrival of four large tin pots into which she proceeded to pour coffee for the superannuated mammies of the family. Tyrell, however, answered me.

"That old gentleman is a man of singular and varied knowledge, and has a simple kindliness which makes his society generally acceptable. He has the good taste to appreciate your cousin Veronica, and worships her afar off, with something of that knightly devotion which makes the charm of old romance. He is an elderly Sir Galahad."

"But who is he?"

"Who is he?" repeated Tyrell, looking at me with a smile. "'Who is he?' is too English a question for us, Miss Molly. We people of the valley, who have few fresh books, do not ask when we meet with a new volume, 'who wrote it?' We interrogate its pages and judge it by what we find. I have told you what manner of man this Mr. Felix is, and you should be satisfied without knowing his profession and his pedigree."

The old man rose from the table.

"He is going back to his work," said Tyrell; "and your beautiful cousin, with kindness beaming in her soft blue eyes, will sit on the steps of the back porch, with her sewing, and draw out his information upon naval subjects, and pour into his lonely, kindly heart the balm of sympathy; and if his gentle spirit has been wounded in his contact with ruder natures, in his daily walk, her refinement will soothe and comfort him. He has been devoted to her ever since her first arrival at Clairmont, when she won his regard by 'responding,' as he said, 'to a few interrogatories.'"

"Cousin Virginia," said I, determined to disappoint Tyrell, who was playing on my curiosity, "in what work is Mr. Felix about to be engaged?"

"Well," said she, "he will begin by cutting out old Uncle Israel's coat. This is a busy time with us, cousin Molly, when the servants are getting their summer clothing."

My look of bewilderment amused Tyrell.

"Do not forget, Miss Molly," said he, "that in leaving England for the interior of Virginia, you made up your mind to pass, by sudden transition, out of a long-established order of things into an earlier phase in the development of society. In lower Virginia feudalism still exists; but in this part of the country, capital is more diffused, and enterprise is beginning to creep in. Our large plantations are nearly all cut up; our slave population is beginning to feel some effects from the competition of Irish labor. Society with us is like a road newly macadamized; it has neither the smooth places of the old dirt road, nor the advantages of a well-beaten turnpike. Every white man counts with us, much as a nobleman does in Poland or in Hungary, where counts and barons are found ploughing, with the sword that marks their order dangling at their sides. They and we have barely the beginning of a middle class between serf and noble. We are expected to admit all white men to our tables, or make suitable apology for their exclusion. I do not say this in reference to Mr. Felix; his company in any circle, upon equal terms, needs no apology. He was born with that native kindliness which is the mint stamp of a gentleman; and his eccentricities make him a very amusing companion to all persons who can forget their reverence for the child-like beauty of his character enough to enjoy a laugh at his peculiarities. Mr. Felix is a tailor by trade, living in Fighterstown, and passes round the neighborhood, from country house to country house, cutting out the summer and winter clothing of the negroes, which is made up at home."

I sat for a moment quite unable to realize that the empty tea-cup opposite my plate had been the tea-cup of a tailor.

"Come, Miss Molly," said Tyrell, at length, "get rid of your surprise, and come with me into the back porch, where I will introduce you to the good old gentleman."

On the back porch we found Mr. Felix, with a large pair of old-fashioned glasses on. He was standing at a long board, raised on tressels, marking out dimensions upon negro cloth with a piece of chalk between his fingers; Veronica was sitting by, and Max was talking to him. The old man's eyes were lighted up with interest, as we joined the group; they were mild, soft, bright, winning eyes, shining under his hair like the eyes of a Skye terrier. Max had been in Paris the year before, when the body of Napoleon had been brought from St. Helena to the banks of the Seine, and he was describing the enthusiasm of the spectators (notwithstanding the extreme coldness of the day) to his delighted auditor. The old man asked all kinds of minute particulars, as if striving to imprint the minutiæ of the scene clearly on his memory. From this description of the closing scene of the great history, the conversation passed into a discussion on the character and history of Napoleon. The old man had no powers of generalization; but I was astonished to perceive how varied and curiously minute his information was. He seemed to have studied the history till the whole period to him was *real.*

Veronica sat sewing. She tried to be intent upon her work, but ever and anon her face was lighted by a bright gleam of intelligence, and several times Mr. Felix appealed to her, when she joined in the conversation with a few words. Max kept it up, I think, because he marked her interest, but, gradually letting it drop into the hands of Tyrell, he seated himself on a low step of the porch facing the beautiful wood, disfigured by pig-pens and a shattered wood-pile. No sooner was he seated, however, than we heard Philip's hearty voice as he came running up from the wheat field before the house crying, "Oigh Tyrell! there's your father coming along the road in his two horse buggy."

Max had business to transact with Governor Tyrell and wanted to see him. Nine o'clock seemed to me early to receive a visit of ceremony, but cousin Virginia did not appear to think so. She who had been busy with a whole tribe of negroes of all ages, giving orders in the kitchen, hurrying up the boy who was out in the wood cleaning knives, and giving directions to two girls who were to sew upon the clothes that Mr. Felix was cutting out—took off her apron as if she had nothing to do and invited us to accompany her to receive Governor Tyrell in the front porch or in the parlor.

She said her servants were all "mighty trifling." A word I soon learnt to understand was Virginian for "careless," "giddy," "untrustworthy"—such a combination of those qualities in short as might be expected in a set of vain and idle people, brought up under a system of scolding, without any aim in life except to enjoy themselves under unfavorable circumstances, and escape punishment, and without any sense of personal responsibility.

As we stood together on the porch waiting for Governor Tyrell, Max whispered something to Veronica. She drew back quietly and answered aloud, "I have placed my poney at your sister's service and do not intend to ride this summer."

The few hours we had been at Clairmont had put a great gulf between Veronica and my brother. He no longer dared approach her on the old familiar terms as his cousin and his play-fellow. Their relations were on a mere footing of distant politeness. Max, who had intended to accomplish a brief courtship, found his intentions ignored or quietly repulsed, and was growing afraid of attempting to approach her. This was not what suited his impetuosity. He felt that every moment he was drifting away from her. He went straight to the point as his manner was determined to draw the truth from her.

"Cousin Veronica," he said, "it appears to me that you forget how intimate we were as children. It seems to me that you are hardly pleased to see us in Virginia. You do not treat us as if you remembered the good old times at Castleton."

Veronica steadied herself against a pillar of the portico and hesitated for an answer.

"Come Veronica," said Max persuasively, though with a tremor in his tone, "relent and give poor Molly and myself a smile of welcome."

"I am sorry to be discourteous, but it is better to be honest than polite," she faltered. "I am not glad to see you here. I wish you had spent this summer at Castleton."

"I should have had no motive in coming to Virginia after that time," he replied. "Fear not, Veronica, I am not going to urge you with unseemly haste to grant me all I hope to ask before the anniversary of the death of your uncle."

"I have no right of course to prescribe where you shall go or whom you shall see," said Veronica. "You have undoubtedly a right to visit your cousins in Virginia and to stay at Clairmont, where you are sure of a kind welcome from Mr. Morrisson and cousin Virginia, but if my wishes had any influence with you, you would leave Molly here and travel into Western Virginia, or go to see Weir's Cave, or the Natural Bridge, or the White Sulphur Springs—all places of interest to the traveller."

"Veronica," said Max, "what am I to understand from this conversation?"

"Precisely what I think you understand," she interrupted him. "It may not be becoming in me to speak so openly, but I am placed in a difficult and exceptional position towards you. Your presence is not welcome to me at Clairmont. Had it been possible for me to go away before you came, I should have done so rather that request a favor. As it is I have no alternative but to beg that you, a man who can go when and where you will, will leave this neighborhood, or else if you stay here that you will take this honest warning."

"Max!" cried cousin Virginia from the grass, "come down, here is the Governor."

Veronica had withdrawn herself, and Max finding that he was left alone, sprang with a long leap upon theg rass from the high end of the portico.

The Governor came up the steps. He was a tall spare man, dressed all in green with a superb emerald pin in his shirt bosom. His hair was white and thin, worn short, and brushed up from his temples. His clear, ruddy face was smoothly shaven. He had been an old diplomatist; had represented his country at divers Courts of Europe, during the days of the first presidents, and served her less by his talents (though those were very considerable) than by the simple dignity of his manners, his polish, and high breeding. So finished a gentleman representing the United States amongst the best society of foreign courts was a letter of recommendation "known and read by all," in favor of his countrymen.

His manners had the precise dignity of the old school, as he came up the steps and made me his salutation.

He had been a young man in Paris in 1785, imbued at that period with all the enthusiasm of the Rights of Man School. It was singular to talk with a man who had gossipped in the *bosquets* of Versailles with *piquante* ladies of the Court of Marie Antoinette; who had mixed up the awful tragedies of Revolution with the petty realities of meat and drink, during the reign of Terror; who had heard Mirabeau thunder from the tribune—had seen Robespierre with his sky-blue dandy coat, and prim bouquet; and shuddered at the dreadful guillotine at work till "all the place ran blood," where now the waters of the further fountain in the Place de la Concorde, leap and sparkle; that fountain beyond the Obelisk of Luxor, the one nearest to the Seine.

The old gentleman had preserved the ideas of that period, tempered by the wisdom of experience. He was not, like most old men, conservative—he was a waif of the old Revolution. No man was ever more thoroughly an aristocrat than he, in all his feelings, habits, and tastes; but in all that related to theories of government he was a democrat of the old democracy. He despised the politician of the modern school. He called them partisans not statesmen; but he believed in the vitality and ultimate diffusion of the ideas he cherished. He thought that Europe was not yet out of the furnace of the Revolution. No untoward circumstances drove him to despondency. He believed with all his soul, that all things worked together for the ultimate triumph of democracy. When the car of Progress alarmed people of less experience by running backward, he knew that it was only a manœuvre to get on the right track when it might get up its steam. There was a loyalty about him that I have rarely seen in other Americans. His patriotism was wider than the boundaries of States. He believed in the mighty mission of the Republic, as the political backwoodsman of the human race. Our cousin Tyrell interested himself more in social questions than in abstract politics. He had caught the tone of the day; but governments and theories of government alone, were what interested his father. No man upon earth was kinder than Governor Tyrell to individuals, but schemes of general philanthropy were not his affair.

He sat in the porch and talked to us delightfully. The flavor of his eloquence would have lent a charm to common-place, but his conversation was altogether out of the common line, both in matter and kind. Cousin Tyrell stood by enjoying his father's talk as much as any of us. Cousin Virginia, forgetting her occupations in the kitchen and back porch, sat by us, with her glorious eyes flashing intelligence. I never ceased regretting, while I stayed at Clairmont, that a woman so fitted to adorn society by every natural gift of wit and beauty, should have had her lot cast upon a country farm, where she was enslaved by her own negroes. And yet powers such as hers must always assert themselves. Her social talents collected round her all kindred elements within her reach. Busy as the mistress of Clairmont always was she—was never like a Yankee woman, too busy to welcome company She was the life of the vicinity, the soul of every attempt at gaiety; she led the laugh on all occasions, and the best efforts of the united neighborhood could hardly keep pace with her cordial hospitality.

Governor Tyrell had come over to Clairmont to engage us to pay an early visit to Stonehenge. He wanted to secure the entire family, children, servants and grown persons. He had plenty of accomodation for all of us, he said. The roads were very bad; and he suggested we should come on horseback,—would send over horses if any were wanted for the party, and had a beautiful little sorrel pony—" the prettiest thing of its size in Virginia,"—that he must place at my disposal while I remained at Clairmont. I gratefully accepted this attention, having heard what Veronica had said to Max, and it was agreed that a ride through the summer woods along the river road would be delightful.

Cousin Virginia arranged the programme of our visit. The following Thursday was fixed on for the excursion, and one proposal made was, that in order to have as much time as possible before us we should leave Clairmont at sunrise.

"My son will send Miss Mandeville his horse and ride with her himself, to make sure that she is safe," said the Governor.

"What is your pony's name?" I said to Tyrell.

"Angelo," he answered. "I believe he is a first rate little horse for a lady."

"Yes," said the Governor, "when Miss Veronica first came I desired my son to place him at her disposal. You used to ride every day with Miss Lomax when she first had him, James," he added, turning to his son, "and you can give Miss Mandeville a good report of him."

"Where is Veronica? Oigh! Mary Louisa, just go and tell your Miss Veronica that she has dressed herself enough," said cousin Virginia.

It had been so much trouble to get Mary Louisa settled to her work, that it seemed to me a pity to disturb her.

"I will call Veronica," said I; and ran up into her chamber. She was not there, and I went on to the back porch in search of her.

As I opened the door Walter rushed up to me. "Oh! Miss Molly," said he, "Mr. Felix says that if he had noble blood, literary distinction, a large fortune, a splendid and youthful appearance, piety, and a perfect knowledge of the French language, he would really feel constrained to offer himself to cousin Veronica."

"I was not so presumptuous as to volunteer any observation of that nature," began Mr. Felix, laying down his shears, and waving the fingers of his right hand, as was his custom, "but young Mr. Walter put the question to me in a direct form, and I was constrained to give it a truthful answer."

"Mr. Felix," said Veronica, "I beg your pardon for this naughty boy, who had no business to be impertinent to either of us. I assure you," she added, with a forced smile, "that I shall never receive a more acceptable offer."

"God bless me," said the old man, in a subdued tone, "you should not say that; indeed, it does not become you to say so. Even a young lady so greatly superior to all others, might find that to confer happiness on one of the other sex who was worthy of her regard, was suitable and becoming. I am most sincerely sorry," addressing me, "that this young lady does not contemplate the silken bonds of matrimony. I should have thought the tenderest relations of life would have had a charm in proportion to her excellence and superiority."

"No, Mr. Felix, I am very happy as I am!" (oh! sad, sad words, that mean so completely the reverse in most cases, when a woman utters them), "and do not mean to give away my independence so long as it can be preserved."

The old man looked at her, but stood his ground. "When a young man of suitable acquirements and of distinguished family and worth, has honestly set his desire on acquiring the attachment of a young lady, I do not consider that she enhances the admiration that all good men entertain for her,when her love of independence induces her to reject his offer."

"Why! Mr. Felix," said the voice of my aunt Edmonia, "I thought you considered Veronica too good for any man."

"This young lady is superior to any other young lady with whom I have ever become acquainted," said Mr. Felix, "but I conceive she will but add new graces to those with which she is so abundantly endowed, when she consents to matrimony."

Here Walter ran away to the front porch, where we heard him telling Governor Tyrell and his son, Max, and cousin Virginia, that Mr. Felix said "if he had noble blood, literary distinction, a large fortune, splendid and youthful appearance, piety, and a competent knowledge of the French language," he would offer these advantages to Veronica; adding that Veronica said positively she never meant to marry anybody, and that Mr. Felix was reproving her.

CHAPTER VI.

Led by my folly or my fate,
I loved before—I knew not what,
And threw my thoughts I knew not where.
With judgment now I love and sue,
And never yet perfection knew,
Until I cast mine eyes on her.

Raised to this height, I have no more,
Almighty Love, for to implore
Of my auspicious stars and thee,
Than that thou bow her noble mind
To be as mercifully kind
As I shall ever faithful be.

COLTON, 1660.

THE sun rose in all his glory over the crest of the Blue Ridge on the morning which had been fixed upon for our Stonehenge visit. The interval between the invitation and the dinner-party had been passed in the busy idleness which is the life of Virginia. I had learned to play cards in the morning, to mix a mint julep and imbibe one, to sit on the porch half the day, and entertain gentlemen. I had planned a scramble through the woods, but found that walking for exercise was unheard of in Virginia; and was consoled by a merry pic-nic, to which we and all the instruments of music were transported in a wagon, with a team of mules. I had been to church, where the minister gave out that the second service would be held at "early candlelight," when the congregation straggled in according to their ideas of that indefinite season.

Gentlemen of the neighborhood, attracted by the news of our arrival, came up to Clairmont every day, and by their assistance we wasted time, and had a dance and concert every evening. Everybody at Clairmont sang—and was singing continually. The drawing-room was littered with flutes, oboes, fiddles, flageolets, guitars and accordeons, besides a venerable Broadwood piano, which had not known a tuning-key for many a day. Not content with all these instruments—on each of which our cousins could all play, without having received instruction—the music of the merriest choruses was eked out by ruder musical inventions. Tyrell was splendid on the sleigh-bells and a tambourine made out of a tin waiter, while Phil whistled like a nightingale to the music of a silver spoon in a glass tumbler, or an *obligato* accompaniment upon the bones; he boasted of a recent whistling-match with the best darkey whistler in the neighborhood, on which a darky jury had been empannelled, and decided, "that Cudjoe had de longes' breath—but Mas' Phil beat him all to pieces in de twisses."

Aunt Edmonia used to sit in her rocking-chair, amongst the perpetual confusion, and laugh at all the funny things that met her ears till her chair shook under her. Little black heads were always popping up from under the tables, from the corners of the rooms, or from behind the doors—for they were kept on hand to run of errands; and participation in the frolics of the "white folks," is a cherished perquisite of all the little darkeys.

Our cousin-in-law, Mr. Morrisson, the impersonation of an easy temper, filled the important offices of Objector-General and Major-General Tease—the duties of which can only be well administered by a person of established reputation for good humor. He interposed the animated "No!" when mischief was on foot—when Phil got up a race down in the clover-field between two negroes mounted upon mules—or when we rode in the wagon, instead of having ourselves transported with "pomp, pride, and circumstance," in the family carriage.

Max and Veronica, thrown into contact in these frolics of the day, were outwardly good friends, though I, who knew what must be passing in my brother's heart, could observe there was restraint between them. Veronica joined in all the nonsense going on with less enthusiasm than any of us. She tried to redeem some of her time, especially early in the day, and used to sit in the dilapidated chamber where our aunt Edmonia passed most of her time, surrounded by white children and black children, and negro women busy in household offices, and cousin Virginia moving in and out from porch to kitchen, with a merry word or a sharp word as the occasion called for. But unfortunately for Veronica's plans of retirement, she was the centre of attraction to all of us; and the whole party used to follow her into aunt Edmonia's chamber, where, for want of chairs, Phil Ormsby, Weston Carter, or Tyrell (if he happened to be at Clairmont), sat perched with their guitars upon the two great beds; and there the ceaseless fun went on, as we played a game of shuttle-cock with every joke; or our cousins, admirable in mimicry, told endless anecdotes, dashed with that broad hyperbole which is the humor of America.

Good heavens! what a power of endless talk there is in old Virginia. Set a Virginian on a porch, with his chair tipped back, and a supply of tobacco enough to last all day, or perch him on a fence-rail with the same condition, and he will talk politics, or argue law, or tell anecdotes till night-fall. Put him with ladies whom he is not afraid of, and take him away from the contagious stiffness of the best parlor, and he will rise to the occasion in gallantry or sentiment. He sows crops of "love in idleness," and indeed is rarely faithful to one charmer, but is always shooting arrows by the sheaf, whenever he gets hold of Cupid's bow and quiver. I doubt if Virginians know what it is to be bored, or if a genuine bore could be "scared up" in the whole state of Virginia.

On the evening before the expedition to Stonehenge, Tyrell had brought over my pony to Clairmont after nightfall. We had had an unusually merry evening. Mr. Jefferson Wayland, rather an admirer of Veronica's, and the great beau of the neighborhood, had been present. He was the only specimen of the exquisite to be met with among these rough diamonds. He was a handsome man, about thirty years of age, dressed in the height of the fashion. Tyrell told me that he boasted that he changed his suit three or four times a day, and had an endless variety of coats and pantaloons at home. He talked condescendingly in turn to each of us; he listened to our music, *en position*, with an air of rapt attention; and having bestowed half an hour of exclusive attention on Veronica, seemed to consider he was bound to make up to me for apparent neglect, by putting my best laced pocket-handkerchief in his pocket, in a fit of gallant vivacity.

Tired at length of being the object of the attentions with which Jeff Wayland thought it due to himself to distinguish the stranger in his company, I made my way through the throng of little servants choking up the door of the drawing-room, and went out upon the porch, where, to my surprise, I found Veronica. Just as I joined her, Max came from the dining-room, bringing a chair which he offered to her. She declined it, and he put it impatiently aside, "If Mr. Tyrell, or Weston Carter, or Mr. Wayland, had offered it to you, I suppose you would have taken it, but you never acccept the most ordinary civility from me, Veronica."

"I have not the least objection to take your chair, cousin Max," said she, drawing it towards her.

"Why is it, Veronica, that you treat me as you do?" he said; "you scarcely look at me. Even in the civilities of the table you will take nothing from me. You won't dance with me. You won't ride with me. In any of the games that are forever going on you never call me by my name or take the slightest notice of me."

"As for dancing," said Veronica, "I never dance, as you know; and cousin Max, I think it is very unjust of you to say that I ever have put any slight on your civilities before other persons. I am the last person in the world to wish to lower you in the estimation of strangers. That I might run no risk of doing so I did more, perhaps, than most women would have done. I told you what my wishes were. I gave you an honest warning, I imagined that I had a right to hope I was dealing with a gentleman who would cease to persecute me."

"God knows, Veronica, that your opinion of me is insulting and unjust," cried Max, bitterly. "Making an honest suit to a woman under the circumstances in which we stand to each other is not persecution. If there is any impassable barrier to my success you ought to tell me so. If there is nothing but the fact that I have not yet been able to win your favorable opinion I shall not despair of gaining it, unworthy as I feel myself of such a woman as you are, Veronica."

"I implore you," said Veronica, "do not force me to say that which will throw Oatlands and all its negroes—human beings Max—body and soul into the hands of Will Williams, a man who is notoriously a hard and cruel master. Some of them are the children and grandchildren of my old Mammy, Max. Hear me plead with you for them. Go away from Clairmont. Let it be understood that I have not pleased you. Be generous, cousin

Max. Castleton ought to be yours, and if it falls to me by the will, I am going to consult Governor Tyrell whether I cannot exchange that fatal inheritance for Oatlands, which cousin Tyrell will manage for me."

"You insult me most of all Veronica, when you consider me a mercenary wretch. I do not despise the noble property that I was brought up to believe myself heir to, but, if I fail, in losing you I lose so much that let whoever will take Castleton! What is it Veronica? What has damaged in your opinion the companion of your childhood—the boy-lover, to whom you gave your childish love. Oh! Veronica—Veronica, if I could only blot out the years that stand between us and our childhood."

"You cannot. And the follies of those unripe years I wish to forget entirely," said Veronica.

"Veronica do you despise me because when I grew up and had not seen you, as you know, for several years, I was attracted by a vain and showy woman, some years older than I am? —ask Molly if I have not had occasion to rejoice over my escape from Lady Ellen MacIntyre."

"Indeed—indeed Veronica, all this is true. You should not judge a man by his boy-loves." I said. "Max has long been truly glad that Sir Colin Nasmyth married Lady Ellen. He has told me often, and has told papa that if there had been no condition in the will he should have come out to Virginia, and have tried to make you love him; and Max is truth itself, Veronica."

"Veronica," said Max, "I not only was not in love with Lady Ellen MacIntyre——"

Veronica shook her head. But Max persisted—"yes, I maintain it was a boy's rash fascination, and not full-hearted love that

I felt for Lady Ellen. I have never loved any woman but yourself, Veronica."

I wanted to go away, but Veronica grasped me by the dress.

"I loved you with the pure, fresh love of boyhood, and though I own with shame that my heart was attracted from you at the opening of my young man's, life, your image lay in its depths and was always my ideal. Veronica, I see you now more beautiful than you have ever appeared to me in dreams. I compare you in my heart with the lady in Comus, about whom you and I have read so often from the same old book at Castleton—you seem to me as she appeared among the satyrs, when I watch you here. Do not imagine that I am chiefly charmed by your beauty, it is every word you speak—sincere and honest on the side of right and truth—that as it drops from your lips is gathered in my heart and becomes precious to me. It is the sweet kindliness which reflects from you on every living thing, insect or animal, or on the little slave, or the infirm old aunt, who loves you. Veronica, why am I alone to have no share in this benevolence? How have I been so unhappy as to be despised by you?"

"Leave me in peace," she said, bursting into tears and hiding her face on my shoulder.

"Veronica, one kinder word!" persisted Max.

"No—no," she cried, "you see that it is only by the old manner that I can prove how unwelcome your attentions are to me. You convince me of it more than ever."

I made a motion to Max, who turned away and walked back into the drawing-room.

I passed my arm around my cousin's waist and she threw hers round mine, in which position we walked for several minutes, without speaking, up and down the porch. At length Veronica broke silence.

"Molly," said she, "perhaps you know that on that evening when he told you all about his love for that beautiful Scotch lady—I was standing in the bow-window at Castleton. I could not get away without being seen, and I was afraid to appear. I overheard all that Max was saying to you Molly. I heard him say, and I admired him for it then, that nothing should tempt him to carry a false faith to a woman he did not love—not though he was bribed to it with two Castletons! I cannot describe to you, Molly, how I felt when I found that all his generous and truthful enthusiasm was considered as the folly of past years, and that he was coming to Virginia, with the object (as I could not but suppose) of fulfilling the condition of my uncle's will, and offering one for whom he had no love, his hand without his heart, bartering his truth and faith for the inheritance of Castleton. It destroyed all my old fancies about Max. I ceased to think him as he used to be—generous and true."

"Veronica, after what Max has said, can you believe these things? Do you not feel, that however he may have swerved from his first love to you to Lady Ellen, he brings you back a manlier love now that his powers are matured. His very confession of that one false step in life, is true and manly."

"Yes," said Veronica, "I know better now; and I am glad—more glad than I can say—to feel he is the Max he used to be: I ask and wish no more. But Molly, while I do him justice, and am willing to believe that in what he says to me he means to be sincere, I cannot but think that you and he are very much deceived, if you believe he cares for me more than he cares for Castleton: the man knows better than the youth the value that a fine estate confers, in the world's eyes, on its possessor. He is no longer in love with Lady Ellen MacIntyre; he no longer reproaches me with his lost happiness, and no other woman having captivated his fancy, he is deceiving himself into the belief that his affections will follow his interests; whereas I am, at the best, but an unobjectionable condition attached to the possession of Castleton. Molly, believe me, these convenient marriages may do well enough for persons who have outlived the probability of more passionate affection. But a woman never so rashly risks her happiness as when she marries a man who does not love her well enough to guard him from the misfortune of sooner or later meeting some other woman he may truly love. No, Molly, my happiness is my own, and at this moment I hold his in my keeping. I am not going to risk the happiness of both."

The next morning I woke early, and saw the first line of golden light break over the mountain. The household had been astir before I was awake. Fifteen or twenty horses were tied about in the wood; for every good riding-horse in the neighborhood had been hospitably placed at our disposal. My sorrel pony was fastened a little apart from the rest, undergoing a course of curry-comb, with cousin Tyrell standing over him, to see it was done properly. I stood for several minutes watching cousin Tyrell, who was looking fixedly at the pony and at the old negro. There was not the same animation about him that there was in others of the party, and he seemed to be indulging some sad train of thought. But he had shaken it all off when we met him at the breakfast-table, where most of us were too much excited to eat anything; and before seven we were mounted, our train being swelled by a good many other guests from Fighterstown and its neighborhood.

Cousin Virginia and her little girls went in the carriage, with "all appliances and means to boot," for our toilets at the dinner-party. Uncle Israel was to take charge of them to the riverside, whence Phil promised to drive the carriage. We had several servants to act as out-riders and gate-openers, mounted on the horses too much out of condition for their masters; and one young fellow, on a Rosinante of the leanest kind, ran the gauntlet of jokes, led by Phil and Mr. Morrison, on the flock of crows said to be following the party for the sake of his horse, which indeed looked like "crows'-meat," until, in a fit of the sulks, he fell into the rear; and neither orders nor persuasions could bring him up again with the main party.

Max was well mounted, and rode by the side of Veronica, whose steed, the Blue-tail Fly, was a beautiful white pony, raised on the estate of Governor Tyrell. I was on Angelo (worthy of his name!) and Tyrell was my cavalier, on a magnificent grey horse, the admiration of everybody.

"We saw you this morning, when you were superintending the toilette of Angelo," said I to Tyrell. "You seemed in a brown study."

Tyrell started.

"Is it possible that you saw me then?—you and your cousin Veronica? But I am not in a brown study now; I should be ashamed to be ill-tempered in your agreeable society."

"Thank you," said I. "But tell me about Angelo: he has a wicked eye; is he perfectly safe? His paces are as easy as a rocking-chair."

"What shall I tell you?" said Tyrell. "It is true that most Virginia horses, like most Virginia men, have something original and distinctive in their characters. Angelo was my horse when I was a boy, and has always been a pet in the family. He is an admirable lady's horse—perfectly safe if I am by to see you mount him; but he suffers no negro and no woman to handle him, unless when in the saddle. Old Uncle Tony, who takes care of him, and whom he follows like a dog, is the sole exception."

"I like him exceedingly," I cried. "How came Veronica to give him up?"

"My father had been raising the Blue-tail for her use, and she sent home Angelo when we had broken him."

After a pause, "Cousin Tyrell," said I, "does anybody read books in Virginia? I have seen nothing since I came newer than Johnson's Lives of the Poets, and a torn copy of Rienzi. As to correspondence—I asked Mr. Morrisson for a pen, and he went out into the yard and pulled me one of a goose's tail feathers, which did not profit me, as it turned out, for Phil had been blacking his boots with the ink, and had not left a drop in the bottle."

Tyrell laughed. "I was once in a valley about sixty miles from here, high up in the mountains with a friend, who wanted to write a letter to his wife in Baltimore. He put a negro on a horse and sent him round the country to borrow a sheet of writing paper. The man was gone all day and returned at nightfall with no better "raise" than the fly-leaf from the Bible of a Methodist farmer. However Mr. Morrisson has quite a library."

"Where does he keep his books?"

"In the attic where I slept last night. I turned the barrel which contains them, bottom up, having in former visits read the books upon the top of it, and sat up untill my candle-end burnt out reading an old-fashioned French novel."

Veronica here passed us riding fast with Max, but attended by Jefferson Wayland, whom she contrived to keep beside her, while cousin Philip, on his crop-eared horse, hovered around. Tyrell and I did not put our horses into a canter, but a long silence ensued as we both looked after them.

"Cousin Tyrell," said I, "are you envying Max?"

"I? No," said he. "What makes you say so?"

"Oh! don't get excited," I replied. "I had no right to attack you. I only meant that as you seem very little disposed to talk to me, you might have been better satisfied with the company of Veronica. I think, however, that Max is to be envied. You know the terms of the will; I am watching them with great interest, and I can assure you he is falling very heartily in love with Veronica."

"And she with him?" said Tyrell. "I venture to ask you this because you introduced the subject, cousin Molly."

"I do not understand Veronica," I replied. "She is not the same frank girl we used to know at Castleton. I do not doubt, however, that Max will win his suit whenever he can convince her that he loves her."

"I wish he may," said Tyrell. "Now, Miss Molly, is the moment for trying Angelo in a gallop; it is a smooth piece of road."

We were nearing the mountain ridge at every step. The road, which was turnpike, skirted magnificent old woods; and noble fields of wheat, stirred by the breeze like the unquiet surface of some green Swiss lake, waved upon either side of us. There was scarcely any grass land, but in the summer season this deficiency was not observed, for the wheat still was in its unripened greenness. Our way to the river was almost a continuous gentle descent, and the only thing wanted by the landscape was a greater abundance of water. I had never travelled through any country so diversified by knolls and dells. There was not a flat ten yards, I think, in any field we passed between Clairmont and the river. Within a quarter of a mile of the Shenandoah the descent became very steep. The high banks dotted with fruit-trees, sloped to the ferry. A picturesque old saw-mill stood a little apart upon the river bank, and a store, a tavern, and one or two frame houses were grouped around the ferry.

We stopped to let the horses rest and wait for the rest of the party.

"How beautiful! How wonderfully beautiful!" I cried to Veronica.

"Yes. 'Every prospect pleases and only man is vile'," was her answer. "This is the scene of an awful tragedy. And that man," pointing to the master of the inn, whose civilities were being declined by the gentlemen, "is a murderer."

"Tell me about it." I cried.

But the Blue-tail was a little restive, and kept backing towards the edge of the river. The man in question noticed it and came forward to take the horse by the bridle and quiet him; but as he approached, and Veronica perceived his purpose, she gave the pony a sudden cut with her riding-whip; it reared, plunged, started, and in another moment horse and rider disappeared over the edge of the bank, plunging as it seemed to me into the water.

I screamed. Phil, Max, and Tyrell at the same moment sprang over the bank after her. But no great harm was done. She was only pale and frightened, and trembled so that she could hardly stand as she dismounted, and stood clinging to the arm of Tyrell.

"What did you do it for? How could you be so rash?" he cried. And she trembling and shrinking gathered her skirts round her, saying in a low voice:

"I could not help it. But he did not touch me."

The rest of the party came up.

"What is the matter?"

"Nothing particular, only Veronica was frightened."

"Frightened at what?"

"At that man," I cried. "What is the story about him?"

"Never mind that story," said Mr. Morrisson.

"'Oh no,—we never mention it' to anybody raised north of Mason's and Dixon's line," said Phil. "Don't tell it to her, pray, sister."

"Are you going to bait the horses?"

"Not *here*. Uncle Israel has brought a couple of buckets and we will stop half a mile further down the river."

Here Tyrell came up to the carriage.

"Mrs. Morrisson," he said, "can you make room for Miss Veronica? After the alarm she feels hardly equal to the ride."

"Certainly," said cousin Virginia. "One of the children will take her pony. Get out Walter, and take the Blue-tail. Bring her here, Tyrell."

He gave Veronica his arm, placed her beside cousin Virginia, saw that she was comfortably established, mounted his own grey horse with a light spring, gallopped to the front, and rode beside me very gravely and silently.

"Who was that man?" I asked him at length.

"A wretch," he replied, "called Jacob Gibson, who in a drunken fit tortured one of his own servants till the man died in consequence of his brutal treatment."

"And he was never tried for it?"

"He was tried for willful murder, but there was not positive legal proof enough to convict him. Your kinsman, William Williams, a sharp lawyer when he's sober, got him off, and there is now nothing to be done, but to leave him to the influence of public opinion, which I hope will drive him from the neighborhood. You observed none of our party would notice him."

"Dear me!" said I, "I came into Virginia, thinking a great deal about slavery, but since I have been here I have had no time to think of anything. The servants about me have seemed very lazy, very obliging, and very happy, and the subject has slipped from my mind."

"Let it," replied Tyrell, shortly. "The less you think of it the better. It is for us to think of it, not you. You have no business in the quarter."

At the halting-place, under the shadow of a mighty elm, after my pony had been watered, Max came to my side.

"This is a very good piece of road," he said, "let us ride on, Molly."

I assented, woman-like always ready for fast riding, and we had gallopped about two hundred yards when we were brought by a deep mud-hole.

"This will do," said Max, when we had passed it. "Draw your rein, Molly, and talk. I seldom get a chance to talk to you."

"Did you have a pleasant talk with cousin Veronica?" I asked, as he seemed to hesitate before opening the conversation.

"No," he replied. "That coxcomb, Mr. Wayland, forced himself upon us. But she encouraged him. She cannot mean to marry him, I should think."

"Oh! no," I answered, "I am sure not. He is such a fool."

"I'll tell you what I have found out, Molly," continued Max, "she does not think me good enough for her."

"Oh! Max," said I, "I do not know where she would find any one more generous, high principled, and affectionate than you."

"Affectionate! God knows, I'd love her as never any woman, I think, was loved before. But I cannot dance attendance on her calmly, and see her smiling at Wayland, and clinging to Tyrell, and finding myself no where. I cannot stand it patiently. Patience is a mean rascally virtue. I like to do things on the impulse of the moment. I am getting frightfully in love with her."

"And Max," I said, "I think she is worthy of your deepest attachment. As Tyrell says, she is a prize worth striving for."

"What does Tyrell know about her?" he said shortly. "Good Heaven! if I only stood in Tyrell's place—if my suit were not hampered by that foolish will! Don't you believe it is that which makes her avoid me?—Or do you think (lowering his voice) that she thinks me a poor devil, quite unworthy of her? You women know each other best. Is that it, do you think, Molly?"

"I do not know," I answered. "I have had so little experience that I am not fit to give you advice, but I think from what she said last evening, that as you were once very much in love with Lady Ellen MacIntyre, she is not disposed to believe in your change of feeling towards her."

"Lady Ellen MacIntyre!" said Max, with contempt. "It was a boy's first fancy for a showy woman of the world, who was half a dozen years his senior. I am ashamed to recollect that business. A man out-grows a woman of that kind, and by the time he is matured, wants freshness, sweetness, and above all, truth. Well! I deserve to suffer, I suppose. I threw away my chance of happiness when I disowned my engagement to Veronica—but then I was not old enough to love her. And as to being worthy of her love—I never shall be."

"Indeed, you think too little of yourself, dear Max. Are you not handsome, rich, and good. And is there not every thing, even in the will, to make her care for you?"

"She will never see me with your partial eyes, dear Molly. But tell me what to do, for she repels my suit at every point, and baffles me completely."

"Be what you are, dear Max," I cried. "Truth is your noblest quality. Be better than you are, and you will win her. I prophesy it with all certainty. But be patient, learn self-discipline. What are we, that all our wishes should be granted as quickly as we form them?"

CHAPTER VII.

> Chacun de vous peut-être en son cœur solitaire,
> Sous des ris passagers étouffe un long regret;
> Hélas! nous souffrons ici sur la terre,
> Et nous souffrons tous en secret.
>
> REGRET. VICTOR HUGO.

HERE Wallie on the Blue-tail rode up to say that we were getting into a worse road, and that cousin Philip said we had better wait for the rest of the party. The road along which we had passed was unusually free from limestone, having been made through alluvial soil on the extreme verge of the bank of the river. Alders, and pollard willows, and low underbrush grew down the sides of the steep bank and overhung the water. On the other side of the Shenandoah, the fir-clad Ridge appeared to rise abruptly from the river. There were awful gaps and chasms in the road, which, to our English eyes, seemed quite impassable for any four-wheeled vehicle; nevertheless, the carriage came on slowly, driven by Phil, and surrounded by a body-guard of gentlemen and servants, ready to give a hand in any emergency—to mend the harness, pry the carriage out of mud-holes, pull down fence-rails to admit it into fields (when the road was completely broken up by the spring freshets), or hold it up by main strength on one side when it tipped too alarmingly towards the river.

A worse road was before us, when we turned into the woods,

where the way was marked only by an ancient wagon-track, or by burnt stumps of giant trees, on one of which, Phil having miscalculated the height of his wheels, impaled the carriage. The party in it all got out, the horses were unfastened, and the barouche was lifted by the gentlemen—each putting his shoulder to the wheel very literally.

We forded a mill-stream at one place—carriage and equestrians passing over the top of the dam—the rushing waters "tottering to their fall" beneath the very feet of our horses, who were slipping on the large, round stones that formed the bed of the impetuous little water-course. Through a second such stream, near its junction with the Shenandoah, we drove up to Stonehenge, cousin Tyrell assuring us with a laugh that we had chosen much the best approach to it—the road on the other side of the house being impassable.

Stonehenge was not a handsome establishment, having been built originally for an overseer. It was a straggling building, of rough, yellow stone, redeemed from ugliness by an abundance of roses, which climbed every where about the walls and porches. The river was two hundred yards or so from the house, and beyond it rose the mountain.

Governor Tyrell met us with his stately welcome, and after the gentlemen had been refreshed by apple toddy at the buffet according to the old-fashioned custom, and we ladies had stood half-an-hour in the drawing-room, we went up stairs to take off our riding-skirts, to repair our toilettes and compare notes of our adventures,

Every room we went into had a plurality of beds, for Virginia hospitality, which has a welcome for every guest, is sometimes driven to accommodate them in very crowded quarters.

"I never was so mortified as to find the carriage had been

left in the woods all night, and the whole flock of turkeys must needs roost there. It took Mr. Morrisson and Phil two hours to get it properly fixed up. Tyrell started the turkeys out of it before day-light," said cousin Virginia.

"Phil and Mr. Morrisson teased George so unmercifully about his horse, that I am afraid he has turned about and gone home, and he has all my combs and brushes in his saddle-bags," said Veronica.

"George thinks himself a mighty great beau among his own folks, and didn't like to have to ride that horse. Whenever George dresses up, he takes his hair out of the little plaits he wears to straighten it. I reckon there is most a hundred of them. Old marm Venus told me he got up in the middle of the night this morning to fix it," observed one of the children who lived more in the "quarter" than she did in the parlor.

In about an hour we were dressed. Cousin Virginia made a point of my wearing the best silk dress I had, which happened to be a sky-blue ball dress, entirely unfit for a country dinner-party. But "the best we had" appeared to be the rule; and the various "bests" were not congruously assorted. Veronica, still in mourning for her uncle, wore a dress of white muslin; and going into the garden where she had observed a smoke-plant, she twined some of its feathery sprays into her hair, till she looked as if her head were dressed with marabouts.

Our toilettes completed, we adjourned in a body to the drawing-room to spend the dreary hour that precedes the call to dinner. The ladies sat apart, and had nothing to say. The gentlemen gathered into knots, and seemed equally at a loss for conversation; till Phil, making an effort, crossed the line in the carpet which divided male and female, and drawing up a chair, asked me confidentially, in a low whisper, "if I was afeard of frogs?"

"Cousin Phil!" said I, "what *do* you mean?"

"Nothing," said he, "except that I never heard that question well circulated, with proper gravity of voice, fail to break up the stiffness of a dinner-party. Pass it on to your next neighbor."

By the time the circle was beginning to thaw under the influence of this "interrogatory," Mr. Morrisson came up and asked what I thought of Stonehenge? Whether I should like it for a residence? Whether I had found my cousin Tyrell agreeable? and other questions at which I could not wisely take offence, because they could be referred to a very natural interest in the home of my forefathers, but which I perfectly well knew were covert allusions to the supposed attentions of Tyrell.

I was thankful when Phil's eyes lighted on an old square piano in a corner, and he insisted I should play on it for the amusement of the company.

Music soon charmed away the stiffness that still lingered in the circle; and when dinner was announced, Tyrell was giving us an endless rigmarole of negro nonsense, set to a plaintive melody, and accompanied by admirable gesticulation, while the company joined effectively in the chorus, which strung together each dislocated stanza on the same thread with its fellows—

'Jenny get your hoe-cake done, my darling!
Jenny get your hoe-cake done, my love!'

Governor Tyrell, in spite of the diplomatic experiences of his younger days, was too genuine a Virginian not to have extended his invitations without reference to the number of his chairs, or to the length of his mahogany. We were a party of thirty-five; the tables had been laid for twenty-eight; and when we entered the dining-room, there were five minutes of inextricable confusion. Suddenly I heard the word "side-table," and made towards it, followed by half-a-dozen others, and we took possession—Phil occupying a seat between me and Miss Jane Dawes, a pretty young girl, to whom the rumor ran that he was paying attentions.

Governor Tyrell had led cousin Virginia into the dining-room, had placed her at the head of the table, and according to Virginian custom surrounded her by the ladies of the most distinction, amongst whom my place had been prepared, whilst the shy young men, of whom there is always a supply on hand at a Virginia dinner party, too diffident to court the company of ladies, clustered round the master of the house at the lower end of the board.

There was not much conversation at the main table. A superabundance of the best fare being provided, the chief business of a Virginia dinner party is to *eat.* Indeed it would be hard to sustain conversation, when in a general way the hosts are busy rectifying the mistakes made by the negroes, a great number of whom are running in each other's way continually, while the little darkeys of the establishment, attired in clean pinafores, and entrusted with butter boats, are continually dripping gravy over you.

Being exiled from the grand feast and placed under the supervision of Tyrell, who in the exercise of hospitality had recovered his spirits and made a famous Lord of Misrule, we had a less supply of things to eat, but much greater abundance of amusement at our side-table. Tyrell detailed a half-grown negro boy, called Adam, for our service, who supplied us with a set of casters, and being repulsed by the elder servants in every attempt to destroy the symmetry of the great table, it was long before we got anything more.

Can I describe how Philip, to the great amusement of Miss Jane, pretended to compose himself to sleep to still the pangs of hunger?—how in despair he helped himself to mustard?—how Miss Jane and I, who had been early served, levied contributions from our own plates for his dinner?—how Tyrell finding Adam's services of "no account," took on himself the charge of foraging, and disappearing for a few moments returned with Phil's plate heaped with some of every dish from the main table?—how quite a *feu de joie* of lively nonsense was let off, and how we laughed and were all delightfully silly, and witty, and merry, till Mr. Morrisson from the great table frowned upon our gaiety?—how Philip and Miss Jane prepared a glass of wine with cayenne, salt and vinegar, and sent it round to Weston Carter at the great table, who being suspicious sent it back, and Philip, by mistake, drank it up eventually?

Ah! me—it was all childish and unrefined, but it was in keeping with the total change of manners and customs, thoughts, characters, and scenery, amongst which I had fallen in four short weeks since I had left England. I enjoyed it. It was genuine. The girls had not begun to put on airs or graces and to ape city life as they have since done. Human nature cast aside conventionality and came out human. And Tyrell, a man of high cultivation and more knowledge of the world than I could ever attain unto, sanctioned my enjoyment of this nonsense by his promotion of the gaiety.

Scenery and characters less novel might not have been able to withdraw my thoughts from the trouble which for months had weighed upon my spirits; but nothing in my present way of life connected Mr. Howard or any recollection of the past with the world around me. And though

I thought of him at morning-tide
And thought of him at eve,

I confess that it was mostly in the solitude of my own chamber. The life I led was unfavorable to serious thought. I caught the infection of the general idleness, as well as the general taste for every kind of broad and humorous gaiety. A month ago I had been drooping in the routine of my home life in our dull English garrison; yet, on looking back to the first fortnight of my Virginia experience, I can but apply to it the words of a French woman of the world, who dwelling upon some such passage in her youth has told us, "I do not affirm this was the happiest period of my life, but I know it was that which contained the most laughter."

After dinner we resumed our music in the drawing-room and sang sentimental songs till the gentlemen rejoined us; when Tyrell, remembering that Max and I must wish to see the place, proposed a walk to us.

The idea was seized by the whole party, but Tyrell with his usual thoughtfulness sent the main body to the meadow where his father kept his colts, whilst he, the Governor, Veronica, Max, and I walked together towards the little grave-yard.

It had been awkwardly placed between the river and the house, and would have been unsightly in the midst of a wide field, had not its low stone wall been covered with the scarlet-leaved Virginia creeper, and the bareness of the field in which it was situated been broken by some ornamental shrubs. Here lay our grandmother and seven infant children, who had gone before her through that rusty iron grating, which was the wicket leading to the pearly gates of the Celestial City.

I was pleased to see that either by the care of Tyrell, or by that of some of the old servants who had been brought up by our grandmother, the little consecrated plot was kept in such perfect order as I never saw in any other grave-yard in Virginia; whilst a beautiful white multiflora rose-tree planted at the head-stone shed its leaves like snow-flakes over our grandmother's grave.

As I stood in silence trying to recall all that my father had told me of her habits or her virtues, Tyrell gathered me one of the white rose buds, and presently he asked me whether I did not see great beauty in the German term, "God's acre," as applied to a burial ground?

I had never heard of it, and he repeated:

"With thy rude plough-share, Death, turn up the sod
And spread the furrow for the seed we sow,
This is the field and garden of our God,
This is the place where human harvests grow."

"A few nights since," I said, "I heard a morbid yearning after death expressed by one who was both beautiful and young."

"It probably proceeded from a want of trust in God's good purposes," said Tyrell. "When smarting from the chastisements of the harsh school-mistress, Life, we are apt to stretch out our hands despairingly towards her calm sister, Death, who waits to take us home. But when we have made more progress in wisdom (and all true wisdom, it appears to me, is based on faith), we no longer look so eagerly for her, who, when the ripe time comes, will beckon us from the tasks in which we shall have become interested."

"Your simile, however, fails," said I. "The child comes back to his old tasks—that which he has learned to-day will profit him to-morrow, but we never come back again. Death cuts us off unfinished, and unripe. What will the lessons we have learned profit those who may come after?"

"I always liked an epitaph that I once read," he said.

"Reader, I was cut off in my spring-time: I had not time to serve God much.
"Wilt thou not serve him for me? And so the purpose that was in me,
"Shall bear fruit in thy life, and God's cause shall be served by the living."

"Can this be so?" I cried.

"Indeed it can. It is a coward's heart that spurns the gift of life, and will not use it thankfully.

"Bear what life has laid on thee,
"And forget what it hath taken.

"When one thinks of what there is to be done—how senseless giant evils everywhere oppress the human race, how the most part of reformers cast out devils by Beelzebub, that is pit evils one against the other—I could wish to have two lives, that I might do my little part in the world's battle. I am ashamed of every moment of past weakness. Not to fear life is quite as brave as not to be afraid of death. Either fear, it seems to me, is only worthy of a coward," and his fine eyes lighting with enthusiasm, he repeated less to me than to himself,

"Wilt thou not feel it shame and grief to thee
That I for thy sake loved less fervently,
Less heartily obeyed, less understood
HIM whom we then shall both acknowledge GOOD?"

"Some men and women, too," he added, presently, "have quenched their 'courage in a vain regret,'—and sacrificed their lives because they could not win affection. How when their

Beatrice shall meet them in another world, will they bear to see reproach upon her face, and how endure the thought that their wasted life dishonored her? The Knights of old did better things. I have a Germanesque fancy for the chivalry of old. Cervantes has found food for ridicule in feelings that commend themselves to every brave man's heart. In the days of woman-worship, each knight inscribed his lady's name on every trophy. He sent each conquered monster to her court to do her homage, each blow of the battle-axe was nerved by thoughts of her—at every thrust of the Damascus blade, her hero called upon her name, and every new danger was attempted in her honor. And thus, whether he lived or died, whether he won her at the close of the romance or never saw her after he set out in search of giants and monsters, she was associated in all his triumphs, and by the hand of him who loved her, she scattered blessings through the world."

The dews of evening were falling round us, I stood in my blue ball dress, with no covering on my head, listening to Tyrell. Max had walked away to join the main body of the dinner guests. Governor Tyrell and Veronica were seated on the low wall at the further angle of the little grave-yard, in earnest conversation, when suddenly several of the Governor's two-year-old blood colts, who had been chased round the forty-acre clover-field by the young gentlemen of the party, eager to exhibit the beautiful movements of twenty or thirty excited untamed horses to the ladies who were sitting on the fences,—leaped over the enclosure and came gallopping past us with streaming manes and tails. They were followed by all the rest of the drove, the heels of the foremost leapers having brought down the highest fence rail. The commotion called out all the negroes, and a scene of dire confusion then took place. The object was to drive the horses back into their pasture. The negroes ran and shouted—the white men issued contradictory commands, and urged them to more daring. The flock of frightened ladies in satin-slippers and gay gowns, sat perched upon the fence-rails screaming, while the wild horses, graceful in every movement, gallopped in wide curves round and round the pasture, indulging, as they pursued their headlong course, in dangerous play with one another.

CHAPTER VIII.

The sun may darken—heaven be bowed—
  But still unchanged shall be
Here in my soul that moon-lit cloud
  On which I looked with *thee!*

MRS. E. B. BROWNING.

THE evening passed in music and gay talk. Veronica said she had a headache, which she attributed to her morning's alarm, and she retired early. The pleasantest part of the evening to me was a quiet half-hour passed with Tyrell in a recess behind the drawing-room window curtains, while he talked of German ballads, and we watched the rising moon. She came with one attendant cloud, which caught her light, full, clear and stately over the green crest of the mountain, and as we watched her, Tyrell repeated some few lines from Shelley's Cloud, a poem which in my ignorance I had never heard of till that moment, but ever since, whenever I have looked upon a moonlight night, and often and often, when with a heavy heart I have stood alone at my dull upper window, commanding only a view of London tiles and variously ugly chimney pots, and watched the Queen of Night close muffled in her foggy saffron veil—the scene on which I looked has changed like a dissolving view, and in place of the tall roofs of Bedford Place, I have beheld the wooded mountain, and over it the summer moon, stealing forth like a bride out of her chamber, veiling her beauty under gold and gossamer, whilst echoes of a full, rich voice, softened into harmony with the summer twilight, rang through the chambers of my memory.

And wherever the beat of her unseen feet,
Which only the angels hear,
May have broken the woof of my tent's thin roof,
The stars peep behind her and peer;
And I laugh to see them whirl and flee
Like a swarm of golden bees,
When I widen the rent in my wind-built tent
Till the calm rivers, lakes, and seas,
Like strips of the sky fallen through me on high,
Are each paved with the moon and with these.

The Governor had made an appointment with Max to take a very early breakfast, and ride over to Oatlands, the estate owned by cousin Lomax in the Valley of Virginia. They set off, I presume, before I was awake, but when I opened my eyes, Veronica, in her white dressing-gown, was sitting in the window seat.

She looked wretchedly ill, but would not acknowledge that she had a headache, and the moment she perceived I was awake, rose up, and with the calm composure with which she met attempts on my part to intrude into her confidence, she shook down her golden curls, and went on dressing.

It had been decided the night before that all the party should remain another day at Stonehenge, and go over to the Shannondale Springs. It was rather early in the season, and there was not much fashion at the little watering-place; but we should have a pretty ride of half a dozen miles through woods, and the Governor and his son were eager we should take it, so about eleven o'clock all the horses were brought up to the door. At the same moment Max and the Governor rode up on their return from Oatlands. The Governor called to Diggory to bring Captain Mandeville a fresh horse, and another pair of gaiters, for to avoid the mud most of the gentlemen wore green baize or brown Holland leggings, frightful to look at, and the body of Governor Tyrell's carriage, which had been ordered out for Cousin Veronica's use, was cased for the same reason in a yellow oil-skin sheath, still more wonderful to behold.

Max sprang from his horse, and without disembarrassing himself of these gaiters, stiff with mud, which he had been with difficulty persuaded to adopt at the instance of the Governor, and which no Virginian thought presentable in the presence of a lady, came impetuously up the steps of the porch and interrupted Tyrell and Weston Carter, who were talking to Veronica.

"Let me speak to you! I have something I must say to you," he began eagerly.

"For any matter of business, cousin Max," she replied, "I refer you to the Governor, who transacts all business for me."

"Miss Lomax's Blue-tail stops the way," cried out Phil Ormsby, and giving her hand to Weston Carter, without another look at Max, she went down the steps and sprang into her saddle.

Max remained standing where she left him. The rest of the party mounted and set off. Diggory was holding Angelo beside the horse-block, while Tyrell, who was to ride with me, was tightening the girths of the saddle.

I looked up in my brother's face, and seeing that something was very much amiss, I hesitated to leave him.

"Come," said he, rousing himself after a few moments, "let me put you on your horse, and see you join the party."

"Dear Max," I said, "I do not want to go until you tell me what has happened. Tell me, dear. I shall be unhappy if I do not know what has gone wrong between you and Veronica."

Here Tyrell came towards us, leading my horse to the front steps, but he understood my look and was walking out of ear-shot, when Max called him.

"Come back, Tyrell. I don't want to send you away my good fellow. Everybody in the neighborhood appears to know that I came out here to pay my addresses to Miss Lomax, and everybody in the neighborhood can see how very little my suit has prospered. We went over to Oatlands to-day, Molly. It is a pretty little house, and an estate in the best order. As we were coming away, the Governor told me that Veronica had spoken to him and desired him to inform me, that she was not prepared to fulfill the conditions of the will; that she had no intention of marrying—that she implored me not to make her any offer—and that as in default of any such proposal upon my part, she should, under the will, become possessed of Castleton, she was anxious to propose to me to exchange her property in England for mine in Virginia, which would better suit her views."

As Max said this Governor Tyrell joined our party.

"I tell this hot-headed young gentleman, Miss Mandeville, that there is no reason to despair because such are the young lady's wishes. She is placed in a very difficult position. Her object at present seems to be to extricate herself from any obligation. The will of Mr. Lomax bribes him to marry her,—an arrangement no young lady would like. If he appears to acquiesce in this proposal to exchange estates, it gives him a much fairer field for courtship. Castleton is worth much more than Oatlands, so that the young lady has the advantage of believing herself to be conferring a benefit—an advantage which all ladies, Miss Mandeville, like to have—this awkward question of the bribe is set at rest, and after the 14th of October your brother will have a fairer field if he attempts to court her. I do not say this arrangement should be final. If it should happen that your brother does not win his suit, I am sure he would not be willing to take any undue advantage of her generous offer; he might saddle Castleton, if he retains it, with an annuity payable to Miss Lomax, but I want him, as a matter of form, to appear to acquiesce in her proposal, for the present. Let her have her own way, and see what it will lead to."

"I cannot bear that she should think me for a moment such a mercenary scamp as to profit by her generosity," cried Max; "and, above all, I cannot bear that she should think that my object is not her hand so much as the succession to Castleton."

"I do not understand," I said, "how Veronica "can deceive herself with the idea that her plan can possibly be entertalned by Max."

"No, Governor Tyrell, I will have nothing so diplomatic," said Max; the expression was not well chosen, and he checked himself with an "I beg your pardon, sir. I meant to say that I am a plain, blunt man—a straight-forward soldier; that I know nothing of the by-ways that might suit a lawyer. I trusted in the fact that I was my cousin Veronica's boy-lover, and that she honored me with her preference when she was about fifteen. I cannot but hope that the remembrance of that early time is not dead within her."

"My young friend," said Governor Tyrell, "you call yourself a soldier. Will the bravest soldier always take a city by assault? This garrison is not disposed to yield. It appears to be abundantly provisioned with a large supply of pride. You had better prepare for a long courtship, and lay your plans to gain the place by regular approaches. Miss Lomax will not be carried by a *coup de main.*"

"I had sooner give up my suit at once," cried Max, "than fall into the ranks with no better chance before me than Jeff Wayland, Weston Carter, or half-a-dozen other men, who, I am told, aspire to marry her."

"I recommend you," said Governor Tyrell, "in the first place, to exercise more command over your own feelings. You alarmed the young lady but just now by your eagerness. You put her in a difficult position, and she had recourse to her pride to extricate herself. Every time you rouse her pride and opposition you will lose a step. Give her her own way; she may be very sorry to have it—if so, it is an advantage to you."

"I do not understand these things," said Max. "If I feared any rival who was paying her his court, I would outstrip all his attentions in my eagerness to make myself acceptable to her. But half the time I think she only distinguishes Weston Carter, or Jeff Wayland, or such other men as are about her, in order to make me sensible of the difference she puts between me and them. Patience, I confess, is not my virtue."

"Then you must make it so, good sir," the Governor replied. "If a man thinks he is to win a Virginia woman's heart without any trouble—that it is to be *veni-vidi-vici* work with him—I say he does not set a sufficient value on his prize. I think that a good wife, Captain Mandeville, is the best gift that a man can ask his Maker to bestow upon him. It will be worth his while to acquire a few new virtues to aid him in the pursuit of her. If I were a woman, I would not yield to any man until my influence had begun to tell favorably upon his character. Impatience should be curbed to a foot-pace, or sluggishness be foremost at the winning-post. If I were a woman, I would assure my triumph over any man before I married him."

"You think my case not wholly hopeless, then?" said Max.

"I do not think any case is necessarily, *a priori*, hopeless, unless it comes under one of three heads," said the Governor. "Provided the lady has no intervening attachment; or unless she has no heart, and is not capable of an attachment (when, of course, she will look out for the largest share of the "pomps and vanities" that constitute an advantageous marriage); or unless (which pretty much amounts to the same thing) her worldliness overrides every thing, and she would strangle Love before he breathed, provided she did not detect the silver spoon in his mouth."

"And," I put in, "in case the man is not a good man, Governor Tyrell."

"Ah!" said he, "I did not contemplate that case. A pure-minded, good woman bears Ithuriel's spear, and turns from a bad man with an instinctive loathing. I will even grant you that my successful lover ought to be a man with a parity of refinement. I never pity a woman much who marries really ill. There must have been something wanting in her moral sensitiveness, when she gave an evil man a chance even to pretend to be her husband. But," he added," it is getting very late for Shannondale; you had better be off, James, with your cousin. Captain, will you stay and dine with me," he added, "and see if you can disappoint your cousin, Miss Veronica; or will you change your dress, take my roan horse, and with a new plan of the campaign in your head, ride forth to reconnoitre?"

Max chose to stay and dine *tête-à-tête* with his new Mentor. Tyrell and I mounted our horses, and rode through the crooked bridle-paths in the woods, and under the boughs of the great trees, so fast that we had no opportunity for further conversation.

CHAPTER IX.

Forget not yet when first began
The weary life, ye know since when
The suit, the service, none tell can,
Forget not yet!

SIR THOMAS WYATT.

WE rode for about an hour through the woods, with no more talk than Tyrell's warning exclamations whenever a bough hung low over the path, and might have caught my dress or struck me on the forehead. In spite of this danger, I like nothing so well as riding fast through these Virginia woods, threading one's way without a path through miles of giant trees. The dead leaves of forgotten years and the dry twigs of the past winter crackling merrily beneath the hoofs of the horses.

It was a warm still day in June. "The tree-tops lay asleep," and the profound stillness of the woods was only broken by our rapid motion; and yet I felt the spirit of life thrilling all around me in those solitudes, which week after week were scarcely traversed by the foot of man. There were not many birds, but everywhere there was a low perpetual buzz just shading into silence, a hum of insects busy in their mission of extracting life from death, and renovation from destruction. Grey squirrels ran about from branch to branch with their lithe bushy tails waving behind them as they ran, or curled above their backs whenever they sat watching us from a safe elevation. Every now and then the summer sun-beams, flickering through open parts of the dim wood, trembled before us on the path, seeming at play amongst the leafy shadows. Huge grape vines trailed their unwieldy sinewy length from tree to tree and branch to branch, and stretching ever upward towards the air and light mingled their unripe clusters and their broad green leaves with the more airy foliage of the oak and elm.

After an hour's ride through the "boundless contiguity of shade," we issued from the woods upon a wagon track which led us abruptly to the edge of the unrippled river. As Hawthorne, the great landscape poet, has told us of that stream that flows by the old Manse, "Gentle and unobtrusive as it was, the tranquil woods seemed hardly satisfied to allow it passage;" for the gnarled roots of the lofty fathers of the forest bound together the loose earth and stones that formed its banks, and their green branches pendent over its tranquil course gave their summer tinge to its unruffled waters.

As our horses, tired and hot, stooped their heads into the flood, a happiness from which horses are not restricted in Virginia, Tyrell raised his voice and sent a long, reëchoed musical cry across the stream, which was answered from the other side of the water; and soon a rudely built old ferry-boat was on its way across, poled by two boatmen in their coarse drab negro clothing.

As soon as it came near enough for speech the one who was nearest to our bank (the other was a mere lad) hailed us with a soft, rich voice from the bow of his little vessel.

"Is that you at last Mas'r Jim—and the English lady? I'se been waiting for you at this bank an hour since I put the rest across, and I had jes done given you up and gone over to the other side to git my dinner. Well, mas'r," springing on shore and taking Tyrell's hand which he shook warmly, "it does my old heart good to see you master. And this is the English lady too—my dear old mistress' grand-daughter! Miss Vera said I was to look out for her and her brother—whar is he?—because they knowed my poor ole mother."

"Cousin Molly," said Tyrell, "I ought to have told you as we came along that you were to meet Uncle Christopher, the son of Miss Veronica's old Mammy. He was born a servant in your grandfather's family."

"Indeed it seems quite like meeting an old friend to see you Uncle Christopher," said I, as he lifted me off my horse, and I stood shaking hands with him.

"My poor old mother!" said he, "she died a long ways off of home, and I reckon she pined after this southern country, but I trust that the Lord, who is in every place, lifted up his countenance upon her. It makes a day of sunshine Mas' Jim to see you or Miss Veronica, and now it will be the same to see this young mistress," looking at me kindly. "I hope she bin going to stop with us, now she done come."

He led our horses to the boat, and as Tyrell and I followed, Tyrell whispered, "He is a very remarkable man. I want to tell you about him, whenever we get an opportunity."

When we were on board the boat, Tyrell stood holding the horses amidships, and told me not to come too near lest they should grow restive. I therefore kept close by Uncle Christopher, who was busy with his pole.

"You'se mighty like your grandma in the face, young mistress," he said, in his soft negro voice, "and thar never was a better saint upon this side of Jordan than my old mistress was. She took me into the house when I was four years old and brought me up to wait upon her in her chamber, and to do sewin' and knittin' an' to pick up her thimble or thread. I wisht she could have lived to know I got religion. 'Oh! Christopher,' she used to say, 'that ar's what I wish for you,' and the Lord heard her prayers, for I know she prayed for me. She lived too near the Lord not to take him *every* wish," he added lifting his old felt hat reverently. "May the Lord bless you, an' make you a blessing, young mistress, an' as good a woman."

"Uncle Christopher," said Tyrell, "how is your wife now, and how are you getting along about that money for Mrs. Williams?"

"Well, Mas' Jim I done pretty well while the cold weather lasted, thank the Lord! I went working down to Harper's Ferry that time with a party of young men on the railroad, an' I come up to the Governor an' he gin me a pass. But the summer is my best time Mas' Jim. I make a fip for every trip in this old boat, and when the hotel at the Springs is pretty full thar's sometimes twenty times a day I have to go back an' forth. An' when my poor old bones ache I can thank the Lord for that too, mas'r."

"Have you got your money all in fips?" said Tyrell laughing.

"Not all. Some of it is put up in mighty big notes on the Valley Bank, mas'r."

"And where do you keep it all? I seriously recommend you to let me or some other white person you can trust take care of it, Uncle Christopher."

"Thank you Mas' Jim. You'se allers ready to do a good turn to your neighbor white or black—and the Lord will reward you. But my ole woman thought it didn't feel jus safe down at her room hid in her chist in a stockin', so she brought it up to the house an' gin it to her ole mistress, an' mas'r said he had better sign a paper for it."

"A receipt?" said Tyrell.

"Aye, that's it, Mas'r Jim—that's what he done tole me."

"And where is that receipt, now?"

"Here 'tis," said Uncle Christopher, producing it from his pocket-book. "I'se done got it all safe, Mas'r."

"Are you sure that's it?" said Tyrell.

"I'se sure I never got nothin' else, Mas'r."

Tyrell began to give a long sharp whistle as he looked at it, but checked himself, and asked how much he had got?

Uncle Christopher thought a moment. "I reckon it's four hundred an' sixty-nine dollars, now," said he; "I done most got all of it."

"How much was it to be? I forget—six hundred dollars?"

"Yes, Mas'r. Old Mistress said I should have my wife, an' her baby, an' the other little boy, for six hundred dollars."

"That was not driving a hard bargain with you," said Tyrell.

"No, Mas'r," Christopher quietly replied. "They would sell for more upon the block."

"Well, Uncle Christopher," said Tyrell, "I begin to think that as you have been five years at this work, the sooner you bring it to a close the better. Your season will be over here by August. If you ask Mrs. Williams to let you have your money back and will bring it to me, with what you earn this summer, I will lend you what you want to make up the six hundred dollars. Your wife's old mistress is failing very fast, and you had better get the business settled before her death. Do you want a bill of sale made out—or free papers?"

The boat by this time touched the shore. Tyrell had only been suffered to make this speech, because if Christopher had left his pole she would have been in jeopardy; but now, with strong agitation on his face, he came up to Tyrell, and shook his hand again with his strong grasp, laying his other hand upon his arm while speaking.

"Mas'r Tyrell, I will bless you, every hour I done live. But I thank the Lord first. He put this thought into your mind, Mas'r."

"It is no great obligation, Uncle Christopher. I mean that you shall work out this money and pay me back again."

But Christopher could hardly speak. His subordinate led the horses to the bank, while Tyrell was looking in his pocket-book for the fare, all of which, but the fip, belonged to the keeper of the Shannondale Hotel, Uncle Christopher's temporary master.

"Good bye, Uncle Christopher," he said, "you have not told me whether you want a bill of sale to some person you can trust, or the free papers?"

"Free papers, if you please, Mas'r."

"There are a great many difficulties, Uncle Christopher, about the residence of free colored people among us; and every year I fear there will be more trouble for you."

"I knows that Mas'r Jim. But you or your father, or Mas' William, I reckon, will go security at the court for me. You see, I'se got a sort of pride of my chil'ens being free. I'se never cared 'bout it for myself. I'se allers had a kind good Master."

"I hope you will always find your master is a good one, Uncle Christopher," I said.

"I'se greatly 'bliged to you, young mistress," he replied. "Miss Vera jus' done tell me she's to be my young mistress; an' dat she'll let everything go on till this money's paid, jus' like her uncle, my ole Mas'r. I was glad to know who it was to be, for Mas'r Warren, up at Oatlands, said ole Mas'r left a mighty oncertain sort of will; an' he didn't know who was to be mistress nor master. So I done troubled about it some at first, an' then I cast that care on the Lord, too,—an' He done brought it out right to me. Blessed be His name! I love to praise Him, Mas'r."

We mounted our horses, and found before us a smooth road.

"I never cross that Ferry," said Tyrell, "without thinking of the Legend of Saint Christopher, '*Der heilige Christopher*,' who was also a ferryman. He carried the infant Christ over the river. You recollect that beautiful Legend?—or if you do not, I shall have the pleasure of finding the ballad for you. It always seems as if that man were conscious of the presence of his God."

After a few moments he said, "But I am very far from satisfied that his money is safe. That paper was not a receipt, as he appeared to think. It was a pass signed by Will Williams, and meant nothing. I did very well to tell him to get the business settled. I will speak to Mrs. Williams about it. How simple these poor negroes are in anything relating to money."

"You do not think that Mrs. Williams, his wife's mistress, would deprive him of his money?"

"No, no," said he, "she is a good weak woman; but her son is very sharp and a bad master. To tell you the truth, she married a Yankee who came down here, and Northern men or Scotch who settle at the South, are generally hard masters."

"Why should that be?"

"They are accustomed to order and to briskness. They expect things to go ahead and earn a profit. The slaves do nothing orderly. They waste their master's substance and are prodigal of their own time. The hard go-ahead man, wanting to make money, gets enraged at their shiftlessness, their laziness, and want of management. He has not been brought up to share his negroes' faults. Absolute power is in his hands, and soon he learns to use it."

"But how could Uncle Christopher, since I gather that he is a slave, make so much money?"

"Most slaves in good families have ten, twenty, or even a hundred dollars in odd change, laid up in a leathern pouch or old yarn stocking, while their masters are riding about the country to raise that much of money. But my father got interested in Christopher's endeavors to obtain his family, who would probably when old Mrs. Williams dies be sold away from him, or see hard times, and he wrote to Mr. Lomax, who gave Christopher his time, and would have freed him but that it is very hard in Virginia to secure the welfare of a colored man who has no legal protector."

As Tyrell ended he put his horse into a gallop, and we went gaily up the first good piece of road that I had seen, which conducted us with several windings up the side of a steep hill which had amineral spring, near which a large hotel had recently been erected. The party from Stonehenge were all upon the porch as we rode up, and greeted us with many inquiries as to why we lagged behind,—together with a good deal of pretty significant banter.

The hotel was a wooden building, staring and white, with a wide handsome porch, extending the whole length of the house, on which many of the guests were promenading, whilst a dozen or more gentlemen, with their feet upon a railing which had been put round the porch for their convenience, sat with their chairs tipped back, enjoying their tobacco.

There was a long bare room in which our party hoped to dance,—a negro band which played native American Quick Steps, "and the usual assortment" of organic airs from the best Operas. There was a cold bare desert of a dining-room, in which fifty people hardly made a show, and where we sat down to a plentiful and well-cooked feast which we pricked our tongues with two pronged forks to eat with the celerity required by custom.

It was not very funny there—not half so funny as at Stonehenge, though some of the party seemed to enjoy the change. My spirits were subdued by the incessant giggle of a party of young girls, who were "carrying on," as their phrase was, with a party of young gentlemen.

"Real torn-down girls," said Phil; but as they were quite pretty in the freshness of sixteen, this was no obstacle to his introducing himself forthwith into their circle.

Tyrell was as grave as I was. Perhaps his thoughts, like mine, were wandering to the affairs of Max; but the giggle that went on amongst the noisy set was such, that it was impossible to think connectedly. He tried a cigar after dinner, on the porch, but threw it away, half-smoked, and came up to me.

"Miss Molly," said he, "let us walk up to the spring, where, perhaps, our own party may follow us. These are the girls who give young men a low opinion of the character and understanding of women. Do you recollect Swift's lines?—I never see a party of girls like that without thinking of them.

"When at play to laugh, or cry,
Yet cannot tell the reason why,
Never to hold her tongue a minute
While all she prates has nothing in it,
Whole hours can with a coxcomb sit,
And take his nonsense all for wit.
Her learning mounts to read a song,
But half the words pronouncing wrong;
Hath every repartee in store
She spoke ten thousand times before;
Can ready compliments supply
On all occasions cut and dry;
For conversation well endued
She thinks it witty to be rude;

And placing raillery in railing
Will tell aloud your greatest failing.

"Well! let us hope that when broken to the serious business of life, they will do better for the sake of the men who marry them. There is nothing like matrimony for bringing out the sterling qualities of our Virginia women."

We walked soberly away to a little spring which bubbled up under a sort of Grecian Temple. We drank part of a nauseous glass, and were standing there quiet and cool when Tyrell said:

"I see Miss Veronica alone upon the porch—do you think she would join you?"

"Go and ask her," said I. . . . .

A few moments after he came back, accompanied by Veronica. "I am tired with all that noise, and am very glad to come away," she said, as they returned together.

"Miss Mandeville," said Weston Carter, who came after them, "what are you thinking of—you looked so serious and pensive as we came up to you?"

"How noble his form and how lovely her face,"

said I. "That is precisely what I was thinking."

"She was thinking of you Tyrell, you see," said Weston Carter, though he really assumed the compliment himself as the handsomest man of the party.

"But where is Captain Max? We wanted him to decide upon getting up a tournament, Miss Molly."

"Max was invited to a *tête-à-tête* dinner with Governor Tyrell," said I. "The Governor promised to give him real Virginia fare, cold hog and fried hominy; and I dare say his ears are being feasted with details of the French revolution."

"Well," said Weston Carter, "I see enough of men in camp. When I come in I would not give one hour of the society of such ladies as I meet here for the company and conversation of any man."

I began to talk to Veronica of Uncle Christopher, and had soon told her of Tyrell's generosity.

She did not say anything for a moment, but when she looked up the light in her blue eyes was troubled by a mist of sympathy, and turning to Tyrell who stood behind her, she put her hand in his, and said in a low voice:

"It is just like you."

"Ah! Veronica!" he said—but checked himself and walked away.

Tyrell was never half so conversable with her as when alone with me. Some mysterious constraint was creeping over us, and I made an effort to dissipate it by telling Veronica that I was expecting to hear uncle Christopher's history from Tyrell.

"Ask him to come back and tell it us," said she.

But Tyrell appeared to have no more story than the Knife-grinder.

> Story—Lord bless you! I have none to tell, sir.

He said I had heard it already—that my conversation with uncle Christopher had supplied the outline, and that I could fill up the details as I increased in knowledge of Virginia. He was constrained and restless. At length he said abruptly, "Let us take a walk," offering his arm, as he said so, to Veronica.

Mr. Carter, whether he liked it or not, had to invite me to follow. He had been talking about a tournament that had been held at Shannondale the year before, and was eager to have another got up that season in my honor. There was a piece of ground on which he wished to have it held, while Tyrell had given it as his opinion that if it took place at all it had better be on the spot which had been marked out for it the year before.

Weston Carter was a little fond of his own way, and now while Veronica and Tyrell walked before he drew me apart down a by-path to the spot of his selection. We spent a pleasant hour there, while Weston with the eye of a surveyor laid off the ground, and stepped it out, and showed how a little knoll to which Tyrell had been disposed to object, in the centre of the lists, could be easily levelled, if necessary, and we built imaginary tents, and saw imaginary banners wave, and talked over the qualifications of the knights and horses that would probably enter.

While we were thus engaged, Tyrell and Veronica emerged from a by-path in the woods and joined us. Veronica wore one of the thick American green veils over her face, but even in the twilight of the forest shade I was struck by the discomposure of the air and manner of Tyrell. She turned to Weston Carter as she joined us, and told him it was high time to depart.

"Then I will leave you and order the horses," said Tyrell, "while Weston collects the rest of the party."

We all kept close together as we rode home through the woods, which were growing dark enough to frighten some of the ladies. Jefferson Wayland was my cavalier, but I was in no humor to accept the attentions which a due consideration for himself as the beau *par excellence* of the society of Fighterstown and its vicinity induced him to offer me. Veronica rode a little in advance with Weston Carter; and Tyrell, whose manly kindness I was secretly comparing with Jeff Wayland's fussy gallantries, rode by himself, or rather hovered in and out amongst the rest, wherever help or encouragement was wanted; putting aside the branches of the trees whenever they bent low over our path; choosing the road for us whenever it was doubtful; acting always with prompt decision and a sort of cheerful kindness, in the triple capacity of pioneer, commander-in-chief, and servant-of-all-work to the party.

CHAPTER X.

Why so pale and wan young lover,
  Prithee why so pale?
Will when looking well can't move her
Looking ill prevail?
Prithee why so pale?
SIR JOHN SUCKLING.

THE next morning after breakfast we left Stonehenge. Throughout our visit the Governor had seemed anxiously to remember that the place had belonged to my forefathers, and to recognize that I had a claim to all interests connected with it. I rose early and went down by myself to the little grave-yard. I gathered some of the white roses, and thought of the goodness attributed to my grandmother as I mused beside her grave. Tyrell joined me as I was coming back to the house, and we stood together on the porch a few moments before any others of the party joined us, watching the effects of sunlight and shadow on the opposite hill. He did not say much, but as we both looked at the landscape, it was pleasant to me to fancy a silent sympathy in our thoughts. On turning my eyes, however, to his face, I saw that he was far from drinking in pleasure from the sight. I was struck by his appearance.

"Cousin Tyrell," said I, "what is the matter? You look wretchedly ill."

"I am not sick," he replied, "I have a headache. A headache

which I am afraid will prevent my riding over to Clairmont with you." He paused a moment and then repeated:

> "And how can any die of that disease
> Whereof himself may be his own physician?"

Forcing the words out bitterly, with rather a tone of sarcasm.

"What disease?" said I, "and where do those lines come from?"

Tyrell laughed—not one of his own genial pleasant laughs; but like many men when they are sick, "having a headache," seemed to have altered him.

"Shall I give you a long Greek name for my malady?" said he. "It was known amongst the Greeks and Romans, and has been covered alike under togas, and white waistcoats, and buff jerkins, and coats of mail! The lines I quoted are from a poem of the sixteenth century, by one Sir Robert Aytoun. You will find it in very few collections. Perhaps if you could I should not quote it to you."

"Cousin Tyrell has a bad headache, and says he cannot ride with us to Clairmont," said I to Veronica, who appeared on the porch at this moment, but she did not stop to give me any answer.

When the horses came up, Tyrell led the Blue-tail to the door and Max helped Veronica to mount. The Governor handed me down the steps, seeming to mark by his consideration that he thought I, rather than Veronica, was the person to be first attended to by the gentlemen of the party, and whilst Tyrell brought up Angelo, lamented that his son should not be able to ride with me that day. "He has not been as well as a young man ought to be of late, Miss Molly. I do not like young men to be fancying they have headaches and such stuff. I shall send him over to Clairmont as soon as he gets well, and you must talk to him and cheer him. I trust to you to cure him."

Tyrell requiring to be cheered, was an idea that had never presented itself to my imagination. He was so universally helpful, and kindly, and cheery—so entirely the person to whom any one else would bring all kinds of griefs in search of remedy—that I had never thought of Tyrell other than as the impersonation of a certain manly strength—strength of mind, strength of purpose, strength of body—held in trust for all whose weakness might demand it. Could Tyrell possibly have need of human sympathy? He who spoke hopefully to others in their trials, could there be moments when his courage drooped under the burden of his own? I rode on wondering what sort of life my cousin Tyrell led in that old crumbling house on the bank of that still river, under the shadow of that fir-crowned hill. They had been laughing at breakfast-time over an advertisement snipped from a Boston paper—"WANTED, a woman to take care of a house and two men during the winter;" but there appeared to me great sense in the advertisement; and I was saddened by the picture conjured up, when I applied its sense in this case, and thought of the Tyrells, father and son, without any woman better than Marm Mona, the black housekeeper, to brighten the dullness of Stonehenge and make a household sunshine when the great hill covered them with its stern shadow. I thought of my seven aunts and uncles who had died in babyhood, and lay buried in the grave-yard by the river, and wondered what might have been the effect upon the dull old place of happy childish voices. I thought how Alonzo Lomax had succeeded to the estate when my grandfather (who could not bear the solitude after his wife's death) had exchanged it with him for the reversion of Castleton; and I heard in fancy the patter of his baby's feet, and saw

Veronica playing with old Mammy on the grass, and fancied she might have given life to the old house as she grew up amongst its shadows. I was roused from these thoughts by the voice of Phil hailing a negro boy on horseback who had come out of a field and was dashing by us without ceremony.

"Oigh there, boy! Is that the way you Jefferson niggers behave to white folks, pushing by them that way without ceremony? Go back and keep behind us till we come to a wood."

"Ole missus mighty sick, mas'r, and I'se gwine for the doctor."

"Who is your mistress?" said Phil, making way at once for him.

"Mrs. Williams, my ole missus," was the answer.

We gathered round the boy, and finding his mistress really was very ill, and that he had been ordered to ride for life and death, we let him pass, and cousin Virginia proposed to Veronica to turn aside and go to Mrs. Williams's at once in order to see if we could be of use to her.

Veronica had seen very little of this aunt, but she was Mrs. Williams's nearest female relative, and in Virginia in a time of distress ties of blood are never forgotten.

"Mr. Morrisson, will you come too? Come, cousin Max—you and Molly, come both of you. It may be the only chance of the old lady's seeing you. You are her English relations, and riding up to the house to ask if you can be of use will be thought kind and attentive of you."

It did not seem exactly the sort of attention that I liked to pay. I hesitated to disturb the dying moments of an aged woman with empty offers of compliment; but Max had turned his horse's head, so I turned mine, and striking into a bad road, made zig-zag between fields separated by crooked and dilapidated worm fences, we made our way up to a house of some pretensions, but in bad repair, dismounted, hitched our horses to a rack, and finding nobody about the place (who ever heard in Virginia of a front door-bell?) we went in at the open door.

Cousin Virginia Morrisson went to the sick woman's chamber and tapped at it. Her knock was answered by a very respectable-looking, stout, yellow woman. She said her mistress "was took mighty sick," and she had sent off one boy for assistance to Stonehenge, and another to Fighterstown, to bring the doctor.

The chamber was a large, square room, superabounding in window sash, from which several panes of glass had fallen, and their places had been thriftily supplied by cotton, thick paper, and paste. There were two double beds, of course, and a great many moth-eaten hair trunks and old deal boxes, piled on one another. There were two rickety old wardrobes, crowned with band-boxes. The plaster was dropping from what had been once a handsome cornice and ceiling. The walls were so broken as to show the lathing in some places; and rat-holes had been eaten along the edges of the floor. There were weather-stains of every shade upon the wall and ceiling, from the faint discoloration of the first rain-spot to patches of the deepest brown, where a huge leak in the old roof drained in the water from every passing shower; and in great rain-storms, I could readily believe the stories told by cousin Virginia, of the floor covered with pails and washing-tubs, and an umbrella fixed by aunt Sapphira, the colored maid, at the bed's head, to protect the poor old lady's pillow.

She lay on the bed quite motionless; there was a lull in the cruel pain, but nature was almost exhausted. We had not been there many moments when the attack returned. It was frightful to stand by and watch her struggling with death for every breath, and to know we could not help her. We thought at one time that to raise her head would give her ease; and Veronica, sitting on the bed, lifted the poor troubled face in her arms and propped her pillow.

In the midst of her worst agony, the door opened, and Aunt Mona, from Stonehenge, came into the room, accompanied by Tyrell. Aunt Mona was a consequential colored lady, who ordered everything about her master's house, and had come prepared to supersede Aunt Saph, and have matters her own way. She was permitted to do this in spite of the presence of white folks—for all cousin Virginia's remedies of relief had failed, though she was skilled in pharmacy.

There seemed nothing to be done but to bathe her temples from a large bottle of rose-water.

The weight of the poor, helpless, nerveless form was too heavy for Veronica, who was beginning to look pale. Tyrell perceived it, and gently took her place, which without a word she yielded to him. A man in a sick-room is seldom serviceable; but it seemed natural that Tyrell, with his grave thoughtfulness, should be there to help us. His presence calmed us, and in his arms the dying woman seemed to lie more easily.

After some moments of stupor succeeding to the cramps of pain, she opened her eyes and looked at our strange faces.

"How do you feel now, dear aunt Barbara?" said Veronica, who was wiping the death-sweat from her clammy brow, as she lay back in the arms of Tyrell.

"Better a little, dear;" and in a faint voice, "who are all these? Is this my son William holding my head?"

"Cousin William has been sent for, aunt Barbara. I am Veronica; this is cousin Virginia Morrisson; and here is our cousin Mary Mandeville, from England, come to see you; and this is cousin Tyrell."

"Is my son coming?—I am most gone," she gasped faintly. We looked in Tyrell's face, and its expression told us she spoke truly.

Aunt Mona here insisted on her swallowing some preparation which revived the spark of life a moment; and seeing her able to understand him, Tyrell said,

"Have you any affairs unsettled, to which you wish me to attend?"

There was no answer. At this moment Mr. Felix, who had been working on the porch, looked in. Tyrell beckoned to him to enter the chamber, and tried again distinctly and slowly.

"Are all your affairs arranged as you wish to have them, if you should not recover."

"I made my will," said she, "and left Sapphira and her children free. Uncle Christopher paid me nearly five hundred dollars for them, and my son got it away from me. I told him if he had it, he must write out my will and leave them free; and Jake Gibson, last time he came here, put his name upon it. Sapphira has been a good servant to me, and I want her to have her freedom. It will not wrong my son to set the children free, because he got most of their value in money."

"Where is the will your son wrote out for you? Shall I see if it is all right, Mrs. Williams," said Tyrell.

She did not answer; but Aunt Sapphira said,

"Missus done told me put it in dat bigges' ban-box, way dar yonder."

"Shall I see if it is signed and is all right, Mrs. Williams?"

"Aunt Saph says, 'please don't ask her any more questions,'" said Veronica.

It seemed cruel to disturb her dying moments; but Tyrell asked again. He was very gentle; and I, who knew his apprehensions about Uncle Christopher, could not but respect him the more.

The dying woman made a sign towards her old wardrobe, and Sapphira, who knew what she wanted, brought her a paper.

"Mas' Gibson done put some writin' upon it," she observed.

"Shall I take it?" said Tyrell.

The dying woman signed assent, as we thought. Tyrell disengaged one hand and took the paper. As his eye fell on it, he gave a sudden exclamation, and was about to speak, but in another moment the cramps seized Mrs. Williams more violently than ever.

While the attack lasted, and we stood around the bed, suffering with her sufferings, as every breath became more faint, the doctor from Fighterstown arrived, leading Mr. William Williams into the chamber. He looked quite wild; he threw himself across the bed in an agony of grief; he clasped his mother's feet, and his sobs shook the bed.

The Doctor shook his head. "There is nothing to be done but to pray for her," he said. "This breath is almost the last one." I hid my face in my clasped hands and prayed for the passing soul. When I looked up, Tyrell was laying back the heavy head, as if in quiet rest, and the dead face that had been so convulsed with pain when I last looked at it, lay peaceful on the pillow.

Then we left the room to Aunt Mona, obtrusively important on such an occasion, and Sapphira, who was kissing her dead mistress' hands, with loud and bitter lamentations. The Doctor, with a whispered word or two to Tyrell, drew Mr. Williams away.

As we stood in the drawing-room, we heard his heavy sobs upon the porch. "I cannot bear to hear it—I cannot bear it," I said to Tyrell, who was standing by my chair. He looked at me a moment with a strange expression of face, and then said, "It is partly liquor."

The shock of this explanation was worse than any other part of the painful scene. That grief and natural feeling should be parodied and profaned!—that vice and death should have met together! Tyrell, seeing how much I was agitated, took me out on the back porch, where a frightened little negro child in a tow-cloth jacket, out at elbows and bare feet, got me a glass of water.

We were summoned shortly by Mr. Morrisson. Our horses were ready, and he was afraid we should hardly reach Clairmont before nightfall.

"I do not like to leave him," said the Doctor to Tyrell, pointing to Mr. Williams, who sat on the front porch, taking no notice of anything around him. "When this fit goes off he is very likely to be wild and rash. He is not by any means sober, and has been for some time past on the verge of *delirium tremens*. Besides which, if he should get better by and by, this is the very moment, beside his mother's death-bed, to bring him to a sense of what he is coming to."

"I will stay with him," said Tyrell. "I have business with him. If he gets better it may be the right moment to arrange it. I will stay—and Mr. Felix."

"Old Mr. Felix was off at once," said the Doctor, with a laugh, "I saw him streaking down the road as fast as his legs would carry him. He would not for a hundred thousand dollars stay in the house with a corpse, nor pass a church-yard after dark, nor sleep up stairs, because of the witches. He believes in ghosts. He thinks he has been visited by one."

"I am sorry," said Tyrell, "for I want a witness. Mr. Morrisson, can you stay here an hour or so, and let Capt. Mandeville ride home with these ladies?"

"I cannot possibly remain," said Mr. Morrisson; "I have a man coming over to speak to me this evening about a note of mine that is out" (Virginia gentlemen have generally a heavy crop of "promises to pay," ripening about harvest-time, all over the country).

"Has anything gone wrong about Uncle Christopher's money?" I whispered to Tyrell. "When you took the will I saw you start."

"Look here," said he.

"What is it?" I replied, turning the dirty paper over and over.

"It is not a will," said he, "though Williams must have made his mother fancy it such. It is a promise signed by the old lady, who was almost blind, that her estate shall pay Jake Gibson all claims against herself or her son William Williams, in full, with fifteen per cent. interest, one month after her death, or shall give up to him the negro woman, Sapphira and her children. Written below it on the paper, is a promise from Jake Gibson to Will Williams to lend him seventy-five dollars, cash, and to release him in full from every claim, on fulfillment of these conditions."

"Oh! cousin Tyrell, what do you mean to do about it?"

"I mean to make use of the first opportunity that offers, to investigate the matter. He may have the will in his possession. It may not be what I fear. I will speak to him to night. If he has any better feelings, this must be the time to call them forth. But I want another white man for a witness to our conversation."

"Max, I am sure, will stay with you," I cried; and going up

to Max, I begged him to oblige me and remain that night with cousin Tyrell.

"What has he got to say to me?" he said with a look of great surprise.

"He will tell you himself."

Max looked at Veronica.

"She will be sure to wish you should remain," I urged; "I will tell her all about it as we ride home."

Max yielded, and Tyrell, as he mounted me upon my horse, promised to bring him over to Cranmer, a little Mission Church, in the woods, and meet us on the Church porch in the morning.

CHAPTER XI.

A letter timely writ is a rivet to the chain of affection,
And a letter untimely delayed is as rust to the solder.

TUPPER.

As we rode along the river's bank I found an opportunity of telling Veronica and cousin Virginia Morrisson, with a great deal of womanly vehemence, of the conduct of Mr. Will Williams towards uncle Christopher.

Veronica was quite as indignant as I. Her color rose and her eyes flashed under her riding-hat; and I was delighted to see that also cousin Virginia's sympathies went in the right direction. I had not been quite sure but that her pro-slavery predilections might throw her on the side of the master.

"Just listen to this, Mr. Morrisson," cried she, turning round to her husband, who being a heavy man was making his way slowly, mounted on a tall bay colt, whose tail untrimmed was becoming fast encrusted with stiff clay (on the dip candle principle) as it dragged through every mud-hole. "Listen to this, Mr. Morrisson. I declare Will Williams is a right bad fellow. He has used that old lady mighty bad I expect during her life-time. I don't know what she would have done without Aunt Sapphira to take care of her. Aunt Saph is a real elegant servant. I wish I had half as genteel a one. Poor thing! I hope Tyrell will be able to do something to help them, for if Will Williams sells them to Jake Gibson it will be an awful fate for them."

Mr. Morrisson listened to my tale and then said quietly:—"Tyrell is putting his hand into a wolf's mouth, I reckon."

"That is like Mr. Morrisson," said cousin Virginia. "He never thinks it wise to interfere about other people's servants. He says it's worse than meddling between man and wife to come between servant and master. But Tyrell is just one of those people who would do what he thought right, I reckon. On the whole it was best that cousin Max stayed instead of Mr. Morrisson. Especially as Uncle Christopher is to be his servant. People might have thought it interfering of Mr. Morrisson. Which is it Veronica, sure enough? When are we to know if the Oatlands negroes belong to you or Max? The 14th October is not so far ahead. Marm Venus brought out one of those fine old hams of bacon to be cooked last week in honor of you, cousin Moll, but I told her to put it by as we were going to have one wedding certain—and *two* I reckoned."

"I should think you knew by this time, cousin Virginia," said Veronica, "that allusions of that kind are very disagreeable to me."

And Veronica was out of temper, a state of mind which she kept up until we neared Fighterstown, when Mr. Morrisson proposed to stop at the post-office and get our letters.

It had been a court day, and on either side of the muddy street stood forty or fifty saddle-horses of every shade and kind, fastened to posts and racks where they had stood since morning. There were no women, save here and there a black girl, in the streets, but everywhere men; men of every condition, most of them in the prime of life, endlessly chewing and talking. There were groups on every house porch, groups at the corners of the streets, groups sitting upon store boxes, groups on the tavern porch and steps, and a large number stood about the post-office.

We rode up there and "hitched" our horses. The mail was not quite sorted. Mr. Morrisson made us alight and go in "next door," which was the principal "variety store and dry goods emporium" in the village. The moment we entered, a knot of men gathered about Mr. Morrisson asking news of old Mrs. Williams, receiving the particulars of her death, and telling anecdotes to her son's disadvantage. I found he had been so miserably drunk at the tavern-bar when the boy arrived to summon him, that the Doctor had him carried to the pump, where after a time they brought him round sufficiently to enable him to mount his horse, in which condition he was carried out to his mother's death-bed. Every body seemed to have the same opinion of this gentleman, that he was "a smart man, but they reckoned a thorough rascal, and a disgrace to that section of the country."

At length the mail was sorted. Cousin Virginia was getting the Colonel, who was master of the store, to put her up some of his "elegant crushed sugar," and Mr. Morrisson, always ready to remember his guests' comfort, had bought a supply of ink and pens in case I had any further demand for them.

"Now, cousin Molly, here are the letters: two for you."

One was from home; the other ——— !

It was a long letter. I slipped them into the folds of my riding-dress, and galloped home as fast as Angelo would carry me, in advance of the rest of the party.

If I were a sculptor, my great work should be the Angel of Letters—he who carries loving words and sweet home interests from heart to heart. I never can bear to think of the materialism of the post-office. Sir Francis Head's revelations of its mysteries, in the Quarterly, jarred upon my feelings quite as much as a philosophical and meteorological explanation of the rainbow ruffled the poetic sensibilities of Campbell.

Oh! most delicious hours passed in the deep window-seat, drinking in the contents of those letters; one of them holding out to me the severed threads of many a domestic interest, whilst each trivial word of the other one was priceless, freighted with precious, precious evidences of remembrance and affection.

True, "their *now* was not my now, nor my *then* their then;" but I lost all thought of that. To obliterate the sense of time is one of the duties of the Angel of Letters. They carried me again to England, reviving the old hopes, and the old thoughts, and the old love, between which and my present life the Atlantic lay like a great gulf since my arrival in Virginia.

With thoughtful kindness, my cousins left me alone nearly two hours, and then Veronica came up to our chamber, and told me that my tea had been long standing, and she thought I had better come down.

It was the first evening we had been without company since our arrival at Clairmont. Phil and his friend Weston Carter had gone into Fighterstown to bring up some men to sleep in Max's room—Max being away. Veronica sat knitting a coarse yarn stocking.

"Who is that stocking for, Veronica?" said I, too happy to compose myself to any useful occupation.

"This is one of uncle Israel's winter stockings," was her reply.

"What! do you knit stockings for the negroes?" cried I.

"Yes, and you will have to knit all the stockings at Stonehenge, by-and-by; you must take into consideration whether you are adapted to hard work when you consent to become a Virginia matron," said cousin Virginia.

"If you please, don't make any more such jokes," said I. "What you allude to is impossible; indeed it is, cousin Virginia."

"I do not see that," she persisted. "I am sure the Governor is thinking of it. He paid you the most marked attention. The Governor was right disturbed at your sitting at the side-table. Nobody is of any account when you are by. He wants you to be mistress of Stonehenge; and your father, I should think, would like to see you take your grandmother's place in the old homestead. It would be recovering more than all the family has lost, if Max had Castleton and you Stonehenge, even though so much of the property has been sold away from you. I declare it would be real good times to have you settled within ten miles of us, Molly."

"Now, don't you interfere with that, Virginia," said Mr. Morrisson. "It is all coming right: I have told Tyrell to come over here as much as he likes, and I'll secure him a fair field to do his courting. When a young lady and young gentleman stand behind the curtains sentimentalizing in the moonlight, and when they lose themselves in the woods, and stay an hour and a half behind the rest of the party, and when the young lady gets up early in the morning, under pretence of visiting a grave-yard, where she is met by the young gentleman, and they take a walk together before breakfast—we all know what it is coming to."

This kind of thing was detestable. I tried Veronica's system of being cross, but I am never very good at being cross, and it was no remedy. So, after enduring a little more of this broad *badinage*, which I could not parry, I got up and said good night, and went to my own chamber. There Veronica soon joined me.

"Veronica," I said, "I wish cousin Virginia and Mr. Morrisson would let alone talking of that notion they have taken up. It was more disagreeable to me than ever to-night. It was particularly annoying to have my name coupled with that of cousin Tyrell."

"Why to-night?" said Veronica, looking at me with surprise.

"Because ——— Sit down, Veronica, in the great chair; I have not been able to tell you anything since I came here, because you have been so cold to me."

"Not cold, not cold, dearest," said Veronica, smoothing my hair, as I knelt before the fire. "Not cold!—Oh! how I wish you understood me, Molly."

I ought to have seized this opening to entreat her confidence, but I was thinking of my own confession, and I let it escape me.

"After all, Molly," she said, "if Tyrell should ever know what is for his own good, and should ask you to be his wife, what obstacle would prevent your loving him? You would make a far better Virginian than I shall make, and be more easily reconciled to this life, which wears upon me. Why do you say 'to-night?'" and again she looked at me keenly.

"Because to-night I know better than ever how much I care for somebody who cares for me," was my low answer. "Because to-night I have had a letter ———;" and I drew it forth, not of course for her to see it, but because I liked to hold it in my hand.

So sitting thus, looking into the fire-light, while the great glowing brands flickered and smouldered in the open hearth, and cold night air came down the ample chimney, I told her all the story of my intercourse with Harry Howard, and of the family pride on either side which had separated us from each other.

And Veronica comforted me, and bid me hope, and listened with sweet patience, while I told her how bitterly poor Harry complained that he could get no news of me. I told her how he called me "prude," and said I could not love him if I would not write to him; but that I could not correspond, because by doing so I should break a promise to my father. I doubted if Mr. Howard quite understood about that promise, and if he did not, he would think me so unkind. How could I let him know that it was not indifference which made me keep my resolution, but that I was bound by my duty to my father?

And Veronica comforted me with her sweet comfort, and told me to ask Max, that he would advise me better than any body; and helped me to undress, as if I had been a little child who wanted petting. And she hung her shawl before the window, to keep out the beams of the great golden moon, which were streaming broadly into our chamber, awakening no thoughts of Tyrell in my heart, as I glided into Dreamland calmly and happily.

CHAPTER XII.

Through the closed blinds the glorious sun
  Poured in a dusky beam,
Like the celestial ladder seen
  By Jacob in his dream.

And ever and anon, the wind,
  Sweet scented with the hay,
Turned o'er the hymnbook's fluttering leaves,
  That on the window lay.

H. W. Longfellow.

The carriage which had brought over bags and bundles and the children from Stonehenge, while cousin Virginia rode on horseback, was ordered out to go to church the following day. Weston Carter and Mr. Morrisson went with us on horseback. Cousin Virginia, Veronica, cousin Phil and I occupied the little carriage. I was beginning to get used to the Virginia roads, and put implicit confidence in the horses Liz and Barney and their driver. So we went as usual over rocks a yard high—through mud-holes a yard deep; ruts and gullies threatening to upset us every moment; stumps in the middle of the road; brooks and streams to drive through, cousin Virginia screaming, Mr. Morrisson scolding, I laughing, and Phil encouraging Liz and Barney (who was blind), over the worst difficulties of our journey.

"Hi, Barney! Get up there, Liz!" cried Phil. "Wake up

old girl, can't you? I reckon, cousin Molly, you couldn't ditto such a piece of road as this among all the institutions of your country. It's enough to break a bird's neck to fly over!"

Divine service was held on alternate Sundays at the pretty Episcopal Church, at Fighterstown, or at a missionary station called Cranmer, a little Chapel in the woods, on the borders of Jefferson and Clarke Counties. Whenever we came to a tolerably smooth "piece of going" through the woods, Phil would strike up some hymn in the Episcopal collection, the whole of which he appeared to know, and Veronica, cousin Virginia, and Weston Carter, would immediately join him. Nothing can be imagined more beautiful than the effect of these four voices echoing the praises of God through the everlasting woods. Here and there, we met parties of negroes in their best clothes, going to church, or making holiday. The women were mostly dressed in white, with colored ribbons round their ample waists, while the men had laid aside the tattered working clothes, the color of clods, the livery of their servitude, and wore broad-cloth or frieze suits of all kinds of curious cuts and dates, either purchased by themselves or the cast off property of their masters.

We overtook Uncle Israel, who was a preacher of some note, and held frequent meetings in the open air in divers parts of the neighborhood, at which the law compelled the attendance of some white person. The old gentleman was sweltering along, it being a hot day in June, in a wadded garment of black camlet, down to his heels, such as was worn in the world of fashion, a generation or two since, when France adopted winter fashions from the Russians—a cross between a great coat and a dressing-gown. He had too great an affection for this raiment, which he thought looked clerical, to sacrifice the dignity of wearing it to any personal consideration. He was going to walk about seven miles to meet his congregation. Mr. Morrisson asked him why he had not taken a mule or a horse. "Laws Mas'r," said Uncle Israel, "the horses done beat out with las' week's ploughin', an' de mules warn't made to be nuffin but a torment to black folks. Ole Uncle Cudjoe says he 'spects dat ar's what white folks buys um for."

"Well," said Phil, "get up behind, old gentleman, and I'll carry you as far as Cranmer, any how."

So we travelled along with this poor black preacher in the clerical skirts, sitting behind us on the foot-board.

The church at Cranmer was built on the slope of a beautiful smooth rounded hill, commanding a superb view of the surrounding country. Farms, amongst which was Oatlands, with its lake, and waving wheat-fields and majestic woods, lay at our feet, clear, bright, and beautiful, glowing with summer sunshine. The little church stood on the edge of the wood. Under the trees were "hitched" the horses of the congregation, stamping and whisking their tails—many of them with side-saddles. Around the church-door stood the men, and about a hundred negroes, it being usual for the male part of the worshippers to stand in the Church-porch and gossip till the beautiful opening words of the American service, "The Lord is in His holy temple, let all the earth keep silence before Him," broke up their talk and they came clattering in together to their places.

Tyrell and Max were looking out for us, and helped us from the carriage.

"Well," said I to Max, "did Tyrell have his interview with Mr. Williams? What have you done?"

"Nothing," said he. "The man is a deeper rascal than we took him for, and as to your friend Tyrell, Molly, he is a trump. One does not often meet with fellows like Tyrell. There is only one thing to be done: we ought to getthe negroes out of harm's way, and I want Tyrell to decide on carrying them off at once, and let me take the risk, but he won't hear of it till everything else possible has been tried. You see he was born and bred in Virginia, and has a master's prejudices about this cursed slavery —the only point we don't agree upon."

Veronica, meanwhile, was getting a clearer account of what had passed from cousin Tyrell. A very few words served to tell her the state of the case; and as we sat waiting for the commencement of the service on the wooden benches of the primitive barn-like little building, where we could see the green woods waving through chinks in the unpainted rafters, as well as through the door and windows, she told me what she had gathered from our cousin.

Mr. Williams scoffed at the idea that his mother had intended to make a will, besides which, he denied that he or his mother, to his knowledge, had received any money from Uncle Christopher, or had given him any paper purporting to be a receipt for four hundred and sixty-nine dollars. He said it was all folly to imagine the negro had laid by such a sum.

After this Tyrell had been to see Jake Gibson, who said that Williams had been a long time in his debt for advances of cash and for his tavern score. He laughed at the notion of selling Aunt Saph and her children for six hundred dollars, as Tyrell proposed, saying, he wanted the woman for his cook, but if he wished to "pocket" them, the negro trader in Winchester would give him double that money. Veronica said *par parenthèse*, that she had never known negroes to be sold to a trader by good families in the neighborhood, except for some serious fault, but that death, debt, crime, and other causes, threw many into the hands of the soul-driver, lying on the look-out for them at Winchester, and that such people as Will Williams and Gibson, who had no characters to lose, were willing enough to convert human property when it fell into their hands, into money.

Uncle Christopher was sexton of the Cranmer Church, and Tyrell and Max had come early and questioned him about his money, amongst which Aunt Saph declared he had had two notes for a hundred dollars. He said that one of his young masters among the engineers at Harper's Ferry had told him it was hardly safe to keep his money wrapped in an old coat in the corner of the tent, and had proposed to get two hundred dollars changed into notes at the office of the superintendent of the railroad. This gentleman was now supposed to be in Baltimore. Tyrell had then asked Uncle Christopher if any white man had been present when he paid Mr. Williams, or if any white person in Fighterstown could identify the money.

But Christopher replied that till he gave it to his wife he had carried the notes about his person day and night, saying nothing to any body except to his young masters at Harper's Ferry, not wishing to have it known that he had cash to that amount about him.

"You are sure you showed the money to no white man, Uncle Christopher?"

"I never shown it Mas'r—yes—stay! My ole woman she asked Mas' Felix one day when he was to work up dar to count it over."

Tyrell was now on the watch for Mr. Felix, who he hoped would come to church, to ask him whether he remembered anything about this circumstance and could identify the money. Mr. Felix, however, did not come to Cranmer, and after waiting at the door till the service was half over, Max and Tyrell came in to the church and took their places amongst the congregation.

After the service was ended Veronica and I both turned to Tyrell.

"What do you mean to do if you get up evidence that Mr. Williams has received and appropriated Uncle Christopher's money?"

"Nothing can be done, I fear, except to deepen my conviction that he's the meanest white man in the country. I may get evidence enough to convince *me*, for I would believe Uncle Christopher on his word in preference to half the members of Congress upon oath, but colored testimony is inadmissible against a white man; and besides, Miss Veronica, I wish to spare your cousin from being publicly prosecuted."

"But Sapphira and Uncle Christopher? How does Uncle Christopher bear it?" said I.

"I did not tell him the extent of my fears, he does not know that Gibson claims his family, but he takes the ill news as far as he knows it in the spirit of a Christian. He said to me, "The matter is safe an' right Mas' Jim, an' whar it ought to be. Whar de Lord says 'all right, Christopher,' I ain't gwine to say 'No, Lord, it's all wrong.' I leaves it in the hands of our kin' Heavenly Father, an' every other thing, thank de Lord I can put that too. The king's heart is as rivers of water, says the Scripture, an' He turneth it whithersoever He will. Just so if de Lord please he'll turn his heart and it shall be jus as it is best to be, I know dat mas'r."

"Oh! but will Aunt Saph be Jake Gibson's slave or be sold away down south? I never could bear that," said Veronica.

"No!" said Tyrell with energy. "These are not flush times with any of us, cousin Veronica, but I can afford to prevent *that*, and I will. The law receives no colored testimony against a white man, but the public will believe Uncle Christopher in preference to Mr. Williams. If I prove to my entire satisfation that Will Williams knowingly appropriated that poor black Christian's hard-earned notes, I shall confront him and charge him with his fraud, and if we can get white evidence enough to take the matter into court my father will threaten him with prosecution on the part of the heirs to the estate of your uncle. The law considers the earnings of the slave the property of his owner, and wrong done to Uncle Christopher is wrong done to his master. I think a threat like this from a man of such weight in our community as my father will bring Mr. Williams to his senses, and that he will sell me the negroes for a small advance on the original bargain of six hundred dollars, after which I shall run them off into a free State or send them for safe keeping to a friend in the District of Columbia. Jake Gibson may bring an action against me if he likes, but I doubt if the paper is valid upon which he might assert a claim, and I rather think that while *he* would dread an exposure in the court room, the public sentiment of the community would sustain *me* in any suit that could be brought between us before any court in Jefferson or Clarke Counties."

Tyrell paused a moment, and the flash in his fine eyes softened as he said: "There is one other consideration, and that is, if I should be driven to this necessity, what ought to be done with Uncle Christopher? If we send Aunt Saph and her two children beyond Gibson's reach must we separate him from his family?"

"No—no!" cried Veronica. "Why cannot he go too?"

"I must know by what authority. Who does he belong to?" said Tyrell.

"He will belong to me. I have arranged that with your father," said Veronica quickly.

"Miss Veronica, it may be painful to you to discuss this business," said Tyrell, "but you had better hear the truth. In case you decline any offer of marriage from your cousin Max, there will be no opportunity to threaten Mr. Williams with a suit, for so far as Oatlands and its negroes are concerned *he* will become your uncle's heir, and will not only lay claims to Aunt Sapphira and her boys, but to her husband."

Veronica flushed angrily at the beginning of this speech, but her anger faded as she listened, and she said "My cousin knows and will respect my wishes. I have every reason to believe and hope that I shall never be placed under the necessity of doing any act which might bring such a calamity."

"If that is the case—if you have reason to be sure that the question of ownership lies between you and Max—I shall venture, in case of necessity, to take the course that I have named if it meets with the approval of both of you."

"It has my sanction; I shall agree to anything you do," she said.

"But you are not of age, nor have you any legal guardian by whom you can act. How is it with Max? Uncle Christopher, though no longer very young, is a valuable servant. Will Max give up his claim if he becomes his property?"

"Max will never wish to profit," I exclaimed, "by an institution he abhors."

"Miss Molly," said Tyrell, with a forced smile, "men's principles differ upon this point, according to their personal relations to slavery."

"He shall tell you himself what his opinion is," said I; and I beckoned him to join our group, which stood apart from the rest of the party.

"Max, Veronica has a request to make to you," I said, and walked away to join my Clairmont cousins.

"I have nothing to say," said Veronica, with tears in her eyes, turning to follow me.

"What is it, Veronica?" said Max, taking her hand and detaining her.

"Nothing!" she said, vehemently, "and when I say '*nothing*,' I desire you to believe me."

Max relinquished her hand, and Veronica was ashamed of her petulance.

"Forgive me, cousin Max," she said; "my temper is not what it ought to be. I don't know what to do, nor what to say. It seems to me you are making a great many sacrifices on my account; but if cousin Tyrell sends Aunt Sapphira to the North, I am quite ready to give up my claim to Uncle Christopher."

Max did not understand what she meant to convey to him, and Veronica, having advanced thus far in her subject, gathered courage and went on.

"I mean that we understand each other. A word from you to me might give Mr. Williams a legal claim to Oatlands, and to Uncle Christopher as well as to Aunt Saph. I —— I —— (and the tears she struggled to conceal rose in her beautiful blue eyes, as she spoke) I can trust your generosity. Will you give your sanction to a plan which would send Uncle Christopher to the North with his family? Without it, cousin Tyrell will not act. Will you do this, because he is the son of my old Mammy?"

"Come here, Uncle Christopher," said Max. "You told me just now you were the son of old Mammy. I do not forget the promises I made at the death-bed of that good old woman. You have my free consent, old gentleman, so far as I have any claim upon you as my servant, to take yourself over Mason and Dixon's line as fast as possible. I shall be very glad to see you out of slavery."

Uncle Christopher, bewildered, looked at Veronica, who said in a low voice,

"And so shall I."

Tyrell, more practical than they, came up and whispered to Uncle Christopher to come over to Stonehenge the next day, for he wanted to have a talk with him, and then we got into the carriage. Uncle Christopher put up the steps. Tyrell and Max mounted their horses, and we drove home, scarcely speaking all the way.

We reached Clairmont in time for a cold dinner at three o'clock. Tyrell, who had quitted us in Fighterstown, came in when it was half over, and after the cloth was cleared away, drew Max on to the front porch, and told him that Mr. Felix said the hundred dollar notes in Christopher's possession had been good notes of the Valley Bank of Virginia. He added that Will Williams had changed a hundred dollar note of the Valley Bank within a few days, to pay his score at the tavern at Fighterstown.

Then Phil was called on to the front porch to join the consultation, and Mr. Morrisson kept out of the way; and that evening, instead of the usual Sunday evening chants and hymns sung by the whole family, every one was grave and silent. Veronica, on the back porch, taught a Sunday class of little colored children, or went into aunt Edmonia's chamber and sat there, with a book shading her eyes.

Tyrell went off so late, having been in conversation with Phil and Max up to the last moment, that aunt Edmonia was unhappy at the idea of his long ride after night-fall, and could not sleep for thinking of him; and Phil and Max made an appointment to ride over to Stonehenge the next day to Mrs. Williams's funeral.

Max was in pretty good spirits all that evening. I think he had gathered encouragement rather than otherwise, from what Veronica had said to him, or rather from the tone and manner that accompanied her words.

CHAPTER XIII.

But wherefore do I murmur thus,
This world is very wide,
My heart shall be an omnibus
And carry twelve inside.

'Tis true that on the way, perchance,
Some to drop off begin,
But can we not as we advance
Take many others in?

PUNCH.

RESIDENTS in the Southern States pay a tax upon their privileges as the dominant race under the "peculiar institution." They are the lawful prey of their dependents, and the tax is levied somewhat disproportionately on "strangers and sojourners," who not only are glad to meet all demands on them for service with unusual liberality, on account of the position of the servitors, but a petty pilfering, very difficult to defeat, is carried on against all the little travelling possessions of the stranger.

Max, either from some hint from Tyrell or from some experience in the first days of his stay at Clairmont, considered his room less safe than mine, and telling me in confidence that he had not a lock and key in his apartment, requested me to take charge of his money, which was all in English gold.

About dusk the next day he came gallopping back from Stonehenge, whither he had gone with Phil to Mrs. Willliams's funeral.

He had ridden in great haste, was flushed and heated, and taking me aside asked me to give him sixty sovereigns, as they were wanted to pay Williams for Aunt Saph and her children, in order that they might carry them out of Gibson's reach as soon as possible.

I went up stairs to get the gold, and looking from the window saw Max upon the grass before the house, talking eagerly and confidentially with Veronica. They had now a subject of common interest, and I paused a moment ere I called him away from her.

As I counted the money into his hand I said, remembering Veronica's advice, "Stop a minute Max—I have something that I want to say to you."

Max looked hurried and fussy, and said in rather an impatient tone:

"Well!—but don't ask me any questions about this business, Molly!"

The human heart is like a pickle-jar—you will get nothing out of it if you shake it in a hurry.

"No," said I, "I believe I will not trouble you Max—only Veronica advised me to speak to you."

"Well! what is it?" said he coming into the room and growing more attentive when I mentioned Veronica.

"It is only something about myself. Only a letter I have had from ——— from Mr. Howard. Veronica seemed to think you were the proper person to advise me."

"Do you mean me to see it?"

"No—not quite. It is a very pleasant letter, and he says I am so very unkind; that he knows nothing about us since we left England. You know I promised papa I would not write to him."

"Write!—no," said Max. "Of course it is not your place to write. I wish with all my heart that that business were given up, Molly. I never had a very great opinion of your friend—though he was just the sort of man to captivate your fancy; but I should object very much to my sister's being looked down upon as she will be if she marries into that family. I should think you were Virginian enough, Molly, to have some pride of ancestry. Think of that black Begum barely tolerating my sister! I declare it makes me angry to think of it."

I began to cry, for this picture was not a pleasant one. It had often presented itself to my imagination, though I kept it out of sight by my attachment to Mr. Howard.

"If we care for one another, Max, that regard will out-weigh all paltry considerations."

"I do not believe it will with him, in the long run," said Max. "It is no joke being a poor baronet with a great unprofitable place like Howard Park, which must be shut up or let for want of ready money. Molly, don't you see that there are better men who show symptoms of giving you their attachment? Don't you know that there are families with better blood than any Howards of Howard Park, who would be honored by an alliance with Miss Mandeville? Don't you know that the deepest regret of our father's life would be dissipated by such a marriage as is open to you? I declare when I look upon the lands that our forefathers possessed it seems to me I would do anything to bring them back into the family."

"Max I won't hear you say such things. They are entirely untrue. I have received this letter and I thought it right to ask you whether, as Mr. Howard does not appear quite to understand about my promise, you would write him a few lines. Will you copy what I have written, Max, and tell him that I cannot carry on any correspondence until better times, because of my promise to my father?"

I gave him the paper and he carried it off, stopping as he passed along the porch to say a few words to Veronica. Aunt Edmonia thought a storm was coming up, and just as he was mounting in the wood, she called from her chamber window, "Oigh! Oliver!—oigh! Tom Tad! Where are those children? I want them to tell Max to take Mr. Morrisson's water-proof cape with him. Veronica, my dear, will you call to him and tell him he will get wet to a certainty."

Veronica took the cape from the table in the hall, and ran across the grass. He did not see her till he had mounted, and then his horse turning somewhat sharply had nearly thrown her down. I watched them from the window. Max sprang from Black Mike in great agitation; then having made sure she was unhurt, he put on the heavy cape, though it was as unseasonable as Uncle Israel's douillette of camlet and wadding, and she stood holding his bridle, patting the nose of his black horse, and passing her soft fingers through the heavy tresses of his mane as he stood pawing the ground.

The letter I asked Max to write for me ran thus:

"My Dear Sir,

"My sister has received from you several long letters, the last of which has reached her during her sojourn in Virginia. She begs me to say that she is bound, by a positive promise to her father, not to correspond with you till the dawn of happier times. She is well, and begs me to assure you of the great pleasure your letters have afforded her, and of her continual remembrance. And with the renewal of the assurance, that only a positive promise which she cannot break, prevents her answering your letters, believe me, my dear sir, to be,

"Yours very sincerely,

"Max Mandeville."

The letter that Max sent was as follows:

"DEAR SIR,

"I learn from my sister Miss Mandeville that she has received several letters from you—one of them within a day or two. I beg to say that her relations have exacted a positive promise that she will not continue to correspond with you. She is well, and passing an agreeable summer among her new friends in this country. She begs me to tell you this, and to unite her best remembrances with the compliments of

"Your obedient servant,

"T. L. MANDEVILLE."

And when I asked Max some months after if my letter had been sent as I had written it, he answered, with the full belief that he spoke the truth,

"Yes, I copied it, but with the omission of lots of feminine trash. That was a woman's letter, Molly, not a man's. I could not copy all that stuff. You all of you, say anything you have to say twice over in the shortest note, and are more diffuse about it the last time than you were the first; just as your only way of arguing is to say over again a little louder what has been answered before."

Old Mrs. Williams was buried the next day, and our gentlemen staid at Stonehenge till after the funeral. Veronica, who appeared to know more about their plans than I, was very restless and uneasy.

It was dull at Clairmont, and had been for a day or two, for the servants and horses were all ploughing corn; and as other horses and negroes were engaged in the same work, there was no visiting amongst the neighboring families at that season. I amused myself that day, for Veronica was too preöccupied to talk, by listening to cousin Virginia's endless anecdotes of queer originals who had flourished at various periods in the neighborhood, and by investigating the domestic arrangements of the family.

I penetrated into the kitchen—a dark cavern of a place detached from the main building, with a large chimney big enough to burn a cord of wood, and roast "a beef," as cousin Virginia told me. The principal light came from the fire, around which three or four of the little darkeys squatted, though I had been gasping in the coolest places in the house, with the thermometer at ninety-two in the shade. Marm Venus was skimming something in a pot, and rapped them over the head with the iron spoon as we came in, and then put the spoon back in the pot again. I felt that it did not do to examine into the mysteries of the delicious, savoury dishes which were there composed.

After an early dinner, I mounted Angelo, but it was only to ride into the corn-field with Mr. Morrisson, and sit by him whilst he discussed with George, or Joe, or Wash, or old Uncle Cudjoe, or Uncle Israel, the relativea dvantages of the old plough, or the Berkshire, or new manures, which he was never likely to apply, or magnificent improvements he had not money to undertake, or the relative merits of his own and neighboring cattle. Any quantity of the servants' time, as well as Mr. Morrisson's, was wasted in these talks, which had no practical advantage that I could perceive, except that they drew out kindly feelings between himself and his negroes. The former asserted their opinions with entire freedom of speech, and to my astonishment, offered to bet on some disputed point with their master!

Mr. Morrisson had no overseer, having too few negroes, and placing great dependence upon Uncle Israel, his head man. He generally sat on the front porch a large part of the day, and gave his orders.

"Oigh! Tommy Tad! you run down and drive those cows out of the wheat! They must have eaten or damaged nigh about a bushel!"

"Why don't you put up hurdles, Mr. Morrisson?"

"Hurdles? I don't know about hurdles; but I am thinking of putting up an elegant wire fence, which will be a great improvement to the property; and as I am thinking of it, it is not worth while going to the expense of any other; so I keep a live fence in the mean time. Oigh! Tommy! Tommy! run and chase that calf, boy! Why have you let it get over that broken railing? It is eating up my celery beds, and doing mischief in the garden."

On the whole, the impressions made on my mind was, that in matters of farming, masters and negroes were all "trifling" alike, to use the expression of the country; and that "the earth brought forth grass, the herb yielding seed, and the fruit tree yielding fruit after his kind," less in gratitude for the assiduities of man, than from observance of the laws of nature. It struck me that on small farms such as Clairmont, where the servants were directly under the eye of the master, the rule in ordinary times must be very mild, and the hand of power light; but I had seen enough of Virginians to know, that when their passions were roused, especially under the influence of toddy, there was no telling what might be the extent of their violence. The house servants I pitied more than I did the people in the field; they were continually fussed over and harassed, till, to use our nursey's expression, they had "no peace of their souls." But they took it quietly, not troubled by any bump of conscientiousness, but evidently under the impression that it was their mistress' business in life to scold and drive them round, and look after them, and theirs to escape her just as often as they could, and do just as little as possible. The pride in work taken by a stirring, smart, sharp-tempered woman in New England, or the sense of duty fulfilled which animates a good servant in the old country, was entirely unknown amongst these people. They waited assiduously day and night upon you if sick, from kind feeling, or if a stranger, from a natural sense of hospitality. Gentle and docile, you could easily make them fond of you. But the whole system was vicious: they were brought up to work when driven like the beasts, without any sense of human responsibility; this feeling was not even cultivated in their domestic relations. A man was not responsible for the maintenance of his wife, or the future prospects of his children; and this under the very best aspects of the system. The faults of the master, reacting on the servants, were visited on the white children, and so on through succeeding generations. The wrongs sheltered under the "institution," avenge themselves very liberally, and, as is always the case (witness the history of Louis XVI. and the horrors of the First Revolution), the retribution of an evil system falls most heavily upon victims the least guilty.

Still the physical and material condition of the servants of the place was so superior to anything I had imagined about slavery, that I was greatly impressed by it at first, as I doubt not any candid person must be, who goes under favourable conditions into a slave country.

I spoke to Veronica about it, and she shook her head. "I have been here longer than you have, Molly—long enough to distinguish between the remorseless working of the system itself and the kindness and good feeling of its administrators. Let a master do what he will to adjust things to his ideas of Christian duty and an enlightened sense of right, sometime or other he gets caught in the wheels of the machinery. I have seen enough to know what death, and debt, and division of property, and laws you can't prevent, will do in time. Watch any set of servants for some years, under as good a mistress or master as you can find, and you will discover miseries which come upon them as inevitably as age or death—evils you can't prevent—which are part of the inevitable working of the institution. They are things which shock your Christianity—things which are "nobody's fault," perhaps, and which you could not help if you were mistress or master. I don't speak of positive cruelty. There is some things that it sickens you to think of,—but cruelty is not a distinguishing feature of the institution. It is kept in check by public opinion, and, on the whole, I am much more astonished that there is so little of it, than that horrid stories come to light from time to time. I don't speak, either, of the want of physical comforts, for, on the whole, it cannot be denied that our slaves are quite as well lodged, cared for, fed, and clothed, as any other laboring population in any country of Christendom; and I call them in general, a happy race, for being brought up with no sense of responsibility (a virtue whose converse is to be "careful and troubled,") they have a singular facility in shaking off cares, and live *au jour le jour* with easy carelessness. But, Molly, look around you. There is Mary Louisa, who waits upon you. She has been three times married, and each time off the place, and both her first and second husbands have been sold away or removed by their masters. Cousin Virginia will tell you that Mary Louisa didn't mind it. Is it a woman degraded into not minding things like that whom you would trust to teach your children their first notions of purity, and their first lispings of truth? Look at little Tom Tadpole (Phil called him that on account of his queer shape), his father struck a white boy over the head with a brick-bat, in Winchester, and the law said he must be hanged or sold out of the state. God knows where he is now among the swamps of Louisiana. And so on, *ad infinitum.* I could not live contentedly and be responsible to God for the well-being and well-doing of these people, with the law watching me jealously whenever I attempted to teach them what all Christians ought to believe and know, and hedging my interpretations of the Scriptures. I must try for the sake of my own comfort to give them self-respect and self-reliance,—dangerous qualities to awaken, I am told, under the institution."

"Tyrell said something which struck me the other day," I said. "He observed that the good that is in us, must act upon the evil that is without us."

"Aye, look at Tyrell," said Veronica. "He has become snarled up in a labyrinth of duties. Duties to God, duties to man, duties to law, duties to society, duties to his country, duties to himself, and duties to his servants, till he does not know, oftentimes, which way to tread, without breaking the meshes of some duty or other."

I thought again of Tyrell, and of another quotation from Goethe, he had made to me, "Do the duty that lieth nearest thee." And wondered whether, till there was a reasonable hope of deliverance for himself and them, it was not his "nearest duty" to remain faithful to his post as the master of his slaves, and make the best of the institution he was born under.

As I was standing at the window pondering these things, there rode up to the house a tall well-looking man, in a new, glossy suit of black, with a pair of saddle-bags.

Presently Mary Louisa came up stairs and handed something to Veronica, saying, "Mas' Parker was down stairs, an' begged the favor of her to read dat paper."

"What is it Molly?" said Veronica, turning it over and over.

It was written in a school-hand, full of flourishes, not particularly well spelled (but then its author might have studied spelling out of Webster or Worcester).

"It's an acrostic, Vera!" said I. "'V. Lomax,' a homage to beauty on the part of Mr. Parker."

"Yes," she said, "paid for in 'drinks,' I have no doubt, and written, by the Yankee district schoolmaster—some ex-pedlar, who came down here from the valley of the Connecticut or the mountains of Vermont, to teach our people. I have known Mr. Parker of old. He came here last year, from his native hills, on the fame of my poor looks, to 'ask the favor' of me to be Mrs. Parker."

"Let us hear how it reads," said I taking up the paper.

"V ery few ladies can bear to be acquainted
L ike her with their own merits when they're painted.
O h, her looks so majestic and handsome and bold,
M ake her eyes seem like diamonds all set in pure gold,
A nd her voice is so extremely mellorific—
X ceedingly reminding me of an ancient hieroglyphic."

"Well, Veronica," said I, when we had done laughing, "don't you mean to change your dress and go down?"

"Veronica! Veronica!" said cousin Virginia, at our door. "Here is Mr. Parker, down stairs, 'begging the favor' of you to come down and entertain him in the drawing-room."

"I am not coming down till tea-time," said Veronica.

"But I can't leave him there, by himself," said cousin Virginia, "Molly, you come down."

Thus ajured, I went down into the drawing-room, and was introduced to Mr. Parker, as "Miss Mandeville, from England." Mr. Parker was a man of thirty-four or thirty-five years of age, who had been born and bred on a spur of the Blue Ridge, in a neighboring county, and had recently succeeded to a considerable property, chiefly in negroes, who were "hired" (*anglicè, let out*) to different families in the county. I had heard him talked about, for amongst the servants upon Mr. Morrisson's farm, was a boy who belonged to him, and whose favorite wish was "dat Mas'r 'd git a wife an' take him home to live," and when he said this he would look out of the corners of his eyes at Veronica. I gathered he was a man kind to his servants, and though still choking with the remembrance of his acrostic, I went down quite kindly disposed towards Mr. Parker.

Mr. Parker looked at me with great curiosity, and got up from his chair, and moved it off a few yards, as if he were a little afraid of me. However, I seemed, doubtless, very tame, and took out my worsted work, willing to be as agreeable as I might, provided I could find interests in common with Mr. Parker.

I began—"I think there is a boy of yours, Mr. Parker, among the servants on this place. He seems very fond of his master."

"Oh! . . . . . I reckon—yes! I seen him ploughing corn as I rid up," said Mr. Parker.

"Did he not recognize you as you rode past?"

"Hey, Miss?" said Mr. Parker.

"Did you speak to him, I mean?"

"Well, now—I reckon! May I beg the favor of you Miss ——— How has that gotten round to you?"

"Nothing has been told to me," I said smiling, "I thought it very likely Joe would wish to see his master."

"Well, now," said Mr. Parker, thoughtfully, "it was that wench Mary Louisa, I reckon."

Mr. Parker's prose proving as incomprehensible as his poetry, a considerable pause ensued. At the close of it Mr. Parker appeared to take a desperate resolution.

"Miss Veronica Lomax ain't going to do me the favor of coming down to see me, I reckon?"

"My cousin is very much engaged," said I. "She begs you will excuse her." Mr. Parker cleared his throat, and edged his chair up close to mine in a confidential manner.

"Have you much preachin' in them parts you come from?" said he.

"Preaching!" said I.—"In England? Yes, there is divine service twice a day in the Cathedrals, and a sermon or lecture somewhere every day, in almost all the large towns."

Cousin Virginia had just come into the room. It was growing dark. "Joe has come up to take your horse," said she. "Will you give him orders what to do. Your room is getting ready, Mr. Parker."

He went out to speak to Joe on the back porch, and cousin Virginia began to be merry. "My dear," said she, "he means to court you instead of Veronica. Joe told him, just now, that there was another young lady staying here, and he reckoned she must be rich, for she had twelve silk gowns. Depend upon it he is thinking of you on Joe's recommendation."

"He is the oddest man I ever saw," said I. "Does he take me for a Hottentot? He has just asked me if there was much preaching where I came from?"

"A regular courting question," said cousin Virginia, laughing,

—"a polite adaptation of his conversation to a topic supposed to be of interest to a young lady. The people in his parts never meet except at church. It is the great frolic of the week to go there. They hitch their horses under the trees and have their talk, and do their flirting, and their business before 'preaching.' I reckon he thought that is the way you go to church in England, at St. Paul's."

Mr. Parker continued this shy, curious style of conversation all the evening, keeping closely at my side, and hardly looking at Veronica, till tired of worsted work and the bore of answering his questions, I got up and went to bed, wondering when Max and Phil were likely to come home again. Mr. Morrisson had gone over to some Mills, some four or five miles off, about a "note," and there was no gentleman in the house but Mr. Parker. I was dreaming of "hitching" Angelo to the railing round the tomb of Edward the Confessor, at Westminster Abbey, when I was wakened by a loud alarm.

CHAPTER XIV.

'If I did despise the cause of my man servant or of my maid servant when they contended with me; what then shall I do when God riseth up? and when He riseth what shall I answer Him?"—JOB 31: 13 14.

A FUNERAL in Virginia is far more touching than any ceremony with which we "bury our dead out of our sight" in cities. There are no Mr. Omers who trade on grief, to interpose professional services between the dead and the living—who if the angel of Death cut himself down with his own scythe would lament over the calamity. The hand of affection composes the stiffening limbs and lays the dead form in the coffin; friends or dependents (who in many instances are friends) carry it to its last resting-place, and the dark vault of death is closed by clods thrown in by hands that have extended their friendly grasp to the hands stiffened on the cold dead breast, and not by hired strangers.

Old Mrs. Williams was buried by her kindred in the Stonehenge grave-yard. No mourners had been summoned by her son, but a few friends unbidden assembled on the Governor's porch, and when the coffin made its appearance (brought over in the carriage she had used in life) they testified their respect by walking in procession to the grave-yard.

The funeral ceremony was over; the funeral guests had gone, but Max remained sitting on the low wall, sheltered by a guelder rose-tree, unperceived by Uncle Christopher, who was smoothing and patting with his spade the sods over the coffin. The servants of Stonehenge, and even those from the estate of Mrs. Williams, had stood round the enclosure during service, and Aunt Saph lingered after the others had gone.

"It ain't no sort o' use ole man," she said, "I ain't gwine to try to reconcile myself if it must come to that. An' Mas' Williams had that man in the house las' night, an' Si he said that ar was what they was talkin' 'bout."

Uncle Christopher paused. "It do seems mighty hard a man can't help, and save for, an' provide for his wife and chile'n."

"You *has* worked for 'em ole man. Your mas'r gin you your time; and that ar's your bag, Mas'r William took down out of his mother's closet right afore our eyes, fore old missus done deceased', an' she done telled him it war your'n old man, an' he done cussed and swore at her about it. An' now he says all niggers tell a pack o' lies, and that you never paid nothin' to ole missus for my freedom. Did you tell Mas' Jim that ar ole man? Wisht I was dead afore he'd sell me an' my chilens to that Gibson? I ain't gwine to b'long to him, ole man—I ain't gwine to," she exclaimed passionately. "He's the worst man in all the country. He can't hire nor buy no niggers. Folks won't sell 'em to him sence he done got his trial for that whippin' he gin Isaac that he died from. Folks of any 'count dat has to pocket their servants 'd rather sell 'em to the soul drivers. Couldn't do no wus than that ar gwine to pick cotton. Oh! ole man what Mas' Jim say when you tole him?"

"Mas' Jim say he'll do all he can, Aunt Saph, but de Lord is my helper, and I will not fear what flesh can do unto me," said Uncle Christopher, uncovering his head. "Here is the grave of my ole missus who is in heaven. She allers said 'put your whole trust in de Lord, Christopher'—an' de Lord he's strong enuff, an' de Lord he's wise enuff, an' de Lord he has love enuff, an' if He don't help us when we cry it is because He hadn't ought to. Jus as you let your chilens cry, Aunt Saph, when day wants what'll hurt 'em—you ain't gwine gin it 'em, ole woman, let 'em cry ever so."

Here Max came forward from behind his guelder rose-tree. "Do not distress yourself," he said, "you have friends who will try to help you. Your master shall not sell you and your children, Saph; there is a better fate in store for you."

"Mas' William done told me that he bin gwine to sell us, Mas' Max. Wouldn't mind so bad gwine into a good family —but I ain't gwine to live with white trash—I ain't gwine whar he want to sell me. Oh! Mas' Max, you'se gwine marry Miss Vera Lomax, an' settle down here—jus you buy us, honey. I'se real good 'bout a house, and I knows Miss Vera likes me right well. Ole missus done bring me up herself, and I knows heaps o' things that dese yere common niggers dunno. Jus you buy us now for de Lord's sake, young mas'r."

"Good heavens—to think of your going back into slavery when your husband has paid more than two thirds of the price asked for you! I have been talking with the Governor and Mr. Tyrell about your case. They believe, Uncle Christopher, that Mr. Williams can be brought to deal fairly by you."

Here William Williams and Gibson, the tavern-keeper, who had stood his trial before the county court for the murder of his negro slave, and been acquitted for want of proof, rode up to the grave-yard. Williams was neither very drunk nor very sober.

"Oigh, Aunt Saph," said he jocularly, "here's a gentleman wishes for the pleasure of being introduced to you. I reckon you'll find yourself at home in the big kitchen at the tavern. He wants to fix you there real smart. Come, now, I reckon if you behave yourself that you'll like to go and live with him."

Aunt Saph drew back nearer to Max, "No, Mas' William," she said, "I'll run away an' git put in jail an' be sold to the negro traders afore I'll go to live with Mas' Gibson."

"Mr. Gibson," said Max, who stood by with the thermometer rising within him, "the title is so fraudulent by which you claim these negroes, that I warn you they have friends who will dispute your possession."

"What right, sir, have you to come here and interfere with our slaves," cried out Williams. "A d——d Englishman and abolitionist?"

"I do not interfere with your slaves," said Max, "*that* concerns yourselves. And this slavery you are hugging to your hearts as the Spartan robber did his fox, is tearing out your vitals. It is working out its curse among you. But the deeds that you have done to this poor black man and his wife will not be tolerated by any institution. You have no right to charge your villainies on slavery. Slavery, Mr. Williams, does not shield a man who keeps back part of the price that has been paid him. Slavery does not sanction men in substituting a fraudulent agreement for a will to be signed by your infirm and aged mother."

"How dare you!" cried Williams, raising his whip, and growing white with shame and rage.

"Dare!" exclaimed Max, springing over the low wall, and confronting him. "Come on, sir; come on—you and this man, who is your fit associate. Add to the list of crimes that now disgrace you a vulgar brawl over your mother's coffin."

Either Will Williams was shamed by this mention of the new-made grave, or he was daunted by Max's attitude. He turned his horse's head, and still muttering something about being revenged another time, and "abolitionism," rode off, and left Max master of the field.

Gibson, as he turned to follow him, stooped and said vindictively to Aunt Saph,

"Look sharp after yourself now, for I have bought you."

"Bought me!—me an my chilens?" cried Aunt Saph. "You hasn't done signed any papers for us yet—has you *yet?* Has you got the bill of sale for us, mas'r?"

Gibson laughed at her confusion and distress.

"I have bought you," he said, "and in good part paid for you—value received. Half the worth of you has been taken out in liquor. I made a bargain for you, and your master and your old mistress signed a paper, and I have trusted your master on the strength of it. You have got to come and live with me, old woman, whether you like it or not, I reckon."

He rode after Williams. Aunt Saph watched him as he went; and then throwing her apron over her face, she sat down upon a grave and rocked herself to and fro. Uncle Christopher, in that silence which is the eloquence of weakness—the mute appeal to that tribunal before which all hearts are open, and from whose scrutiny no secrets are hid—went on with his employment, and Max, turning from the grave-yard, walked to the house, and poured forth his indignation into the ears of Tyrell.

"I have thought about it anxiously; I have thought of little else for the last two days, and agree with you that it is time to act, if we mean to act at all," said Tyrell. "I had some scruples at first about following the guidance of my indignation; but I have talked with my father, who thinks it is our duty, as owners of plantations, interested in the support of slavery, to put down rascality like this, which throws discredit on the institution."

"The more the system is discredited, the better, I should say," said Max.

"A sentiment capable of being carried out into the most unchristian action, and which is fast becoming at the North a party principle," said Tyrell. "Turn any system over—or society itself—into the hands of the unscrupulous, and you set going the pendulum of revolution, with its action and reaction; you will have the 'twin Dioscuri, Oppression and Revenge," that Carlyle talks of, stalking about, and lighting up fires that never will be quenched in this century."

"You are extremely fond of generalization," returned Max. "I wish you would suggest what we can *do*. Here are Phil and I ready to carry out the plan that we talked over yesterday evening."

"I have explained it to my father," Tyrell said. "He is willing to lend his sanction to our plan, and approves of it. But I hoped there would have been more time to mature the scheme, or that some means would suggest themselves by which we might avoid it. I meant to have had another interview with Gibson."

"I had that just now," said Max, "and he was bent on getting his prey into his clutches."

"Yes," replied Tyrell; "but I should have more weight with him than you in a matter of that nature. The best and the worst of us are extremely sensitive about the interference of foreigners with slavery. There is such terrible inflammation now round the "vexed question," owing to unskillful treatment, that a man should have been long familiar with the wound before he ventures to touch it—and then he must deal gently.

That which we freely admit to be evil amongst ourselves, we warmly defend when it is alluded to by strangers. That is the reason why I discourage your enthusiasm. A little indiscreet zeal upon your part might draw on us the indignation of our neighbors, whereas it is my object so to act as to enlist on our side the public opinion of the community."

"I want no prominent share in anything that may be done," cried Max. "'But if it is done, when it is done, then I would it were done quickly.' I am ready to lend my aid in any post in which you will employ me."

"The difficulty is," said Tyrell, "that—— The truth is, that to carry out the plan proposed, we want in hard cash three hundred and thirty dollars, which we agreed, and which my father agrees with me, is the least it would be judicious to offer Williams, in addition to the four hundred and sixty-nine dollars which he received from Uncle Christopher. My father hopes to frighten him into acknowledging that he has received that sum. But we have not three hundred dollars in the house, and in this part of the country even a small sum of money is not to be raised in an hour."

"I have plenty of money at your service," exclaimed Max, "in English gold. I am the proper person to advance it; for under every contingency but one, contemplated in the will of Mr. Lomax, Uncle Christopher becomes my slave, and it is my place to secure the safety of his wife and family. I can ride over to Clairmont and get my English sovereigns. I have put my money into Molly's keeping. She has it locked up in her chamber."

"Come into the house," said Tyrell, "and let us take counsel with my father. I do not wish to take any step in a business of this kind without his advice and sanction. Few men have ever stood higher in the good opinion of the men amongst whom their lot was cast than my father."

And having talked over the new features in the case with Governor Tyrell, who approved the plan proposed, Max mounted Black Mike and galloped to Clairmont, promising to be back in time for the old-fashioned early tea hour, adhered to in the family of the Governor.

CHAPTER XV.

Drunkenness is a pair of spectacles through which to see the devil and all his works.
OLD PROVERB.

LATER in that afternoon, Uncle Christopher might have been seen hanging round the kitchen at Mr. Williams's, waiting to get speech of his wife, who was busy in-doors. When he saw her it was in so hurried a manner, that she had no time to ask the questions he was cautioned to avoid answering. He simply gave her a message from "Mas' Jim," to the effect that she was to keep her children up and dressed till after nine o'clock, and have a small bundle of their clothes and her own made up, in case any one should call for them.

Lyndgate, an old poet in Dan Chaucer's day, solves the mystery of races, white and black, by telling us, that some years after the expulsion from Paradise an angel came down to visit Eve, who, having a large family of children, was a little behindhand in getting them ready for company. When Eve beheld the angel at her gate, she thrust the unwashed children into a dirty barrel, told them to keep quiet, and gathering around her the newly washed, prepared to receive her visitor.

"Eve," said the angel, after caressing the group, "is this all your little family?"

"All," replied Eve, woman-like, putting the best foot foremost, for the sake of appearances, and not cured of her old, unhappy propensity.

"Nay," answered the angel, as a dirty little face peered over the edge of the meal-barrel, "and those children hidden away unwashed you shall never be able to wash white any more."

Thus Aunt Saph, being a daughter of Eve, inherited her mother's wish to have her children in their best clothes before company.

The curiosity of Eve beset her for the remainder of that evening. It was getting dark as her husband gave her the message from cousin Tyrell, and in the multitude of her distresses, this poor daughter of the boy and girl hidden by our universal mother in the dirty meal-tub, thought more of the mystery than she did of her cares.

The other sentiment inherited from Eve awoke, however, about eight o'clock, when she began to get impatient to get her eldest boy, young 'Siah, washed and dressed with his best clothes on, ready for the occasion. But 'Siah was in the dining-room, where his master for three hours had kept him standing, till the child was nearly ready to drop down from sleep and weariness. Mr. Williams had a black bottle of whisky on the fire-place, and was mixing glass after glass of toddy for himself—tossing the heel-taps into 'Siah's face, cursing him in the intervals of his drink, throwing the ends of his cigars at him, and once a lighted chunk of wood—for the boy was alone with his drunken master, and the man had nothing else to vent his passions on. The child had to take alike his anger and his ribald jocularity. Better had it been for that man to be cast into the sea, with a millstone round his neck, than to reckon with God for the lessons given to that young, immortal soul.

Aunt Saph came once or twice into the parlor, and called the boy, but their master, with an oath, bade her begone, and she dared not, for the child's sake, anger him. Her other little fellow was a child of three years' old. She had dressed him, and put him in a sort of pen or cage, where she imprisoned him, and let him scream unnoticed while she went about her daily labor. She was stirring round the kitchen, anxious to leave as little undone of the usual household work as possible, when sudden shrieks startled her, proceeding from the dining parlor. She knew it was Si's voice, and ran towards the sitting-room—not to interpose between the boy and his intoxicated master, but at least to be at hand to see what was taking place; to watch in the entry, and to hear the blows; to have the mother's heart within her bleed, while as her own child's fellow-slave, she passively stood by, "with no help in her hand," whatever might be done to him. But as she got into the entry, which was dark, she ran against the Governor, Max and cousin Tyrell.

A carriage that she had not heard had driven up, and as they met thus in the darkness, the door of the dining-room was suddenly flung open, and Si ran out screaming into the passage, while his master rushed after him, flourishing a half-burnt hickory stick which he had snatched up from the fire. The glow of light proceeding from the open door into the corridor revealed the group to him. Will Williams, drunk as he was, stopped short, and threw his brand back on the hearth, sending a shower of sparks into the dark, and uttering a curse against the boy who had eluded him.

"I have not touched the little rascal," he exclaimed, as if admitting that some apology for the scene was needed by the Tyrells. "He stood there, first on one leg, then on the other, dropping asleep, till he gave way at the knees. I was just going to teach him that it is his business to keep awake. What can I do for you, Governor?"

"A little business, Mr. Williams, said Governor Tyrell, who

entered, accompanied by Max, while cousin Tyrell said a few words to Aunt Saph, who was receiving her son with no particular demonstrations of tenderness, for negro parents are seldom very gentle with their children.

"Take a seat, gentlemen. Have a drink?" said Williams, who was in a hospitable mood, having drank alone till he was weary of his own company.

Governor Tyrell picked up a chair which had been overturned in the scuffle between the master and the boy, and sat down by the table. Max remained standing by the door.

"Mr. Williams," said the Governor, proceeding on the principle that there are some men a great deal better for being knocked down at once, "it is my opinion that you have proved yourself of late a great rascal."

"Don't know as I think so, Governor," said Williams, not in the humor to be offended by words, and the Governor's manner was bland; "but reckon I am something of a sharp man, Governor."

"So sharp, Mr. Williams, that you have been overreaching yourself, of late, or, as the negroes would tell you, 'playing fool for cunning.' I think I have gotten legal evidence—white evidence—which will win our case if we take it into court; evidence to prove that a $100 note which can be identified as having been taken from a wallet given you by Mr. Lomax's negro man, Christopher, was changed by you at the tavern at Fighterstown."

"Come on, then. Take it into court; and what will you do then?—Who prosecutes?" said Williams, insolently.

"I am the prosecutor, Sir ———," began Max, but Governor Tyrell stopped him.

"A slave cannot hold property by law, therefore, the money paid by Uncle Christopher to your mother, and received by you," the Governor said, "belongs, by legal right to the estate of Mr. Lomax. Mr. Williams, we are unwilling to have any dispute with you. We will not reclaim that money, nor by exposing your other frauds hold you up to the contempt of the community, if you will sell us those negroes (taking the money you received from Christopher in part payment) for eight hundred dollars. This is two hundred dollars more than Mr. Gibson offers you."

"I tell you I ain't going to sell you those niggers," Williams said. "Gibson has got me in his power. Two years before he got that paper signed he got verbal promise from me, pledging me to sell them to him when they came into my hands for six hundred dollars. He'd levy an attachment on them for debt even if he had no other claim upon them. He's advanced me money upon those negroes. I ain't going to do that thing, I tell you, Governor. I ain't going to, nohow. Gibson's got me in his power."

"How much money has he advanced upon his bargain?" said Max, impatiently.

"Well, now, there's my bill down at his place—two hundred dollars, more or less, in cash, I reckon."

"And if we pay you three hundred and thirty one dollars down, that is £66, making eight hundred dollars, in all, as the price of this woman and her children," said Max, "will you pay Gibson what you owe him and so be off that bargain?"

"I reckon he wouldn't be off his part of it," Will Williams said. "It's less by one third than the traders would give him for that lot. The children are mighty likely. Cotton is rising every day, and the prices of negroes running high. He'll bring an attachment on those negroes—he said he would—and have them, anyhow you could fix it, Governor."

We will take care of that," cried Max. "They will be sent out of Virginia. Eight hundred dollars which we offer you is more than six. Think of it, Mr. Williams. If you don't, you will be prosecuted about that money you received from Uncle Christopher; Miss Lomax and I are determined on it. Whichever is heir to the old gentleman's estate will follow up this matter."

"I reckon, if all accounts be true, that I'll come in for Oatlands yet," said Williams, with a laugh. "They say it's more than likely you will get the sack, and that she'll marry Jim Tyrell."

"Now Mr. Williams, make haste with your decision. We want your answer at once," the Governor said, emptying a roll of glittering English gold upon the table. "This purchase, to be of any use to us, must be made to night, and we shall carry the negroes out of the way of Gibson's claim, or sheriff's writs before morning. Jake Gibson may content himself with his money, not his pounds of human flesh. No gentleman ought to sell that fellow negroes, and none of us would do so but yourself, in this county. Make up your mind, sir, for the time is brief. Will you give me a bill of sale, and take the money?"

"I'll tell you what, Governor, there'll be the devil to pay when Gibson knows of it. He wanted that woman for his cook. He finds it mighty hard to hire one or buy one. I'm bound to sell her to him, that's a fact. Suppose you let her go and take the children?"

"We must have all or none," the Governor replied. "Now, Mr. Williams, my carriage is ready at the door to take them off, —will you sign a bill of sale? This is my last offer. Three hundred and thirty-one dollars, down, and the money in that wallet you received, of which you changed a hundred dollar note, in Fighterstown. Eight hundred dollars in all, a very sufficient price for those negroes. Two hundred more than Mr. Gibson offers you."

"I am going to be beggared by that man," said Williams, who was getting into the querulous stage of his intoxication. "I am a miserable man, Governor Tyrell. I was brought up by one of the best of mothers, and led to expect a fine estate, and my uncle Lomax has appointed other heirs to his property. I am an ill used man, and people come over to my house to triumph over me and to insult me, by heaven! and to force me to give up my property, and to get me into an infernal fix with a man who is the hardest creditor and hardest master in the State, and who has me in his power. No words can tell you, Governor Tyrell, what he has been to me the last two years. He's tortured me, sir, as bad as ever he did that negro of his, Isaac, that he was tried for. I'm a miserable—miserable scoundrel—that's what I feel myself, and he has driven me to this—and now you threaten me with prosecution for a fraud, and come here to triumph over me. I wish I was dead—that's what I do, Governor," and Mr. Williams took another glass of whisky toddy.

"Deliver yourself out of that man's power, sir, and be a man. Pay him his money and be done with him. Here it is. Are the negroes mine as executor of the will of Mr. Lomax, and his agent for the Oaklands property?"

"Mr. Williams," said cousin Tyrell, looking in suddenly, "in three hours it will be daylight, in another half hour it will be too late to start. Yes or no? Give us your answer."

Williams had fixed his eyes upon the coin. It seemed a great sum of money to give up.

"Are the negroes going to belong to the old man's estate?" he said with a cunning look.

"Yes," exclaimed Max. "Now there! is it all right? Are they ours, Mr. Williams?"

"Well I suppose so," said Williams. "Count the money. Oh! Lord I feel so sick," he continued, throwing himself groaning on the lounge. "You had better run the lot right off if you don't want Gibson to get hold of them. Oh! Lord—he'll come here to-morrow and threaten me, but I shall tell him they are off. I shall have *mania potu* before long. I wish I had. I wish I was dead. There ain't a more miserable sinner, I reckon, this side of judgment."

"Where do you keep any ink, Mr. Williams?" said the Governor, as Max and Tyrell searched around the room.

"Oh! Lord I don't know. I flung something at that cursed boy to make him wake. I reckon it was the ink-bottle."

Sure enough in one corner of the room an ink-bottle lay broken, while the ink was dripping on the wainscoat or had soaked into the floor.

"Is this all the ink you have in the house, Mr. Williams? How shall we sign the bill of sale?" said Cousin Tyrell.

"Oh! Lord—Lord! come to-morrow, and take the niggers off to-night. I am too sick to attend to any more business. Help yourself to a drink, Governor."

"I shall carry off this money for to-night," Governor Tyrell said. "I cannot leave this drunken man in charge of all this money, but you, my son, and Captain Max had better be off. You have no time to lose. Even if Gibson should resign his claim, the creditors are very likely to oppose the sale of any of his negroes, unless by a sheriff's order. When you get to Washington take care my horses have a three days' rest, and drive them slowly home."

Williams was already in a drunken sleep. The Governor followed Max and Tyrell to the door.

Phil Ormsby, always ready to perform a driving feat, was holding the reins and hiding himself from observation. Sapphira and her children, and a large, awkward bundle of their effects, were thrust into the body of the carriage. Uncle Christopher closed the door with a quick slam and jumped up beside "Mas' Phil." Tyrell and Max mounted their horses, and the Governor returned to gather up the pile of money in the dining parlor, where Williams in his drunken sleep had rolled from the lounge on to the floor.

CHAPTER XVI.

> To have pursuit of honourable deed
> There is I know not what great difference,
> Between the vulgar and the noble seed,
> Which unto things of valarous pretence
> Seems to be born by native influence,
> As feats of armes and love to entertaine,
> But chiefly skill to ride seems a sciënce
> Proper to gentle blood.
>
> SPENSER: *Faërie Queene.*

THUS arranged, the carriage and its attendants proceeded on its way into the darkness. Phil and the horses seeming by instinct to avoid stumps, rocks, and mud-holes. After going some way down the road Phil checked his horses, and putting his head out for the first time, asked Tyrell whether he meant to cross the river by the ferry or the ford?

"By the ford if we can cross it," Tyrell replied; "I was apprehensive lest the recent rains had raised the waters and went to look at it when our relay of horses crossed the ferry this afternoon. The river is full and rising, but not 'out of ride,' as several persons have crossed it since the morning."

As they approached the place, where at the junction of the river road and turnpike stood the tavern by the ferry, they saw lights gleaming from the bar-room, and Tyrell pointing them out to Phil, asked if it seemed worth while to draw the attention of Jake Gibson, the master of the inn, by rousing up his ferryman, and whether they had not better try the ford, which was a couple of hundred yards further from the inn, and higher up the river.

"Try it yourself," said Phil. "If your father's horses will pull true I can take them across with the water over their backs, I reckon. But you can't swim a carriage over the river."

"Come on then, Phil. I'll pilot you across," said Tyrell.

They passed the tavern apparently unnoticed, driving noiselessly upon the grass at the road-side, and having reached the ford Phil drew up on the river's bank, at a spot that was sheltered from observation from the inn, and waited the result of the experiment of Tyrell.

As a resident of the neighborhood he knew the ford well. His gallant grey was well under his command, but nevertheless snorted and eyed the ford suspiciously as he was urged onward by his master's spur into the dark mass of rapid waters. Tyrell sat erect upon his horse, with his feet thrust out in the stirrups to their natural position, for he knew that there was danger in what he intended to attempt, and that it was necessary to keep a firm seat in the saddle. Most of the gentlemen in the neighborhood, when crossing fords, were in the habit of keeping their feet dry, by drawing them out of their stirrups and stretching them out in front, or crooking them up behind, and some of the most venturesome would draw their legs up under them and sit cross-legged, or tailor-fashion in the saddle, till it was a wonder how they could preserve their equilibrium. But Tyrell knew it was no time for such experiments, and preferred the position which would give him the greatest command over his horse, even at the cost of a thorough wetting. As at each step the flood rose high around him, he rose up in the saddle, and fixing his gaze earnestly upon his horse's head, just visible to Max in the moonlight, gathered his reins in a firmer grasp, and kept his horse diagonally across the current, his head well up the stream. He reached the middle of the river, and the way before him was probably not worse than that behind. The water became so deep that the back of the horse was barely visible, and the party on the bank wondered how the brave animal could keep his footing. The current was strong, as could be seen by the piling up—as it were—of the muddy water against the chest of the horse, with almost force sufficient, as it seemed, to have swept horse and rider down the stream entirely at its mercy. Thus they proceeded silently and slowly onward, the action of the horse entirely concealed from those on land, and as less and less of his neck remained visible Max expected every moment to see him lose his foot-hold and float down stream. But now the worst was passed, the horse's back rose, as it were, slowly out of the water, the rider relaxed his attitude of fixed attention, reached forward and patted his horse's neck, Uncle Christopher uttered an ejaculation of pious thankfulness, and Max and Philip Ormsby breathed more freely, as the moonlight shone upon the dripping sides of the brave animal who had so nobly borne himself. He acknowledged his master's caress with a neigh and toss of his head, and Tyrell waved his hand to the party left behind as he issued from the ford splashing the water right and left around him like a shower of bright sparkles in the moonlight. Max thought of William of Deloraine's midnight ride, and his passage of the mountain torrent, and repeated aloud:

"The warrior's very plume I say
Was draggled by the dashing spray,
Yet through good heart and our Ladye's grace
At length he gained the landing place."

Phil drew a long breath and said, "He has had a deep ride."

"Do you intend to attempt it?" asked Max.

"Yes, I reckon so," said Phil. "There is certainly some danger in it. Still I have crossed here with a carriage when the river was certainly as high, if not higher than it is now. By keeping some twenty yards higher up the stream than where he crossed, I reckon we shall find the water not so deep by six inches; these horses are half a hand higher than his, and with a firm hand and a cool head I reckon we may venture through."

"'Tain't allers the highes' horse, Mas' Phil," said Uncle Christopher, "dat is de safes' in de water. I'd liefer hab some on em with de ribber runnin' over dere backs 'mos', dan some other when it didn't reach the shoulder. Reckon though dese horses got good sperrit; dey ain't gwine to jibe, Mas' Phil, 'long as dey feel de bottom under 'em."

"But," exclaimed Max, "a horse can have no chance to swim in harness, and if these should lose their footing, it would be a desperate case, Phil, for your party."

"Better fall into de hands ob de Lord dan into de hands of man, Mas' Max, 'specially when dat man Mas' Gibson," said Christopher, raising his hat reverently.

"There is little or no drift-wood running," said Philip, who had been looking round him. "I believe I will try it;" and alighting, he threw Christopher the reins, while he commenced loosening the bearing-reins and martingales, and giving a critical examination to the state of the harness.

"Mas' Phil he done know what him 'bout," said Uncle Christopher to Max, and turning to Aunt Saph, made her put her feet up on the the seat of the carriage.

"Now then, Captain," said Phil Ormsby, resuming his place and pointing across the water; "you take notice of the remains of the old fish dam by that ripple running almost all the way over, we will keep immediately above that, and we shall have shallower water, I reckon, and a smoother bottom."

"All right," said Max; and the horses responding to Phil's admonition, boldly entered the water, encouraged by his voice, and the perilous passage was begun.

Max kept as close to the carriage as he could, so as to be able to render assistance in case it should be necessary, and watched attentively and admiringly the coolness and tact which Phil displayed in managing and directing his horses. No one spoke a word, and a half-smothered exclamation from Aunt Saph as the carriage jolted over the rough stones at the bottom of the river, was the only sound which broke upon the ear, save the dull roaring of the waters, and the splash of the horses. It was certainly an undertaking of great danger to attempt to cross the current, with a carriage loaded to its utmost capacity; but there were stout hearts and cool heads to guide the enterprise. As Phil supposed, the place that he selected for crossing was not so deep by six inches as that where Tyrell had crossed the ford; and in the slight eddy caused by the fish-dam, the water was smoother and the current less violent. They had reached the middle of the river, and the horses were tugging patiently at their heavy load, while the whole party began to breathe more freely, when Max's attention was attracted by a noise of shouting on the left bank of the river. He stopped—listened more attentively—and assuring himself that something unusual was going on, called out to Philip, who checked his horses, and taking a rapid glance behind him, exclaimed—

"By the gods, it's that party at the tavern, and I hear Gibson's voice above all the rest. See, they are making for the boat; they have noticed us, and perhaps have got wind of what we are doing, and they are going to try to cross the river and intercept us. They can do it too; for with this current running, they can put the boat across in five minutes. Well, Aunt Saph, what do you say to getting into Gibson's clutches after all? But you shan't if I can prevent his having you."

"But what's to be done?" said Max, "as you say they can get across the river before us; and even if they did not, they will raise a hue and cry after us, and it will not be long before we are overtaken. Blood might be spilled, and the consequences would become far more serious than we anticipated."

"There is but one thing to be done," said Phil, "and that is dangerous; but if you will undertake it, I think we can keep Mr. Gibson and his party on the other side of the river."

"What is it?" replied Max. "I'll do any thing to accomplish our object."

"You must swim your horse down the river, and cut the rope on which the boat works—they will then be unable to cross; and you have no time to lose, for they are about starting. Have you a knife long enough to cut a small-sized cable?"

"No—mine is only a penknife."

"Well, here, take Uncle Christopher's—he has a jack-knife, I am sure. Lend us your knife, old man;" and reaching out, Max took the knife from the old negro, and turned his horse's head down the stream without another word—Phil calling out after him,

"If you can get to the other shore, do so; but if you can't, make the best of your way back to Clairmont; we can take care of ourselves, if we can only keep the river between us and Gibson."

Max was not a man easily frightened, and having undertaken an enterprise he did not let himself see the dangers of it, except to guard against and overcome them. There was little time now for reflection, for the horse swimming in the direction of the current, was carried along with great rapidity, and all the rider's watchfulness and care were necessary to retain his seat in the saddle. But Max had received an English officer's thorough training in horsemanship, and with a light and steady hand he directed and sustained the struggles of his horse, keeping his eye on the outline of the rope which he could distinctly see stretched in a graceful bow from shore to shore, reaching about midway to within a few feet of the surface of the water. To this point he directed his course, and as he approached it, calculated whether he could reach the rope from his horse's back, and whether he might not be carried past it. But he was not long left in doubt, for in less time than it has taken me to describe, he found himself under it, and stretching out his hand above his head, seized fast hold upon it. And now a difficulty presented itself which he had not anticipated. The rope hung so high above his head that he could barely reach it with his outstretched hand, and to use the other in cutting it would oblige him to let go the reins, and, consequently, give up control of his horse. To keep the horse under him while he hung half suspended from the rope, would be impossible, and he saw at once that he must give up the horse and take the chance of reaching the shore without him. So swinging out of the saddle, he raised himself to the level of the rope, and sustaining himself by one arm over it, he drew the knife from his pocket and commenced his work, while Black Mike, free from his master's control, turned his head towards the shore, and struck out boldly to reach it.

In the meantime, Gibson's party had freed the boat from its fastenings, and not perceiving the object of Max's exertions, had already commenced the pastage of the river. Max saw their approach and worked with might and main, but the rope was several inches in diameter, made of hard, closely-twisted hemp, and not to be severed as easily as he supposed. When, however, the boat was within a hundred feet of him, the rope parted with a loud crack, and Max found himself in the water. The men in the boat now perceived the object of his manœuvre, but had only time to vent a few disappointed curses, when the peril of their own situation required their attention. The boat, deprived of the support of the rope, and being broad-side to the current, fell rapidly down the stream, and there seemed every probability of the party being carriod down the Shennandoah on a voyage of discovery, but fortunately the tackling which fastened the boat became entangled in the main rope, the end of which, loosened by Max's exertions, swung around within reach of them, and they lost no time in making it fast, thus securing a connection with the shore, by means of which they were enabled to make a safe landing. They never thought of rendering assistance to Max—or if they did, the thought was suppressed as soon as entertained, for in their chagrin at the disappointment he had given them, they would gladly have seen him sink to rise no more. His first thought on finding himself in the water was a feeling of satisfaction that the progress of the carriage could not now be interrupted, and casting a glance towards the right bank of the river, he saw it had reached the shallow water, and was within a short distance of the shore. His next thought was of his own situation, which was, indeed, very perilous. He was a bold and expert swimmer, and under favorable circumstances would not have feared to undertake the classic feat of swimming the Hellespont, if Veronica had been on the other shore, but now he was much fatigued by his exertions in clinging to and cutting the rope, and felt the necessity of husbanding all his strength, for the struggle before him. He was near the middle of the river, about two hundred and forty yards from either bank, and as he suffered himself to drift down with the current, hesitated for a few moments, as to which course he should take.

He observed that the current set in towards the left, caused by a bend in the river below, and recollecting that Black Mike had taken that direction, he thought the animal's instinct an excellent guide, and determined to follow the same course. He did not waste his strength in useless efforts to cross the current, but making up his mind for a long swim, suffered himself to be borne along with it, satisfied that if he could keep himself afloat long enough he should be able gradually to make his way to the land. He might have to swim a mile, or more, before this could be accomplished, but he felt himself freshened and strengthened by his immersion in the water, and struck out vigorously and fearlessly.

As he floated down the stream he saw the party in the boat accomplish a landing and linger on the shore, apparently watching to see what had become of him. He did not suppose they could see him, and never thought of trying to make himself heard in the hope of assistance, for he knew the character of Gibson and his associates, and felt that no assistance could be expected from them. He thought at one time he heard Tyrell's voice shouting his name from the right bank of the river, but the sound came upon his ear so faintly that he concluded it was mere fancy, and did not attempt a reply. He knew that neither Phil nor Tyrell had it in their power to render him any help, and did not care to give them useless anxiety—besides he saw with much satisfaction that he was making considerable progress, and felt quite confident in his own ability to reach the land.

A bend in the river formed a headland jutting out from the left side, and as Max saw its outline distinctly visible before him, he made up his mind to attempt a landing at that spot, knowing that if he were swept past it, the current would set in towards the other shore, and the dangers of his situation would be very much increased. This headland was now not more than a couple of hundred yards distant, directly before him, and he kept his course steadily towards it. As he advanced, however, he found that the current was bearing him off to the right, and as he found his strength failing him, the hope of being able to land on the headland seemed more remote—still he struck out boldly, making every exertion to counteract the tendency of the current, and still made considerable progress towards the shore. He lessened the space between it and himself by more than half the distance he had to swim, but alas, found that the current, stronger than he, was bearing him round the point, and would soon carry him out to the middle of the stream again. He kept his head directly towards the shore—determined to make a desperate effort to reach it before he was carried past the point—and soon exhausted his little remaining strength in a useless struggle with that powerful, rélentless current, which seemed fated to bear him on to "that bourne whence no traveller returns." He was not more than thirty yards from the river bank, and the boughs of the large sycamores which fringe it might be reached in less distance, but while he made one yard in that direction by his exertions, the current carried him down three, and at this rate of progress he saw, despondingly, that he would be swept past the point before he could reach it. He still struck out boldly, but it was hoping against hope; his over-strained strength was spent, his feeble limbs refused their office, his heart sank within him. After all his efforts, to perish within reach almost of safety!—one prayer to God—one thought of Veronica—one pang of regret for the bright world he was to leave for ever—a rushing in his ears—a gurgling in his throat, and he went down in his agony.

But he was not doomed to die thus, though Death was close beside him. As he was carried down the stream he struck against something, which he had consciousness enough to grasp and try to raise his head above the water. He succeeded in doing so; a breath of air revived him, and he found he was lodged among the sunken branches of a tree, which formerly stood on the margin of the stream, but having been undermined by the action of the water, had fallen along the bottom of the river, holding out its friendly arms to save him from destruction. He made himself secure in his new position, returned thanks to God for his almost miraculous preservation, and paused to recover his strength before making any further exertion. To reach the shore was a matter of little difficulty; the branches of the tree stretched almost to the surface of the water, and were so intertwined as to afford him a secure hold, and he worked his way from one to another until he came to the main trunk, where he was so much out of the current as to be able to walk along it until he reached the shallow water, through which he waded to the shore, and again stood safe on the left bank of the river.

CHAPTER XVII.

Oh! they will murder thee!
It may be so,
But I hope better things; yet this is sure,
That they *shall* murder me ere make me go
The way that is not my way for an inch.
H. TAYLOR: *Philip Van Arteveld.*

THE struggle between Death and Life was at an end, and Lif had won it. Once in the existence of each of us, the pale Ange will have his hour of victory. Will it be an everlasting triumph —or will the Angel of Life, shouting the battle-cry, "Thank be to God on high, who giveth us the victory through our Lor Jesus Christ," rise at the moment of defeat and snatch us fror the power of the enemy?

Max walked slowly up the bank of the stream, wonderin what had become of Black Mike; and after going a couple o hundred yards, was agreeably surprised to find his gallant stee quietly feeding on the grass, which grew along the bank, an apparently waiting for his master; he had landed at a poin much higher up the stream. Max found him fresh and gay, an returned with a kindly pat the affectionate nicker with whicl Mike recognized his master. He mounted, and was preparin to set out for Clairmont, when his attention was attracted by th hoarse cries of the rowdies on the bank two or three hundre yards above, apparently making an examination, to see whethe he had landed on that side of the river. They had lighted pine torches, which threw a lurid glare over the dark water, while the moon, peeping in and out amongst the clouds, left deeper darkness for each fitful gleam, with which she silvered the ripple of the old fish-dam higher up the river. As Max sat on his horse, making up his mind what he had better do, and watching their next movements, the shouts grew louder and more fierce, and there appeared to be increasing excitement among the rowdies at the Ferry. Suddenly Max heard a horse galloping furiously, and drawing up a little on one side, prepared to let the rider pass him. It was Williams, who had been roused suddenly from his drunken sleep, and vaguely recollecting what had passed, and finding no money lying upon the table where he had left it, and Governor Tyrell gone, maddened by drink, had taken it into his head that he was robbed; and now, with his coat off and head bare, was mounted on a stout plough-horse, galloping like a madman after the party. He passed Max and saw him, but could not check himself in mid career. As soon as he could do so, he turned his horse's head across the road, so as to block the passage, and raised an Indian yell, which was answered by the party.

Max perceiving he was thus hemmed in, struck spurs into Black Mike. There was a farm road, leading to a mill almost in front of him. He turned into it at full speed, and in a very few moments the whole hunt turned in after him. After passing through the first gate, Max and Mike found themselves in a corn-field, across which the rider (used to steeple-chases and fox-hunts in Old England) guided his horse diagonally in the direction of the turnpike. A leap over a low fence brought them on to the turnpike, with their pursuers far behind. Max drew his rein and listened for their voices. They were coming on, but he thought they would probably give up the chase after they reached the highway; nevertheless he shook his rein and put Mike into a canter. But soon he heard their horse-hoofs, hard and fast, increasing in speed as they came nearer: a hand-gallop was not enough. Max was brave as man could be. For one moment he checked his horse, determined to confront them; but it was no bravery to meet a dozen drunken, infuriated men at night, in a strange country. Once more he touched his horse's flank, and the gallop was increased to Black Mike's utmost fleetness. The horse had travelled twenty miles before that day, and Max, willing to spare his favorite steed, had sent another horse ahead to meet him at the top of the mountain; nevertheless, notwithstanding his extraordinary exertions, the noble animal put forth his utmost strength, and again his speed and mettle distanced the pursuers.

Forward they went, still at this desperate gallop; at every pause the clang of horses' hoofs was heard behind. Many times Max doubted whether it would not be better to turn at bay, and meet Judge Lynch—and had he been an American he would probably have done it; but he had no acquaintance with his worship, and less faith in his equity than those have who live in districts over which he occasionally presides. At length he approached Fighterstown, and felt relieved as the negro opened the turnpike gate, and seemed to admit him through its pale into the security of civilization. He rode slowly through the dim and quiet street. For two miles he had heard the sound of no pursuing feet; and, whereas his first purpose had been to put up for the remainder of the night at the tavern, it seemed to be so nearly dawn that he made up his mind not to stop short of home. But as he walked his weary horse up the hill before you reach the avenue to Clairmont, a hideous yell burst suddenly upon the silence in the direction of the sleeping town.

It was too late now to turn back, and Max pushed onward, to seek the advice or claim the protection of Mr. Morrisson. He galloped up the avenue. His first act on dismounting was to take the bridle and saddle from Black Mike and fling them on the grass, and then he rapped loudly at the closed front door. It was this noise which, in my dream, had startled me in Westminster Abbey. I sprang up in my bed, and heard not only quick steps on the porch, and a loud knocking, but a murmur of hoarse voices in the distance, where Fighterstown lay white and calm under the summer moon.

It was about three o'clock. I threw open the window and looked out. Max stood upon the porch, looking down the turnpike, and counting his pursuers as they came up from the town; the horse lay rolling on the grass; the sounds towards Fighterstown grew more distinct. I heard mens' cries and horses galloping.

"For God's sake, Molly," cried Max, "where is Mr. Morrisson? Call him up and let him open the door."

Before I could close the window and obey him, Veronica, in her white dressing-gown, with her red Indian cashmere wrapped around her, had glided from the room and opened the hall-door.

"What is it, Max?" she said. "What have you done? Are you in any danger?"

"For heaven's sake," he cried, "go in. Where's Morrisson?"

"He is gone to Laurie's mill."

"And there is nobody to protect you but me; and I have brought that drunken rabble here!" he cried; "I who know too little of the character of these people or their designs, or even the cause of their pursuit, to be your defender. Let me go, Veronica—let me go, I say," for she had seized his arm with both her hands, and was trying to draw him into the house, "and I will meet them in the avenue."

"Max," she cried, "come in. They will not attack a house where women are; and we will send for help. Only let me speak with them, and remain passive; it is a case where women can act better than men. Go up stairs,and for all our sakes, keep quiet. These men, let them be drunk or angry, will not hurt a woman."

By this time every creature in the house was in the hall. Mr. Parker roused from his sleeping-place was leaning over the staircase. Cousin Virginia stood with her back against the door of her house. Mary Louisa was putting a bar across it. Max was seized upon by all the women, and Veronica ran up-stairs to Mr. Parker, imploring him to go to Fighterstown and bring us succor.

Veronica imploring, lovely as she was, in that red shawl and white drapery, could not implore in vain.

"You must go through the woods," she said, "and over the fences. Keep to the right of the house. They are coming up the avenue. Bring any one who will assist with you. Bring the Colonel, he is a justice of the peace. Mr. Parker we depend upon you."

"Just so," he replied. "I don't like leaving you, though."

"My cousin, Capt. Mandeville, is here, and will take good care of us."

"Well, now—I don't know as he can take much care of himself. I tell you what, Miss, he has gotten himself into a tight fix, I reckon."

But in a minute or two he was out of the house by the back porch; and striking into the woods, went on his errand, unperceived we hoped by the party of excited rowdies who came straggling up the avenue. Within doors, several servants who had come hastily from their "quarter," were, under Max's directions, barricading windows and doors. Cousin Virginia was giving rapid orders, and nobody had time to attend to her. Wallace, who knew where fire-arms were kept, produced a bowie-knife, belonging to Weston Carter, and a great pair of unserviceable horse-pistols; the little girls were crying with fright, and aunt Edmonia, in a queer night coif, sat trembling in her chair, wringing her hands and groaning aloud.

"Veronica," said Max, stopping her as she was drawing a large table, greatly too heavy for her strength, to barricade the door, "you must go away quickly. Go to your room, and let me act. I must clear the hall at once. These people, unless I go out to them, will break open the door."

Veronica shrieked and threw herself before him.

"Max! I entreat you!—You do not understand these people. A woman will do it better than you. The worst Virginian has consideration for a woman. There will be help in a few moments. They might tear you in pieces. Think of those to whom your life is precious. Oh! for the love of heaven, Max!"

"Will *you* care, Veronica?—Will *you* care?" he said, bitterly.

"I did not mean that," she said, growing cold, as she remembered her position. "Come up-stairs, let us all come up. If they break open the door we will stand at the head of the stairs. They will not hurt women."

We went up stairs, for in her excitement her air of command was irresistible, and we obeyed her as one born to rule.

"Where is Max?" she said, when we found ourselves at the door of our room. "Molly, implore him to keep quiet. It is the hardest part that can be assigned to a man."

As she spoke she threw wide open a window that opened on the top of the porch, a movement for which I was quite unprepared; she stepped from it and stood before the crowd. I followed her.

There was a lull among them as she suddenly appeared. Some had dismounted, and were standing on the porch. Some were trying the weak door, whose hinges were not likely to resist. Others had gone round to the back of the house, but they all came to the front and stood upon the grass, when we stepped out and confronted them. There were about a dozen men by this time, for all along the road as they came on they had called upon recruits. Most of them were young, all, more or less, excited by whisky, all influenced by the strongest passion that excites men in a slave state, and some of them were honest, for believing Max had been concerned in the escape of slaves, they looked upon him as an abolitionist and incendiary. Foremost in the group was William Williams, falsifying, by word and deed, his own acts, with blasphemy and violence. He was foremost in calling Max incendiary and abolitionist, and appeared in the character of injured slave-owner with great effect, declaring that the negroes run off, were his property. Gibson, the tavern-keeper, sat on his horse, excited, but more clear-headed and stern. He also declared he owned the negroes.

"What do you want, gentlemen?" said Veronica, her clear tones breaking on the silence that was made as they looked up at her.

"We want that Englishman who has been running off slaves —Will Williams' slaves—(here several voices broke out, and cried 'Jack Gibson's!') Tell him to come out! We don't want to molest you ladies, but we ain't goin' to have strangers coming here and meddling with our institution. We ain't going to have any foreigner interfering with our niggers. He must quit it. Let Englishmen and abolitionists stay at home, and look after their white niggers, who are starving in their manufacturing towns. Send him down to us. We'll teach him a thing or two."

"It is false, gentlemen, that my cousin had any intention of interfering with property belonging to any man but himself. The servants in question have been purchased for the estate of Mr. Lomax. My cousin, Capt. Mandeville, and I, are heirs to that estate. We had a perfect right to send our servants to Washington. It is you who are interfering with the rights of ownership. If Mr. Williams or Mr. Gibson think otherwise, they can sue for damages in the next court at Fighterstown. I am ashamed of you, gentlemen—ashamed of my countrymen, who attack women and strangers. Let me beg you to do us no further violence, but disperse, and let us alone."

"Look here, now; just you go in. What are you defending *him* for?" Will Williams cried, and laughed a drunken laugh, the echoes of which caught the ear of Joel Parker, half way upon his road to Fighterstown.

At this moment Veronica felt an arm thrown firmly round her, and she was drawn into the house by Max. The dawning day flashed its light upon his face and Will Williams laughed the louder.

"Forgive me this liberty," he said. "But that was no place for a woman, Veronica, nor can I suffer myself to be dishonored by allowing any woman to put herself forward in my defence. You must not interfere in this matter."

"*Must not* . . . .!" It was different from Max's usual tone, she thought he was displeased and hurt, and the idea of his dissatisfaction moved her.

"Will you take care of yourself then?" she said, laying her hands upon his arm with a soft pleading grace. He seized those hands and kissed them, and wrung them, without answering, by which movement the advantage he had gained was lost, Veronica resumed her coldness. He had time to feel the chill that came over her warmth of manner, before he sprang two steps at a time down stairs and opened the front door.

"If there is any man among you who calls himself a gentleman, or who retains any of the feelings popularly believed to belong to gentlemen in Virginia," he cried, "he will restrain those drunken scoundrels who may desire to molest these women. Disperse or I shall fire among you."

As he stood there alone, tall and calm (to all appearance), though with quick beating at his heart, as he thought how drunken wretches pressing through that door, which Mary Louisa, at his orders, was again making fast on the inside, might profanely rush into the presence of her he loved; the golden glowing sun scattering the clouds and mists that lingered in the train of darkness, rose red and majestical over the crest of the mountain.

"One—two; I give you warning, I shall fire. Three!"

Then rose a yell, for somebody was hurt, and the crowd answered with a flash; a ball glanced against his heavy horse-pistol, and without wounding him, struck the side of the front door. Gibson had fired it. The crowd perceiving he was now disarmed pressed forward in a body on the porch. He struggled with the foremost ones—one against half a dozen. They over powered him and dragged him from the porch. Veronica from our window saw their violence. Her limbs trembled under her, she gave one loud, wild shriek, rising louder than the yells and imprecations of the crowd, and then was silent, watching, as the rising sun lighted their faces, if there were any one among the group whom she had ever seen before. Suddenly she saw the overseer of Jeff Wayland's place, who had been roused from his bed by the cries of "abolitionist," and had hurried with several others, with no knowledge of the case, to lend his aid to exterminate such vermin.

"Oh! Mr. Wylde, save him!" she shrieked—"save him, Mr. Wylde. Oh! gentlemen, for God's sake listen before you act. Hear what he has to say!"

"What do you want me to do, Miss Lomax?" said Wylde, coming close up to the house, and speaking under the window, unheeded by the crowd without, so great was the excitement and confusion.

"Get delay—delay," she said, "at any price. There will be help from the town soon. I have sent a messenger!"

Whilst she said this there came help. As the pistol had been fired, horsemen coming along the highway, put their horses to a quicker gallop and hurried to the rescue. It was a party led by Tyrell. He and Phil had been so anxious to ascertain the fate of Max, that in spite of their own danger they had lingered on the right bank of the river; and, when they discovered vengeance against Max was set on foot, and that a presentment before Judge Lynch was in question, Tyrell left the carriage under the command of Phil, and without a word turned the head of his weary horse, and plunged again into the river. This time he made no attempt to find the ford, but swam across the current; and in a few minutes landed safely.

A negro at the tavern told what had taken place, and he galloped steadily towards Fighterstown, falling in along the road with gentlemen on horseback, roused by the rowdies who had stopped at all the farms along the road, to call upon their male inhabitants to lend their aid in putting down an attempt to run off slaves—that worst of high treason, in their eyes, against the institutions of their state, and the interests of their community. To all these, Tyrell in few words explained the facts. A few after hearing him turned homeward to their beds, but the greater part, indignant against Gibson and Will Williams, joined him in pursuit of their party.

For a long time they heard no sounds ahead, only the tramp of their own horses. After a while, however, they began to hear occasional hoarse noises. As they passed through Fighterstown its inhabitants were all afoot. The exasperated rowdies had pulled up before the tavern and yelled until they roused the landlord and obtained more liquor. The colonel, who was justice of the peace, was lingering in the street, hesitating on which side to place the majesty of the law—a few words from Tyrell decided him. Tyrell's party was swelled by all the respectability of the place; as much of it, at least, as could be mounted at a moment's notice. They hurried on to Clairmont, passing Joel Parker on their way, who was approaching the village from an opposite quarter.

Some of the gentlemen impetuously galloped straight into the midst of the rioters, scattering and dispersing the drunken rowdies. On Tyrell's ear, Veronica's wild shriek, as she beheld Max seized, rang like the blast of a war trumpet.

"Cowardly ruffians!" he cried, "disperse! The colonel will be here almost immediately, with a party of constables. I know your ringleaders! Release Captain Mandeville."

There were confused cries about Judge Lynch and "abolitionists."

"Bring him before a magistrate, and arrest me too, for I am as guilty as he. I wish to have this matter sifted and brought to light before the whole community," cried Tyrell. "And if it costs me all the value of my farm I will punish the ringleaders of this disgraceful proceeding."

"Bring him down to the court house and confine him in the jail. *There* he will be safe," said some of the party.

"Yes," exclaimed Max, "give me fair play—a fair examination is all I ask. Stay with the women Tyrell."

But the alarm had spread to Lawrie's Mill, and Mr. Morrisson arrived at that moment, so that Tyrell left him to guard Clairmont, and placing Max upon Mr. Morrisson's horse, rode by his side, with a great body-guard of friends and foes, into the village.

CHAPTER XVIII.

Reserv'dness is a mighty friend
  To form and virtue too,
A shining merit should pretend
  To such a star as you.
Maintain a modest kind of state,
  'Tis graceful in a maid;
It does at least respect create,
  And makes the fools afraid.
Let baffled lovers call it pride,
Pride's an excess o' the better side.

[COTTON, 1660.

CLAIRMONT was left with trampled grass and broken window-panes to its inhabitants; and Veronica, while every body else was pointing out evidences of devastation, or relating with one voice his or her share in the night's experience, went up into our chamber, where I found her an hour after, kneeling by the bed, with her face buried in the bed-clothes. When she rose up from prayer she was the calmest person in the place—the only one of us who was not boastful of experiences, though she had been the only one exposed to real danger. I saw her after breakfast, patting Black Mike, who was grazing in the yard, apparently not the worse for his night's work; and I heard her asking Tommy Tad to inquire if his Uncle Israel had seen him fed that morning.

Max meanwhile was at the court-house, undergoing an examination before the colonel. The charge preferred against him was for firing at William Williams, with intent to kill, maim, wound, &c. Tyrell was involved in the abduction business, and Williams and Jake Gibson knew their own interests too well to bring any action in which Tyrell's wide-spread popularity would damage their cause. A man's character is worth dollars and cents to him in a small community, where every juryman sets his own value upon evidence; and so the business before the magistrates ended by Max being bound over for trial at the October court, which would be held at Charlestown.

When this business was over, the presiding magistrate, who was also the militia colonel, post-master, and keeper of the dry goods emporium of the village, came up to Max, as he and Joel Parker were standing on the steps of the court-house, having a few last words with Tyrell, who was going home.

"If you'd take my advice," said he, "capt'n, you would quit the neighborhood till this matter is blown over. There are persons who accuse you of abolition views, and who would not be sorry to see you get into difficulty with the rowdies who have taken up this business. If you were as favorably known in this community as Mr. Tyrell, I should advise you to stand your ground, and shoot one or two of these rascals, as you are not a professor of religion, I understand, and so would not object to fight on Christian principles."

"I hope I am sufficiently religious not to desire to shoot a man on any principles," said Max; "but I am not afraid of threats, and have no intention of leaving the neighborhood."

"Well, then," rejoined the colonel, "I reckon you had best put a couple of pistols in your pocket, and let it be understood that you go armed."

"Well, now, I reckon that warn't bad advice, of the old gentleman's," Joel Parker said, as the colonel turned back into the court-room. "I live beyond here a piece, and I am going right away up into the mountain. I reckon, capt'n, you had better come and stay a month or so at my place: I'll fix you up the best I can. I can give you elegant parched corn, and I've got lots of persimmons.

"The temptation is not extravagant," said Tyrell, in an aside to Max, as he got upon his horse, and bent over his side to fix the martingale. "We shall hear from Phil at Washington, I hope, in a day or two. I told him to write as soon as he had placed Uncle Christopher and the rest under the protection of Mr. Gregg, an honorable senator, who is my father's great friend, and who, when the affair has been arranged, will see them all booked for Philadelphia. My father will ride over to-morrow, and see Gibson about this business. Gibson's position in the community is such that he cannot afford to quarrel with respectable persons."

So saying, Tyrell rode away at a brisk trot, and disappeared under a grove of walnut-trees, spared in the middle of Fighterstown, in the unenclosed play-ground of the academy.

Max and Joel Parker prepared to walk to Clairmont. They would have done better to cross this plot, and avoid the main street of the muddy little town; but they were not acquainted with the short-cuts, being both of them strangers.

They therefore walked together into the main street, at the corner of which stood a grocery. As they approached, Will Williams, who was drinking there with some others of his set, got up from a store-box upon which he was sitting.

"I reckon, I know a trick 'll serve you yet capt'n," said he coming out into the street and squaring his arms. "Promise to pay me ten thousand dollars cash down, and I'll sign you the claim to Oatlands, which on no other terms are you going to get. Lord! what a fool you were to swagger out here like an Englishman, thinking a thorough-bred Virginia girl would snap at you like a duck at a June-bug."

"Stand aside, sir. Let me pass," said Max, for Williams was balancing himself in the middle of the side-walk, and Max did not choose to go out of the road.

Williams made some gestures of impertinence, Max knocked him down, and stepped out of the path, while Joel Parker strode over him, as he laid prostrate, and they passed on their way, without a word, through the main street of Fighterstown.

The friends of Williams picked him up and carried him into the grocery. Max and Parker heard drunken curses, hoarse and loud, bawled after them as they went along the highway.

At Clairmont, standing on the porch, was Mr. Morrisson.

"Where is that rascal, Williams, captain?" said he, 'see what his gang has done to my plantation—trampled my grass and loosened my door-hinges."

"Reckon you'll have him up here before long," said Joel Parker. "The capt'n ran at him just as savage as a trout runs at a bait, and knocked him down as we came out of Fighterstown. If I'd been the capt'n I'd have whipped him when I got a chance. I wouldn't have left a grease spot of him.'

"I gave him enough to quiet him," said Max.

"Enough to make him mad—and not enough to make him quit it," Joel Parker said. "Mad! he's as angry as a stump-tailed bull in fly-time."

Max laughed at the comparison. He caught sight of Veronica's head at the moment. She was sitting in the drawing-room, busied about some trifle of woman's work, looking so still, so cool, so feminine, as she sat in her white dress, with her eyes bent on her sewing, that it was hard to conceive she was the Veronica of the night before. Max forgot Williams and Joel Parker, and the annoyances of the court-house, as he gazed at her, though only her head and ear, and one of her eyes, with its soft lashes, bending towards her cheek, could be seen above the window-frame. He gathered a red rose from a cluster that climbed up a pillar of the porch, and went up to the window and offered it to her. She put out her hand and took the rose, and laid it down beside her.

"Wear it Veronica," he said. "I have been thinking as I watched you, how much I wished to see it in your hair."

A blush mounted on her cheek, and words unuttered seemed to tremble on her lips, but with a laugh as careless as pride could make it, she replied, "It is easy to gratify any one who makes so trifling a request," and putting up her hands, she fixed it in her hair.

There was a pause. "Are you not tired," he said, "after such a dreadful night? I cannot blame myself enough for having brought those ruffians to disturb you."

"Ask cousin Virginia how she feels," replied Veronica. "She has been on the verge of hysterics ever since the danger was over. Some people expend all their heroism in a great effort, and when the fever is past, lie crushed and languishing. My excitement passes gradually off, and is not yet over. But you must be exhausted, cousin Max. Let me get you something to eat? I was wanting in Virginia hospitality not to think of it before."

"No," said Max, "I had some breakfast in the court-house, which the colonel sent to me. I had some sleep there, too. I was apprehensive of tobacco stains if I took up my quarters on the floor, and so bivouacked upon the judge's table."

"Mandeville," cried Mr. Morrisson, at this moment, "Mr. Parker and I have been discussing your assault upon young Williams. If you stay here this house is not safe from another attack. I shall have to collect a guard of gentlemen to protect my family, which will be very inconvenient to the friends that I might call upon, as it is just harvest time. I do not know what to do about it. I recommend you to take advantage of an invitation from Mr. Parker, and go with him to Rappahannock for a while, till this matter has blown over."

"To Rappahannock, sir!" said Max, "what should I do in Rappahannock?"

"You endanger my property, and my family," said Mr. Morrisson, "and it is very foolish upon your part to expose yourself to the anger of these persons, who will not stick at anything."

"I had best take you along with me to Rappahannock, if you will come," said Mr. Parker, in a hospitable way. "It's a mighty pretty country 'way yonder where I come from. In another week or two we'll shoot a deer."

Then, observing that Max hesitated, he continued:

"I reckon you'd best make up your mind right away, and we'll set out cap'en, afore any of them rowdies get about again. They'd have a precious time if they was to attack my house. They'd have to come up a narrow pass, single file, where we'd pick 'em off, one by one, as they came up, I reckon."

"You are very kind, Mr. Parker, but . . . ."

"Now, then, I'll ask Miss Veronica what *she* says," said Joel Parker, turning to our cousin. "Don't you think, now, he ought to, Miss?—let us hear what you say."

"I am of Mr. Parker's opinion," said Veronica, in a low voice. "I think that by staying here, he may expose himself, and, perhaps, others, in a very needless way."

Max looked at her, till the blood rose in her cheek.

"You advise me to accept, then?" said he.

"Indeed I do," she said. "It is my best advice to you."

"And when may I come back to Clairmont?"

"When Molly wishes it," said Veronica.

"When Molly wishes what?" said Max, trembling himself, as his fate trembled in the balance.

"When Molly wishes to return to England. Molly," she said, turning to me, as I came in, "there is a proposition before us which involves the safety of Max; persuade him to adopt it if possible."

Cousin Virginia Morrisson came in too, and when she heard that further mischief might perhaps be afoot, and that Mr. Parker proposed to take Max with him into the mountains, she was pressing in her advice to him to go—were it only for a few days—into Rappahannock county. I seconded cousin Virginia, for I, too, was seriously alarmed.

"The only thing to be apprehended now," said Mr. Parker, aside to Mr. Morrisson, "is that they should waylay him on the route. I recommend that the young ladies should ride along with us a piece. I reckon they won't much mind going."

I overheard him, and carried the proposition in a whisper to Veronica.

"I do not see," said she, aloud, "why we may not ride as far as Front Royal, if you will go with us and bring us back, Mr. Morrisson. Molly, can you ride twenty-five miles before dark, and come back to-morrow morning?"

"Oh! yes! indeed I can."

"Come, now,—that's real elegant of you," cried Joel Parker. "I like that in you,—you're an old soldier."

"If you consult the wishes of us *all*," said Veronica, with a slight emphasis, turning to Max, "you will accept the hospitality of Mr. Parker. I hope," she went on to say, in her quiet way, "that Mike has mettle enough left for another journey. We shall ride slowly—it will not be like the race that he ran yesterday. Mr. Morrisson, will you call to Uncle Israel, and tell him to get up our ponies? Molly, let us get ready."

"It is time we were off," said Mr Parker.

Cousin Virginia protested we must have "a snack." Veronica hurried me up-stairs to put on my riding-dress, and pack our necessaries into saddle-bags, to be carried by Mr. Morrisson, and thus it was arranged, almost without the will or consent of Max, that he should become the guest of the eccentric mountaineer, who had dropped, the day before, into our company.

Oh! how bitterly he repented the self-confidence which had anticipated no difficulties in his courtship, which had looked upon Veronica as a girl, young and facile—easy to be won. Had he known more of her, the six months he had stayed in England after her uncle's death, would have been passed in endeavoring to render himself acceptable to her. Fool! to have based his pretensions upon her uncle's will! Fool! to have thought that the immature girl who had returned the love he paid her in her teens, would retain her regard for him when she became a queen amongst women! Fool! to have lingered in his courtship, dreaming she could be won by a few lover's speeches, a few attentions, a little offering of his pride made to her vanity, a gift to be resumed when the wedding day was over, and the prize was won.

And yet the thought arose and tempted him, that until evening he might be riding at her side, and that during those hours, an opportunity of testing his fate might be afforded him. And at the prospect his heart beat fiercely in his breast, though it sickened as it beat, when he thought of the probability of losing her.

"But I cannot go without leaving some word or message for Mr. Williams," he said, suddenly.

"What do you want to say to William Williams, I should like to know?" said Mr. Morrisson.

"I wish to let him know where I have gone, in order to protect your house," said Max. He will not seek me here if he knows that I am not to be found, and in the next place I wish to tell him where to find me. You will not object to my informing him that I shall be your guest, Mr. Parker?"

"I rather presume not capt'n. Let him bring on his rowdies. We could pick off the whole gang of 'em, one by one. I reckon we would make the fur fly," said the belligerent Parker.

CHAPTER XIX.

> I turn to thee, and say, "Ah! loveliest friend
> That this the meed of all my toils may be,
> To have a home—an English home—and thee."
>
> COLERIDGE.

WHILE Max sealed a note he had written to Will Williams, lest any suspicion of flight should attach to his departure, Veronica and I stood on the porch waiting for the gentlemen. Mr. Parker, with his saddle-bags over his arm, and in a full dress suit of black, was standing by the horses. He helped me to mount Angelo, while Max put Veronica upon her pony. She did not oppose his riding by her side, thinking, indeed, that her presence would protect him more effectually than mine, should any violence be offered him.

They rode under the green trees, through the summer-woods, and both were silent. The heart of the young man stirred with the breath of life and love like the leaves that waved above him. He was more nearly alone with her than he had been at any moment since his arrival, for Mr. Parker was bent on paying court to me, and kept me as much as possible in the rear, while Mr. Morrisson upon his long-tailed colt, being a heavy man, was always behind the rest of his party. The opportunity Max sought was afforded him. Pensive—her sweet face shaded by her riding-hat—she rode beside him. Her right hand almost touched him.

What would he not have given to guess one of her thoughts? One of those thoughts which lie too deep, in the deep waters of the heart, to be drawn up to the surface by every bucket, and spilled carlessly abroad in idle words. Serene and beautiful, did her daily life flow, scarcely ruffled, over these hidden thoughts, catching the reflection of passing influences,—as the brook reflects the trees that wave upon its banks, and the birds that skim over its surface, and the colors of the skyscape, as the sun goes down?

Max was not accustomed to draw analogies. At this moment his own feeling was, that he had neither need of speech nor wish for it. He imagined what he would say to her when he broke silence. His enraptured fancy imagined the possibility of that gauntleted right hand which held the riding-whip, being laid in his firm grasp, while the beautiful fair face was turned away with the sweet shyness of surrender. And then that other awful possibility which seemed like an eclipse of life! Max thought nothing of the loss of fortune and position now. His thoughts were only of the inexpressible happiness of knowing that the fair woman at his side was to continue his for ever, or the bitterness of that other alternative—an alternative which would make him wish that he had never been born. He thought how fondly he would cherish her if the little hand were laid in his, how the weakness of her womanhood should be shielded by his strength. How he would keep her safely from all danger, as she leaned upon his arm, and looked up to him for manly tenderness and kind protection. He thought how every noble purpose in his heart would ripen into fruit of noble action. He thought of the blessedness of coming home from the rude bustle of the race of life, and being welcomed under the shadow of his roof by those kind eyes. Queen, as she was, to him she should be doubly queen. "Queen of my life!" he called her in his frantic thoughts, and looked at her with earnest eyes, when he had named her thus, as she sat beautiful and calm, at his side, on her white pony.

Still they rode on in silence, Max, busied with his thoughts, did not perceive the flight of time, or if he did, he felt the present silence would explain itself in the question and answer of the future.

Oh! solemn silence, when the earthly destiny of two who may be one, hangs trembling in the balance. And one of them may perhaps be walking heedlessly beneath that trembling fate, while if she knew what was to come, prayer (if she ever prayed at all) would rise up to the lips so soon to utter the answer which will bring the highest human joy, or deepest human sorrow. Max felt inclined to pray. The situation awed him. Every holy feeling in his heart was stirred within him. There were aspirations after goodness and perfection in his heart, such as he had never been conscious of since nursery days. "My Veronica," he called her in his thoughts, "my own Veronica!" And his heart leaped up as he said it, for though the words had not been uttered with his voice, they startled him so much that it almost seemed as if she must have heard them.

At length she broke the silence. It was only a question about the adventures of the night. He answered her briefly, without any of the assiduity of attention with which a lover in less pre-occupied moments answers the questions of his mistress, and they relapsed into silence. At last Max spoke. "Listen to me," he said, "cousin Veronica." She turned her eyes on him, and the old coldness settled on her features.

Max was chilled by her look. Instead of the warm words which he had just been saying to her in his thoughts, he became constrained, and approached his question very differently from the way in which he had addressed her in his heart, but a few moments before.

"It may be some weeks before I see you again, cousin Veronica; and though I risk your displeasure—perhaps your fortune, if I speak, it seems to me but right that we should part with some better understanding with each other."

What could be colder? and Max felt that it was cold; but the cold look in her eyes took from him all his confidence. He began to feel that it was but a forlorn hope that he had staked his all upon.

"It seems to me that every way I turn, my freedom of judgment is hedged by the provisions of this unhappy will, Veronica. If it were possible to delay what I now wish to say, till I should be in a freer position to offer you disinterested love, I should prefer to do it. As it is —— Veronica, may I speak to you of all my hopes?"

For a moment she did not answer; then she replied.

"Do as you please; my only hesitation is on account of the negroes whose welfare is connected with the answer I may give you. Cousin William is notoriously a bad master."

"Your answer would certainly be unfavorable to my hopes?" said Max in a low voice.

"Do you mean that for —— for the question contemplated in the will?" she replied. "Am I to give you an unequivocal answer?"

He looked into her face and turned away. The path became narrow, and he suffered her to ride before him for a hundred yards or two. When he resumed his place beside her, he said, "Veronica, I have saidall that I intend to say. You know my hopes—I think you know my heart; it is for you to decide our fate. Give me some sign if you are disposed to be favorable to my suit—if not, let us say nothing more about it. We are placed in a position of great difficulty and delicacy, and I think that any further advances ought to come from you."

She said nothing—still nothing. They rode on a mile—two miles—five miles, till they approached the bank of the winding Shenandoah; then Veronica spoke, and said,

"Cousin Max, I have consulted your true interests, as you will find, when a few weeks have softened any mortification you may feel at what has past. Let us be good friends. There are several subjects that concern us both on which Governor Tyrell will consult with you."

She held out to him the little hand, but it was now no pleasure to him to take it.

"Won't you be friends with me?" she said, with a tremor in her voice. "Believe me, cousin Max, you will soon thank me, and feel that I have acted as I ought. I wish you may have a wife who will make you very happy. Cousin Max, to be happy, and to make her happy, you must love her, you know."

"Good-bye, Veronica," he said.

They were standing under the trees near McCoy's Ferry, waiting for the ferry-man to push his boat across and put them over.

Mr. Parker and I came up. He had been paying his addresses to me all the way, and was dreadfully hard to convince that it would not at all suit me to become Mrs. Parker.

"Max, I am sorry to interrupt your conversation with Veronica," I said; "but you really must keep beside me for the remainder of our ride. I cannot have any more conversation with Mr. Parker."

"Veronica and I have said all we have to say," he replied.

I knew what had taken place by his tone and his look.

"Oh, Max!" I said.

He stopped me with a glance which said, "Be silent if you please." I thought of

> The busy hand of consolation,
> Fretting the sore wound it could not hope to heal.

and I *was* silent.

Mr. Morrisson came up, and we all crossed the ferry. There were heavy hearts amongst us, as we began to ascend the mountain on the other shore, and after riding a couple of miles further we put up for the night at Fennel's tavern—a little roadside farm-house, which provided entertainment for man and beast, more simple, but far cleaner, than any we should have had by stopping at the larger public house in the little village of Front Royal.

The people were Methodists. It was the close of the working man's day with them. They were preparing to retire for the night, and were singing a plaintive Methodist hymn, the burden of which was the happiness of passing over Jordan. They broke off as we rode up and made us welcome. The gentlemen went into the barn to see the horses well rubbed down. Veronica begged to be shown our room, and allowed to go to bed, for she was very tired. I felt as if I did not wish to have any conversation with her, and remained till a late hour on the porch, talking to our host's family, who asked innumerable questions about our relationship one to another, our family history, and other particulars of private life, which an American of the back-woods, who knows his neighbors all by heart, desires to learn of strangers; and at last finding I had come from England they turned their powers of interrogation upon Queen Victoria, who they appeared to imagine must be a lady with whom I had considerable personal acquaintance. Fortunately I knew many anecdotes—some of them drawn from private sources—illustrative of the good sense, industry, and domestic virtues of her Majesty. I happened to have an English postage-stamp in my pocket-book, and on leaving in the morning I stuck it on a card, and presented it as the Queen's likeness, to the family. They were so delighted at the attention, that they did not wish that I should pay any bill; and in the excitement caused among us by amusement at a speech, in which mine host told me, it was worth fifty cents any day to have my company, we parted from Max and Mr. Parker with less embarrassment than I had feared, and turned our horses' heads towards Clairmont, with Mr. Morrisson for our companion and protector.

CHAPTER XX.

Afar from thee! the morning breaks,
  But morning brings no joy to me;
Alas! my spirit only wakes
  To know I am afar from thee.
In dreams I saw thy blessed face,
  And thou wert nestled on my breast;
In dreams I felt thy fond embrace,
  And to mine own thy heart was pressed.

REV. GEO. W. BETHUNE.

THERE are moments in a man's life when all things seem against him. Misfortunes seldom "come in single spies," and prosperity sets in with a flood. This was a dark hour with Max. He had nothing to do in Rappahannock but to ride about the country, and brood over the situation in which he found himself. Fortune and love both risked—both lost. Happiness had been in his power once, and trifled with, had passed beyond his reach, as it appeared, for ever. His beautiful Castleton was to become the inheritance of Veronica, while his would be the fate that he had once predicted for himself in a moment of passionate irritation; he would be sent to some distant colony with his regiment, and wear out his days in garrison inactivity. But the loss of Castleton, severely as he felt it, was not the prominent distress that troubled him. He was a young man, and a lover. Castleton could have been resigned without a sigh, if by that disappointment he could have purchased the attachment of Veronica.

I do not believe in theories of compensation. When we can bear prosperity, God gives it unmixed to us, and when trouble is what we need, disappointments are apt to succeed each other like the messengers of misfortune that came to Job. We talk vaguely about runs of good fortune or of evil—each comes as the servant of God, accomplishing that which He pleases, and prospering in the thing whereunto He sends it.

The life of Max had been the careless life of a young man, with little purpose beyond the pleasure of the passing moment. He had not advanced beyond the simplest moral of the book of life, that fault and error work out pain and punishment. He was about to pass on to another lesson. He was to learn that troubles (not the lineal descendants of error), often meet us as God's messengers upon the path of life, and turn our feet into the ways of peace.

As he paced up and down his chamber, long after Joe Parker and his household had retired for the night, impatiently reiterating the inquiry why, without any especial faults for which he could reproach himself, he had been brought to shame and loss, he was led to look more deeply into the problems of life than he had ever had occasion to do in days of carelessness and of prosperity.

The point in his conduct upon which his mind rested with most satisfaction, was his determination not to risk Veronica's inheritance of Castleton. Sometimes, convinced of her indifference, he would have returned to England at once, but for the suit hanging over him before the court of Charlestown. Sometimes the thought chafed him, that if he could have been with her, his silent devotion might have touched her. Sometimes he was glad he was away, that he might not see other men attentive to her.

During the watches of the night, when Fancy fits her patterns on the woof of life, schemes rash and wild as the adventures of romance, shaped themselves into what seemed practicable. Man is Gulliver in Lilliput by night. The slender threads of circumstance that bind him are Lilliputian cables to the strength of which he feels himself possessed—but waking he finds himself beyond the borders of the Land of Giants, and the first difficulty that looks him in the face seems like the maid of Brobdignag.

He passed a miserable fortnight at Joe Parker's, where the solace provided by his host was only of two kinds, whisky-toddy and tobacco, and when he found they were refused, the resources of his hospitality were at an end. Max was not in the humor to sit talking by the hour on the porch. To the great astonishment of Mr. Parker, who would have "run a mile to catch a horse to ride half a mile," he took a fancy to long, solitary walks upon the hills, among the rattlesnakes—hills covered by the mountain strawberry, where mountain children who had never heard a church bell, nor had seen a book (unless some *colporteur* of tracts wandered into their vicinity), gathered the fruits of nature's garden, and brought their strawberries down the mountain to sell.

He wrote many letters to Veronica and destroyed them, and as "great events from little causes spring," only a sense of the rarity of letter-paper, when he had covered his last sheet, was the cause of his sending her at length a finished letter.

Veronica was sitting with me on the porch at Clairmont, when the boy brought up the bag that held this document. I eagerly opened the post-bag, for which I watched day after day with sickening hope, but found only that letter. Veronica's hand trembled very much as she took it, and I, feeling that she must wish to be alone, went into the house and left her. She did not open it upon the porch, but shortly after I watched her in the wood, with the letter lying open in her lap, as she sat on a rock under one of the great oak trees.

Tyrell was at Clairmont that evening, but whilst I talked to him as he sat with his cigar upon the upper steps of the porch, I could not forget Veronica. In any moment of agitation it soothed me to be with Tyrell. I could see I exercised on him a corresponding influence—a sure sign, had I but known it, we were not in love; for unacknowledged love is always feverish. It agitates its possessor and it irritates its object. I imagine that the pleasures of the most successful courtship, and especially the intercourse of lovers immediately before the declaration of attachment, are far outweighed by its anxieties and pains. Tyrell and I exercised upon each other no such disturbing influence. On the contrary his voice soothed me, his opinions strengthened me. When we were apart, I might sometimes disturb myself by reflections on the reports in circulation which made him my admirer, but when we were together I forgot them. I found him the kind, sympathizing friend, whose influence was strengthening and refreshing, who showed me the path of right, because he walked in it, who leaned on God, and invited me to lean upon Him. The only safe test in cases where we half suspect ourselves or others of attachment, is to observe the nature of our personal influences. It is safer than any deductions drawn from circumstances.

The evening star had risen after a day of weariness and heat, and the mellow evening light that flickered through the trees lighted me upon my way, as I went in search of Veronica. I found her sitting at the edge of an old quarry, on a huge fragment of blasted limestone. Max's letter had been folded up and put away, for Veronica was not the person to whet the appetite of grief or love which "grow by what they feed on."

"How long is Max going to stay in the mountains, Veronica?" said I, not knowing very well what other question to ask her.

She started. "Not very much longer, I imagine," she replied. He has some intention of going to the Springs, and of visiting Weir's Cave, and the Natural Bridge, as I have recommended him."

I was silent for a moment, and then throwing my arms round Veronica, I whispered, "Vera——! if I might ask what that letter contained——!"

She looked up quickly. "Nothing pleasant, Molly, and yet something. You may read it if you like." She drew it from her dress and held it out to me. "I am going to the house. Stay here and read it. You can give it back to me by and by."

She went away. Not with the elastic, tripping step that had been once one of the graces that distinguished her. She had grown quiet and listless. There was little in her daily life to call off her thoughts from hidden troubles. Her face was grave, and her smile was fainter, and she rallied her attention with an effort when anybody talked to her. But these were indications of the state of things unseen that only watchful love was likely to detect, and no such tender interest waited about her path and bed at Clairmont. No one there loved her as well I did, and alas! I thought too much of my own position with respect to Mr. Howard, to have been the friend she wanted at this crisis. And I had a grudge against her too, for Max's sake. I was not tender to the wounded spirit of my cousin.

I opened the letter, carelessly written, and somewhat blotted, as everything Max wrote always was. It ran thus:—

"I have thought of little else than our conversation at Front Royal, since we parted, Veronica! It is hard for a man to resign his dearest hope—to feel that he stands at that point in his life, where two roads meet, the one leading to disappointment, the other to prosperity and happiness, and deliberately to choose between them. But calm reflection in the past ten days, has taught me my duty. No question of worldly prosperity need come between us, for I feel that a disinterested and deep attachment, is, of itself, a worthiness, and constitutes a claim upon the favorable notice of its object; but I can no longer disguise from myself the conviction that you do not, and may never love me. I ask myself if the follies of boyhood and the unhappy position into which we have been forced, must outweigh all other claims that I could make to your affection? And in the silence of the night, the answer comes. I withdraw, for the present, all pretensions to your regard; I resign all claim to Castleton. I leave you free to choose amongst your suitors. But, Veronica, if I can bring my pride down to my fortunes, I shall enter their ranks. Hereafter, when questions of property can be no longer affected by the fortunes of my suit, it may seek at your hand acceptance or rejection. *I think it may.* I cannot be quite sure it will. I think, Veronica, I love you better than my pride, and I know that unless I do, I am only worthy of your rejection. You need not fear me, therefore. You need not meet me ever armed, at all points, and never off your guard. But it would be unworthy of my manhood if I resigned all future right to attempt to win a recognition of any attachment. I will not resign all hope, until more has passed between us than it would be generous to urge upon you, before the expiration of the year after my uncle's death has ceased to attach consequences to your refusal. Meantime, I shall take your advice, and travel through Virginia, unless (is it possible that this might be?) some word from you should reach me before the 14th October."

It was truly a lover's letter, with all its mixed ingredients of hope and of despair, of pride and feeling, of renunciation, and reliance on the power of a strong attachment to compel good fortune.

"Ah! Veronica," I said, as I returned it to her that evening, in our chamber, "is there nothing I may say from you to him?'

"Nothing, Molly, except that he is doing as he ought. If it be a sacrifice, I respect him and admire him for making it."

"I do not understand you, Veronica. You seem to me disposed to be very harsh to Max, and yet there are moments when —— Veronica, if all obstacles and difficulties were removed, and Max, as he says, were your suitor at this moment, I believe you do not know whether you would accept him or refuse him."

"I do *not* know. You are right," she said.

"Then, Veronica, you are not sure you would refuse him?"

"You have no right to ask me questions," she replied.

"But, Veronica, is it not loving, if you care for him enough not to be quite certain you should refuse him if he renewed his suit?"

"Hush, Molly!" exclaimed Veronica, wringing her hands. "It 's bad enough to have a treacherous heart, you need not tempt me with suppositions that have no foundation, and questions I cannot answer."

I sat down by her side, and put my arm around her, and said, "May I not tell you how sincerely he loves you?"

"No, you may not," she said. "The future may disprove or confirm my doubts. Meanwhile, I wish to be left entirely to my own thoughts. There is indelicacy in discussing such a subject; and allusions and suggestions such as you might make, would do no service to your brother."

I was silent. She resumed presently—

"It would naturally be a great disappointment to him to lose Castleton, and I shall not know what to do with it. Governor Tyrell has promised to use his influence with Max, to make him consent to a more suitable arrangement. My present object is to keep my cousin William from being the possessor of the negroes at Oatlands. I could not feel my duty was performed if he obtained possession of them through my fault. Molly, did Tyrell say he had heard from Uncle Christopher? I thought I heard him saying something about it to you at tea-time."

"Yes," I replied, "the family is safe in Philadelphia—safe and free. They are able to earn a living for themselves, and their children will grow up to be free men. It is sweet to think of the benedictions they will draw down by their prayers on those who helped them."

"True," said Veronica. "I hope they will be very happy in their new condition. Not that they have been unhappy hitherto—for Aunt Saph was the best friend of her mistress, and every body respected Uncle Christopher, who was known to all men, white and black, in the community. They would have been happy, without change, if no event had thrown them into the hands of a bad master."

"They are better off, now," I said. "A gentleman in Philadelphia wrote to cousin Tyrell, that it was delightful to see the airs of self-importance which marked their appreciation of freedom—the sense of the duty of self-reliance and self-protection, which seemed suddenly to have come upon them in middle life,—their *naïve* realization of their obligations and responsibilities to each other and their children, which, he said, spoke volumes against the system which had stunted their feelings. They had only been two days out of slavery when he saw them, and he said it would rejoice Tyrell's heart to witness their enthusiasm; and that they talked of little else than him, and you, and Max; and that he would let us know, from time to time, how they were getting on."

"That one good deed is the sole pleasant memory of this sad season," said Veronica. "Gibson has been arranged with about Aunt Saph and her children. His reputation is such, that he dared not risk a quarrel with people of the Tyrells' standing in the community. But cousin William still is very angry."

"And says," I added, "that if he should get Oatlands, he will reclaim Uncle Christopher, and sell him south to pick cotton."

Veronica shuddered, and closed her eyes. I think she was praying that she might never be under the necessity of refusing Max's offer.

I did not care to write to him, for I had nothing more than what he knew to tell him; and Veronica seemed so sensitive on the subject of my interference, that I was reduced to remember that "speech is silver, but silence is gold."

So Max went morning after morning to the little post town, five miles from Joel Parker's plantation, where on more than one occasion he found the postmaster in his harvest-field, a mile from home, with the mail unsorted in his pocket; and though he sat down on a stump, and looked the letters through to find the one for which Max hoped, it was not there.

"I've 'most a mind to write you one myself," he said, "'cause you look so disappinted. I never see a man come for his mail, and look like that, that he isn't thinking about some gal or other. Stick close and brag high, and you'll get her yet, I reckon."

CHAPTER XXI.

Then let us cheerfu' acquiesce,
Nor make our scanty pleasures less
By pining at our state.
And even should misfortunes come
(I here wha sit hae met wi some,
An's thankful for them yet),
They give the wit o' age to youth,
They let us ken oursel;
They make us see the naked truth,
The *real* guid and ill.
Tho' crosses and losses
Be lessons right severe,
There's wit there ye'll get there
Ye'll find no other where.

BURNS.

DAYS came and went; very monotonous days; for the bloom of novelty was brushed off of Virginia life. By the end of September I had had only one letter from Max, dated at Weir's Cave, containing nothing but guide-book information about petrifactions and stalactites, and saying he should remain there four days in hopes that I would answer his letter, but as it had taken a week to travel by cross-roads a hundred miles to Clairmont, and as I had nothing pleasant to communicate, I, not unwillingly, concluded that before my answer could travel back, he would have pushed his way into another part of the country.

Veronica was sad, the house was dull, the society which had

been so merry and amusing when my spirits were tuned up to the key note of its romping jollity, was miserably discordant to my present tone. My heart sank within me. Twice a week the mail came in from Washington, and when little Tad with the post-bag was dispatched to Fighterstown, my heart sickened with the hope deferred, that some news from Mr. Howard might, perhaps, arrive. Not a word, however, reached me. My home letters did not mention him. But in an English newspaper (as I scanned every line of its columns, in a vain hope that the movements of his regiment might be recorded) I had seen the death of an old relative of his who had promised to leave him a considerable legacy.

> "And e'en as life returns upon the drowned
> Life's hopes returning roused a throng of pains."

After seeing this I grew so restlessly wretched that it seemed to me sometimes as if the suspense were more than I could bear. In the night watches and in the hours when I sat sewing by the open hearth, heaped with light brush and hickory, even in September, the voice of my heart cried out with anguish to my brother, and begged him to return and take me home. Then I had vague notions that Mr. Howard himself, now that the independence we had looked forward to was his, might, perhaps, arrive and claim me. Every day I expected Max. Every afternoon at six o'clock, the hour when any arrival from Simpson's Depôt was to be expected at Fighterstown, I stood upon the porch straining my eyes along the road between Clairmont and Fighterstown, or if I rode out I always insisted upon taking the road to the depôt. In vain I reasoned with myself that I had not the smallest right to hope that Mr. Howard, on the strength of his small independence, would come to America in search of me, but

Something within would still be shadowing out
All possibilities, and with these shadows
My mind held dalliance.

I blamed myself for want of womanly pride, I tired to acquire more self-discipline, but every afternoon the tide of hope was at the flood, rising and swelling, till the brief autumn twilight faded into greyness, and then it slowly ebbed and left my life bare as a sandy shore. Tyrell came frequently to see us. He was capricious in his attentions and his visits. Sometimes he was constantly, on slight pretexts, at Clairmont, on other occasions he would stay away, apparently without reason, for a week at a time. If it had not been for the reports that went about the neighborhood, that he was paying court to me, I should have been glad to see him. But I was too sick at heart to feel complacency in that kind of homage. And whereas under ordinary circumstances a woman secretly feels a certain prepossession in favor of any man who is supposed to acknowledge her merits, and whom public opinion declares her suitor, the contrary is the case, provided she is embarrassed by an attachment to another person. So when cousin Virginia tormented me by insinuations that Tyrell was in love with me, assurances not borne out by anything that came under my knowledge, it perplexed and worried me. I began to be uneasy in his presence, to treat him no longer with frank cordiality. The pleasant relations between us were in a measure broken up. I found myself on the lookout for anything that I could persuade myself might be his faults. The geniality of Tyrell deserted him. The merry light in his eyes was troubled. When he came to Clairmont he was often lost in reverie.

"See how earnestly he looks at you," said cousin Virginia. "Must not a man be in love to watch you so closely?"

And Veronica—even Veronica—would listen to these speeches, and never checked them in her quiet way.

One afternoon Tyrell came over to Clairmont; he had stayed away ten days, and everybody had missed him.

"I reckon we are right glad to see you, Tyrell," said cousin Virginia from the porch, as he was "hitching" his grey horse to the rack under the trees. "Cousin Molly has been very uneasy about you."

Tyrell made her no answer. He came slowly to the house, and saluted us all gravely. He seemed to be troubled in spirit, and to have nothing to say. By and by he found himself near me, and asked me in a low voice if I would ride with him. I was delighted at the opportunity of mounting Angelo, and went up stairs to put on my riding-dress. While I was there Veronica came up to insist that I should take her riding-hat with feathers, because she said my own was less becoming, and then she pressed me to take her riding-whip, with its handle of carved ivory, and as I stood dressed, drawing on my gloves, she abruptly threw her arms round me, and said:

"Dear Molly, may God bless you!" and then as suddenly turned away and went down stairs.

Tyrell placed me upon Angelo, and mounted his grey horse.

"Where shall we go?" said he. I chose the road leading to the depôt; and we rode slowly, conversing about indifferent things—the burden of the conversation falling upon me, for Tyrell was very silent till we found ourselves in the woods, about two miles beyond the noisy, muddy, disorderly streets of Fighterstown.

"Miss Molly," said Tyrell, "I have a story to tell you." I looked down with apprehension of what I thought was at hand. How should I answer him?

"I am not happy," he went on to say, "and for the last six

weeks I have not even enjoyed the luxury of feeling that my unhappiness, so long as it could be borne silently, concerned myself alone. I think you will know why I speak to you thus, when I tell you my story. It is an old legend—old as the first pages of the Hero-book, and older—old as the first poetry which sprang out of the first heart-sorrow."

I was silent.

Tyrell turned deeper into the woods, and thus began:

"A German writer tells us, 'With Renunciation alone can the real life of man be said to begin.' This is a story of renunciation; it is the story of the pine tree of the forest, which shot up with no luxuriant foliage clothing its rugged trunk; and when it came to a sense of what the beauty was that it had not, it prayed the vine to climb up its rough bark, and clothe it with her green broad leaves, and make it fruitful with purple clusters of bloomy grapes. But the tendrils of the vine yearned towards a tree with broader boughs and of a foreign growth, and she clung to it, and graced it with her beauty. It is the common story of a man who has grown up without anything of womankind to cherish, who has nourished his fancy with books, and worshipped ideal loveliness, suddenly brought into contact with her who realizes all his dreams. I will not say that the creature of his fancy is all real. Perhaps he endows her with spoils borrowed from the pages of his favorite authors, and brings fancies of gossamer, caught up during the hours he has slept on fairy ground, with which to invest reality. But when he finds her, he bows down to her; and if he loses her, 'the affection that in this world will ever be homeless,' shrinks back upon himself. It wanders ever after in dry places, seeking rest. It comes back like rejected gifts, to shame and grieve the giver. Perhaps womanhood owes something of its loveliness to the pious worship of the men who have bowed down to it; perhaps nothing can attain its highest beauty till viewed by the light of the lamp of sacrifice. The hero of my legend, which I was beginning to forget, was not a hero, but a child, who set his desire on a magic rose, which grew in a fair garden; but it blossomed into beauty beyond his reach. Day after day he inhaled its magic fragrance: it was sweeter to him than all the other roses. He saw the happy bees, those 'heavy-winged thieves,' nestle unreproved among its leaves, and suck its liberal sweetness. He saw a rain-drop steal into its bosom; he saw the sunbeams kiss its petals, and he cried, "why am I alone to be deprived of this inheritance of happiness?' and he struggled to be tall enough to reach it—until struggling, he tore his hands with the sharp thorns that guarded it, and with the rusty nails that fastened it to the wall above him. And then he sat down, sore and wounded, by a springing fountain, and tried to forget his disappointment. But it was a charmed rose, and had a fairy power over his fancy. In vain he said to himself, 'there may be other roses as beautiful as this in the garden of sweets in which I find myself:' no other rose was half as fragrant to his senses: he gathered none of them. I mean," said Tyrell, "that perhaps they were all enchanted roses—perhaps they all grew above his reach; but he never had the heart to try them. He looked up at his magic bud, and had no heart to offer them. You understand me now, I think. He never loved any more."

I understood him and was silent. With the first understanding, there came womanly pique for the fear which evidently moved him, that I had lent ear to the 'reports,' and expected him to care for me.

I was quite silent for several minutes, during which it seemed to me as if no answer upon my part could be needed, and then

I looked at him and saw the anxious, suffering expression of his face, and all my pride went from me.

"Cousin Tyrell," I said, "it is very kind of you to tell me that story. I can sympathize with it. My magic rose-tree grew in England. The bud I wished for was within my reach, but a sharp east wind came, and wafted it too high for me."

"Thank you, dear cousin Molly, for this frankness—for the generous frankness—which has made us for ever friends." And Tyrell stretched out his hand and took mine in his warm, kind grasp, which seemed to say, what he did not suffer to transpire in word or look, "Thank God you have not suffered injury from me;" and my heart warmed towards Tyrell in his loneliness; almost it said,

> "Might I but be the wild-flower on the wall
> Of that war-wasted tower. A weed, alas!
> But with a perfume."

"Is there no remedy for the past," said I to Tyrell.

"None," he replied. "I had no sister, and my mother died when I was very young. I have lived always among men, yearning for woman's tenderness. The one affection which taught me all a woman's love might be, has been unfortunate. But even as it is, I would not part with it. It glows with new beauty from the back-ground of sad thoughts. It is the holier and the lovelier from a sense of disappointment. Do not imagine," he went on to say, "that I will waste my life in weak regret, and that a vain appreciation of my loss will quench my courage. If God sends tears, they are to water a soil that is not yet sufficiently fruitful. He from whom God has taken away the hope that children and wife shall eat of his bread and drink of his cup, should carry strength and gladness to the homes and hearts of others. Gather up the fragments that remain, that nothing be lost. If we cast the bread of our feast underfoot, because we have no appetite to enjoy it—if we spill our wine of gladness because our heart revolts from it—we despise the gifts of God, and waste the happiness that He intended should be used, either for ourselves or for others. There is no remedy for unhappiness, that I know of, but an interest in the happiness of other persons. Work was the boon God gave to our First Father when he turned him out of Paradise; and the five thousand years that have since passed have given disappointment no better remedy."

"And I have been wasting life in unreasonable longings," I said sadly, "while you are so courageous and so loving, so full of generous endurance and endeavor—so worthy of the happiness that you say is denied you."

"There is truer happiness than mere good fortune," replied Tyrell; "as I read it in a review the other day, 'Man is not dependent upon mere worldly gifts of luck in life. These are possible, not promised. Happy he who can rule over them; but *doubly* unhappy he who cannot.' 'God shall choose our inheritance for us,' says the Psalmist. I accept my lot in life, though its bleakness is discouraging. I shall not attempt to grow fruits and flowers on it. I will dig into the bowels of the earth, and strike, perhaps, some hidden ore."

"But this idea of never-ending work—not for dear home's sake, but only to be thrown into the common fund of human effort—seems to me so profitless and wearisome."

"Would you rather, then, 'have leisure to die of love?' as my reviewer says," asked Tyrell. "You did not mean *that*, cousin Molly. And yet I dare say a woman yearns for her own garden spot; while I, if I am never to have children and wife, thank God for other people's wives and children, on whose welfare I can bestow that money, time, and interest I would have given to my own. As for rest—I fear it. My heart would be like an old sword in an old scabbard,

> And eat into itself, for lack
> Of something else to hew and hack.

'Work while it is yet day—the night cometh when no man can work,' is the trumpet-call of the Life-angel sounding in my ears the signal for the battle. '*N'avons nous pas toute l'éternité pour nous reposer?*' said Arnauld to Nicolle, the Port Royalist; and at present I feel as if I dreaded any rest short of that deep repose that broods over eternity.' "

"You soar above my ordinary range of motive and of thought," I said. "But I can feel it would be glorious if the words of the Saviour could be written on our tombstones: 'I have glorified thee upon the earth. I have *finished* the work which thou gavest me to do.' "

"*That Thou gavest me!*" repeated Tyrell. "There is comfort in that thought. Work or happiness are alike his gift. 'There is no want to them that fear Him;' and He denies our reasonable wishes for love's sake when disappointments come. Our lesson in trouble is taught us by George Herbert:

> Thy Father could
> Quickly effect what thou dost move;
> For He is Power; and sure He would—
> For He is love."

"It seems so strange that He does not give us all happiness," I said. "It would be so easy for God to make every body happy, even in this world."

Tyrell laid his hand upon Angelo's silken mane, and a beautiful light of love and trust was in his face as he said confidently,

"Interpret His dealings by His character, not His character by his dealings: they are not fully known to us. 'Rejoice in the Lord alway'—'Thank Him for an unknown blessing.'"

He seemed to be speaking to himself, forgetful of my presence; but a moment after, turning his face full to me with a smile of hope and trust upon his lips, he said gently,

"Tarry thou the Lord's leisure, be strong and he shall comfort thine heart, and put thou thy trust in the Lord."

CHAPTER XXII.

God sends country lawyers, and other wise fellers,
To drive the world's team when it gits in a slough,
So John P
Robinson, he
Says the world will go right if he hollers out "gee!"
J. R. LOWELL: *The Biglow Papers.*

TYRELL was greatly more cheerful after our conversation. Pleasant relations were established between him and me. We understood each other, and I found the happiness of having such a friend to draw my thoughts out of myself—to "point to brighter worlds, and lead the way." All social questions interested Tyrell. My own range of reading and of thought was confined exclusively to Belles Lettres and to Art, and to a taste for what appealed to the fancy. But Tyrell's tastes all pointed to the real and true. Noble actions inspired him, social problems interested him. If he received a new idea, he wanted instantly to set it working. He took his place amongst the little band who labor in the rough ploughed field of life, waiting for the harvest. And it seemed to me as if nobody about him understood him as well as I did, and that my sympathy, though so imperfect, was a solace to him.

All the gentlemen of the neighborhood were full of excitement about politics. All Americans are fluent, and all natives of the

Southern States have an extraordinary familiarity with the operations of Government. It seems as if, like citizens of Ancient Rome, leaving the cultivation of their soil to slaves, they busied themselves in keeping watch over the interests of the Republic, and this is very probably the reason why the Southern States enjoy a political influence, vastly out of proportion to the number of their voters, which are enormously outnumbered by the voters of the North. The interest felt in measures of the General Government, is lukewarm in the Northern States, confining itself to those whose interests may become affected by particular bills, but in Virginia every man makes the proceedings in Congress his own concern; and bills are discussed in coteries, upon the tavern-stoops, or on the porches of country houses, or at the post-office, with more vehemence and enthusiasm by country gentlemen, than they would put into any affairs of their own. There is an *esprit du corps* throughout the South when certain questions are attacked, which supplies the place of patriotism, a virtue in which, in its largest sense, Americans are very deficient.

Now Tyrell was not a politician of this stamp, and though he could sit upon the porch at Clairmont, or Stonehenge, with his cigar, and hold his part by the hour, in a political arguefication, it was without the personal excitement of his neighbors, for as he said to me, on more than one occasion, "Our American government is never in advance of the people. Nor does the press do more than keep up with public opinion. The people have the bit in their teeth, and guide the government. The country must go on, no matter who may hold the reins at Washington. The worst government will not injure a prosperity which depends solely upon material advantages. I am only concerned when I think of our foreign relations, and happily it has always been the policy of every government to put its best man at their head."

The church, too, and religion, were very frequently discussed, but I soon found out that Tyrell was a Christian on a different pattern from the persons who surrounded him. While they argued upon doctrines, and discussed the legislative proceedings of Conventions, and strained at gnats in matters of amusement, and swallowed enormous camels in the practices of daily life, Tyrell sat commonly silent.

"Christianity," he said to me, one day, "has a double aspect. It is individual and social. Individual Christianity, earnest, but narrow-minded because it has cut itself off from the sympathies by which God meant it to be nourished, is illustrated by many beautiful examples in our community, but social Christianity, which hastens the coming of the day of the Lord, which weaves its net around all human relations, which recognizes the claims of brotherhood, which never says, "am I my brother's keeper?" which knows Christ died for *all*, and knowing that truth acts upon it—has not 'begun to begin,' as our Virginians say, to hide its leaven amongst us."

It was in hearing Tyrell talk thus that I began to find a thousand new thoughts, and new interests, stirring within me. I began to recognize new obligations. I desired to search into things of which I had not thought before.

The trial of Max, who fired on the rioters, and of the rioters who assaulted Max, was appointed to be held in the October court, at Charlestown. Max had not returned. About a week before the day appointed, notice was served on him to appear at that same court, and to show cause why William Williams, Esq., of Clarke county, should not take possession of the estate of Oatlands, together with the negroes belonging to the personal estate of Thomas Lomax, Esq., deceased.

"What is the meaning of this?" I said, to Tyrell, to whom I now always turned for advice or sympathy.

"It means what I have for some time past feared," he said, "that Mr. William Williams claims Oatlands, which your brother inherits from Mr. Lomax, because your brother is an alien, and cannot hold real estate in Virginia. The negroes, who are personal property, he claims in virtue of that clause in the will, which says the negroes shall in no case be separated from the landed property."

"And what will then remain for Max?" I cried.

"Nothing," he answered, "except some old furniture in the house now inhabited by the overseer, at Oatlands."

"And how would it be settled if Max had offered himself to Veronica, and had been refused?"

"Will Williams would have had this estate, and Castleton would have been sold and divided between Max and Veronica."

"Do you suppose that Max knew this before he went away?" I answered.

"I cannot tell," said Tyrell. "Jake Gibson, who has quarrelled with Will Williams, and is anxious at present to curry favor with me, put the idea into my head about three weeks since, by telling me that Williams had threatened Max with such a step, and offered him a compromise, while he was too drunk to know what he was about, the day Max knocked him down in Fighterstown."

"I wonder if Max understood what he said?"

"I imagine not. One pays so little attention to what a drunken man may say. Your brother would not be likely to understand his vague allusion to a law of doubtful application, which we have seldom occasion to remember, and it was Williams's policy, of course, to keep his intentions dark as long as possible. My father does not think that Williams's claim is certain, and did not expect it to be brought so soon, but we should have sent a warning to Max, if we had known where to direct to him, and have been hoping for his return from day to day."

"Oh, if we only knew," I cried, "where a letter would find him!"

This conversation took place as the evening was growing dusk. We were sitting on the porch, and as I said this, little Tommy Tad stole up the steps with his bare feet, and held before my eyes the post-bag. I opened it. It contained a letter from Max. He said he should be at Joel Parker's the night after he wrote, and on the 15th of October, would be at Clairmont.

I read the letter aloud to Tyrell, and then exclaimed.

"The court is to begin on the day after to-morrow, the 14th of October."

"I will send Diggory on my horse into the mountain. He can ride from here to Parker's in a day on my grey steed. Black Mike will bring your brother down by the afternoon of the 14th. Don't cry, cousin Molly. It may not be so bad, after all," Tyrell said soothingly.

"Do you suppose that Veronica knew this?" I cried, "Perhaps——perhaps she would send him a note or message if I explained to her all the loss that her continued unkindness will entail upon my brother."

Tyrell rose and looked suddenly with interest at a wasp's nest in one of the pilasters.

"I never observed that nest before," he said. "Yes, perhaps so."

"I shall go and ask her," I said. "Would it be improper? Oh! cousin Tyrell, give me your advice."

I looked up in his face, and there, by the light of the moon that was just rising, I read something that I had not anticipated. I read the secret of his life—the interpretation of his legend.

"You had better ask somebody else," he said; each word came slowly. "I am not the proper person to advise you in this matter."

I turned away, and he went down the steps. I had hardly the heart to go to Veronica, and ask her to do for my brother's sake what would crush all hope out of the heart of cousin Tyrell.

I went up into our chamber and threw myself on my bed, in a passion of tears. Before I could compose myself or think what I had better do, Veronica came hastily up stairs.

"Molly," she cried, "what do you wish? Tyrell told me—Why, Molly, what is the matter?"

"What did Tyrell tell you?"

"Merely that you wanted me; and had gone up stairs in search of me. I thought something was the matter by the way he looked. What is it Molly?"

"It is this, Veronica," I said, "that Max is on the eve of being ruined for your sake. It is that he will lose all his inheritance if you reject his suit." And I explained it to her.

"Oh! Veronica, write him a little note, and tell him it is not too late. Tell him you will love him again if he comes back to you."

I threw myself upon her neck, and said these words in a whisper.

Veronica caught her breath with nervous agitation, and trembled so much that she put me from her and sat down.

She sat silent for some minutes, shading her face. It was dark, for the closed blinds kept out the moonshine.

Suddenly Mary Louisa came up the stairs, and said:—

"Miss Molly, Mas'r Tyrell want 'know if you'se got dat letter ready?"

As she opened the door, a draft of wind blew open one of the green blinds. Veronica started up as if pierced by a sudden arrow.

"No, Molly," she said, standing up, "I have tried, I have examined my feelings before God. I can send your brother no message nor letter."

"Veronica," I cried, "answer me one word further. Had you rather that he did not come?——Answer me, Veronica!"

"He must do as he likes," she said, and left me. It was useless to write to Max. I had nothing satisfactory to tell him. After five minutes' consideration, I went down stairs to Tyrell. He was waiting by the porch, mounted upon Angelo, his object being to ride to Stonehenge, and bring back Diggory to Clairmont, to ride his own grey charger into the mountains of Rappahannock—to ride him nearly to death, perhaps—that horse which I knew he suffered no person but himself to mount, and on which, it sometimes seemed to me, he had concentrated the tender affections that no woman, child, or infirm parent called forth from him.

He held out his hand in silence for the note from Veronica.

"She has not written," I said, "nor have I any idea of what she feels for Max. I cannot, therefore, write him anything satisfactory. Is it necessary to do more than send this notice from Will Williams? I know not what to write to him."

"I will write to him myself," he said. "Good bye."

His face was pale in the moonlight. He turned the pony's head, and went slowly through the intricacies of the darkening avenue. But the moment he was on the highway, he mended his pace; and I stood on the porch at Clairmont, listening to the patter of the hoofs of Angelo, till the echo died away as he neared Fighterstown.

CHAPTER XXIII.

Such is the fortune that I have,
To love them most that love me least,
And to my pain to seek and crave
The thing that other hath possessed.
So thus in vain always I serve,
And others have that I deserve.
SIR THOMAS WYATT.

THE relations of Max with Veronica became the talk of Fighterstown. Groups gathered on the tavern-steps, and in the principal stores along the street, and in the post-office, put up their feet, cocked back their hats, tipped up their chairs, spit their tobacco-juice, and talked over it. Gentlemen rode over to their neighbors', sat in the porches, and discussed it.

When "time shall be no longer," we shall know what sum of human existence was wasted in unprofitable talk over the affairs of Max and Veronica.

Where was he? What did it mean? Had she given him the mittens? (as they called it.) What were the rights of the story?—and whose were the wrongs?

Tyrell, who came back to Clairmont about daylight, and who rode over to Winchester to lay the case before two eminent lawyers, whom his father wished him to retain on behalf of Max, was beset with questions. One man stopped him as he was fording the Opeccan, and in the middle of the river, with the water up to his saddle-girths, began a searching cross-examination.

The next morning, October 14th, the anniversary of the death of cousin Lomax, the household rose up before the red sun came glowing over the mountains, ushering in a ripe Indian summer day. Before we had had breakfast the lawyers from Winchester rode up, upon their way to Charlestown, mounted upon handsome horses, with their papers and briefs in saddle-bags, which, as they ate, they put under the table.

As soon as the meal was over they handed us into the carriage. Veronica and I, Tyrell and Mr. Morrisson, were to go over to Charlestown. It was possible we might be called as witnesses, and they smiled at each other as they thought of the delicate nature of our evidence. Veronica might be called upon to testify that she had or had not refused the offer of Max, and cross-examination might bring out for the amusement of the court all the particulars of a love-story.

One of these gentlemen had had a few minutes' conversation with Veronica upon the porch, before we got into the carriage. She was pale and flushed by turns. York and Lancaster contended in her cheeks. She wore a white chip bonnet, and a lilac muslin dress, and took her red shawl folded on her lap in the carriage. Tyrell rode Angelo, who notwithstanding his exertions of the day before, seemed fresh, but Tyrell looked worn out and miserable.

After driving from sunrise to ten o'clock, over an odious road, where now—by grace of Irishmen—there runs an excellent new turnpike, Uncle Israel drew his horses up before the principal tavern in Charlestown. The person who opened the carriage-door for us was Max. Diggory had done his errand faithfully. Leaving Clairmont about sunrise, he had ridden sixty miles by sunset, and it was a relief to hear Max telling Tyrell with some eagerness, that the grey horse had not looked the worse for his long journey. Max had mounted Mike, and had ridden sixty miles in time to reach Charlestown two hours after sunrise. He had gone over to Stonehenge at once, where the old Governor had "posted him up" in his own business, and had accompanied him to Charlestown after breakfast, where they had been waiting in the street looking out for our arrival. Max looked as rough as a back-woods-man, with a full, handsome beard, and a slouched hat shading his sunburnt cheeks, and leaving his forehead fair when he removed it at sight of Veronica. His appearance was greatly Americanized, and I thought that, in spite of the stains of tan and travel upon his dress and face, he had never looked more handsome.

He helped us from the carriage in silence. Veronica flushed scarlet, and another blush rose burning on the traces of the first, as she caught Tyrell's sad eyes looking at her. I saw him too. I was almost more interested in him than I was in Max and Veronica.

We went up to the room labelled the "Ladies' Parlor." A large square room, with a musty smell about it, ornamented with portraits of wooden-looking men and women, staringly like the people they were meant for I am sure, but looking as if they had been painted after lay figures and not from living models. There was a side-board, and a pitcher of fresh water, a table with an empty lamp upon it, and a Bible, such as is supplied to every room in inns by the Bible Society. There were some queer old gim-cracks on the fire-place, a piano, covered with a table-cloth, a horse-hair sofa, and a dozen Windsor chairs. A small door opened on a balcony, overhung with a grape-vine, with rich clusters of ripe fruit. Veronica went out upon this balcony, and I turned to my brother. The lawyers were in the room, and they were talking to him. I did not dare to interrupt them.

I heard him say distinctly,

"No, gentlemen, Mr. Williams is not entitled to Oatlands by the terms of the will. I have not made any such proposal to Miss Lomax as the will requires me to do within a year after the decease of her uncle."

"Just tell me what this to-do is about?" said a stranger, joining the conversation.

The stranger had considerable political influence; and one of the lawyers, who was a candidate for the legislature, explained to him the business, going into all the particulars (for each man's business is every man's on such occasions in Virginia). He told him how old Tom Lomax had left Captain Mandeville his English estate, provided he married Miss Lomax within the year that was expiring, and how the Oatlands property in that event was settled upon her, and on her children, and old Mrs. Williams, or her heirs, were to receive a legacy. How, if Miss Lomax refused the captain, the Oatlands property and negroes were to go to Mrs. Williams or her heir, and Castleton was to be sold and divided between Max and Veronica. He explained how, if Captain Mandeville made no offer of marriage, as appeared to be the case, he retained Oatlands and the negroes under the will, and Miss Lomax had the English property; and finally, how Mr. William Williams laid claim in this event to Oatlands, on the ground that an alien could not hold landed estate in Virginia; and claimed the negroes on the clause in the will which said they should in no event be separated from the landed property. Several strange gentlemen gathered round to listen to this information, and being well primed with the main facts, retired below into the bar-room, to be the centre of a knot of men, sipping cool drinks, and talking over the matter.

The lawyers continued to converse with Max. I pulled him by the sleeve.

"What do you want, Molly?" he said; and the lawyers paused to know what I could want with him. They were interested in the case, which was a novel one; and of course I could not tell him, when they all paused with an interrupted look, that I wanted him to go on to the balcony, and talk to Veronica. I did whisper something to this effect at last, and he went out, but Veronica received him very coldly. He could not win any encouragement on which he dared to speak. He came back in a few minutes, and said,

"It will not do, Molly; and listen," he added: "I forbid you to speak to her about it. I will not have her interfered with. She knows how devotedly I love her; and knowing my heart as she does, and the position in which I am placed, this is a case in which she must make the first advances."

He went down into the street; he went into the court-house, where his case about the riot at Clairmont was called up, and talked over, and defended, and witnesses examined; and little dogs ran about the court, and got between the legs of the judges; and the counsel made a great display of eloquence, indulging largely in stale similes—the orator's cheap tinsel—and they stuck their fingers through their hair, till they looked as if they had seen ghosts. Max told me afterwards that it was a vastly more animated scene than the sleepy decorums of Westminster Hall. Men sat packed together, listening and chewing tobacco; and the plash in the spittoons alone interrupted the eloquence with which the case was argued; and Tyrell and his father gave evidence, and the judges wagged their heads; and their private opinion was known to be, that the merits of this case depended a good deal on the result of that other one coming up for decision the next day: that should it be decided that the slaves belonged to Mr. Williams, it was a case of abduction of negroes, which justified a certain amount of excitement in the neighborhood. But if it were decided that the negroes were the property of Captain Mandeville, then Captain Mandeville had had a right to carry his negroes to Washington in any way that he thought proper. And so the case was adjourned, after a protracted sitting, and endless talk which resulted in no decision.

This had been during the afternoon session. During the morning one, Max had been kept hanging about the court-house, waiting for it to come on. We had all dined together at the public table—private meals or private sitting-rooms being, in a place like this, too great an advance in civilization. Every body was looking at us. Governor Tyrell was placed next to Veronica, and I was on the other side of her, flanked by Tyrell, beyond whom sat Max and Mr. Morrisson.

I wish I could describe the endless variety of pies, baked in flat plates, which the lawyers did not stay to partake of. Justice was not done to them that day, for Tyrell and Max had no appetite, and I am sure Veronica and I had none.

After the court adjourned, late in the evening, Tyrell came to our parlor and told us that nothing had been done, and that the case of Mr. Williams and his claim would not come on till the next morning, so that we should have to sleep in Charlestown, or drive over to Stonehenge and partake of the hospitalities of their bachelor establishment. We had chosen clean and cheerful looking rooms and preferred to remain in Charlestown.

Nobody can imagine the dreariness of that dreadful day, sitting on the Windsor chairs in that dull drawing-room, with strangers coming in and out, and looking at us with curiosity, and a woman doing nothing, but fanning in a rocking-chair, and no possibility of comfort, or even of conversing privately together. Still Veronica did not go to her bed-room—nor did I urge her, for I fancied she was thinking that, perhaps, Max might come and speak with her.

"Don't let us go to supper, Molly," she said, when the great tea-bell rang its summons. And I agreed. I had no appetite for a second edition of dinner.

When we were left alone, Veronica threw herself into the rocking-chair, vacated by the lady with the fan, with a sigh of suppressed suffering.

"Veronica dear," I said, kneeling at her side, "can I do anything to help you?"

"Nothing Molly," she said, "but to leave me alone. I wish ——— Oh! I wish ———" But what she wished she did not say. Her thought was that her pride had ruined him for life, and she wished she could have brought herself to make an advance for which it was now too late. Her bitter remembrance of the way in which he scorned her love at Castleton, and reproached her for too facile an attachment, had checked the impulse of her generosity.

She got up and walked to the balcony which looked upon the street. Reeling down that street came William Williams, with his hat off and some boys following him. A decent looking negro man, in his working clothes, was passing with a dejected look along the narrow side-walk.

"Hallo! you Oatlands nigger! What's your name?" cried out Williams.

"Dey calls me Pete," replied the man, but not very respectfully.

"Pete!—you're the brother of that runaway nigger Christopher, that all this shine is about, ain't you?"

"I'se Uncle Christopher's brother sure nuff," replied Uncle Pete, continuing his walk. But Williams placed himself in his path.

"Who's your master?" roared he.

"I dunno," said Uncle Pete.

"I'm your master. D'ye hear me?" cried Williams at the top of his voice, brandishing a cowhide, which he drew from under his coat. "I'm carrying this cowhide to give a whipping to the English rascal who helped your brother to run off from me. I reckon I'll commence by giving a taste of it to you."

Veronica shrieked and started back. In the door-way of the balcony stood Max. He had been there for more than a minute watching her. Her look and gesture were a mute appeal. He obeyed it instantly. He ran down the balcony steps on to the street, and snatched the cowhide out of Will William's trembling hand, and threw it over a high fence, with a contemptuous exclamation, and turning on his heel strode back to the house. Will Williams sent after him a peal of long, loud, vulgar drunken laughter.

Max hesitated a moment, as if he would go into the house by the lower door, but changed his mind and came up the steps of the balcony again.

It was nine o'clock. The court had sat very late. As he came up upon the balcony Veronica retired into the parlor. The lamp was lighted on the table, and as he came into the room she was standing beside it. The light shone on her face and she was greatly moved. She looked up and saw him.

"Ah! Max," she said in a low voice.

He came near her. Her hand was resting on the table. Her pretty white hand. He laid his hand upon it. And it did not stir. It was resting on the Book of God. His hand was laid on it, as it had been five years before, over the Bible upon Mammy's bed, when they plighted their first troth to each other. Both thought of that moment as their hands met. Each was silent till Veronica gave a sob.

"Oh, Max," she cried, "that man was Uncle Pete, one of old Mammy's sons, whom we promised to be kind to. Those poor unhappy people at Oatlands will belong to that miserable drunken wretch, through my fault. And I have ruined you—and it is too late to repair it."

And Max replied by passing his arm round her, and drawing her closer—closer to himself, till her face rested on his shoulder.

"Too late," she said, with another sob.

I looked up and saw Tyrell standing in the doorway. I never can forget the expression of suffering in his face as he stood there and saw them. And yet my impulse to appeal to him in any moment of distress was so immediate, that I cried out,

"Oh! cousin Tyrell, is it too late? Can we do nothing?"

Veronica started as I spoke, drew away from Max, and looked up with a tearful face of half appeal into the pale, fixed face of Tyrell.

"Is it so, Max?" said Tyrell, recovering himself.

Max grasped his hand. *He* did not know the secret guessed by me, and shared by Veronica—the secret of Tyrell's deep attachment to the woman who had just surrendered herself to him. He did not know that as his sun of life arose, the paler star of Tyrell's hope set at the other extremity of the horizon. He did not look into the face of the friend, whose generous hand, icy as it felt, returned his eager pressure.

"It may not be in time to quash our worthy cousin's suit; and yet ——." He looked at Veronica—he looked at Tyrell, and repeated an interrogative "and yet ——?"

Tyrell hesitated a moment.

> O'er his face,
> The tablet of unutterable thoughts was traced;
> And then it faded as it came.

"Stay here," he cried, "and I will see: it may not be too late." And he departed.

I next heard his voice in the court-yard, calling firmly, loudly, yet with a change, which my ear noted, in its tones, for Diggory to ride to Stonehenge and bring the Governor.

Max and Veronica stood by each other, with whispered words, and hands clasped close, and sobs, and many a "too-late" of self-reproach from Veronica. And there were the low tones of Max's manly voice telling her (and oh! how earnestly our cousin Tyrell could have said the same) how true and tender he would be to her—how fondly he loved her.

They took no note of time—for Love (sly rogue) ties feathers to Time's feet when they travel in company. Perhaps they partly knew what was in preparation—perhaps reality was swallowed up in the joys of that moment when the affection which had been repressed by pride, declared itself.

But I became sensible of a bustle in the house—of a great stir below us in the bar-room—of lights glancing across the street and in the court-house; then forty or fifty men seemed suddenly to turn into the street; then half-a-dozen of them came under the window and gave a sort of cheer; but they had been tippling all day, and were in a state of excitement. I doubt if the lovers heard them.

Then there was more running with candles across the street, and lights began to blaze in all the windows of the court-house. After an absence of half-an-hour Tyrell came back again.

"Come," he said, "all is ready;" and he gave his arm to Veronica. She clung to it—hardly understanding, I think, what she was going to do. I followed with Max. We went down stairs, and at the door were joined by Mr. Morrisson. In the street there was already a considerable crowd—thickest, however, about the doors of the court-house. Tyrell made his way through this—the people making way—and we entered the building.

Veronica's face was hidden in her handkerchief. Ah! Tyrell—poor Tyrell—why did she cling so closely to your arm?

Poor Tyrell . . . . .? I mean noble Tyrell. There must have been joy in heaven, as the recording angel wrote down a sacrifice, that angels "who neither marry nor are given in marriage," could not emulate.

We went into the court-room. It was full of light and full of people. All the lamps and candles of the inn, and of the neighboring stores and offices, had been collected and brought in there. The judges sat on their high bench. The clerk of the court sat ready, with pen and paper.

We advanced to the table before the bench, and Tyrell gave up Veronica's hold upon his arm. There was perfect silence in the court-room.

"Will your honors have the goodness to appoint a guardian for this young lady, who is not of age?" said Tyrell to the presiding judge, "in order that the necessary legal paper may be made out for her marriage."

The judges asked two or three questions that I did not understand. They were going through a form, the preliminaries of marriage being more strict in Virginia than in any other state in America.

The judge turned to his colleagues, and after a whispered word or two, said, "Mr. Tyrell, the court appoints you guardian of Miss Lomax, feeling sure it could not bestow on you a more agreeable duty than to assist on this occasion."

Veronica stood clinging to Max, with her head a little bent, like that of some tall lily. She hardly realized, I think, what was going on. Tyrell walked up to the clerk of the court, whose pen was flying swiftly over his paper. There was some swearing over a book and sundry formulas, and Max and Veronica were several times appealed to. At last a paper was handed to the judge and he rose up.

I looked around for Tyrell. He was close at hand, standing a little behind Veronica, and I could not take my eyes from his fixed face, so well composed that no one who did not know his secret, would have remarked the pain.

"Thomas Lomax Mandeville," said the judge, "do you take this woman for your wife?"

"Veronica Lomax, do you take this man for your husband?"

They took each other by the hand affirmatively.

Max saw a small gold ring on Tyrell's finger (his mother's wedding ring) and with the feeling that a man must marry his wife with a wedding ring, he made a sign to him to lend it for the occasion. Tyrell, drew it off. Perhaps he had often imagined the day when he himself should give it to this woman as his love gift.

"I pronounce you man and wife," fell on his ear, as Max placed the ring on his bride's finger.

CHAPTER XXIV.

> And that high suffering which we dread,
> A higher joy discloses;
> Men saw the thorns on Jesus' brow,
> But angels saw the roses.
> MRS. S. G. HOWE: *Passion Flowers.*

THE hurried marriage ceremony over, we went back to the hotel, where a great banquet of pies had been set out by the landlord, as a complimentary feast on the occasion, and we afterwards understood that the judges, and lawyers, and sheriffs, and newspaper editors, who had assisted at the ceremony, partook of it, and drank the bride's and bridegroom's health in whisky-punch, with roars of three times three.

Meanwhile Max and Veronica and I went up to the inn parlor. Veronica threw herself upon the horse-hair sofa, and cried from agitation. Max sat by her and soothed her. I walked out upon the balcony, under the grape-vine, through whose leaves the moonshine twinkled and threw fantastic shadows.

By and by Max came and called me. Veronica was more composed, though she would not acknowledge herself married. Governor Tyrell had arrived and was sitting beside her on the sofa.

"I have promised Max that our real wedding-day shall be this day week," she said, blushing deeply. "Do you suppose that Marm Venus can make wedding-cake enough by that time?"

* * * * * * * * *

It was the wedding afternoon. Marm Venus had put forth all her powers, and will boast of her exertions to her dying day. As a great battle to a commander-in-chief, so is a wedding in the family to the black Soyer.

"Laws, honey," she says, whenever you remind her of it, "couldn't never bin married if Mammy Venus hadn't kep up three days an' three nights sure 'nuff, jes winkin' 'tween whiles —an' sure 'nuff dat weddin'-cake turned out real elegant, honey! Aunt Mona dar, way dar from Mas' Tyrell's, she done turn up her nose cos I got a roas' pig with a lemon in his mouth, way dar top of 'e table, an' I says to her, 'nebber hab no weddins' in your house sense you was little black gal. Reckon you dunno nothin' 'bout it anyhow.'"

A large number of guests had been bidden to the wedding, for this was not a case in which "sober privacy was comelier than public display." The wedding at the court-house had formed the subject of so many newspaper paragraphs, that it was the object of all concerned to mark by all possible bridal display, their resolution to consider the religious ceremony their true marriage.

The servants had been so occupied all day that I did not feel justified in sending Tommy Tad to Fighterstown, though I had seen the stage pass up the road, and knew it was the day when we should probably receive our English letters.

While I was still in my chamber putting the last touches to my dress (for it wanted but an hour to the time fixed for the arrival of the company), I saw Tyrell riding towards the house, accompanied by Diggory with a carpet-bag. I put my head out of my chamber window and called to him; for calling in Virginia, where bells are hardly known, is not considered an unlady-like proceeding.

"Cousin Tyrell, did you stop at the post-office, and ask if there were anything for us, as you came through Fighterstown?"

"No I did not," said he, putting his foot in the stirrup again "But there is plenty of time to spare, I will ride down and bring you your letters?"

It did not take me long to complete my toilette, and leaving our chamber to Veronica and to the many cousins and friends, anxious to add last touches to her bridal beauty, I went down upon the porch and waited the return of Tyrell. He soon arrived, though no horse could have "kept pace with my expectancy," and riding up to the porch he said "A letter for Max—not any for you." I took it from him. It was an English letter in our father's hand. I ran up to Max's chamber and knocked. Max, nearly dressed, opened the door.

"Please Max tell me what does papa say?"

He opened the letter and glanced over it. Tyrell was coming up the stairs. I knew he intended to make his toilette in Max's room. But I was watching the change in Max's face, and did not stir as he came into the chamber.

"What is it Max?"

"Nothing," he said, crushing the letter in his hand. It is business for me."

"Max you must tell me!"

I clasped his arm. I looked wildly into his face, for I saw that something had gone wrong with him by its expression. Fatigue, anxiety, and "hope deferred," had unnerved me completely.

"Nonsense," said he, trying to laugh. "You are absurd, Molly."

"Then let me see the letter, Max."

"No—no. Be a good girl. I will tell you about it when the wedding is over. Go away now, Molly—that's a dear!" he said. And something in his tone struck on my ear compassionately.

"Oh! cousin Tyrell," I exclaimed, "ask him to tell me what he knows. I shall be wretched till I know the worst. There is such vague uncertainty when there is everything to fear."

"Don't think about your fears," said Max. "Let it alone till after the wedding."

"Oh! tell me ———!" I stretched out my hands in supplication. I was growing very pale, and Max became frightened at my expression.

"For pity's sake, dear Molly," he exclaimed, "take my advice. Try to bear up until the wedding is over, and then ———."

"I will bear up. I will not spoil your wedding—only tell me."

"Mr. Howard is going to be married. So my father tells me," he replied.

"To whom?" I said, trembling, but chilled into proud calmness by the presence of cousin Tyrell.

Max was deceived by the composure of my manner, and having taken the first step, and not finding its effects so bad as he had feared, he hurried over the remainder of his information.

"I always told you that he was not a man we could depend upon, situated as he was, with the whole Howard influence in favor of his marrying that wretched little half-caste daughter of Sir Howard and the Begum."

I turned to leave the room. My first thought, even in that agony, was to conceal my agitation from the eyes of Tyrell.

"Cousin Tyrell, I beg your pardon, for having been in your way," I began to say with a smile, but suddenly the room rocked under my feet, like the deck of an ocean steamer. I seemed to have no foothold. The floor of the room was like a great sheet, lifted at the four corners. Everything heaved around me. I staggered and fell. One of them caught me. When I remember anything more, I was lying with my rose-garland crushed and drooping, in Max's arms, who was supporting my head upon his shoulder, while Tyrell bathed my temples.

"How do you feel now?" said Max.

"Oh! I don't know," I said, trying to stand, "so weak and dizzy."

"Oh! Molly, try to bear up for Veronica's sake," Max whispered. "Just bear up bravely until this is over. It will grieve her so much, if you, who are her bridesmaid, should be unhappy or absent. Take courage, for my sake, don't give way."

"Come along, captain! The bishop has come!" shouted Philip Ormsby, on the stair-case, "and my little charmer, Miss Jenny Dawes, looks like an angel, in rose-buds and white slippers. I am to stand up with her. Where is the other bridesmaid? All the house is looking everywhere for her. Tyrell is her groomsman. That will be a match yet. Ain't you most done fixing yourself up, Tyrell?"

I raised myself from Max's arms, and stood up. *I felt pale.*

"Can you bear it?" said Tyrell, in a low voice. "If you can do it trust to me. No one shall notice you."

I looked into his face, and read my lesson there. "Blessed is he that overcometh!" I made an effort to collect my scattered senses, and to rise superior to suffering. Between us, at that moment, were established the true relations between man and woman. The one imparting strength to every noble purpose, and receiving it from a consciousness of his protecting superiority. Some lines that Tyrell had quoted to me, came into my memory at that moment. Rising, as it were, by inspiration to my thoughts, as quotations do continually, for we know not whence they come, nor whither they fade from our remembrance. They prosper in the errand whereunto they have been sent, and leave celestial messages at the heart's door.

> "BE NOBLE! and the nobleness that lies
> In other men, sleeping, but never dead,
> Shall rise in majesty to meet thine own.
> Then wilt thou see it gleam in other eyes,
> Then will pure light around thy path be shed,
> And thou wilt never more be sad and lone."

Perhaps the spirit of this quotation was fulfilled to Tyrell in that hour, when half his thoughts were of another who was suffering at his side, and when he must have known that I caught the reflection of his self-devotion. Perhaps God's kind angels smiled more kindly upon us than they did on happier hearts in that gay room.

The large square dining-room, cleared for the wedding, was full of flowers and lights. Guests to the number of one hundred and more, were assembled. The bishop was waiting, book in hand. Cousin Philip and Miss Jane, a rustling cloud of pink and white, preceded us into the presence of the company, and Tyrell and I followed. I, clinging to his protection, and feeling each throb of that true heart, as it beat against the hand that lay upon his arm. He stood back amongst the guests to the injury of the "*coup d'œil*," but to my great relief, for I could still lean upon his arm, and we hardly looked like groomsman and bridesmaid.

And thus we heard those wedding words, which strike so sadly on the ear of many a wedding guest at every wedding. Some hear them and think how far their lives have drifted from the hopes of brighter, purer days, when their lips uttered them. Some hear them, knowing in their hearts, that such dear vows will never pass their lips, and, perhaps, as their thoughts follow the bridegroom's words, another voice takes up the answer,—a voice that should have uttered the companion vow—a voice that only echoes in their dreams, or in sad hours lifts its lonely wail in that sad, haunted, carefully closed chamber of the heart, where walk the ghosts of memory.

I heard the words of marriage, and they struck a knell upon my heart.

"I Max, take thee, Veronica."—Was Tyrell's heart rebellious at that moment? Did it seem hard that it could never be, "I James," instead of Max? It seemed to me as if the doors of hope closed with an iron clang, as I thought no voice would ever say, "I Henry, take thee, Mary." That bright dream had faded into grey, and Hope must never more mix rainbow-tints, and paint it on my fancy.

"O stern word—nevermore."

They crowded round the bride, with their congratulatory kisses. Tyrell led me away on to the quiet porch; under the eyes of heaven. We sat down on the lowest steps of the porch; I blessed the coolness and silence. I leant my head upon my hand, and tears came fast, trickling in the starlight, down my arms, and falling on my wedding finery.

After a time Tyrell said, "I intended to ride over to Oatlands this evening, and see if everything were in order for the reception to-morrow, of your brother and his wife. What if we take Diggory and Aunt Pomona (who came over here to assist at the supper, but Mrs. Morrisson says she is only in the way of old Aunt Venus), and you come with me? It will only be an hour's ride, and you can tell them better than I can what they should do."

I did not answer.

"A quiet ride by star-light will be better than the garish glare of a ball-room."

"Oh! so much better!"

"Come then, get on your riding-dress; old Warren's wife will find a room at Oatlands for you."

I rose up to obey, and he went to call his servants and to saddle Angelo. I know not how it was, but without fuss, he arranged it so that, with no servants in the way, we mounted our horses—cousin Virginia coming down the steps of the porch to see us off, and taking charge of my excuses to the rest of the wedding-party.

Diggory, with Aunt Pomona mounted *en croupe*, were waiting for us. Every body obeyed Tyrell, without fuss. He was like a skillful rider, who manages his horse with a firm hand, but never frets his mouth, as is the case with most men.

So again we were on horseback, riding fast away from Clairmont with all its windows gleaming with light, conspicuous even from the gap in the distant mountain.

We rode in silence for a mile or two. We were taking a short cut, and struck into the woods, where we had to ride more slowly. Nothing could have quieted my throbbing nerves like that still, fast ride by star-light. Suddenly, as we came to an opening in the trees, a growl of thunder struck upon our ears; another and another, and the lightning began to play across the sky, flash after flash. The wind was gathering up its strength. It was a real Virginia thunder-storm.

"The voice of the Lord breaketh the cedars," said Tyrell, quoting that magnificent description by the poet David, of the rise and progress of an Eastern thunder-storm.

As he said it, there came a crash, followed by sudden silence. A great tree, only two hundred yards from us, was struck by lightning. There was a blinding flash: a sudden glare succeeded it, and about fifteen feet of blasted wood came crashing, splintering down upon the smaller tree-tops: the monarch of the forest was discrowned. For years he had courted and defied the lightning, which at length remembered him in wrath.

The horses reared and plunged with starting eyes. Diggory and Aunt Pomona disappeared into the darkness. Tyrell leaped from the saddle and seized the head of Angelo. "The dark grey charger," with his bridle hanging loose, galloped away in frantic terror. Tyrell calmed Angelo. The blazing tree died out. The heavy rain came, soaking through the arches of the forest, wetting us to the skin.

"There is a blacksmith's shop not far from here," said Tyrell, "where we may find shelter."

The rain was so heavy, that at every step set by Tyrell or by Angelo, there was a spongy, quashing sound, as if we had been going through a morass, as the water was pressed out of the fallen leaves. The rapid lightning showed us the narrow path, while the great drops of rain came tearing through, and breaking down, the broad oak foliage; and ever and anon "the tempest held his breath," before another effort more fierce and sudden than the last, sent the hail rattling on the tree-tops with redoubled violence; and the fierce voice of the thunder muttered in the distance—then roared nearer and nearer, and died away towards the mountain, where we heard it growl from rock to rock, like some fierce monster driven to his lair.

We reached the shop at length, a ruinous old shanty, insufficient to keep out the rain, which found its way abundantly through the shingles. Tyrell swung himself through the little window, and unfastened the door from the inside. He led Angelo in; and he and I, and the pony, found partial shelter.

It was past eleven at night, as Tyrell's watch showed by one of the sudden flashes. I sat down on a rude horse-block, and Tyrell, after a little while, placed himself near me. We tried to talk about our situation—the prospect that the rain would cease—what we had better do when it should be over; but by-and-by the conversation flagged. I moved my seat to escape a heavy stream that was pouring through the roof, and Tyrell, who was fast lapsing into a reverie, roused himself suddenly.

"Cousin Molly," he said, "don't think me careless of your comfort."

"Indeed you have been all kindness," I replied. And then, after a moment's pause, I ventured to add, "Cousin Tyrell, I believe you can appreciate that kindness more than you think I can. You have been very generous. I owe you thanks for more than attention to my comfort—for your example." I went on hurriedly—"Believe me, cousin Tyrell, I am not incapable of understanding it." I laid my hand on his hand as I spoke, and he took it and pressed it kindly.

"Did your sister tell you ——— ?" he began.

"No, no!" I cried; "she is too honorable to have breathed a word on such a subject; but I have seen it since you told me the legend. Oh! cousin Tyrell, words are weak to tell you what I have learned through watching you."

"Yes," he said sadly, "it is true. I loved her—I loved her" (he dwelt upon the word as if lengthening out its sweetness), "with the exclusive devotion of a lonely heart—a heart that had never opened its closed leaves to any woman till I knew her. And when I loved her, minor interests in life and lesser joys seemed to blossom in the sunshine of the great hope and happiness. My care must be to tend these; they are all that is left. I pray and strive they may not die in this the Arctic winter of my life, in which the sun withdraws himself.

'That love for one from which there does not spring
Wide love for all is but a worthless thing.'

I want all that is good in me to be counted as her triumph. I want every deed of kindness that I do to be reckoned to her. The madness is past. Her memory will shine as a true light. But I am glad she is going to England, otherwise I must have gone myself. I am not strong enough to look unmoved upon their happiness, and know that while Veronica says kindly, 'I am sorry for his suffering,' the remembrance of that suffering will be effaced by the sweetness of the first word of love that is uttered by another."

I was silent. But with all my love and sisterly admiration for Max, I yet wondered why she had not preferred our cousin Tyrell to my brother."

"I loved her from the first day I saw her here," he went on to say, "when she welcomed me with rising tears, and kind, bright smiles, because I was a waif from Castleton; and every succeeding interview made her more dear. She liked me very cordially. In conversation with her opinions took a higher tone, my thoughts blended with her thoughts, as rain-drops run into each other. My hidden fancies shrinking from the light, came forth and claimed her recognition, and I remarked with rapture that she caught my tricks of thought, and in the quiet and calm beauty of her soul, I saw my dreams reflected, as one sees the sky on the still bosom of some lake or river. I had no reason but this to imagine that she loved me, and yet I feared no rival, there was nobody else here whom I imagined she could love. I knew nothing of your brother. Suddenly the news came of old Mr. Lomax's decease and of his will. I thought I ought to test my fate, to win or lose it all. I spoke to her. It was nearly a year ago that I first spoke to her (I have spoken to her once since), and then found I had been guilty of self-deception. "In my gay silk-mongolfier I had risen to the highest regions of the Empyrean, by a natural parabolic track, and returned thence in a swift perpendicular one." I am not a man to sue for love withheld, and lower my own self-respect; nor was Veronica Lomax the woman to be moved by that which would degrade her lover. I went home to the old house, which now seemed doubly dreary, and shut myself two days into my own room. It was my wilderness of temptation—and then after the devil left me, angels came and ministered unto me. There was the Angel of Hope in skyey-robe, and she said, "Be worthy of the happiness that you have lost, and God will make up in Himself that which He withholds from you." There was the Angel of Love, who stood beside me in my dream, and wore the likeness of Veronica, and she laid her hand upon my brow, and said, "Arise, for I have work for thee." And the Angel of Peace stole after her, and left the Saviour's legacy. Cousin Molly, let me assure you, from experience, that God, like kings of old romance, flings his jewels in a cup—and that cup is the cup of sorrow. Anything that teaches us heart-knowledge of the commonest religious truths is blessed to us. Watch and pray that having sown in tears you may not fail to reap the blessing. Pray that you may watch, and watch that you may pray. Bereavements are ambassadors from heaven, bearing precious gifts to us. More precious than anything we offer in exchange is their gold, frankincense and myrrh. Shall we refuse their gifts, especially as they will assuredly fulfill their errand, and carry off that which they came to seek and find? Refuse to entertain the messengers of heaven as we will, no embassy of Death or Grief goes empty away."

"Ah! cousin Tyrell ———!"

"All this is vague," he said, "but these are truths, which each of us must work into the woof of life, according to the design that lies before him. I have been trying since that time to find out what I have to work at. Cousin Molly, there is the same task for you. Though in what form it may be set I know not. Each one for himself, by the light that God affords, must determine it. One reason that a married life is best (what woman's heart does not acknowledge *it is best?*) is that the line of duty lies so plainly before you. But where marriage is impossible, the path to happiness is somewhere, if we can but find it. It is our part to look for it—near at hand, most probably, and not far off; often under our very feet; so close at hand we overlook it."

And as he spoke, the first light of the dawn streamed in through the dilapidated rafters. The chirp of birds, rejoicing after the rain-storm of the night, began. The waters still splashed from the leaves in heavy drops, but in every drop when the sun rose would shine a tiny rainbow.

We were startled by the suddenness of the change. Morning had come unexpectedly upon us. Tyrell rose and led out Angelo. I mounted and we retraced our steps along the forest path which we had traversed in the darkness. Just as we neared the opening in the wood, where the storm had burst over our heads during the night, the sun rose red over the Blue Ridge, and we saw Tyrell's charger, with his broken bridle hanging from his neck, grazing quietly beneath the ghastly ruins of the blasted tree, but a few yards before us.

CHAPTER XXV.

Facts with her are *accomplished*, as Frenchmen would say,
They will prove all she wishes them to—either way;
And as fact *lies* on this side or that, we must try,
If we're seeking the truth, to find where it don't lie.

Fable for Critics. J. R. Lowell.

I ought to have said, perhaps, in an earlier place, that the whole tide of public sentiment turned in favor of Max after the hurried wedding in the court-house, and quashed all proceedings against him; whilst the claim of Mr. Williams was made null and void, since Oatlands and its negroes, by the terms of the will, fell to Veronica. There were persons in the community who still bore enmity to Max for his anti-slavery tendencies; but Mr. Felix advanced, and maintained, a theory that when a man came to own slaves, he was enlisted in support of the institution, and he "mightily convinced" the frequenters of the post-office, illustrating his position with many and illustrious examples. What Max would have said to that line of defence I cannot say. He was occupied with the civilities he had to pay to the guests who assembled in honor of his happiness at Oatlands; and after he and Veronica and I were left in peace, there came endless business arrangements with old Warren and the Tyrells.

Oatlands was a mean and inconvenient house, though good enough for Warren and his wife; and it was little likely Max and Veronica would ever do more than pay their Virginia property an occasional brief visit of inspection.

It was a great satisfaction to Max and Veronica to find every reason to believe that Warren (an old English yeoman, imported as a sort of steward in the time of our grandfather) was a conscientious guardian of their people's interests; and had he not also been true and just in his dealings with his employer, he could hardly have failed to take advantage of the repeated injunctions he received, to make the interests of the owners of the property secondary to those of the negroes who cultivated it.

"*L'un n'empêche pas l'autre*," said Tyrell. "The true interests of the negroes are best promoted by the prosperity of the master. They take their full share of the advantages of a good harvest, while the penalties of debt and difficulty are more apt to fall heavily on them than on their owner."

"The misfortune is," said Veronica, "that in attention to the physical comfort of our slaves, and often to their enjoyments, we are apt to imagine we have done our duty, and that all the reproach that the North heaps on slavery, is unjust to us; whereas the real responsibility laid upon us is heavier far than to provide food, clothing, and good treatment for them."

"Yes," replied Max, "the insensibility around me, constantly reminds me of an anecdote my father tells of Mr. Randolph. He was at an anti-slavery meeting in Exeter Hall, in London; for, twenty years ago, Exeter Hall was a young power in the state, and a public man in America was not liable to be bothered through all his after career, because some simpleton raised doubts about the principles of the company in which he indulged the freedom of speech-making. Mr. Wilberforce was chairman of the meeting, and on seeing Mr. Randolph come into the Hall, he requested him to come up upon the platform, and as the great American orator, to oblige them with a speech. Mr. Randolph complied, and in a happy effort of half-an-hour's length, spoke highly of the philanthropic intentions of the Society, and then branched off to the subject of slavery in Virginia—lauding highly the general condition of the slaves, and forcibly contrasting the plenty they enjoyed with the scanty comforts of our English peasantry. Mr. Wilberforce, after the speech, came across the platform and complimented Mr. Randolph, at whose side was standing an English admiral, of American origin.

"'I am happy to hear you say so much on the subject of the good treatment of the slaves,' began Mr. Wilberforce.

"'It is all true, sir—all true,' interrupted the admiral.

"'I am more glad, sir, to have it confirmed,' said Mr. Wilberforce; 'but think *of their souls?*'

"'Hang their souls!' cried the admiral with a laugh. 'How should we know any thing about their souls? We never saw them!'"

"And yet," said Tyrell, "the number of black communicants in the Baptist and Methodist societies is very large indeed. If you take a census of the whites and blacks, I think you will find a double per-centage of black to white communicants among our southern population."

"I don't see what that proves," said Veronica, "except that the rain of heaven trickles down into the valleys, and does not lodge upon the hills. You are arguing away from the main point, like a slave-owner and a Virginian. Can you say, upon your conscience, that you think that the conscientious care that ought to be prominent in a Christian community, is taken of our servants' religious interests, or even of their morals?"

Tyrell was silent. Perhaps he was recalling sins of omission on his own estate; or perhaps, with the characteristic promptitude with which he set each new idea to work, he was forming resolutions for the future.

"The practical point is, I conclude," said he, "what shall be done in favor of the little Oatlands darkeys?"

"Mrs. Warren tells me she has some sort of Sunday-school for them," said Max.

"True," said Tyrell, "so there is on almost every estate; but you just now seemed to say, that these classes, conducted as they are by the women and children of the place, are inadequate to meet the master's responsibility. I am ready to propose to ride over here, and do my best to impart oral instruction to the people on this place every Sunday."

"You are the best of friends and neighbors," exclaimed Max. "It would be too bad to give you any trouble of that sort, old fellow."

"I am not sure but cousin Tyrell has illustrated another principle," said Veronica with a laugh. "He rounded his moral so quietly, that it reminds me of the figures that we draw for children—distracting their attention till we cry out suddenly 'and so they found that they had made a goose.' Is it not true that all the wise *talk* on this subject is in England or the Northern States, and when anything is to be *done*, the burden falls upon the South?"

Cousin Tyrell did not answer this remark. He had ridden over upon business, and that business being wound up by this discussion, he took his hat and was gone.

After a month spent at Oatlands, receiving visits of felicitation, and making preparations for a long farewell to "Ole Virginny," Max, and Veronica, and I, found ourselves one morning standing on the platform of the railroad, at Charlestown, waiting for the train from Winchester, which was to carry us the first stage on our way home. The time had been changed, the depotmaster told us—the train "would not be along there for an hour or so."

"Come with me, Molly," said Veronica, for Max seemed busy in conversation with a knot of friends. Tyrell watched us as we left the group, but did not offer to accompany us. We went alone to the hotel, and Veronica stood again in its dull parlor.

"How was it, Veronica?" I said. "What induced you so suddenly to change your mind?"

Veronica looked down. "It was not suddenly, but very gradually, as you see in nature, all things working together for a result which comes like a surprise upon you. I have never had even a girl's passing feeling of preference for any one but Max; but oh! Molly, I was wounded to the heart by a conversation that I overheard between him and you at Castleton. To be accused of want of proper pride—to have my timid, girlish love, which only sought to do him good, considered forward—out of place—was worse than to have it flung back in my face and trampled on. To have him say of me—of *me*, who would—

'Have laid my soul down at his feet,
That images of fair and sweet,
Might walk to him from God on it,'

that I was the barrier to his happiness—and that though he perhaps might marry me, he could never give me his love! Oh! Molly, as I think of it the shame comes burning in my cheeks. It seems to me that years of tenderness—and Max is tender and gentle to me beyond words—would never quite soothe my bruised and trampled pride—that pride which cannot be a sin, because it is given to a woman as a safeguard, like her timidity. I came out to Virginia not only to be beyond the possibility of injuring his interests with uncle Lomax, but because I wished to be where nothing would remind me of 'that old love whereon we both did live,' and the shock by which all ties between us had been broken. But Time seemed rather to *wear in* than to *wear out* of my heart that strong impression. I was wretched. The very pain that accompanied remembrance served to fix my thoughts upon old times, as when a wound is sore and stiff we bend and touch the aching part to ascertain how much we suffer. God forgive me! but I tried to wean my heart by taking pleasure in the attentions of other men until I found I had done cruel harm to one who should have been too good to have given *me* such power—so that was a new bitterness still flavored with the old one. And then you came;—and I believed Max only came to court me because he *must;* and I resolved that he who had once accused me of too little pride, should find I had enough to reject such mercenary advances. And when I began to see how much my refusal might injure him I was glad to give him pain. And then I began to think he really cared for me, and that he was really good and true, which when he first arrived I had not thought him.

'Doubts tossed me to and fro.'

I was unutterably wretched, Molly. Then came his danger in the riot at Clairmont, and I almost forgot pride in my sense of it. And he began to speak to me again upon the journey to Front Royal, and I was foolish, Molly. He seemed to think that I cared for him, and then my pride rose up, and the old feeling came back that he would ask me only because it would be unjust to my interests, under the terms of the will, not to ask me, and I answered scornfully, and so we parted. And then Max would not make me any more advances. That suit of cousin Williams's came up—he no longer thought I should accept him, and he would not risk my fortune by giving me the opportunity of refusing him. When he came back—all through that dreadful day that we passed in this room—it was my prayer that if he really loved me, and if I should make him a good wife, he would come back and ask me; and the hours went on—he did not come, and I would not make any advances. Molly, I don't know whether I blame myself even now. It was a dreadful day. Pride and affection struggled for the mastery. Whatever I might do seemed wrong. I tried to trust that God would make things work together for the best; yet every lost moment was making it too late, until it was so very late, that hope was gone. And then when it was over—in the anguish of that moment when the struggle was ended, and there only remained the certainty that he was ruined through my pride and foolishness, my fortitude of purpose all gave way, and I said something,—and he came to me, and then . . . . Oh! Molly, you know all the rest. Did I do wrong to believe that after what I overheard he would think lightly of me if I yielded readily to his suit? Must pride be always wrong, Molly—*womanly pride?*"

As she said this Max and Tyrell came in in great haste to say that the cars were already in sight. We hurried down to the depôt without further words. The train had just come up, and on asking the conductor why it arrived before its time, he said, "They was a' most full half an hour earlier than usual at Winchester, and they thought they might as well be going."

Tyrell put me into the car, and took both my hands in his and pressed them close. We were so much hurried that I believe he got out of the car without taking leave of Max or Veronica. The last we saw of him he was standing by

Uncle Pete upon the platform; and the old negro was bowing and waving his old hat to the master and mistress, whose last directions to Warren had been to make him comfortable; for the old gentleman had married off of the estate and it would have been small mercy to have given him a freedom which would have obliged him to leave the State, and have separated him from his family.

Tyrell was probably not conscious of the expression of his face. It was unutterably miserable. He looked very ill and thin. I was grieved that my last impression of him should have been so painful.

We travelled to Baltimore and thence to Philadelphia, where we stopped two days in order to see Aunt Saph and Uncle Christopher. They came to us at the hotel and no words can express their satisfaction and delight at seeing our familiar faces. But after a while, when the broad smiles upon Aunt Saph's face had worn off, we began to perceive she was dejected.

She was full of complaints about "mean white folks." All her aristocratic prejudices had had their fur rubbed up the wrong way by her residence in Philadelphia. She was cooking at a boarding-house, and heartily despised the people she was working for; while Uncle Christopher was out of employment.

"Laws honeys," said Aunt Saph, "can't even have my chil'ens in de house with me. 'Bliged lock 'em up when I'se 'way feared o' harm. Oh! Miss Veronica, so you done left 'em all in ole Virginia. Do'n see hows you could! Wisht I war back in de ole State. Nebber done no good sence we comed 'way from thar. De Lord He knows if I'se gwine live to see ole age in dis here northern country."

We inquired at some length into her grievances. They did

not seem to be great. She had a tolerable place, and could not have expected to have her children squatting about a northern kitchen; and Uncle Christopher had formed a connection with a Baptist church, and had had work since he came to Philadelphia. At that moment he was out of employment, and winter was coming on, and Aunt Saph's six dollars a month was little enough to support the family upon, but that was no more than every laboring man must expect occasionally.

He seemed much more contented than Aunt Saph. "Thorns an' briars you knows, Mas' Max, dey grows on dis earth ebbery whars. Nebber seen no place free from 'em yet. Grows in ole Virginia like they does here."

"Jus wisht I'se back agin, old man! Wisht I war back!" was the burden of Aunt Saph.

At last Veronica proposed to send them back.

Their faces brightened. "Ain't no place in dis worl," said Uncle Christopher, "like ole Virginia."

"But your children?" cried Max, "they will be slaves again if you go back to Virginia."

"Do'n want 'em to be slaves, Mas' Max, but do'n want bring 'em up here." Then after a pause. "Dunno as de laws 'll let us go back dar. Dunno as de gemmen 'll like to hab us come back. Nebber welcomes black folks back when dey's done run away."

"I don't know about that," said Max. "What can be done, Veronica?"

"Write to cousin Tyrell," I said, "and ask him to arrange it."

It was a piece of advice taken by Max, and we quitted Philadelphia, leaving Uncle Christopher and his wife with a half hope that before Christmas they might be suffered to return to the way of life in which they had been brought up amongst their old friends, and in their own country. They had not been fitted by previous training for an independent position. They had been accustomed to depend on whites, and all their virtues fitted them for dependence. They were admirable servants, and respectable members of society in their own place, but they were entirely out of their element when called upon to stand alone.

"This is the case," wrote Tyrell, "with very many of our better class of Virginia servants, when they find themselves removed from old associations. They do well, if they can take a master or mistress with them into freedom, so long as they keep up the old relations; fugitive slaves do better at the North than manumitted ones. In the first place, Bacon's rule about bad marriages contracted without friends' consent, applies equally to them. They will 'be sure to make good their own folly.' In the next place a fugitive slave is sure to have had a bad, or at the best a careless and indifferent master; besides which, it takes a large amount of spirit, energy, and earnestness of purpose to effect an escape from a slave state. Those who have accomplished it have shown some of the qualities that make poor servants but good freemen. And lastly the fugitive finds friends and assistance among a large class of persons at the North, who have little sympathy for the emancipated slave—always pining like Aunt Saph, after the aristocratic associations of his earlier days. Remember that it was all Moses and Pharaoh together could do to wean the Israelites from a taste for Egypt."

Tyrell went on to Philadelphia, and had great trouble in arranging their return to "ole Virginny." I think his expedition had the advantage of having done him good, for his letter was written in more cheerful spirits, and had a gleam of his old fun in it when he described the difficulty with which he smuggled his *protégés* out of freedom into slavery.

Max was mortified at this untoward result of his first experiment in amending "the institution," and could only write to Tyrell that he intended to give Uncle Christopher's children the freedom they were entitled to when they came of age, and that he hoped they would be brought up in such a way as to have a higher appreciation of the blessing he intended to bestow upon them.

"You are right," wrote Tyrell in reply. "You are beginning at the right end of this subject of emancipation. We of the South have John the Baptist's mission to perform—'preparing the way' for means of future deliverance. We have to call our own age to repentance for participation in, or careless indifference to, the miseries, and sins, and evils, engendered by this institution. And if in individual cases we attempt emancipation, let us 'prepare the way' for that also, by such previous care and instruction as may fit the objects of our bounty for the new station of life which we assign to them. Nor does the duty of a master who emancipates his slaves rest here. No Christian man, who is a slave-owner, can reconcile the possession of such property with the instincts of his conscience, unless he looks upon it as a stewardship which binds him to consult the true good of those committed to his care. Emancipation does not set him free from this responsibility. It is not enough to transplant a family of helpless servants out of the homes in which they have been sheltered—friendless and houseless, ignorant, simple, and dependent—over Mason and Dixon's line. Cheap benevolence—I mean the benevolence that contents itself with a single effort, whether of alms-giving or of emancipation—is apt to do small service. The duty of the master to the slave he would emancipate, obliges him to send him forth provided with a trade by which to live, and such instruction as may fit him to get an honest living. Were this the case, we might not hear such complaints from the free states of negro crime and pauperism. Beside this, his benevolence, or rather his *duty*, in this case—(a duty incurred by his benevolence)—must contemplate the future. In the sight of God, he who has reaped a profit from slavery, or won men's praise for his benevolent self-sacrifice in emancipation, will continue to be responsible for the well-doing of the slaves he has sent into a free country. He should keep his eye upon them, and, if possible, raise up friends for them, and as opportunity shall offer, should promote their interests, long after those interests have ceased to be his own. We have no right to tear away the prop and then expect the creeping plant will flourish and do well without some pains or training. I do not think that a certain moral obligation of assistance and protection ever ceases to be binding on the master of an emancipated slave. The negro tacitly acknowledges this bond to be of permanent continuance. You very rarely find a respectable emancipated southern servant in a free state who does not keep up a sort of feudal feeling of retainership towards his 'old master.'"

END OF THE SECOND PART.

PART THIRD.

Still through the paltry stir and strife
  Glows down the wished Ideal,
And longing moulds in clay, what life
  Carves in the marble Real.

J. R. LOWELL.

Think'st thou thy work at an end, and thy discipline perfect?
Other pangs still remain, other labors and sorrows;
Other the crises of Fate than the crises of Being.
Let me round my words with one brief admonition:
Take for the bearings of life, thine own or another's,
This motto, blazoned on cross and on altar, "GOD'S PATIENCE."

MRS. S. G. HOWE: *Passion Flowers.*

PART III.

CHAPTER I.

Oh! square thyself for use—a stone that may
Fit in the world is left not on the way.
PERSIAN PROVERB.

Poor indeed thou must be, if around thee
Thou no ray of hope or joy canst throw—
If no silken cord of love hath bound thee
To some little world through weal or woe.
MISS WINSLOW.

WE made a stormy passage across the Atlantic, in the middle of November, and as the newly-married pair stayed a week or two with our father (then quartered in North Wales) it wanted but a few days of Christmas when we arrived at Castleton.

More than two miles away from it, we heard the merry English bells ring out their chime of welcome; and the enthusiastic villagers had put a green arch, decked with shining holly, over the bridge, and cheered us as we passed under it.

Max stopped the carriage, and I loved him for the tear that I saw glitter on his eye-lashes, as he stood up and took off his hat, and waved an answer to their welcome.

"God bless you my good people—one and all. Thank you

for your kind welcome to me and to your lady: you know her of old."

"Yes! and God bless her!" from the people around the carriage. "Three cheers for our lady."

"I hope," said Max, "to be always your good landlord; but if I should ever fail in doing what is just and right, you must seek a friend in her, and she will use her influence for you."

"Hurrah!" from the crowd.

"Drive on," said Max.

We swept through the iron gates, and through the long oak avenue. Veronica was leaning forward, flushed with eager expectation.

"Mrs. Mayhew is there, dear Max, and all the rest of them. The only changes seem to me to be in us. And there is Miss Alicia—and I see the Rector!"

There was no stately presentation of the bride to the assembled servants, for Veronica springing out of the carriage as soon as it stopped, was among them, shaking hands with all of them —more as if she had been amongst a crowd of colored servants at the South, than as if she remembered the etiquettes that English custom had set about her dignity as mistress and matron.

She had used up her queenly dignity during her courtship, and since her marriage, had thrown the stiffness of those days aside.

She was as gay as a bird—the merry, loving, winning Veronica of the old happy years.

"I shall do better by-and-by, dear Max," she said. "I shall take up my dignities, and make a very stately mistress of Castleton."

"I would not have you any better, nor any thing, my sweet one, but what you are," replied Max, catching her hands and drawing her to himself, as they went together into the great drawing-room, which had been opened for the occasion.

"Oh! Max!" she said, when she saw the bow window, drawing away from his side.

"No, no," said he, laughing, "do not look that way, love, but this."

He drew a large red chair up to the marble table—the very chair into which on that unhappy evening he had thrown himself; and again placing himself in it, and holding both her hands in his, he made her stand before him.

"Now, Veronica," said he, "I will tell you an old story, a story which you like me to repeat, if you will tell me once again you love me."

"Let go my hands, then," said she.

"Very good," said he, grasping her dress, "say it prettily. Brush back my hair from my face—just so, with those two little white hands."

And as they lay upon his glossy chestnut locks, she stooped and whispered the assurance that he asked, with a half coy look.

He sprang up in his own quick way, and caught her in his arms, and gave her, ere she could prevent him, more than one of his rough kisses, exclaiming,

"When you say that, you make me the happiest fellow upon earth, though we have been married two honey-moons. Now come and see old Luath, and the swannies, and the pony."

The venerable hound, a very Old Parr among dogs, had never quitted the stable since Veronica left; but he knew her at once, and to the admiration of every one, followed her to the house, and resumed his old place at her side.

That evening in the gloaming, she, and Max, and Luath went together to the church-yard. They took the key of the church with them, and stood long in the chancel over Uncle Lomax's tomb. Then they came out and visited Mammy's humbler grave; and Veronica said, as she leant lovingly upon the arm of Max,

"Everything I love is at Castleton. You could not have chosen any wife whose affections were so completely centered in your home. I was so unhappy all the time I was away, that I formed no attachment that it wounded me to sever. There is poor Molly, like a grape-vine clinging to everything that comes within her reach, but I am ivy and was made to grow upon the walls of Castleton."

"Poor Molly," thus they had already learned to call me. I was indeed a grape-vine, torn from its supports, and trampled under foot. Our roving life had not enabled me to form ties of locality. I was like a flower transplanted constantly from pot to pot. No sooner did my roots accustom themselves to the soil and begin to strike, than I was torn up and moved elsewhere. I had naturally a great deal of adhesiveness and suffered terribly for want of a home-feeling, as we moved about from garrison to garrison. I had a strong attachment to Castleton; and Max and Veronica urged me to live with them, but my heart asked for occupation. The charities and interests of Castleton could be sufficiently managed by Veronica and Miss Alicia. Veronica liked to see me there, but she was just as happy in my absence—my presence supplied no want in my brother's home.

My father's household was not peaceful nor orderly. Six children of his second marriage were growing up, and Mrs. Mandeville was more their mother than his wife; it seemed to me as if in my duty to my father, lay my one tie to existence—as if wherever he was were the germ of home.

I devoted myself to him. I tried to make him comfortable.

I tried to soften the rude boisterousness of growing boys, for his sake, and teach order and refinement to the little girls, who, with their hair about their ears, were always looking out of the window after the officers. I used to write a great deal for my father, who called me his "home-secretary," and it was in that way that after a time I became acquainted with cases of distress, and began to take an interest in the soldiers' wives and children.

He took me on his arm to slatternly low houses in the suburbs where they lived, and taught me that to persons of that class our influence may be more useful than our money. He taught me that the charity which is most largely blessed is the charity of *time.*

Before long I gained the hearts of a good many of the women connected with the regiment, a disorderly, unthrifty class, but "therefore there is so much the more need that we should teach them rightly to manage what they have," said my father.

"You women all know something about cookery and household matters, I suppose, and you can do them more good by teaching them good management and thrift than by giving them money. I have a strong dislike to the indiscriminate distribution of alms."

So, though I carried but little money in my purse, I went among them chiefly on the authority of the colonel's daughter, and was surprised to see how glad they were to welcome me, even where I feared at first I might be considered an intruder. As soon as they believed I was their friend they brought me all their troubles with a sort of dependence upon me as a superior authority. I did not give much money, as I said, but I soon saw a great change. "Dear papa," I exclaimed one day, laughing at some news from America, about a Womens' Convention, "I have more than all those women are contending for. I have no diploma it is true, but I can practice medicine to what extent I like, for though I chiefly preach the soap-and-water-cure and total abstinence from Godfrey and Daffy, my people would swallow any drug I recommended them, and quite frighten me by receiving my opinions as authority. As to preaching!—I read the Bible constantly from house to house, with a few words of explanation, and as I read the neighbors gather round me in sick-chambers; I teach a Sunday class of great boys, who are almost men; and women eager to be taught, frequent my Bible classes. Dear papa, these people have been like sheep having no shepherd. It has been a field in which the enemy sowed tares and no one reaped the wheat. Now almost all of them are going to some church, and the children are baptized and sent to school. Papa, it frightens me to think how little I have labored and how much has been done."

"I do not mean to disparage your zeal or usefulness, my daughter," he replied, "but I told you from the first that if they learned to look upon you as their friend, no one could measure the influence you would exercise through their appreciation of your social position. The English mind is unduly influenced by adventitious superiority, and when that is all on the side of religion, virtue, and improvement, you cannot estimate how much it elevates people of the lower class to be brought into contact with persons of higher rank in society."

When I first came from Virginia, I learned that the report of Mr. Howard's engagement was *true.* I hoped I should escape hearing more about the marriage than the mere announcement of it in the London paper. But unfortunately, the editor of the county journal of the town near which the Howards lived, was under obligations for kindness shown him by my father; and whenever there was any thing of especial interest in his paper, he sent us a copy. Thus I read, almost against my will, of the feast for all the tenantry at Howard Park, of "the gallant bridegroom," and "the whole roast ox," and "the lovely bride," and "attendant train of bridesmaids," and "the hymeneal altar." This was about six months after our return—before any answer of peace had come to my wild question,

"What has God given me His fatal gift of life for? Why am I taught to thank Him for creation and preservation?"

Thank God, who gave me interests and occupations, and led me through "the duty that was nearest to me," into a wider range of interests, and let me see the fruit of my labors—a privilege I did not merit; for I marred my own share in the work by a restless impatience of spirit, which carried selfishness into the vineyard, where I labored,

"Not for love—yet nothing for reward,"

but for the luxury of labor—for the satisfaction of crowding out the thoughts that would look backward—for the gain of doing journey-work—for the privilege of shutting out all view of that bleak, lonely path which I saw stretching towards the sunset, over the barren moorland of the future.

My brother, be not exquisite to cast
The uncertain shadow of uncertain evils;
For grant they be so—while they rest unknown,
What need a man forestall his date of grief,
And run to meet what he would most avoid.

May God forgive me that despondency! I am punished for it every day, when I look into my glass and see the silver streaks in the hair that should be still all brown upon my forehead.

My dearest father's health began to fail, and I waited on him assiduously. Every day drew us closer to each other. There was so much of his inner life I shared, which was not guessed at by his wife or younger children!

His tall form began to show some signs of age. I heard somebody call him "an old gentleman," and was inexpressibly shocked at his being so described. The surgeon of the regiment recommended change, and we went down to Castleton. It was glorious autumn, and those days were rest and peace. On the very last evening of his life, he walked with us through the woods, and was talking of Virginia. His thoughts strangely overleaped the sixty years that lay between that hour of calm twilight, and the period that they dwelt upon, as he told us stories we had never heard before, about Stonehenge, his mother, and his boyhood.

That night he died quietly. I went into his room to wake him with a kiss, and found he slept the sleep that knows no waking!

They buried him at Castleton, on the estate which should have been his own—he who was born to the fortunes of a prince, and owned so little beyond his pay as a lieutenant-colonel!

Max and Veronica urged me to live with them; but they were too happy. I could not add to, nor take from, their happiness by my determination. Their eldest little boy, Charles Lomax Mandeville, could totter alone along the floor of the long drawing-room, and hide behind the draperies of the bow-window, and play at peep-bo with his baby sister Thomasine, whom he looked upon with *naïve* curiosity and boyish pride. My place was not at Castleton; I was wanted at home.

I never went back to the regiment. I never saw those soldiers' wives who called me friend, but I heard that others took my place, and that where I alone had "sown in tears," three or four entered into the field of my labors. The work was in better hands, and better done. I did not deserve to be God's instrument, because I had begun it so selfishly.

I never saw my boys again—poor fellows, each laboring over his verse of Scripture; great fellows—almost men—in semi-regimental dress, with touching humility getting little fellows, who could read better than they, to prepare them for their turn, by telling them the big words of the lesson. My last lesson (strange coincidence!) had been from the twentieth chapter of Acts, "And now brethren, I know that ye all, among whom I have gone teaching the kingdom of God, shall see my face no more." They looked at me with their intent round eyes, and interrupted me with strange, irrelevant questions, such as they used to put to their best friend; and we none of us were conscious we were reading prophecy. An officer took charge of of them after I left—for, thank God, the spirit of Christian usefulness has of late years crept in, even among the officers of our regiments—and he wrote me of their progress from time to time.

My father's widow moved to London. There had been talk before he died of sending the boys to the London University. Max undertook their schooling and establishment on their entering into life, and I thought I might best do my duty to my father, by living at home and superintending the domestic discipline of his family.

I have told in another place, of those dreary days when I stood at the window of my attic-chamber, watching sunset or moon-light, and thinking about that last bright sun-light spot in my sad life—my visit to the Valley of Virginia. I yearned in spirit over the recollections of that time. Its memories were "dear as remembered kisses after death" are to the mourner. I had tried to keep up a correspondence with my cousins, but it is not in the nature of Virginians to write letters. If there were not a mixture of foreign blood in the old Dominion, and if there were no candidates for office, I believe there would be little inconvenience felt from shutting up the Post Offices all over Virginia.

Cousin Virginia wrote me at long intervals, and Phil sent me a letter once or twice. But Phil was not funny upon paper. Indeed, as I learned afterwards, he got Mr. Morrisson to write him rough copies of these epistles which the family called "First and second Philippians," and paid him for the first in a second-hand white waistcoat, and for the second in a chain made from the hair of Miss Jane Dawes, which he kept on a shelf, in an old boot, which contained his keepsakes and valuable papers.

I should have learned little enough of what was going on over the Ridge, had it not been for the letters of Tyrell. He wrote to Max very regularly about Oatlands. Max abhorred writing, and would constantly enclose the letters to our father, during his lifetime, begging him to get "the Home Secretary," to answer them and say, "Yes, yes, yes," to every proposal. And thus a sort of desultory intercourse was established between me and Tyrell.

Strongest and dearest of all my recollections of Virginia were my remembrances of Tyrell. As the memory of Harry Howard faded into the back-ground of my life, the image of Tyrell, as that of the best and noblest man whom I had ever intimately known, came out in strong relief. Even in the days of my love I had acknowledged his superiority. I had never compared him with Mr. Howard *then*, because I shrank from the comparison, but *now* as my love for the one faded, my appreciation of the other brightened. I grew angry with myself for thinking so much of Tyrell. I chid myself as Pharaoh chid his bondsmen with "Ye are idle—ye are idle," and plunged into more work than I could get through. But to have known a truly good and noble man makes an epoch in one's life. It is a thing to thank God for. I went more cheerily about my work in life, when I remembered that cousin, whose path was so widely different from mine, but whose example animated me in another field of duty. I was more hopeful as to the result of human effort, when I thought that in the world (to me unknown) there might be other men like cousin Tyrell. And when I thought of "the shade by which his life was crossed," of his deep, manly love (so nobly overcome by unselfishness) for the woman who had preferred a man whom I could not but acknowledge was less worthy, I learned that success is not what God deems the best prize of life, and that "whom the Lord loveth he chasteneth," answering our prayers and aspirations not according to our *will*, but to our *well*, as St. Augustine hath it.

If God did not give Tyrell happiness, why should he give happiness to me? And the object upon which the passion and the tenderness of Tyrell's noble nature had been spent, was worthy all the wealth of gold, and frankincense, and myrrh, his love had lavished at her feet, and which she stepped on—lightly it is true—and passed by disregarded. But Harry Howard . . . . ? Oh! doubt—Oh! dreadful doubt—that now arose on the horizon of my life. I had made my venture for happiness and it was wrecked.—Was the boat upon which I had embarked it seaworthy? Could it have brought me back the golden summer fruits for which I pined? Would it have been better to have seen it wrecked in sight of port, and, having married, for the sad remainder of my life been forced to draw up from the ocean of Time—that ocean salt with human tears—fragments of stranded hopes, from which to eke out an unhappy destiny? My little bark had foundered out at sea;—she had gone down all standing; her white sails glistering with the summer light, and "not a wrack was left," to connect the present with that sudden misery.

It was a warm spring day in May, and London glowed in all the brightness of the season. The parks and gorgeous Regent street teemed with the press and turmoil of human existence. Max and Veronica had come to town for a few weeks, and had taken rooms in a hotel in St. James street. Max had long wanted to have his beautiful wife presented at court, and Veronica had always shrunk from the expense and turmoil of a London season, but now that she had yielded to her husband's wish, she was anxious to gratify him by her appearance, and took a thousand-fold more pains and care in selecting a court-dress that should show off her beauty to advantage, than ever she had done in her unmarried days to win his admiration. We had consulted milliners, and chosen feathers, and held committees of taste over *point d'Angleterre* and *point d'Alençon*, till I was tired of my post of consulting counsel.

The important day had come, and as I was to make my appearance at Veronica's toilette at twelve o'clock, I gave my little sisters a whole holiday. I was not sorry to have the early hours of the morning to myself, and opening my desk began to look over some papers. Among the contents of that desk were the half-dozen letters I had had from cousin Tyrell. As I sat looking them over—arranging them according to their dates—proudly and almost fondly lingering over the justness of the views he held, or watched the sparkle of froth upon the wave—good sense made graceful by his playful fancy—I did not notice that my little brother Marmaduke was looking into the desk, and had possessed himself of a paper.

"Don't Clara! if you push so you shan't look," he cried.

"What have you there, Duke?" said I.

Duke opened the paper and Clara snatched at it at the same moment.

"Oh! Clara give me that," I cried. "It is a little yellow pimpernel, which I value very much. It was given me in Virginia, by your cousin Tyrell."

"Come," I resumed, when Clara had restored the pimpernel, seeing they were not not likely to be quiet, and that their quarrel had broken the bubble of my reverie, "I will tell you a story about cousin Tyrell." And the children, who liked nothing better than to hear about my Virginia visit, gathered around me eagerly.

I told them about our journey to Harper's Ferry—I described the American railway cars—I told them how the railroad track was scooped out from the mountain side—and then I told them of Harper's Ferry, and of our meeting with cousin Tyrell—of Jefferson's rock—and of our pic-nic dinner.

It was a great pleasure thus to talk of Tyrell. To these children to whom I spoke of him as their cousin, I could dwell upon his manliness and goodness without risk of misconstruction. He was little more real to them than a prince in the Arabian Nights' Entertainments, and I pleased myself by dwelling on his virtues with enthusiasm.

It was a story so agreeable to relate that it lasted far beyond the limits of an ordinary fairy tale, and I was startled by the arrival of a cab, from which my brother Max jumped out and rapped at the front door in a great hurry.

"Molly," cried he, as he came running up the stairs, "Vera wants to know if you have forgotten her?"

"No, indeed, I am going to set out this very minute, Max. I did not know it was so late."

"Make haste then; put your bonnet on as fast as possible," he cried.

I did not keep him waiting, and as we went down the stairs he said:

"Veronica fancied that you might be detained by Tyrell. Susan, if a strange gentleman comes here and inquires for Miss Mandeville, tell him she is at Fenton's Hotel, in St. James street, where he had better come and find her. And tell him, too, I did not get his letter till this morning."

"Tyrell in England, Max?" I cried.

Max nodded, as he placed himself in the cab beside me. "Here is a letter from him, dated a week ago in Liverpool, and directed to Castleton. I thought it likely that when he found that he received no answer, he would come up to town, and, as he knows your address, that he would come first to you."

CHAPTER II.

> Fate's pure marble lies so whitely,
> Formlessly between us cast.
> I have wrought and studied slightly,
> Thou who knowest all things rightly,
> From my heart's love, but not lightly,
> Mould a friendship that shall last.
>
> MRS. S. G. HOWE: *Passion Flowers.*

> Nor would it derogate from her fair perfections,
> If she should hold her best affections free
> To change as times change; with no wanton lightness,
> Nor on vain pretexts; nor from those that *are*,
> To those who are not worthy.
>
> H. TAYLOR: *Isaac Comnenus.*

IT was past one o'clock, and Veronica was dressed when we arrived. She was standing in the middle of their sitting-room, in full court costume, and my first involuntary exclamation was,

"Oh! how beautiful!"

She made a court courtesy to her husband, and her eyes danced with pleasure at the sight of his admiration.

Her dress was white—all white, as it should be for a first presentation; and on the glittering folds of the train of watered silk, the priceless lace she wore (an heir-loom from George the Second's day) lay with singular advantage. Soft feathers drooping from her head, added to her dignity, and the beauty of her *point d'Alençon* lappets was as "rich as it was rare." The last touch had been given to her beauty by a present from Max.

"I should not have known my wife had she worn nothing red," he said, pointing to his gift of diamonds and carbuncles.

"White and red is my favorite combination," said Veronica, shaking her head, till the red light glowed from the jewels in her ears; "but it is in defiance of the rules of taste, I know, for any *blonde* to deck herself in that color."

As she said this, the door opened, and the servant brought in a card.

"Oh! ask him to walk up," she cried, and in a moment after cousin Tyrell came into the room.

I watched the effect upon him as he entered. He was startled by that radiant vision, as holding her train with one hand, she came forward with the other held out to give him an eager greeting. I fancied he changed color. My heart beat fast with sympathy for what I thought it likely he must feel when he thus beheld her.

His greeting, however, was self-possessed, cordial, cheery, and cousinly—not different from that he gave to me. He was very little changed—a trifle stouter, perhaps, and his bearing was a little freer; and he had paid a traveller's respect to the great city of the earth "in all its glory," by a little more attention to his dress, than in the days when he wore old coats at Stonehenge, or rode about the country in green baize gaiters.

"Are these your children, cousin Max," he said, smiling at Charles and Thomasine, who were wondering at their beautiful mother from a corner of the sitting-room. She went across the room, and taking Charlie by the hand, led him to cousin Tyrell, saying, as she did so,

"This little fellow is too small to take your name in vain; you must let him call you uncle."

"Uncle Tyrell," he repeated, with a certain thoughtfulness, as if the word had struck upon a chord of feeling. "Uncle Tyrell! Come here, my little nephew, and make acquaintance with your new uncle."

Max, who had retired to prepare for court, soon came back in his handsome scarlet uniform. Before they started, the luncheon was brought up, and he insisted that his wife should eat a plate of soup. She took it standing. Little Thomasine, who was watching her, begged hard to taste of it; and Veronica, whose management leaned to the side of indulgence, told her to get upon a chair and she should have a spoonful.

The carriages were beginning to pass the window, and Max had called Tyrell and me to view the plumed ladies, handsome horses, and gay liveries, but we turned from the show as the beautiful mother, standing behind her child, who was mounted on the chair, put her white, jewelled arms about her neck, and gave her the promised spoonful.

I never had been so struck with the beauty of motherhood. Her womanly, sweet action, crowned her with a higher grace than all her other loveliness. My first feeling was a *fear* lest Tyrell noticed it as I did. My next was to despise myself. Why should I not wish Tyrell to acknowledge the beauty of my sister? It had been no anxiety that he should suffer which had given rise to that bad feeling; it was a selfish consciousness that I, in the background, in my plain grey dress, could bear no comparison with Veronica. I was afraid to meet the eye of Tyrell.

The carriage was at the door.

"Good bye, good bye," cried Max. "Molly, you have promised to stay here and take care of the children till we return, and we shall keep you and Tyrell to dinner. We shall drive round to your house when we leave the drawing-room, and show ourselves to Marmaduke, and Clara, and the other children. I promised them we would. And I shall tell your mother not to expect you home till after dinner."

They were gone, and Tyrell and I were left with the luncheon, and the children, and the window overlooking the procession. We stood there some time silently, and watched the ladies in court-plumes, as they passed us in their well-appointed carriages, carriages so strangely different from those in Old Virginia. I saw several persons that I knew, amongst them Sir Colin and Lady Ellen Nasmyth, the latter with a harassed look and a disdainful air, as she looked out upon the crowd that fringed the kerb-stone.

"There is a gentleman bowing to you in that carriage," said Tyrell. "He seems to want to catch your eye. A handsome aristocratic man, who looks the high-bred Englishman, beside a dowdy, little dark woman."

"That," said I, with no touch of faltering in my voice, "is the new Sir Harris Howard, going with his wife to be presented on his accession to the Baronetcy."

"Do they live in London?" said Tyrell.

"No," I replied, "but they have come up here for the season, and have been quite attentive to Veronica and Max, since they have been in town."

Tyrell said nothing more, and we continued to watch the carriages. When nearly all had passed, we left the window, and sat down. Tyrell began to tell me of the people, white and black, over the Ridge. He had lots of funny stories about cousin Phil; he was just as merry as he used to be—he laughed, and talked, and played with the children, and the afternoon passed away so rapidly and pleasantly that I was startled when the door opened and Veronica and Max, accompanied by Marmaduke, came back from the drawing-room.

"Well," said Tyrell, "did you have a pleasant time?"

"We had a real, first-rate time," said Veronica, laughing, as she answered his Americanism in American. "It was a great deal less formidable than I expected, Molly."

"Did you find many people whom you knew?"

"Yes, several. I talked a long time to Lady Ellen Nasmyth, whom Max introduced me to."

While our chat about the drawing-room was carried on, the table was being set for dinner, and Veronica sat down to eat it in her court-dress, laughing at the inconvenience of her costume, as she disposed her train over the back of her chair.

Marmaduke, who had had his eyes fixed upon Tyrell ever since he came into the room, leaned over to me and said something in a whisper.

"What is that, Duke?" exclaimed Max. "No whispering in company. Say out what you want to say to your sister."

"I only wanted to know," said Duke, "whether that is the cousin Tyrell Molly was telling us about this morning, who she said was so good, so much better than anybody else in the world, and she hoped Charles and I should be just like him when we grew older."

I felt that I was blushing distressingly. I had no objection that Tyrell should know my high opinion of his character (or rather I should have had no objection a few hours before, that he should know it), but now I had grown shy and conscious, and to have it blurted out in this way by Duke, was very disagreeable.

After the coffee, when I had helped Veronica to resume her usual dress, and kissed the children sleeping in their cribs, I put on my bonnet to go home with Marmaduke, but Tyrell insisted on escorting me. When we were in the street, I found him so eager about London sights that I asked him, laughing, how he could have wasted a whole afternoon at Fenton's, instead of going in search of St. Paul's and the Tower, which he appeared to be looking for round every corner. He answered he had been better employed, but that he meant to be very eager about sight-seeing the next day; and finding that the children knew nothing of the London sights, and that I was not familiar with half the objects that made up his idea of London, he went into the house with me and urged Mrs. Mandeville to let him bring a carriage the next morning and take me and all the children to see the Tower and the Tunnel. Mrs. Mandeville was very willing. Tyrell's cousinship, distant as it was, was allowed to meet the question of propriety, and for a fortnight we were all engaged in seeing traveller's sights, not merely those the ordinary visitor to London sees, but we visited all sorts of queer localities connected with the past history of London, which Tyrell's extensive acquaintance with the literary history and private memories of the 18th century, made very interesting. We walked down Bread street, and asked a grocer's woman if she could tell us in which house John Milton had lived.

"Lord no!" said she. "I've lived 'ere fifteen year, and in that time there's been so many broke and gone away, that I'm sure I can't tell you anything about 'em."

"And such is fame," said Tyrell, "even the fame of Milton. We talk of a literary reputation as more enduring than an empire, we talk of extending it by translations into all manner of strange languages, but what if, after all, our greatest chance of extending it among our race were by letting the knowledge of our greatest minds soak more into the masses, by making Milton and Shakespeare familiar among the millions who already speak and ought to read and write our English tongue?"

But the place where Tyrell liked to go the best was to afternoon service at Westminster Abbey. Transplanted as I had been from spot to spot, there was no place upon earth for which I had so strong and personal an attachment as for Westminster, and it was pleasant to find that Tyrell shared it. We sat together evening after evening under the glorious fret-work of the roof; the variegated light falling, as the sun-set shone through the west window upon the fretted arches, on our faces and my drapery, and then the evening shadows quietly stole in, making the tracery of the roof misty and vague, till all the place was dim with solemn twilight. I have knelt there with an aching heart—knelt beside Tyrell, who could not read my thoughts, and prayed to be delivered from impending evil and temptation.

"Molly," cried Max, bursting, about noon one day, into the little front parlor, that I called my school-room, "Veronica says that she is tired of London, and she thinks the children are looking pale, and we are going home next week. Tyrell has promised to go down with us, and we want you to pack your trunk and spend a month at Castleton."

"I do not think I can, Max," I said in a low voice. "I will come a month later if you like, but at present I do not think I can go down to Castleton."

"Nonsense!" cried Max. "Why, you promised Veronica to go back with us! She depends upon it. You are the oddest girl! I shall ask Mrs. Mandeville about it. Why a day or two ago you were talking of your visit. She is going to take the children to the sea-side and can perfectly well spare you."

Tyrell, who had entered with Max, was standing by when this was said, and he looked troubled. As Max went out of the room, he said in a low voice:

"Is it because I am going to Castleton?"

The question took me by surprise. I could not answer it for a moment; then I said: "It would be impossible for me to go now. Max will not be much disappointed."

Tyrell made no answer. There was a painful pause.

"Come along Tyrell," said Max looking in. "We promised to be back at the hotel by two o'clock. Molly, I am sorry I have no better news to carry to Veronica."

"I will follow you presently. In a half an hour, perhaps," said Tyrell.

He waited a few moments till Max had left the house, and then he asked me if I would walk with him that afternoon to Westminster Abbey. There was something strange in his tone. My instinct told me that a crisis was at hand, of what nature I could not guess, but I put up my work and said I should be glad to go.

When I came down Duke was asking Tyrell to take him too, but Tyrell, with his gentle, but decided way, against which no one could appeal, said: "No, my man, you must stay at home this afternoon. I have something that I want to talk about to your sister Molly."

An object in this walk was thus announced. I took his arm and we walked on in silence, through Oxford street, down Regent street, and Waterloo Place, and descended the broad steps that lead into St. James' Park behind the column; still Tyrell did not speak nor did I.

It was but two o'clock when we passed the Horse Guards and it was too early for Westminster Abbey. Tyrell drew me to the ornamental water, and choosing a vacant bench beneath a tree, placed me upon it, and was about to seat himself beside me. A little hesitation in my manner made him pause.

"Do you object?" he said.

"It is very like nursery-maids and Life Guardsmen," I replied.

"Is that all? I am about as much like one of those giants in bear's skin, as you are like a nursery-maid. You are tired, and we cannot do better than take this bench," he said, seating himself at my side.

Again we were both silent. My thoughts had been busy ever since we set out, with reminiscences of our acquaintance and intimacy. I had been trying to look into the depths of my own heart, but the waters had been troubled, and I could see nothing clearly. That heart was like a troubled sea that could not rest. Its waters cast up mire and dirt, and gold and gems. Sometimes there was a thought that Tyrell might, perhaps, care for me, and then I flung that thought away with all my strength. It was not so—he did *not care.* Of all the people in the world I was the one who ought least to have suspected him of a second attachment. What was I that I should succeed to such a woman as Verónica?

Another fear presented itself—presented itself with a *refrain.*

"Why did he marry Fulvia and not love her?"

That unanswered question from the lips of Cleopatra. And I strengthened myself with the thought that if, unhappy in his bachelorhood, he stood upon the brink of such an error, he would be rescued from it by my resolution.

At length I saw he was about to speak. I turned to him. But the words failed him.

The pause became more painful. I felt that I had probably been in error—had deceived myself into the belief that Tyrell had something of consequence to say to me; and I despised myself for having given audience for a moment to the vain, rash thoughts which I had been indulging.

At length, and while I was yet chiding myself for imagining he meant to speak, words came.

"Cousin Molly," he said, "if you knew nothing of the past, it would be easy to speak to you of my present feelings. 'I love you,' could be quickly said; but in this case there is so much that ought to be said first. You know that if any man ever cherished a strong, true passion for a woman, I did for your sister Veronica."

"I know it—indeed I know it, cousin Tyrell;" and my old sympathy for his disappointment was so strong, and so habitual, that I overlooked for a moment that he had just declared himself my lover, and laid my hand on his to enforce my sympathy.

"When I knew you in Virginia," he went on to say, "my thoughts were full of her. The goodness and the beauty of other women seemed to pass before me like the shadows of a dream, and I regarded them not. But, cousin Molly, after you went away—after the suffering past, I found something in my heart that I did not expect, and that something was your image. I do not say I loved you—that would be untrue; but you were different to me from all other women; and the thought strengthened. Every thing I heard about you, every one of the few lines I have received from you, strengthened this fond remembrance, and where the rose had been cut down grew up the violet. I formed an ideal of true womanhood, and found it was made up of what I knew of Mary Mandeville. I distrusted myself. I thought, perhaps, that this ideal was all fancy; and still more, I doubted whether I had any right to intrude this love on you. I came to England at length to solve these doubts. I find you a great deal more than all my memory or my fancy shadowed you. And now it is to you I bring the other doubt. Cousin Molly, tell me, shall I go away, or may I from this day begin a courtship, whose chief object must be to convince you of the possibility of a second attachment?"

My tears were falling fast—great, slow, heavy drops, falling one by one.

"Oh! cousin Tyrell," I said, "I did not dare to entertain the thought that you were feeling thus."

"Molly! shall I ever make you love me?"

"I think so, cousin Tyrell."

"Do you care for me, dear Molly?"

"Oh! Tyrell, I have tried not to—so much."

Tyrell started up; a happy light was in his eyes; he seemed like a new man.

"I never dared to hope for this. I thought you had discovered my wishes, and that you wanted to prove to me my suit was vain, by avoiding me at Castleton."

"Oh! no, I was afraid to trust myself."

And happy moments came and went. It seemed so strange to think our happiness was for life, and could not be disturbed. It seemed impossible to believe, that when we broke the stillness of those moments of bliss, the happy feelings would not pass away.

As we sat there, the great clock at the Horse Guards rang out three. Tyrell started and said,

"We shall be very late for service at the Abbey."

I thanked him in my heart for that suggestion, for it seemed to me as if the calm half-hour of cathedral service would consecrate our happiness—as if under its influence I could grow composed.

And when I knelt by Tyrell's side, and prayed for the blessings of heaven upon us both—and yet, in praying for both, felt I was praying for one—a holy, happy calmness stole into my heart, and I looked up at Tyrell. He was gazing upwards to where the evening sun threw purple, gold, and crimson shadows. But it seemed to me his thoughts were beyond shadows or sun, and had entered into the very presence of the Eternal.

At that moment the anthem began, sung by the boys' sweet flute-like voices; and the last words of that anthem sank into both our hearts, reminding me of the evening when Tyrell told me of his earlier love. It was a sort of comment on our past history, and we prayed that the lesson which it taught might never be forgotten. "Oh! tarry thou the Lord's leisure. Be strong and he shall comfort thine heart; and put thou thy trust in the Lord."

CHAPTER III.

> I would have brought so clear a light
> Between the slave and his oppressor,
> That straight the greater had become
> The loving guardian of the lesser.
>
> MRS. S. G. HOWE: *Passion Flowers.*

WE walked in silence from the abbey. I knew that Tyrell was looking at me, and I would not look up. At length he said, pressing the hand that lay upon his arm, closer to his heart:

"Are you happy?"

"Ah! Tyrell —— *so* happy!" Then after a little pause I said. "There is but one thing to mar the fullness of my happiness—and that is slavery. Oh! Tyrell, how I wish that you were not a slave owner!"

Tyrell was silent a moment, then he said: "Will you shrink from bearing with me the weight of that responsibility?"

"No," I replied, "but I wish it were any other."

Tyrell looked grieved. "I cannot make it any other," he replied. "I have foreseen that this subject might make trial and difficulty for you. But I hoped that you might share my views of the duty and responsibility that God has laid on me."

"Will it never be possible to emancipate them," I suggested timidly.

"The day is more distant than it once appeared to be," said Tyrell. "But suppose I set them free at once—remember dear

Molly, that my place in life has made me the guardian of their happiness and welfare, and that I ought not to be drawn aside from the fulfillment of that duty, by the pursuit of any theory or experiment. You will grant, of course, that the duty of all others, that 'lies nearest to me,' is to do the best I can for the real good and real happiness of my people."

"Of course," I said, a little wondering, for these were hardly the views I had expected to find a slave owner taking of the subject.

"Well then, to do unto others as we would they should do unto us, means that so far as in us lies, we must seek what we conscientiously believe to be their true good. There are sixty-seven servants, little children and aged included, at Stonehenge, suppose I set them free to-day, what is to become of them?"

"Could not they continue to live as laborers on your estate?"

"The State discourages a free-colored population, and the laws are becoming every day more stringent. They must emigrate. They will not be suffered to remain amongst us."

"What a cruel law!"

"That is not the point. You are wandering away from the practical view that I am wishing you to take. I am not a legislator, but only an individual anxious to do his duty under existing circumstances. Archbishop Leighton says: 'Would to God men were but as holy as it is possible to be under the worst forms now amongst us!' It is a good working principle applied in any case. Perhaps you are right about that law. It gives rise to misery, which falls the heaviest upon the best class of our servants. Maryland, in which the free colored population outnumbers the slaves, is very prosperous. Well then—since my people must emigrate, where shall they go?"

"Into the free States!"

"Who wants them at the North? Are you in the least aware to what unfavorable influences you would consign people who are particularly susceptible of influences? Did you ever watch the history of the decline and fall of nine out of ten families of colored emigrants to the northern States? I believe, upon my conscience, that the worst sufferings of the colored race are in the North, and in the great day of account we shall know more than we do now, of the sin of the prejudices which have trampled them down. Many of those prejudices are due to the misguided zeal of men who call themselves their friends, and use them in the war of party as offensive weapons. What is done by society—by philanthrophy—for their social, moral, and religious elevation? It is a blot on the humanity of the free States. Missionaries and missionaries' wives are sent to die in pestilential Africa amongst the heathen, while no man gathers into Sunday-schools and churches colored children and adults, who grow up like heathen in northern cities. Men who are crying out against our institution are making it impossible for us to emancipate. The great missionary work of the nineteenth century, the civilization and Christianization of a mighty continent, is lying neglected at their doors. Rum has been at the bottom of almost every case of native American destitution, unconnected with ill health. You might as well hold water in a cullender as to attempt permanently to benefit any family of pauper Irish, who besides are removed from your influence by their religion; but there is a race docile and fond of guidance—and who labors to elevate it? They are thrust out of all trades—they are crowded out of churches—they share little in the boasted benefits of school-funds and northern education—they have no place made for them in Sabbath-schools. Every ship, as it lands its freight of Celtic or Saxon laborers upon our shores, drives one or two of this unhappy race out of an honest living. Ignorance, oppression, degradation, and the influence of political agitators foster the *classes dangereuses*, and the North may be thankful that the rigors of the climate, unfavorable to the constitution of the negro, keep down the increase of the colored population, though 'Was I my brother's keeper?' will be no answer to God's accusation against society, when the voice of their blood is calling from the ground. They have none of the ambition, spirit, energy, and self-devotion to an abstract principle, which carried the Puritan fathers across the ocean, 'not knowing whither they went.' It rarely occurs to the more intelligent and educated amongst them to seek their fortunes under more propitious influences. The enterprising and educated take up the trade of political agitation. The mass sink into squalid streets in the black quarter of large cities. The parents may have striven to live honestly, but the children, exposed to vicious influences, and never brought into elevating contact with the better class of whites, succumb to evil habits. I am not going to expose my people and their descendants to that fate. Have you no better way of disposing of them?"

"Liberia," said I.

"Aye," he replied. "I look forward in faith to Liberia. We may live to see a mighty Exodus which shall carry civilization and Christianity to a continent whose climate places it beyond the influence of any other Christian emigration. The experiment has been nobly made—by noble men—the noblest being of that race which has not elsewhere had the opportunity of proving itself noble. If everybody took the same interest in Liberia that I do, they would make it their duty to attempt, so far as possible, the elevation and improvement of the colored people round them. We have no right to swamp the colony with ignorant paupers. We ought to do our part to make those who come under our influence Christian and industrious, to give them trades that may be useful to them as colonists, should they ever become such, and, so far as is possible, an education. Education, however, is not confined to book-learning. Believe me, my Molly, I never forget that many, or all my people, may yet emigrate to Liberia, or at least, their descendants. I am quite ready to send any one from my estate desirous to go, at any time. But there have been great prejudices among the colored race against Liberia. Prejudices founded upon ignorance, and many absurd negro notions. These prejudices are beginning to disappear as the colony grows prosperous, but still at present there is little to tempt an ignorant and unambitious negro laborer, on a kind master's estate, to give up a home where he is happy, and go out to an unknown country, merely for the boon of freedom. The negro does not think of Liberia except under the pressure of necessity. Few spontaneously turn their attention in that direction. It is always an alternative. As I have said, any of my people may have their freedom if they want to emigrate to Africa, and rather than pass into the hands of a new master I do not doubt they would accept it; but many have married off the estate, they could not take their families with them, and are bound by many ties to the soil."

"It is a risk too," I said, "to expose them to the climate and the fever."

"As civilization increases," Tyrell replied, "the danger of the acclimating fever grows less and less. With respect to health, I think I would rather send my people to Liberia than Massachusetts. Of two emigrants with an equal number of children—one to New England and the other to Africa,—the latter would be likely to have the larger number of descendants. The hardships of emigration to Liberia fall upon the people you send out,—their children are nearly sure to prosper. The contrary is the case with emancipated slaves who settle beyond Mason and Dixon."

"Then there is nothing to be done," I said, "but to do our duty, and wait."

"Dear Molly," said Tyrell, "this has been a strange conversation for to-day, but I am glad that we have had it over. And while I respect and understand your English feelings, on this subject, I am sincerely desirous to bring you over to my views. This matter, as a practical question of everyday life, has greatly occupied my thoughts. Will you not trust my judgment, and share in my responsibility? I feel assured that time will remove many difficulties—meanwhile, let us do the present duty that lies nearest to us, and see that our servants, when the day of emancipation comes, are fit for freedom. I wish very much I could persuade you to talk as little as possible on this subject in Virginia, even with persons who espouse your views. The question has been so inflamed by poisoned tongues, that it is best avoided. The influence of your quiet home efforts for the improvement of those around you, will circulate more widely than your opinions on the abstract right of slavery."

I looked up in Tyrell's face. It was a little grave, a little anxious, and I could not bear to grieve him.

"Dear Molly," he said, "let it become only a practical question with us."

And I answered, "You are right, Tyrell. I will trust your judgment. We will be of one mind on this as on all other subjects, as nearly as we can. I have taken upon me to share all the interests and duties of your life. We will together meet this great responsibility."

"Preparing the way for better times, beloved," he said, looking at me kindly. "We will not betray our trust, by shrinking from the responsibilities of our order, like the émigrés of the old Revolution."

"And when may we expect the time when the freedom of our slaves may be less difficult than at present?"

And Tyrell answered me in the words of the Anthem which had thrilled in our hearts that evening,—"Tarry thou the Lord's leisure—and put thou thy trust in the Lord."

Our marriage was one in which everybody rejoiced. It was celebrated at Castleton, and then we passed the winter on the Continent, returning to the Valley of Virginia when the perfume of the locust bloom was scenting all the fields. We kept open house for a week after we reached Stonehenge, and I had a second edition of festivities upon my marriage.

I know now how the old place looks when happy children frolic on the grass, for as I write I watch my eldest boy, who has his father's merry laugh, and sunny deep blue eyes, throwing roses at Aunt Saph, as she sits on the lower steps of the porch, with the baby in her arms. But to-morrow Uncle Christopher is to cut down my rose trees and transplant their roots to our new home.

I have been wandering about the house all day. That house under the mountain, that was once so gloomy, where Tyrell suffered so much in days that are forgotten,—that house which has been long brightened by the love, and peace, and happiness of home. Tyrell says my worst fault as a wife, is, that I am always sticking pins and needles in the table-cloth in his library, —that library in which he used to shut himself up, and be unhappy, but I know he likes to find me in that room, and thinks it brightened by my presence. Only last night I heard him whisper to himself, as he stood a moment on the threshold:

> "The very place 'cos she was in
> Looked warm from floor to ceilin."

To-night is our last night in that room, for a new house with all sorts of modern improvements, and better situated, has been built by Tyrell—we move into it to-morrow, and Stonehenge, when we have left it, is to be pulled down.

Old Warren died at Oatlands, and Tyrell wrote to Max upon the subject. Warren, as I said, had been an English yeoman whom our grandfather brought with him to this country; he superintended the property with great success, and Tyrell, who could not devote much time to the details of management on Max's estate was unwilling to place an ordinary Yankee or Scotch manager upon the property.

Max answered his letter by a proposition that Tyrell should buy the Oatlands farm, on which condition he was anxious to give us all the negroes who would not consent to emigrate to Africa. Tyrell and I hesitated a few weeks. It was adding to our responsibility, but it seemed a duty of mastership put into our hands; it was difficult to replace Warren with a person we could trust to do his duty to the servants, and there seemed nothing better to be done.

The change of ownership made a better opening for our persuasions in favor of Liberia. Two families consented to emigrate, the heads of which were old Mammy's sons, Uncle Joe, and Uncle Pete, for whom Tyrell purchased his family. Tyrell saw them embark at Baltimore, and provided for their favorable start in life in the colony. They have done well there, and are happy. We have strong hopes that as our people through the communications from them become familiarized with Africa, others may voluntarily follow their example.

The person who most neutralizes our influence upon the subject is Aunt Saph, whose aristocratic predilections for white society of the better sort, make her an enemy to the colony.

"Laws honey," I heard her say last week, "dere ain't nothin' dere but black faces to look at. I never see no good come of niggers widout white folks among 'em."

In the Fall we hope to go to England for a visit, and shall spend the fifth anniversary of our wedding-day at Castleton.

THE END.

www.ingramcontent.com/pod-product-compliance
Lightning Source LLC
LaVergne TN
LVHW021138110826
845150LV00005B/1062

* 9 7 8 1 4 2 5 5 4 8 7 0 4 *